ÉREC REX

THE SECRET OF ASHONA

ALSO BY KAZA KINGSLEY

Check out all the books in the Erec Rex series

EREC REX

THE SECRET OF ASHONA

KAZA KINGSLEY

Illustrations by James Ng

Simon & Schuster Books for Young Readers
New York   London   Toronto   Sydney   New Delhi

SIMON & SCHUSTER BOOKS FOR YOUNG READERS
An imprint of Simon & Schuster Children's Publishing Division
1230 Avenue of the Americas, New York, New York 10020

SIMON & SCHUSTER BOOKS FOR YOUNG READERS
is a trademark of Simon & Schuster, Inc.
For information about special discounts for bulk purchases, please contact Simon & Schuster Special Sales at 1-866-506-1949 or business@simonandschuster.com.
The Simon & Schuster Speakers Bureau can bring authors to your live event. For more information or to book an event, contact the Simon & Schuster Speakers Bureau at 1-866-248-3049 or visit our website at www.simonspeakers.com.
Also available in a Simon & Schuster Books for Young Readers hardcover edition
Book design by Lucy Ruth Cummins
The text for this book is set in Adobe Caslon Pro.
The illustrations for this book are rendered digitally.
Manufactured in the United States of America
0113 MTN
First Simon & Schuster Books for Young Readers paperback edition February 2013
2 4 6 8 10 9 7 5 3 1
The Library of Congress has cataloged the hardcover edition as follows:
Kingsley, Kaza.
The secret of Ashona / Kaza Kingsley. — 1st ed.
p. cm. — (Erec Rex ; bk. 5)
Summary: With a romance brewing between him and Bethany, the discovery that his brother and sister are secretly king and queen of the Fairy world, plus the Stain brothers growing more and more underhanded, fourteen-year-old Erec is not in the right state of mind for his next two tasks.
ISBN 978-1-4169-7992-0 (hardcover)
[1. Fantasy.] I. Title.
PZ7.K6153Sf 2012
[Fic]—dc23
2011021081
ISBN 978-1-4169-7993-7 (pbk)
ISBN 978-1-4169-8560-0 (eBook)
erecrex.com

For Sarah, my muse and inspiration.
May I someday grow up to be as wise and wonderful as you.

CONTENTS

CHAPTER ONE
Tarvos the Great

TWO SNAILS SAT ON THE KITCHEN TABLE. Their eyes drifted back and forth on their long stalks, tracking a teenage boy as he paced the room. From the snails' perspective, the tall fourteen-year-old looked quite normal—although his dark hair was straight in front and wildly curly in the back.

But normal was the last thing Erec Rex felt like.

Normal kids would not have dragon eyes that let them see into the future.

Normal kids would not be forced to become king of a magical land.

Normal kids would not have to do twelve ridiculously dangerous quests to become king.

Erec sighed. Weird or not, it was his life. He could live with that. But what was hard to live with right now was doing absolutely nothing. Normal kids would be having fun in the summertime. Erec had been sitting around for over a month reading books and staring at the walls. He didn't want to go on a quest again—there was no mistaking that. But he had to do *something*. Instead, he was pacing this dingy apartment kitchen, stretching out the time before he opened the letters that the two snails had brought him. Once he finished reading them, it would be back to complete boredom again.

Normal kids, Erec thought, would at least be able to hang out with their friends. But all of his friends were far away in another world, and he was stuck here alone.

Well, he wasn't *exactly* alone, and he wasn't *exactly* doing nothing. He was babysitting, as usual, for his younger siblings—red-haired Trevor and little Zoey. It basically amounted to reading to Zoey and watching her play house. His sister Nell had found a friend in a nearby apartment and she hung out there all the time, and their adoptive mother, June, was working. Erec didn't know anybody around here, but at first that hadn't bothered him at all. The idea of a little rest time with the family sounded great. Peace and quiet. But he soon realized that doing nothing but babysitting for weeks felt like being chained to a couch watching maternity channel reruns.

He paced some more, watching the two message-carrying snails watch him back. They eyed him impatiently until, finally, Erec grabbed the one on the left and pulled a letter out of its thin shell.

Dear Erec,

Ashona is amazing! Every day that I'm here I keep finding secret passages, ancient spell books, and other incredible surprises. Queen Posey gave me a master key, and yesterday I discovered a huge room filled with buried sea treasure that had been dug up and brought from all over the world's oceans! I can't wait until you see this place.

What are your plans? I still haven't gotten a letter from you—write me back!

Love, Bethany

Without thinking, Erec crushed the letter into a tight ball. It wasn't fair! He understood why June wanted them to stay in New Jersey, hoping to give Trevor, Nell, and Zoey something close to a normal life. But how could New Jersey hold a candle to the undersea world of Ashona? Bethany was Erec's best friend in the world, and she was there with his father, the King of Alypium. King Piter's powers were gone, and for safety he had to stay close to his sister, Queen Posey, who ruled Ashona. Alypium, the land where magic was still real, was where Erec was destined to become king, and it was out there waiting for him. Bethany was probably having the time of her life in Ashona, and Erec was here . . . stuck.

He stared a while at the *Love* in "Love, Bethany," trying not to think about exactly what that meant. Bethany had become close to a girlfriend . . . more than just a friend, but it was hard to know exactly where they stood. He should be glad she was having fun . . . but he

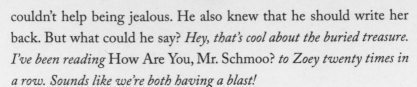

couldn't help being jealous. He also knew that he should write her back. But what could he say? *Hey, that's cool about the buried treasure. I've been reading* How Are You, Mr. Schmoo? *to Zoey twenty times in a row. Sounds like we're both having a blast!*

He would have to wait on that letter back to Bethany.

Plus, he already knew what she would say. She would tell him to get on with his next quest—the seventh out of twelve that he had to finish to become the next King of Alypium. Once he was ready, his mother would find a way to let him go. Nell would have to babysit, and Erec could leave here and start his next adventure.

The only problem was, he didn't *want* to do any more quests at all. He had almost lost his life in the last one. Actually, he *had* lost his life to the three Furies—huge, all-powerful creatures that had taken his soul to escape their prison. But through some ancient magic, dragon's blood, and a grateful cat, he was brought back to life again. After that, who could blame him for his lack of desire to do any more quests again—ever?

He wondered if his mother would let him go to Ashona just to have fun instead of doing his next quest. But he could imagine the look on her face and the firm *no*.

Something moved in the family room, jolting Erec out of his thoughts. He walked in and peered around with interest even though he had barely seen the thing. It was gone, but Erec was suddenly alert. It almost felt like nothing else mattered. But then the feeling passed as quickly as it had come on.

He tried to shake off his strange reaction. Maybe his mind was playing tricks on him after all these weeks of boredom. He picked up the other snail and took the letter out. Just then Trevor bounded into the kitchen. "Snail mail?"

Erec smiled. Even though Trevor did not talk a lot, he was a brilliant kid. But before Erec could answer, he was distracted again by something moving in the family room. Curiosity overwhelmed him this time, and he took off running into the room, nearly tripping over a kitchen chair. What could it be in there? He searched, grabbing cushions and looking under the couch. All through him there was a sharp need to find . . . what was it that he was looking for?

The feeling wore off, but left him confused. What was wrong with him? Was he paranoid?

Trevor stared at him and Erec felt his face turn red. He picked up the other snail mail, pretending nothing had happened.

To: Erec Rex

This letter is to inform you that the three new kings, Balor, Damon, and Dollick Stain, have completed their twelve quests. They will be crowned on June 25. At that time we will need all three of the royal scepters for their use. King Pluto's scepter is in our possession and Queen Posey's will be soon. We request that you immediately return King Piter's scepter to President Inkle at the Green House. If you do not do this in the next three days, we will be forced to send the armies of Alypium and Aorth to track you down.

Rest assured, when you return the scepter to us, you will leave here unharmed. The Shadow Prince no longer has a need for you, and he wishes you all the best. Thank you, and have a great summer!

Signed ----------- ~~~~~~~~~~ --------------------------

Scruffymat, the Secretary of Preplanning of Protocol Development

The snail cocked one of its elongated eyes at Erec, watching his stunned reaction.

The Stain triplets were going to be crowned kings? If Balor, Damon, and Dollick became the next rulers of the Kingdoms of the Keepers, they would hand their scepters to Baskania, the evil Shadow Prince, who would destroy the world with them. Well, Erec had one of the three scepters, anyway, and there was no way he was giving it up even if Baskania did send the armies of Alypium and Aorth after him.

His heart sank. If he wasn't going to do the quests to become the next king, then what did he think was going to happen? He was the one who was supposed to rule. But how could he risk losing his life again doing another quest? The next time he might not get it back. He just wished there was another way to stop the Stain triplets from becoming king. Maybe if he used his scepter somehow . . .

The thought of his scepter brought back memories so intense that Erec had to close his eyes. Visions of the golden staff filled his mind. He could feel its electricity surging through him as if it were in his hands right now. He fought against his cravings for the thing by putting things in perspective. He really wasn't ready for it—it was far too powerful. Only after he completed all of his quests would he have the strength to use it without falling under its influence. That was why he had sent it away—

Something moved again in the family room. *What* was running around in there? He had to get it this time, whatever it was. He darted forward as if he were hypnotized, stalking back and forth like a panther searching for its prey. There was a flash of white—he dove and grabbed it . . . but it was just a blanket.

Erec hugged it to his chest, annoyed. Where did the thing go? What was it? And why was it driving him so crazy? Frustrated, he threw the blanket onto the couch.

Trevor stared at him in shock. "What's wrong with you?"

"I don't know. Didn't you see that thing . . . ?" Erec gestured around the room, but Trevor shook his head. "I guess I need more sleep—"

But just then, the thing moved again, right behind Trevor. Erec dove, compelled to grab it—

And tackled his younger brother. Whatever it was was gone again.

"Man, I'm so sorry, Trev. You okay?" Erec dusted himself off and pulled his brother up.

Trevor stared at him with wide eyes and nodded.

"Something weird is in here," Erec said. "You better stand back while I look for it." He searched under the coffee table and by the front door. Nothing was there. . . .

Suddenly, the entire world froze. A tiny man in white raced from under the couch, toward the curtains. He was moving too fast to see clearly, but Erec was captivated. The little guy stopped, spun around, and gazed at Erec with painted, wide-set eyes. That was when Erec realized that it was a toy—a little wind-up bullfighter. But it was the most fascinating thing Erec had ever seen. He could not pull his eyes away from its face. The harder he looked, the more it drew him in.

"What are you staring at?" Trevor followed his gaze with a confused look on his face.

Erec barely heard Trevor. It sounded like his voice was far away. The painted eyes of the little toy sparkled and filled Erec with curiosity. Their gaze looked right through him, as if it were reading his mind. Erec could feel himself tremble from fear, excitement, or maybe both.

Trevor shook Erec's shoulder. "Why are you looking like that? What's wrong?"

Trevor's words were meaningless background noise. Erec pushed him away and headed toward the little bullfighter. Its eyes were glowing. Erec had to follow wherever it went.

The bullfighter pulled out a small swatch of red cloth, and swished beneath its arm. Seeing the flash of red made Erec lose his last bit of control. He dove toward the thing—nothing was more important than grabbing that patch of red and having it for his own. The toy darted away. Erec charged, tripping over Zoey's doll. The thing spun out of reach.

"Erec! What are you doing?" Trevor clutched Erec's elbow, but Erec shook him off.

The toy buzzed back into view and then disappeared behind the couch. Erec pounced, scraping his face on the wall. "Get back here!" His voice sounded strangled, but he could not think clearly enough to question why. He scrambled behind the couch after the shining toy.

"Stop!" Trevor grabbed Erec's ankle, pulling him back.

The little bullfighter spun around again to look at Erec. Its painted eyes taunted him. Behind it, Erec noticed a small black spot in the wall. As Erec watched, the spot grew larger until it became a hole that was the size of his fist. The bullfighter disappeared inside its darkness.

How could that thing leave without him? Erec was filled with rage. He reached a hand into the hole, which was still growing in the plaster. The bullfighter was out of his reach, but the gap kept growing wider. Soon it got big enough to climb through. Without a thought, Erec plunged in headfirst. He was in a tunnel that led out of his apartment. It was warm inside, although pitch-black. As Erec surged forward, he felt that his right leg was being yanked back. He shook it, but he couldn't get it free.

It was too dark to see what was wrong with his leg, so instead he kept pulling himself forward. The tunnel was soft, like it was made of felt, but it was strong enough to support him. The little bullfighter was somewhere ahead of him, Erec could feel it. In the back of his mind, he realized that he had never been this determined to have something in his whole life. For a second he wondered why, but then all thoughts beyond the little bullfighter toy left his head.

A dim light appeared ahead. Erec crawled toward it, dragging his right leg behind him. The light grew into an exit from the tunnel that emptied into a giant cavern. Erec had to grab the walls of the cave and pull his body from the tunnel against whatever was tugging on his ankle. As he slid out, the tunnel tightened around him, closing as he was leaving it. A sharp scream issued from the tunnel as the gap narrowed snugly around his legs. The sound jolted Erec out of his obsession with the bullfighter, and for a moment he looked around and wondered where he was.

He was almost out now . . . if only his right leg would come. Why was this so difficult?

Erec yanked and pulled, and then with a pop his leg shot out of the closing tunnel . . . with Trevor attached to it.

Trevor looked terrified. "What's going on?" he gasped. "How did we get here?"

With his brother's words, the spell on Erec seemed to lift completely. The bullfighter was gone. He couldn't see it anywhere. But now they were stuck in a cave with no way to get back.

For a moment, neither he nor Trevor moved. Erec tried to collect his thoughts. Someone had obviously used magic to lead him here. Could it have blinded him that much? And where was he now? The rocky cave was enormous and empty, no sign of the little bullfighter anywhere. In fact, there was nothing at all except for a corridor at the other end of the cavern. It seemed silly to just stand there, so Erec walked toward it. Trevor followed him, grasping the back of his red T-shirt. When they reached the hall-like tunnel, Erec was afraid that there would be nothing but more empty cave and no way home again . . . but something around the corner made him stop in his tracks.

A gigantic bull sat on an ornate golden throne that filled the far end of the hall. The bull must have been fifty feet tall. Fluffy dark brown hair stuck out from its face and body in all directions. A thick gold ring dangled from its nose, and another from its right ear. They both waved in the air when the bull snorted.

The beast reared back and majestically pointed a hoof at Erec. Erec shrank back, half expecting lightning rays to shoot down at him, but nothing happened. The beast shook its hoof and frowned. "Something is wrong with you." Its deep voice echoed through the room. It raised its hoof toward Erec again, but then dropped it, growling. "You're not normal. It's like you're indestructible. But don't worry. I'll figure out how to get rid of you soon enough."

Three giant snow-white cranes with spindly long black legs were perched on the bull's shoulders. Red circles surrounded their beady black eyes. They eagerly turned their long necks toward Erec, chomping their long, sharp black beaks

Erec shook from head to toe. What was going on? Why was this strange giant bull trying to get rid of him? Then a thought occurred to him—maybe this was all a dream. It was certainly strange enough.

Trevor yanked his arm hard enough to hurt. This was no dream. "Erec?" His voice sounded weak. "Let's go. Quick."

Erec nodded, but his feet were stuck as if they were glued to the floor. "I . . . I can't move." He pulled harder but could not budge, as the bull watched in amusement. "Just go on without me."

Trevor twisted, but his feet were also fixed to the ground. He stared at the bull in terror.

It dawned on Erec that the bullfighter toy's spell had brought him here, but Trevor hadn't even been able to see the thing. He probably wasn't supposed to have come. Someone was trying to kill Erec, and now Trevor was in just as much danger. He had to get Trevor to safety, if not himself.

This had to be a trick of Baskania, the Shadow Prince. He must be trying to capture him. But that didn't make sense—the snail mail from the Green House in Alypium said he had three days to give them his scepter. Why would they trap him here now if they wanted him to bring it?

The bull roared with anger. "What have you done to yourself, you pathetic boy? I can't *take* you like this."

"Who . . . who are you? Where am I?"

The three white cranes looked at Erec like he was crazy. "'Ee's actually talking to the master! Ee's asking 'im questions!" one said.

"No doubt that'll end badly."

A third scratched its feathers with its pointy beak. "Not that it won't end badly for 'im either way, now, will it?"

The bull gnashed its teeth. "Don't bother me with your stupid questions. You *belong* to me, and I am going to put you in my army. Something is wrong, though. I can't seem to change you into one of my slaves. . . ."

"Let my brother go!" Trevor tugged against his stuck feet.

The bull nodded toward Trevor, frustrated. "Where did this other boy come from? Did you bring him here? Nobody does this."

"He's my brother. He followed me." Erec squeezed his eyes shut. Why hadn't Trevor stayed home where it was safe? "Please let him go. You don't want him, right? Just keep me."

"I don't send people back. Ever."

Erec was overwhelmed with panic. It was bad enough that he was trapped in this awful place, but how could he have let Trevor follow him? Why had he been so obsessed with that dumb little toy that he didn't stop to look at what was tugging on his leg?

He tried to calm down and talk his way out of this. "Why do you want me? Maybe we could make a deal. Send my brother home and you can keep me as long as you want."

"Tarvos does not make deals," the bull roared. "I'll keep you forever, and I'll dispose of that boy as soon as I turn you into a Golem. But you have *ruined* yourself, so I can't do it. I have to figure this out fast, so I can move on to the next person on my list."

Erec and Trevor exchanged looks. Erec had no idea what the bull was talking about, but it didn't sound good. What was a Golem?

This time the bull pointed both of its front hooves at him. Searing pain flashed through both of Erec's eyes, like they were being torn from his head. He screamed, covering them with his hands. Soon his entire body burned inside. He dropped to his knees and wrapped his head in his arms, rocking. Tears streamed down his face.

Then the pain stopped.

"'Ee thinks that was bad," one of the birds commented. "Just wait till 'ee gets the rest of 'is soul ripped out."

Another bird tsked. "Yup. 'Ard to get used to watching it, but like I says, better 'im than us."

Erec saw his brother frozen in terror, tears streaming down his face, so he tried to pull himself together. "I'm . . . fine. It's all right, Trev. Pain's all gone." He tried to smile, to show his brother that he was okay, but it was a pathetic attempt. Whatever this bull-thing wanted to turn him into, Erec didn't stand a chance.

The bull's brow lowered in annoyance. "What did you do to yourself? I can't pull those eyes out of you. I can't burn off that blood." He snorted. "Something is all wrong here. Those parts of yours are indestructible. I don't understand. It's like they're not even human. Are they from another creature?"

Erec heaved a sigh of relief. Maybe he did stand a chance after all. The bull was referring to the fact that he had dragon eyes. They must have stopped the bull from doing whatever horrible thing he was trying to do. And his blood . . . did he have dragon blood? "Why are you doing this? I don't understand—"

"I'll ask the questions." A waft of smoke drifted from the bull's nostrils. "Tell me where you got those eyes. I need to figure out how to remove them."

Did the bull think that Erec would really help him do that? "I—I didn't get them anywhere. I don't know what you mean."

The cranes on the bull's shoulders started pacing, agitated. "This ain't good, I tell ya."

"I know, chum. The boy's odd, all right. Causing all kinds of problems, ain't 'ee?"

Tarvos sneered. "You're making me look stupid and I don't *like* to look bad." It roared in frustration. "You're wasting my time. I have important work to do." Then the bull sighed and shook its head. "I suppose I'll just have to kill you, then. What a waste. You would have made a fine soldier."

Erec threw his hands up. "D-don't kill me! I . . . I can help you get my eyes out if you want me to." Better blind than dead, Erec thought. He had to stall for time, figure out what to do. "Just . . . um . . . explain a few things to me first. Then I'll tell you how to pull my eyes out, okay? I'll even do it for you."

The bull looked at him quizzically. "You can do that?" His eyes narrowed. "I don't like having to ask for help." He laughed. "Then again, once I turn you into a clay fighting machine, you won't be able to tell anyone about it. All right, then. I'll answer a few questions. But make it quick."

"'Ear that?" one of the birds said. "'Ee's going to talk to the boy. I can't believe it!"

"No tellin' what will happen. Kid is strange, all right."

"Who are you?" Erec said. "And why am I here?"

The bull's bloodshot eyes bored into Erec's. "I am Tarvos the

Great. Ruler over you and your kind. It is my right to collect all you living beings without souls and turn you into my army of clay Golems. The Fates have bequeathed you and your soulless brethren to me to use as I please."

Erec was too stunned to speak. This didn't make sense. Why did the bull think that he had no soul? This sounded more like a strange mistake than a plot of Baskania's.

"Listen . . . Tarvos. There has been a big misunderstanding. First of all, I *have* a soul. And so does Trevor here. I just saw this strange little bullfighter toy and ended up crawling through a tunnel into this place—"

The cranes exploded in laughter. "Listen to 'im! 'Ee thinks it was all a big slipup!"

"Oh, don't they all."

"Cut it out!" Erec yelled at the birds. "You don't know what you're talking about."

"Oh, now, *that* was a slipup, all right," a bird said. "Insulting me like that."

"Yeah, that there troublemaker *deserves* to become one of those icky Golems."

"Look," Erec said. "You're all wrong. You have to let us go home. There are a few things that are . . . different about me. I've done six quests to become the king of Alypium . . . and I've used the king's scepter. Maybe that did something to make you think I have no soul?"

The bull's eyes remained hard. "Of course that's not it! You think I'm stupid, don't you?" His eyes drifted above Erec's head. "Everyone thinks I'm stupid. But I'll show them. Once my Golem army is ready I'll wipe out everyone who has ever laughed at me." He focused on Erec again. "Don't think you can talk your way out of this. I know your soul is missing. Souls are more visible to me than the bodies that they rest in. You do have a tiny piece of one left, but it's not much to speak of. Definitely not enough for me to spare you." He grunted. "Your kind need to be removed from humanity and destroyed before you cause damage. That is why the Fates have given you to me to dispose of."

This sounded crazy to Erec. "Why do you think my soul is gone? What if you are wrong—?"

"What?" the bull yelled, enraged. He dragged his claws on the ground, making a harsh scraping noise. "I'm never wrong! How dare you question Tarvos the Great? Of course I can't tell *why* your soul is missing. *You* are the one that should know that."

Erec searched for an answer. Could he have lost his soul? He had done nothing but sit at home for a month. Before that, his last quest was to give himself to the three Furies—terrible, powerful creatures who were about to be unleashed upon humanity. He had to let them out of their prison. Luckily he had managed to change things so that they were at peace when they escaped.

Not that he had gotten out easily himself. He had died and was brought back with the help of a bee locked inside amber and a healthy dose of dragon blood.

Erec's jaw dropped open. Something else had happened when he died. . . . He had given something to the Furies. . . what they needed to escape Tartarus . . .

It all seemed so vague and long ago. . . . His dying had literally made it seem like it was another lifetime. But now everything made sense. He had given his soul to the three Furies. After being killed and brought back to life, he assumed that he had been brought back to his normal self, how he started off. But that was not the case at all.

He was alive . . . but the Furies still had his soul.

CHAPTER TWO

A Horrible Deal

EREC'S MIND SPUN, trying to take in this new information. Tarvos had said that Erec had a little piece of his soul left. And that was all he had been living with this last month? It was strange that he could not even feel that his soul was missing. He felt exactly the same as he had before he had lost it. The whole thing seemed so strange. Did the Furies still have his soul with them? That thought lit a small spark of hope in Erec. Maybe they didn't need it anymore, now that they were free. . . .

But before he could get too excited, another realization hit him. Tarvos had not made a mistake. That meant Erec would never get out of this cave alive.

"You said people like me have to be destroyed," Erec said, "before we do *damage*? But I feel totally fine. I'm not going to hurt anybody. I didn't even notice that my soul was missing."

Tarvos growled. "You're a hazard. It's a matter of time before you'll turn bad. You all do. You're a danger to society."

Erec couldn't believe his ears. This couldn't be right. "Can't you just give me a chance? Let me try to stay under control . . . before you destroy me?" He gulped.

Trevor looked back and forth between his brother and the giant bull, then blurted out, "Let him go! I'll make sure he's okay."

Tarvos's glowing red gaze bored into Trevor's. "That's not so easy. These *things*"—he pointed at Erec—"lose track of right and wrong completely. They all turn evil. I do a great service by ridding the world of these terrible creatures."

Erec felt sick. He was a terrible creature now? He would soon become evil? How much of what Tarvos was saying was true?

"What if . . . what if I could get my soul back again?"

The cranes burst into laughter. "'Ee thinks 'ee can just get it back again. Like 'ee could buy it at the local Burger Rama, or one of the Herman Howl's UnderWear stores or some'pin."

"If dat's right, I want to buy a few extras me'self."

Tarvos snorted. "Give it up, boy. That's not going to happen. When some people die and come back to life, their soul moves on without them. They won't come back by themselves . . . and there's no way to contact them, so don't think some psychic will find yours."

"But—"

"Your time is up. Pop those eyes out now so I can move on to the next soulless one on my list. I have an army to put together." He rubbed his hooves together, and then said thoughtfully, "I could just tear your head off. That would get rid of those eyes . . . but then you would be a Golem without a head, and what good would that be? No," he grunted. "I'll just have to kill you both."

"Stop! Wait!" Erec took a breath. "I *can* find my soul again. I—I didn't just die, I gave my soul to the three Furies to help them escape Tartarus. They probably still have it. Now that they're free, they might give it back to me. Please, just give me a chance to ask them."

Tarvos's eyes lit up with wonder. "Did you say the Furies? Alecto, Tisiphone, and Megaera? *You* helped them escape Tartarus?" He stood and began to pace in the small space in front of his throne. "Well, this is interesting, indeed. The *Furies* have your soul. Good luck getting it back." He stared at Erec for a moment. "Then again, if they really owe you, like you say, then maybe they would work something out."

Erec could not believe his ears. Hope surged through him. "Do you know where the Furies are? Where my soul is?"

"No. They keep their captive souls near them in some prison. Pretty nasty, even for my taste—keeping souls locked up like that forever."

Erec was confused. "Do the souls know they're in a prison?"

"Of course. Wouldn't you? They're miserable. Yours will be the lucky one if you get it out of there."

The idea of three thousand souls locked in a prison, including his own, was horrifying. He had to try to get it out of there. But what about all the other ones? It didn't seem right to leave them all there to rot. But before he could do anything at all about it, he had to get out of this place.

Tarvos smacked his lips, hungrily. "Actually, I need to talk to the Furies too. They have something I need. In fact, now that they're free I might be able to get it." He eyed Erec appraisingly. "And you say that they owe you a favor, that you released them?"

"I did. Maybe I could help you if you let me go." Erec's mind raced with excitement. Maybe he could fix everyone's problem at once—get his soul back, get whatever Tarvos wanted from them, and go home.

A smile flickered on Tarvos's lips. "Perfect . . . Ask them for a little thing called a 'Master Shem.' It would help me get control of things down here."

"A Master Shem? What does that do?"

"Nothing that concerns you," the bull snapped. "Just get it and I'll overlook that you're going around out there without a soul."

"So, you'll let us go, then?"

The bull shook its head. "Not both of you. I need a guarantee that you'll return. Once you have your soul back there is no way for me to bring you here. This boy is your brother, right? I'm sure you'll return for him." A smile lit his wide face.

Erec broke into a sweat. "No—wait. That won't work." He could never leave Trevor here. "Keep me instead."

"How is that possible? I need you to get the Master Shem from the Furies. If you bring it to me before one month passes, then I'll let this boy go."

Trevor looked so small and pale. How could Erec even think of leaving him with this monster?

As if Trevor was reading Erec's mind, he said, "I'll be fine." His voice shook. "You can do it, Erec."

"I can't leave you here!"

Trevor shook his head firmly. "That's the only way we'll *both* be free."

"Not quite." Tarvos shook his head. "Only this boy will. That is our trade. You will still belong to me—that is, unless you get your soul back. Then you will be your own person again, of course." He tapped a hoof on the ground. "You'll need a way to get back here. I'll leave a passage open for you, but it will work only one time. Find the giant Bubble Boulder of Racks Rocks in Quiet, a part of Otherness. There will be an entrance that only you will be able to see."

"Racks Rocks? Bubble Boulder?" Erec was trying to keep the bull's words straight, even as he was thinking of ways to get out of this craziness.

"Good luck, Erec." Trevor closed his eyes. "I know you can do it."

Fear raced through Erec. How could this be happening? He couldn't leave his little brother alone with a beast that turned people to clay, and then hope to do the impossible in order to set him free. But then again, what other choice did he have?

The bull roared, "Is it a deal?"

Trevor shouted, "Deal!"

A moment later, Erec was back in his house. Surrounded by the world that he knew—his kitchen table, Zoey's dolls in every single chair—he almost felt that the whole thing had been a terrible dream.

Except that Trevor was gone.

Erec felt shaky. What was he going to do? He looked around his apartment desperately, as if the answer might be right in front of him. Then, confused and feeling sick, he lay in his bed and stared at the ceiling. How was he going to get out of this mess? Poor Trevor . . .

Then he jumped up. Paper. Pen. He had to write down the way back to Tarvos before he forgot:

The passage to Tarvos is in the giant Bubble Boulder of Racks Rocks in Quiet, which is in Otherness.

He stared at the paper a while, committing it to memory, then shoved it into his pocket. Not knowing what to do next, he decided to make a list to put his mind in order and sort out the problems.

1. Trevor is being held hostage by a giant bull.

This he underlined three times and circled. Then he wrote:

2. My soul is missing. And I might turn evil at any minute.
3. I need to get the Furies to give me a Master Shem, whatever that is, so I can get Trevor back.
4. If I don't get my soul back from the Furies, Tarvos will turn me into a clay Golem thing.
5. The Furies are keeping three thousand souls prisoners.
6. Balor, Damon, and Dollick Stain are going to be crowned kings in a few weeks.
7. In three days, when I don't give my scepter to the Green House, the armies of Alypium and Aorth are going to come after me.

Then he added, just in case his life wasn't totally impossible already:

8. I have to do six more quests before I become King of Alypium. If I do them I can stop Baskania from destroying the world.

For a moment he felt better that he had gotten it all down on paper, like he was on the verge of a plan. But at second glance, everything seemed way out of control. Any one of these problems alone was more than he could face. He took a deep breath. The most important thing was to save Trevor as soon as possible . . . and also to find his lost soul. If he really did start to turn evil, then it would all be over.

That thought terrified him. Would he realize that he was going down the wrong path? What if he began doing bad things and he didn't notice? Erec thought about his last month at home. Hadn't he taken a big bite of Zoey's Popsicle last week, before she was finished with it? He hadn't thought twice about it at the time, but she had gotten upset. Later Zoey calmed down and didn't care anymore—did that make it okay?

What else had he done? Yesterday—yes, that was right—he had snapped at Trevor for turning up the television again and again when Erec was reading a book. The thought made Erec sick. He had felt justified at the time, but now poor Trevor was trapped in a cave with a vicious beast, held hostage because of him. Why hadn't Erec been more patient?

Was he turning evil now? Those things he did hadn't seemed any different from normal. Nobody had said anything to him, anyway. Maybe, he thought, someone should keep an eye on him.

Bethany was the obvious choice. She knew him better than anyone. And she was honest enough to tell him if he was acting different. Maybe she could also help him find the Furies. But even that seemed impossible. How *would* he find the Furies? They were superhuman creatures with power beyond his imagination, just like their sisters, the three Fates. . . .

That was it! For the first time, Erec had a spark of hope. He would speak to the three Fates. There was a well in Delphi, Greece, called the Oracle, where he could talk directly to them. They knew everything. They would tell him how to find their sisters. Maybe, if he was lucky, they would even tell him how to get his soul back.

Zoey burst through the door. Cherry Popsicle juice dripped down her hand, leaving red smudges around her face. "Erec! Erec! Mommy got me Flying Count cereal and Tummy Smacker Jumping Jelly Beans! You can have some—I saved five for you, five for Nell, and five for Trevor. Where is Trevor?" She looked around, candy-stuffed fist waving in anticipation.

Erec bit his lip. "Trevor is . . . he'll be back soon. Okay? I need to go . . . help him out." He hesitated. In their apartment there was a Port-O-Door—a magical door that would take him anywhere he wanted to go. It was tempting to leave right now before he had to face his mother. His heart sank at the thought of telling her what happened to Trevor. And what if she tried to stop him from finding the three Furies? He had to save Trevor and get his soul back again. . . .

Erec fought his urge to run away. He made himself wait until June walked through the door, carrying overflowing bags of groceries. She took one look at him and stopped in her tracks. "What's wrong, kiddo?" She set the bags down. "You look awful."

Erec's throat squeezed shut as he started to talk. He had to take a breath and start again. "I . . . Trevor . . ." What could he say? The truth was too horrible to spit out.

A look of alarm grew in June's eyes. "Where *is* Trevor?" She headed down the hallway, looking behind doors. "What happened?"

Erec followed her until he found the courage to say, "He's not here. Sit down, Mom."

June dropped into a kitchen chair. "Did someone take him? Is he kidnapped?" Tears formed in her eyes. "I was afraid this might happen. Did you call the police yet?"

"Mom?" Erec was confused. "You thought Trevor might be kidnapped?"

"No—I mean, not now at least, or I wouldn't have left him here. I was just worried about it. Of course. I mean . . ." She looked at Erec apprehensively.

"What? You mean what?"

June put her face in her hands. "We need to find him. And I don't think the police will be of any help." Her face crinkled and tears streamed down her cheeks. "I should have taken him with me. I should have been more careful. . . ."

"Mom—it's okay. It's not that bad. Trevor wasn't kidnapped. Not exactly."

Confusion wrinkled June's brow. "What do you mean? Where is he?"

"Well . . . it's not good." He managed to calm his breathing so he could tell her about Tarvos, and that Trevor was still there.

June jumped up and immediately started pacing. Erec recognized that she was going into action mode. She raised a finger a few times before she spoke. "A bull? In a cave? I don't understand. And you say you don't know where you were? Show me where in the wall that hole opened up."

Erec pointed to the spot and June felt for gaps, with no success. He hesitated a moment before dropping more terrible news, but he knew that he couldn't keep it a secret for long. "Tarvos had brought me there because my soul is gone—at least most of it. The Furies still have it, so maybe I can get it back. That's another reason I have to find them."

June stared at him. "Your *soul* is gone? What are you talking about?" She rested her hand over her eyes for a minute, thinking. "Do you mean that when you gave your soul to the Furies so they could escape, you didn't get it back again? I thought since the Hermit brought you back to life, you were back to normal. . . ." She eyed Erec critically from head to toe as if she might see his soul somewhere. "Could that be true? Do you feel different?"

"I feel the same—but Tarvos said that he could see that it was missing—and that I'll turn evil if I don't get it back. It's one of the three thousand souls the Furies keep in some awful prison, feeling miserable."

June winced, but then looked even more determined. "This is crazy. We have to find the Furies." She took a breath. "And try to figure out where Tarvos's cave might be. We need to go get Trevor out of there now."

"I have no idea where we were. We just climbed there through the tunnel."

June closed her eyes. "I'll call King Piter and see if he knows anything about this."

"Okay. And I'll see if Bethany will come with me to find the Furies."

June's eyes narrowed. "You mean with *us*, right? Just because you've been off cavorting across the globe before doesn't mean you can go on your own again. You understand?"

"Yeah. That's fine." Erec actually felt relieved that his mother was coming with him. It was too much to have the responsibility for rescuing Trevor all by himself. "We need to talk to the Fates at the Oracle and see where we can find the three Furies."

"Good idea. I'll call King Piter first." She went down the hall to the computer that had the MagicNet loaded on it—their connection to the Kingdoms of the Keepers.

Erec sat on the couch and held up a pair of magical glasses that were on a chain around his neck. He carried them with him everywhere—they let him see the person that he was missing the most. And right now that was his friend Bethany.

He put the black plastic frames on his face. All of a sudden, everything glimmered brightly around him. It seemed like the room was moving, and it made him dizzy. He focused on the wall, and it was oddly rounded, shiny and clear. It took a moment before he realized that he was inside a giant bubble—or at least that's where he was seeing that Bethany was. The shiny bubble wall was lined with a multitude of smaller bubbles, each shimmering with rainbow hues. Darker striped things on them were hard to make out, but on closer look they were books. Tons of books were everywhere, lining the bubble shelves.

It took a minute to find Bethany within all the wobbling, book-filled bubbles. She was sitting at a wooden desk which contrasted strangely with the bubble room, scribbling on a pad of paper and furiously paging through a thick math book.

"Bethany?"

She dropped her pencil. "Erec? Is that you?" She searched all around, unable to see him—Erec's glasses only let her hear him, even though he could see her.

"I'm here—I mean, I have my Seeing Eyeglasses on. Are you okay?"

"Hey, Erec! Yeah, I'm great." She settled back in her chair, a smile appearing on her face. "This place is so cool. Queen Posey gave me a huge suite to stay in with a bunch of rooms and servants. It's kind of like when I lived at King Piter's castle." Her eyes gleamed with excitement. "It's been great having time to read and work on my new math book. This one disproves my last book, which is pretty neat 'cause it totally changes the whole basis of math. The upper-level topology was all wrong, but there was no way to show it by proofs. So now the time-space continuum can be seen more realistically . . ." She laughed. "I'm sorry. I could talk about this for days. How are things going at your mom's place?"

"Terrible." Erec told her about everything from the bullfighter to losing his soul. "I have to fix all of this right away. But if Tarvos is right, then I might turn evil at any time. You know me better than anyone—would you hang out and keep an eye on me? If I start acting weird you can let me know when I still am able to do something about it."

"Of course! Oh, poor Trevor. We have to find him, fast. Do you have any ideas? I can't believe he's still in that cave! And your *soul* . . . This is awful." A hopeful look crossed her face. "I'm really glad to help, and of course I'll keep an eye on you if you want. But . . . is that the only reason you wanted me to come with you?"

Erec wondered what she might be thinking about. Why else

would he want to be with her? "No. I also need someone to hold in front of me in case the Furies attack."

She laughed, and then blushed a little. "I thought so. Yeah, I'd love to go with you." She crossed her arms and shivered. "I know you're upset, but don't worry. I'm sure this will all work out okay—it has to." She laughed. "And I miss hanging out with you, too."

Erec felt his own face turn red. He was glad that she couldn't see him right then.

Jam Crinklecut, King Piter's butler, followed Bethany through the Port-O-Door into Erec's apartment. He bowed low when he saw Erec.

Bethany ran up and gave Erec a hug. "Jam said he'd come with us! This will be like old times, the three of us exploring the world together...."

Jam blushed with pleasure, but June cleared her throat. "Not just the three of you. I'm here too, and the kids are out of school. So we'll all be together this time." She smiled at Jam. "It's good to see you, Jam. Thanks for coming with us."

Zoey ran up and hugged June's leg. "Where do we get to go, Mommy?"

Erec frowned. "You're bringing Zoey to find the Furies?"

June put her hands on her hips. "Of course not. For now we're just going to talk to the Fates and find out what to do next, right? We'll see what they say, and then I can decide what to do. King Piter didn't have any idea where that cave might be." She thought a moment. "Erec, do you think you can look through your Seeing Eyeglasses and talk to Trevor?"

"Great idea, Mom." He sat on the couch and put the glasses on, concentrating on his brother. When he opened his eyes, he found the cave walls surrounding him. Before him, Tarvos sat on his giant throne. Trevor squatted in a corner, pale arms tight around his knees. In between the bull and the boy, a young blond woman looked around herself in wonder. She squirmed, trying to pull her feet from the ground where they were stuck.

When she realized that she was trapped, she bared her teeth, hissing in anger at Tarvos. "What's going on? Where am I? And where's that little . . . bullfighter I followed down here?"

Tarvos laughed and leaned forward hungrily. The cranes preened on his back. "You belong to me now. And you will make a fine fighter when I am ready for you."

Tarvos pointed a hoof at the woman's face. She raised her hands to her head with a look of shock, then screamed as hundreds of cracks split deep through her skin. She looked like she was breaking into tiny pieces. At the same time she grew taller and heavier, her screech lowering into a deep, heavy moan, lower than a grown man's voice. She kept expanding until her clothing shredded, revealing a chunky gray bricklike body. Clumps slid off her, hitting the floor and bursting into sprays of sand. Blond hair streamed onto the floor like hay, and her features flattened until only slits remained for her eyes and mouth in her blocklike face.

What had once been a woman looked down at her arms and body, unable to speak. A door slid open in the cave wall, and Tarvos motioned for her to go through. She mutely lumbered past the doorway, leaving behind a trail of sand.

CHAPTER THREE

Terrible Visions

S WEAT DRIPPED DOWN Erec's face when he pulled off the glasses. That . . . thing was the Golem that Tarvos had tried to turn him into? A giant warrior made of sand?

"Is Trevor okay?" June was poised above him, a terrified look on her face.

"No . . . I mean . . . yes." Erec tried to calm down, knowing he was frightening her. "He's fine. I—I don't think he'll be hurt there."

June didn't look too sure. In a second she was already in the

Port-O-Door, pulling Zoey in behind her. "Let's go, quick. I want him out of there now."

"Modom, would you like me to wait here with Zoey? Or would you like to stay here with her? I will watch over these two."

June looked back and forth between her daughter and Jam.

"What if Nell comes back here when we're gone?" Erec asked.

June's shoulders dropped. "What am I thinking? I'm so upset, I forgot all about Nell coming home. I'll just call her now. . . . No." She sighed. "I'll stay here. You two will be fine with Jam. Just hurry back and let me know what is going on."

"Okay, Mom." He gave her a hug, and Jam and Bethany followed him into the Port-O-Door. They closed the vestibule door behind them and a screen lit up with four colored quadrants and an orange bar at the bottom labeled UPPER EARTH. He pressed the orange bar, and a world atlas sprang into view.

"The Oracle's in Greece." Erec tapped a finger on the eastern Mediterranean Sea and that part enlarged to fill the screen.

"There it is." Bethany touched the city of Delphi, and when it enlarged she found Mount Parnassus. "The Oracle is right here. Remember?"

Erec did not want to think about the last time he had spoken to the three Fates at the Oracle—back then he had thought that Bethany was dead. But now poor Trevor might be soon if he didn't work fast. He placed the Port-O-Door into a tree trunk near the base of the mountainside and swung the door open into the sunshine.

The Castilian spring that trickled from Mount Parnassus sprung into view as soon as they stepped out of the Port-O-Door. Erec took off running for it, hope building, but then his mind filled with questions. What would he find out from the Fates? They knew the future. What if they said that he could never talk to the Furies again? Then he would not be able to save his brother or his soul.

Which brought another thought into his mind. What about his other lost brother? And his missing sister? Now was the time to ask the Fates about them, too. Erec was one of King Piter's triplets. His other two birth siblings were supposed to join him on his quests so that they could become the next three rulers of the Kingdoms of the Keepers. He needed to find them—they would help with everything that he was doing. It would be great to find his missing mother, too. Queen Hesti had disappeared at the same time as his siblings did, and he was raised by June, who used to be one of the castle nurse-maids when Erec was little. The Fates knew everything, so maybe they could help. They usually didn't mind telling him things—at least when they were in the right mood.

Soon the Oracle, a plain-looking stone well, was in view. Nothing about it seemed unusual at first glance, other than that the water inside was extremely dark and deep. Erec swallowed his nervousness and thought about what he had to do.

"Oh, no." Bethany backed away, her hand up blocking her vision. "I don't want to watch this."

"Sorry." Erec flashed her a grin. "It's probably going to look awful."

"Oh, yes." Jam cleared his throat. "I forgot . . . I mean, you look perfectly respectable when your dragon eyes are out, young sir."

Erec took a breath. In order to call the Fates to the Oracle, he had to act as a medium, using his dragon eyes to look into the future. With all of his excitement about talking to the Fates, and worries about Trevor and his soul, he had forgotten that he would have to glimpse into his own future. And it was the last thing he wanted to do right now.

Sometimes Erec could direct what he saw in his future. His magic tutor and guardian, the Hermit, had told him that deep inside his heart he already knew all of the answers. When he looked into the future with his dragon eyes, he was simply showing himself what he needed to see. Maybe he would just ask himself to show what would happen to Trevor, and find out if he would be okay.

Then again, he was terrified to learn the answer to that. What if Trevor would *not* be okay? Then Erec wouldn't be able to keep on going.

He fought to overcome his fear, then he leaned over the well so the Fates would sense when he looked into the future. He closed his eyes.

Please, show me something that has nothing to do with Trevor. Or whether I'll get my soul back.

Erec followed the steps that the Hermit had taught him. First, he imagined himself entering a small, dark room in his mind. The moment he did, a feeling of calmness spread through him. Things would be all right, he knew. It felt good being back in this place, and he rested there for a while before imagining a second, smaller room within this first one. He pictured himself going through another doorway. Inside, he felt wonderful. Pure peace filled his being. Before him a box sat on a table. This box held all of the knowledge of the universe locked inside. Erec was ready to see what it would show him.

But first his fingers were drawn toward the box. It was warm, as he remembered it, and it seemed to hum a happy sound. All of his fears were gone. Life was good, and he was ready to enjoy it.

Before him, two windows perched on a wall, their shades drawn shut. When he opened them, they would function like his eyes, showing him a vision from his future. He reached for the soft cord that hung between them and pulled.

Erec ran fast, holding on to an ax and swinging it wildly. He was sweaty and out of breath. Anger and hate surged through him. Before long he came to a small house made of logs. He had to break into it. Erec raised the ax above his head and brought it down onto the door, splitting the wood. He yanked it out, then did it again and again. Pieces clattered to the ground as he kept chopping.

In a rage, he reached inside and unlocked the knob, then flung the door open with a growl. Before him, a family trembled. The mother held a young child tight, his arms wrapped around her neck. An older girl clung to her knee, crying.

The father stepped in front of them, arms out in a gesture of protection, but his hands shook badly. "Leave us alone. You can take anything you want from here. I don't care what happens to me, but stay away from my family."

"Jewels. Necklaces. Watches." Erec squinted around the room. "Where do you keep them?"

The man stuttered, upset. "D-don't take those. Please. Anything in the whole house is yours—but don't steal our jewels."

Erec swung the ax back over his shoulder, aiming at the man's neck.

"Sorry!" The man stepped back in shock. "I'm sorry. Go ahead. They're upstairs in my wife's dresser. But we don't have much. T-take what you want."

Erec shoved past them and went upstairs. He rooted through drawers, dumping out piles of clothing and old notebooks. . . .

Erec dropped the window shades and stepped back. His hands shook violently. He was robbing an innocent family of their valuables? That didn't even make sense. Unless . . .

He gulped. Yes, it did make sense. He was going to turn evil.

Tarvos had warned him what he would become if he didn't have a soul. Now he had seen it with his own eyes. He could not let that happen. If Erec could not find the Furies, he would give himself to Tarvos and get it over with. Thinking about the giant clay creature he would turn into made him sick, but that was better than being pure evil.

Then a horrible thought occurred to Erec. If what he saw in his future was right, and he ended up evil, then that meant he would not succeed in getting his soul back from the Furies. . . .

The warm box pulsed next to him, sending waves of calm into his mind. He put a hand on it until he started to feel better. Then he imagined himself leaving the dark rooms. He could feel his eyes turn in their sockets, bringing his normal blue eyes forward and rolling the dragon eyes back into the darkness. When he opened them, he squinted at the bright sunlight.

Below him the dark water in the well began to churn, racing in circles. The waters took on vivid colors, some of the shades strange like nothing he had seen anywhere else. All of a sudden, the well water frothed up. Bubbles raced toward him as if they would overflow the stone walls. Then they settled back into still blackness.

They would be there, listening now, he was sure. "Um . . . hello? Fates? Can you hear me?"

No one answered. Jam glanced at him, worried. Then three shrieks of pleasure echoed at once. "It's him, girls! Like, no way! This is sooo, like, totally cool."

"Oh, I love that boy! He is *so* to die for!"

"Eeek! That is so funny! Like, because someone *is* going to totally die for him!" The three exploded in laughter.

Erec didn't like the way that sounded. "What does that mean? Who is going to die for me?"

"Oh, that is so cute," one of the girl's voices said. "He wants to know who is going to die for him this time."

"This time?" Erec felt irritated and a little confused. "Someone died for me already?" But then his heart sank, and he knew what they were talking about. His dragon friend, Aoquesth, had died for him, and given him both of his dragon eyes. "Who else is going to die? When is that going to happen?"

"Now, if we told you that, it would take all the fun out of the surprise," one of the Fates chirped cheerfully.

"Fun?" Erec felt himself get upset and tried to calm down. Anger wouldn't get him anywhere with these powerful creatures. "Okay. Please would you tell me? I don't want someone to die because of me."

A fountain of laughter exploded from the depths of the well. "Oh, I love him. He is so cute!" They were beginning to fade away.

Erec realized that they were leaving already, and he had not gotten any information from them at all. Before it was too late, he shouted, "Wait! I need to know how to find your sisters—the three Furies! I have to try to get my soul back from them. I also have to get something to rescue Trevor . . . how can I do that? Where should I go?"

A few more giggles issued from the well, but Erec sensed a somber tone that had not been there before. "Of *course* we know that you want to find our sisters. We can tell you how to do that—but you have to trust us. Okay, lil' tyke?"

"Sure."

The voice that answered him back sounded deep and serious, not at all like the Fates he knew. Multiple tones spoke in unison, and their echo made the rocks around him vibrate. "You can find our sisters, Alecto, Tisiphone, and Megaera, in the Gray Mist Valley, in the land of Alsatia where they now live. They choose to remain there because it is blanketed by a special magic that keeps us from seeing what they are thinking and planning. This concerns us greatly.

"We once were forced to imprison our sisters in the caves of Tartarus to protect humanity from their wrath. For eons they had plotted revenge against us for shutting them in there. They had planned to wage war on us once they escaped, even though they knew it would cause the complete destruction of the world. Their anger was so great that they wanted everything to end.

"But when they met you, Erec, you were able to do something that nobody else could. You used the Awen charm that you carry around your neck to give them an inner peace that they had never felt before, and the Furies came away from that changed. We gave you the quest to go to them because we knew that you might be able to sway them this way. But we did not know if you would succeed.

"Now, it is impossible for us to tell what they will do next. We are sure that even they do not know. They might choose to make peace with us, or to create chaos. It could go either way. We have no power in Alsatia, so they have complete freedom to prepare to attack us if they wish.

"You can speak to the Furies about the questions that you have for them. They will talk to you. Our sisters hold you in the highest regard. You gave yourself to them to help them escape, and you asked for nothing in return. But be cautious. You will have to make important decisions, and your choices will affect the outcome of everything. Do what is right, don't forget that. The Furies may give you what you need to free your brother. But that will come at a price too.

"You will not succeed in speaking to our sisters if you go now. First you must draw your next quest from Al's Well. That quest will give you something you will need in order to approach them. When it is time to speak to them, you can find Alsatia by falling into Mercy's Spike in Pinefort Jungle in Otherness. Good luck."

A deep silence followed, rather than the usual giggles coming from the well. Erec was glad that Jam was furiously taking notes. There was no way he would remember all of the places he had to go. And what was Mercy's Spike? What kind of a place does one have to fall to get into? The whole plan sounded strange. The Fates had said to trust them—and how could he not? They had only been right before, always helped him. His mind whirled—what was he forgetting? He needed to ask them something else. . . .

"I need to find my birth siblings—the two missing triplets. Can you tell me where to look for them?"

The voice that bubbled back sounded amused. "He wants to know where they are, girls! Should we help our little prince? I don't want to give away all the fun!"

"Here's a hint, hero. Your brother is near, and your sister is far. Your sister is close, and your brother is distant. Your sister needs help, and your brother needs more. But you need the most help of all, so you better find them!"

Another voice chimed, "That was *so* good, Nona! I love your riddles!"

That answer didn't help him at all. What she said was more confusing than anything else. But right now he was elated that he would actually be able to find the Furies. It sounded like he would even get that Master Shem thing to help Trevor escape. Which reminded him . . .

"What about my soul? Do the Furies still have it?"

"Like, *of course* they have your soul! Unh! How do you think they escaped that Tartarus place? I mean, like, you don't think they want to go back to that gnarly prison, do you, hero? For real! They want to keep their sweet hind claws out of that place, so they're going to hold tight on to every one of those little souls. Like, wow."

"Well, how can I get mine back, then?"

The voice sang back, "Like, I don't know. Maybe you'll have to send our sisters back to Tartarus. You know, free all of those poor souls again."

Another voice added, giggling, "Good luck!"

Back in the apartment, June leaned on Erec's shoulder, face pale. "I didn't want you doing any more of those quests. They have been ridiculously dangerous. And what have they gotten us? Things are worse than ever. King Piter's castle is gone. He's stuck living with Queen Posey now, in Ashona. He has to be near her scepter if he wants to stay alive, since he's so old. Baskania is in a better position then ever, using those Stain triplets as the next kings. And he found out that Bethany's brother is the one that holds the secret of the Final Magic that he has been looking for. The Furies are out of their prison and could end the world at any minute." June looked from one person to the next, waiting for them to agree that Erec should just stay home.

Erec was surprised. "So . . . you don't want me to try to save Trevor? And get my own soul back?"

June squeezed her eyes shut. "Of course I do. It's just killing me to let you go do this again. I convinced myself we were through. You don't know how hard it is to let you go off and do dangerous things. And sending you to meet the three Furies—those horrendous beings—in person . . ."

Jam put an arm around her. "Modom, I will accompany young sir the entire way and watch out for him. And during his quest, the Hermit will also be keeping an eye on the boy. I assure you that he will be well taken care of."

"Don't worry, I'll watch out for him too." Bethany grinned. Erec knew that she looked forward to having an adventure with him. He only wished he could be as excited about it. Bethany hadn't seen the Furies in person or she might have a different attitude about going anywhere near them.

June shook her head. "What can I do? I guess we don't have a choice. Thank you, Jam. It means more than I can say to have you with him."

He blotted a few tears from her face with his handkerchief. "My pleasure, Modom."

Erec tried to reassure himself as much as he did her. "It's okay, Mom. We'll just go do the quest quick—it's probably no big deal. The Fates said that we'd be fine talking to the Furies after that. I'm sure they know what they are talking about." He paused a moment. Had the Fates really said that they would be okay? Not exactly. They did say that he would be able to talk to the Furies only after he finished his next quest, not that he would survive meeting them again. It wasn't worth bringing up and worrying his mother about—but he would have to make sure Bethany didn't go anywhere near the Furies, just in case.

A wooden door appeared in the wall of Erec's apartment, and somebody knocked on it. It was someone else's Port-O-Door, but who could be knocking?

June and Jam both seemed as surprised as Erec was. Jam put his hand on the knob, but then thought better of opening it. "Who is there?"

"It's me, Rosco Kroc. Are you busy?"

Jam glanced back at June. "Ma'am?"

"It's okay," Erec said. "Rosco has been helping us."

The corners of June's mouth turned up. "I know, Erec. I got to spend a little time with Rosco in Smoolie, remember? He's been a good friend."

Jam opened the door and waved Rosco inside. Erec cracked a

smile when he saw Rosco's green scaled face. Rosco grinned and waved for a moment before Bethany ran up and threw her arms around him. "It's so great you're here, Osc—I mean Rosco. We have a lot going on, and we could use a little help."

June nodded to Rosco. "That would be great. Anything you could do . . ."

Rosco looked confused. "Are you having problems? I'd have come sooner. I was just stopping by with some news for Erec. What's going on?"

Everyone took turns filling Rosco in on the horrible details of the day. Rosco sat on the couch, stunned. "I have heard of Tarvos. Baskania has mentioned him. I think he's working with him on something, but I don't know the details. I'll find out, and I'm sure I can learn where his cave is."

"You see that?" June pointed at Rosco, excited. "There is another way! Erec, you don't have to do that next quest or see the Furies after all. We'll just get the information from Rosco and go straight to Trevor."

Although that sounded tempting, Erec knew that it wouldn't work. "Mom, you know that when the Fates tell me what I have to do, it's the only thing that will help. That's proven itself every single time."

Before June could protest, Rosco nodded. "Erec, you're right. Do what you need to, but I'll be looking into things from my end too. I'll get back to you once I get any details. But I can tell you that Baskania wasn't behind trapping Erec and Trevor in that cave. He's still hoping you're going to show up at the Green House in a day or two with your scepter."

"That would never happen," Bethany said. "So, what did you come here to tell us?"

Rosco looked around in thought. "Not to be rude, but maybe if Erec and I can just have a few minutes alone . . ."

June gave a nod, then Rosco motioned for Erec and Bethany to follow him down the hall. As soon as Bethany closed the door to Erec's room, she spun around. "What's going on, Oscar? I've been worried about you! Have you been okay?"

Rosco laughed. "Never worry about me, Bethany. I'm too powerful and connected now to be hurt. Remember, Baskania can't read my mind, so I'm pretty safe. It's you two that have to be careful, not me. That's what I came to tell you about."

"Is this about the letter I got from the Green House?" Erec asked. "The one saying that all of the armies of Alypium and Aorth are coming after me if I don't give Baskania my scepter?"

Rosco shook his head. "There is even more bad news, unfortunately. I don't want to upset the rest of your family, but you need to know this. The Shadow Prince has stepped up his game. He has tons of detectives and hunters out searching for Bethany's lost brother—the one that knows the secret to the Final Magic he's been searching for. And when he's not obsessing about that, he's plotting to find the scepters. The Stain triplets are going to become kings in a few weeks, and he's going to get them one way or another. The Stain boys understand that they're working for him—he's the one in control."

Bethany put her hand to her head. "My brother . . . we have to find him before Baskania does. What can we do?"

Erec could feel the stress inside himself rise thinking about what she was going through. Bethany had a missing brother, just like he did. But now hers was in mortal danger.

"I'll let you know as soon as I find out more. Just try to think of any clues about where your brother might be. For now, be on the alert. I'm keeping an eye out at the Green House." He tapped his eye, the one that he had once given to Baskania and Erec had returned to him. "Thanks again for this."

"It's okay, Oscar." Bethany smiled. "We're just glad that you stopped by."

"If anything else comes up, let me know. Don't trust snail mail, though. Nobody would spy on mine, but yours might be read. It's best to be safe. When you want me, just drop me a snail with nothing written on it. I'll figure out where you are—I'm good at that."

"Thanks, Oscar. It's great to see you."

"You too, kid." Rosco got up and headed out. "Don't forget—if you ever need me, just let me know."

Jam packed more things into backpacks for himself, Erec, and Bethany than they would ever need. Erec was glad to see that he was taking their favorite Serving Tray along—the silver tray that magically produced whatever foods they wanted to eat.

Jam's brow wrinkled. "You have to get to Al's Well to draw your next quest, but I don't think going there is safe. The last time, soldiers and guards were surrounding the place and Harpies were flying overhead to keep watch. I'm sure that hasn't changed. I wonder how we should proceed. Do you think we should fly in aboard a dragon again?"

Erec shook his head. "The last time I did that, I almost got shot out of the sky. Bethany and I found a way to get to Al's Well through the waterways under the city. They lead right up to it. We can go in and out safely from there."

Jam frowned. "That's odd. I didn't pack bathing suits. You know me—it's my magical gift to always be prepared. I should have them somewhere."

"Don't worry," Bethany said. "We usually go in our clothes. Last time we didn't have time to change. It won't matter, anyway. Once our Instagills start to work we feel perfect in the water, even with wet clothes on. We don't get cold or hungry. . . ."

It occurred to all of them at once that Jam did not have Instagills to let him breathe underwater. Erec and Bethany had won theirs in a contest last year in Alypium. "I suppose . . ." Jam tapped his chin. "I might slow you down, paddling on top while you are swimming underwater."

Bethany shook her head. "That wouldn't be a problem. But I don't know if there is any air at the top of the water tunnels. You might not be able to go at all."

Jam cracked a grin. "Wait a minute. I suppose that I am prepared, after all." He opened his backpack and pulled out a small tank. "Oxygen. I wasn't sure why I brought one of these." He laughed. "Now I see why I had the odd impulse." He slung it over his shoulder and tucked it under his backpack. "Where do we find the underwater tunnels, young sir and modom?" He raised his eyebrows politely.

Bethany said, "They're everywhere, but the closest place to Al's Well is the swimming pool outside King Piter's house in Alypium."

Erec said, "One other place might work better—the Oracle, where we just were."

Bethany smiled. "That's right! That well led straight into the tunnels."

In minutes, Erec, Bethany, and Jam were walking under the sparkling blue skies of Delphi, Greece. Bright sunshine warmed their backs, and rushing water bubbled near their feet. Soon Erec was gazing down into the Oracle's blackness again.

"I should see if the Fates will help send us to Al's Well like they did last time. That way we won't get lost for sure."

Bethany frowned. "I don't know. Aren't you worried that you're calling them back too soon? I wouldn't want to bug them. Maybe we should jump in and see if they'll help us on their own."

"I doubt it," Erec said. "They probably won't know that we're here unless I call for them again." He thought a moment. "I don't want to bother them either. But we could drift around in those tunnels forever and never find Al's Well. I better just ask them."

As soon as he said that, a bad realization hit him. He would have to look into the future again with his dragon eyes so he could call the Fates. The vision he had seen last time was too much—he was robbing a terrified family like a sick criminal. It was obviously the end result of being soulless and turning evil. What else would he see himself doing in the future?

He took a breath and leaned over the well, eyes closed. After a moment he visualized that familiar dark room deep inside of his mind. It felt warm and comforting to be there again. Erec found the second door within it, opened it, and went in.

The second room was even darker and more peaceful. The humming box on the table nearby radiated a calm wisdom. He was ready for whatever he needed to show himself. So Erec reached for the silken cord hanging between the two windows and pulled. . . .

Kids ran all around a playground, handing out candy. Anger seared through Erec, making him shake. Give that to me!" He dove at the kids with a snarl. A low growl escaped from his throat as he grabbed candy from their hands. People stared at him with wide eyes, as if he were a maniac. But there was no time to stop— so many kids, so much candy. And he had to take it all!

Mothers darted toward their children, trying to save them. But Erec could run faster than they could. One of the toddlers was surprisingly strong, and Erec struggled a while before yanking the sweets out of his hand. His mother looked equally confused and terrified. Right behind her was a kid about to put an opened lollipop right into her mouth. Not when Erec was there—he'd get it first! Shoving the mother out of his way, he snatched the sucker out of the little girl's fist, leaving her crying and rubbing her hand.

A few kids got knocked into one another as lollipops in their hands sailed into the air—Erec grabbing each one. Some kids still sat on the swings. They looked small and defenseless —taking their candy would be easy. He scooped the lollipops straight from their little fists.

One of the mothers stepped forward, outraged. "What's wrong with you? These are little kids. . . ." She tried to grab his arm, but he shoved her back. There was still a lollipop he had missed, and she wasn't going to get in the way. "Ow! Somebody call the police. This guy's crazy! Let's get out of here, Dougie."

The last kid was older, and he struggled with Erec before letting go of his lollipop. Erec hadn't meant to trip him, but the kid ended up on his face, his cheek cut and bleeding.

That wasn't important. Erec had all the candy now, so he patted his pockets and turned away. He had won—he had taken every child's candy in the whole park. But it wasn't enough. Now he had to steal something else. . . .

Erec dropped the window shades and stepped back. He could feel himself shaking. It did not seem right to touch the black box next to him and calm down after seeing this—he did not deserve to feel good. Instead he quickly left both of the dark rooms. After he felt his dragon eyes swivel into the back of his eye sockets and his regular eyes come out, he opened them in the bright sunlight. He was blinded after the darkness, but he was too angry at himself to care. Why should he be comfortable, knowing the awful things that he was going to do?

This was worse than the first vision he had today. Stealing candy from kids? And not just taking it but practically beating them up?

He could think of only one possible reason. By then he had lost his soul. He would not get it back. Instead, he would become evil and do horrible things to people.

Bethany was watching him, with a curious expression on her face. He thought about telling her what he saw . . . but the words wouldn't come out of his mouth. How could he let her think of him that way?

No, he would keep this nasty secret to himself. He would try not to think about it until he started to see signs that he was deteriorating. Then he would have to find a foolproof plan to give himself to Tarvos before he hurt anyone else.

CHAPTER FOUR

The Erec Rex Fan Club

"**F**ATES?" Erec called into the blackness of the well. "Sorry to bother you again. Can you help me?"

Nothing but silence issued from the well. Bethany also peered into the black water, and Jam looked concerned.

Erec went on, "I won't ask you any questions this time. I'm sure you don't want to be bothered again. But we have to get to Al's Well so I can draw my next quest. Could you send us there through the water tunnels?"

A faint giggle echoed from far away. Maybe they had heard him.

Erec gave Bethany a half smile. "Ready to jump in? I guess they're either going to help us or they aren't."

Jam fitted a tube into his mouth and attached it to his oxygen tank. The tank seemed awfully small. Erec sure hoped it was magical, so there might be more inside of it than it seemed. Likely, Jam was prepared with what he needed.

Erec climbed up the well and jumped into the clear water. It felt strange in a familiar way—boiling hot and freezing cold at the same time, yet not exactly painful. The sensation was intense, the same as it always felt in the Oracle, or near Al's Well—waters that were touched by the Fates.

Bethany slid in next, followed by Jam. Both of their eyes flew open in shock from the feel of the water. The Instagills in Erec's wrists opened and he relaxed, breathing through them. He felt warmer and more comfortable, floating with ease. Bethany looked relaxed as well, but Jam was fidgeting with his mouthpiece and shivering.

They floated for a minute, not going anywhere. Then a rush of warm water shoved them to the bottom of the cistern and around a bend into a rock-lined channel. Erec tumbled through the water, arms over his head so he didn't hit himself on a wall. The current catapulted them past forks and passage openings, around sharp turns and down steep holes.

Bethany was the only one able to control herself in the water so that she could travel headfirst most of the way. Erec could not stop laughing when he saw Jam spinning wildly in the water. Jam squeezed his backpack and oxygen tank to his chest as he whizzed by. His hair waved around his face like a lion's mane, and his eyes were bugged out in shock.

Erec recognized a few of the wider turns and passages, but most of the tunnels looked alike. It felt good soaring through the water, almost like he was flying. Before long they slowed down, and the water began to have that strange feel again. A hole in the roof of the tunnel let in a beam of bright sunlight, creating a lit circle in the water. When they swam into it, they found that they were looking up at the sky through an open toilet lid.

Jam popped his head into the air and took out his mouthpiece. When he realized he was inside a toilet, disgust crept over his face. He bit down on the mouthpiece again and sank next to Erec and Bethany.

A shadow fell on them as a large head leaned over the opening. Looking down through the toilet seat was a man in overalls. Tools hung from his belt, and a patch saying AL was sewn onto one of the blue straps. His mouth hung open in surprise, and then he burst out laughing. Erec and Bethany could hear him perfectly through the water, and they could speak as well—some of the perks of their Instagills. "Boy, do dose three girls have a sense of humor. Dey were complaining that deyr water was clogged with three pieces of . . . Well, never mind. I'm glad dey let me know you were coming. It's about time you came back to pick your next quest, kid. Things in Alypium ain't lookin' so good, wit the Stain boys 'bout to become kings and all. You hear deyr coronation is on June twenty-fifth? Dat's in just three weeks, enough time to prepare for whatever massive kind of celebration dey're planning. Do ya think you can finish the rest of your quests before then so's you can stop them?"

Erec had not even considered finishing all of his quests in the next few weeks. It actually wasn't a bad idea—that is, if this and the other quests were a little safer. Once he had accomplished them all, he would be the true ruler of Alypium. The scepter would be his to command, and he would be able to build a huge new castle for himself with its magic. The Stain boys would be no match for him then. Even Baskania might not be able to hurt him with all the power he would wield.

Then a horrible thought occurred to him. What if he got the

scepter and then he turned evil? He tried not to think about how horrible that would be.

"What's wrong?" Bethany eyed him suspiciously. "You should see the look on your face."

"Um . . . nothing." Erec wasn't ready to tell Bethany about his visions of his future. "I'm just thinking about those quests. You know how hard they've been."

"Al has a point. You might as well try to do them as soon as you can. What's the use in waiting when the Stains are about to take over?"

"Yeah . . . we'll see. Right now I need to get this one done fast so I can get Trevor out of that cave." He looked up at Al. "Is the quest paper floating around in here somewhere?" He waved his hand around in the water hoping to find it, but nothing appeared.

Al shook his head. "Nah. You need to sign Janus's paper pad first. Da ya remember how ya got there last time?"

"Oh, yeah." Janus was the guardian of the quests, and he was in the Labor Society building right next to them. "I'll be right back." Erec dove deeper and found the water tunnel that tracked under the foundation of the building. Multiple pipes tracked straight upward from the tunnel. Most of them were too small for him to enter, but a few were wide enough. He swam up into one that he was sure he had been in before. Around the corner was a row of openings with light shining through. He cringed as he swam past those, remembering that they were openings from toilets in a bathroom.

The pipe narrowed, but Erec was able to fit all the way to the end. A small hole opened up above him through a sink drain. Yes, this is definitely where he had found Janus before.

Last time he was here, Janus had sobbed through the drain. The poor guy had been so lonely, with nothing to do but wait with his paper pad for the few moments of company he would have when Erec signed for his next quest. So Erec was confused when

he heard what sounded like dance music playing in the room.

"Woo-hoo! Shake it, baby!" The voice was definitely Janus's, but Erec had never heard the little man actually sound like he was having fun. Laughter and voices tinkled through the room.

Erec had no idea how Janus would hear him with a party going on in the room. He shouted through the drain, "Janus! Janus! Help me—it's Erec Rex. In the sink!"

His words were lost in the loud music. He had to think of another way. . . . Desperate, Erec wiggled the drain with his fingers. After poking it awhile, he gave it a punch and it popped out into the sink. His hand just fit through the drain, so he stuck it through, wiggling his fingers.

In a minute he heard a scream. "Eew! Look at this! A *hand* is coming out of the sink. *Janus!*"

"It's okay there, sweetie. Just let old Janus here take a look and—ugh! You're not kidding. What is this thing?"

Someone grabbed Erec's fingers and tugged as if his whole body would come through the little sink drain after it. He figured that it must be Janus, so he yanked his hand back out, put his face up to the hole and shouted. "It's me—Erec Rex! I need to sign the paper pad with you so I can get my next quest!"

"Oh, my! Is it really . . . ?" Then Janus's tone changed from amazed to commanding. "Stop! Turn down the music, Lenora. We have an important guest here with us today! The *most* important one—the hero I have been telling you all about. It's Erec Rex!"

The music stopped, and a hush settled over the room. "It's him!" "Erec Rex is here!" "Now we get to see him for ourselves!"

"You have quite a following here, Erec," Janus said. "Seems these good folks have come at the right time. Now they can witness the magic of you signing your name. I'll go get the pad."

Janus stuffed a pen through the drain into Erec's hand. "So, old friend, how have you been doing?" Erec had the odd feeling that Janus was bragging—playing up how close the two of them were . . . but that didn't make sense. Why would these people care about him? And who were they, anyway?

"I'm okay," Erec answered. Then he thought about his fate to become a Golem. "If you call having only a few months left to live being okay."

There was a gasp in the room. Someone shrieked, "Erec Rex is going to die!"

Chaos ensued, with screeches and yammering. Someone was crying, accompanied by an odd sound like castanets clicking.

"Quiet!" Janus peered through the hole. "Erec, what is going on? Tell us what's wrong. A lot of people here care about you. Can we do anything to help?"

Erec found himself speechless. It was still unthinkable to him that he could have fans in Alypium, let alone people that liked him at all. The last time he had been here, everyone despised him. They all had believed Baskania that Erec was a villain, trying to take over as their king even though the Stain triplets were the rightful rulers. People had booed him in the streets, called him names. . . .

Could people really be on his side? If that was true, the last thing he wanted to do was to tell them all that he would soon turn evil. "No, really, I'm okay. I just mean . . . things have been pretty dangerous. That's all. I get worried about doing the quests."

Janus sounded victorious. "You hear that? Erec Rex is as human as you and I. Which only makes him that much more remarkable. He does dangerous quests, risking his life, even though he is terrified of what might happen next. And he does this for you and me, so that we may live safely, protected from Baskania."

Was Erec hearing right? He grinned from ear to ear. This was the first time he had had a pat on the back for doing the quests. Janus was right—Erec had been risking his life for their sakes. He was starting to feel pretty good about himself. That is, until he remembered he would soon be stealing kids' lollipops. . . .

"Thanks, Janus. Do you have the pad for me to sign?"

"Here it is." Erec saw the paper through the hole and pressed the pen against it, marking it with his name. In a moment the paper split where his pen had touched it, opening deep into the pad. Bright light streamed through the cracks.

"There it is." Janus waved the page in the air. "It is definitely his signature."

Wild applause filled the room, and Erec could feel his face grow hot. He wished that Bethany had come with him so she could hear this as well. "Janus? Why are all of these people with you? Who are they?"

Janus's voice filled with pride. "It's your fan club, Erec. And it's growing. You can thank your friend Jack for all of this. When he sent a mouse in here with a message for me once, it gave me an idea. I'm not allowed to leave this place, but there is no reason I can't have visitors. I trained a few mice carefully, feeding them by hand. Then I strapped notes on their backs and let them go outside, hoping they would approach people for food. Well, a few of them did, and my notes got out. Next thing you know, life has been wonderful!"

"What did the notes say?"

Janus cleared his throat, embarrassed. "Well, they said I was having a party here, of course."

"A party?"

"Um, yes. I figured that if I was going to invite people to visit, I might as well give them a good reason to come. So I always have a party going now. We have a great following. Some people bring music, others bring food, and I bring . . ."

Erec waited to hear what Janus had to offer. A few voices shouted, "Tell him! Tell Erec what you bring to the party!"

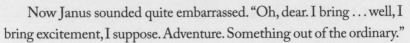

Now Janus sounded quite embarrassed. "Oh, dear. I bring . . . well, I bring excitement, I suppose. Adventure. Something out of the ordinary."

How could Janus, the person with the most boring job on the planet, someone who had to sit and wait all the time, bring excitement to anybody?

Another voice shouted, "He brings *you*, Erec Rex. Illegal, unapproved, risky, dangerous you. That's what's exciting. It wasn't just a party he invited us to, it was an Erec Rex party! On top of all our fun, we knew that at any time you might show up and do that magic with the paper. That was really cool!"

Someone else chimed in, "We all thought you were some kind of criminal mastermind before Janus told us the truth about you. That's the word around Alypium—you are pure evil. Which is actually why most of us came here to begin with. None of us had seen you in person, so the chance that we'd get to glimpse the underworld villain we'd all heard about was kind of thrilling."

"But you're not like that at all!" a girl's voice shouted. "Janus was *so* cool, telling us the real story about you."

Erec flushed with excitement. People had heard the truth—and they believed it. Maybe he did have a hope of ruling them someday as a good king. . . .

But no. He didn't have a soul.

"Come in here, Erec! We want to see you in person!" A chorus of cheers arose, along with shouts of agreement.

When it quieted down, Erec said, "I can't fit through the drain. This is the only way I can get here now."

Dissatisfied murmurs filled the room. Janus sounded uncomfortable. "Well, Erec, maybe you could stay there awhile and let people take turns looking at your eye through the hole?"

"Yes!" People sounded happy with that suggestion, so Erec agreed. When he put his eye against the drain hole, he finally got a good look at Janus. In the past, the man had been covered in dust, dressed like a shabby survivor of a desert island. But now he wore sunglasses, a suit, and a bow tie. His long white hair had been cut and pulled into a neat ponytail, and he looked more like a movie star than a prisoner in a dungeon. The partygoers took turns staring at Erec's eye, waving at him and peering inquisitively. Finally, Erec pushed his fingers through the drain hole and waved good-bye.

"Where were you? We were worried!" Bethany's arms were crossed. "I was going to come find you, but Jam talked me into waiting. Are you okay?"

"I'm fine. Sorry, Janus had a party going on in there—and the people were all part of a fan club for me. I couldn't believe it."

Bethany looked like she couldn't believe it either. But before she said anything, Erec felt something warm in his grip. "It's the quest!"

His hand was shaking now that he was about to find out his mission. How dangerous would this quest be? And how long would it take? He needed to find the three Furies right away so that he could save Trevor.

Slowly, he brought the paper to his face. He read it out loud, his voice dropping off by the end of the unbelievable words that came out of his mouth:

"'Trade your life for the next five people to be killed by Baskania at noon tomorrow in the Diamond Minds of Argos.'"

Trade his life? Die? Erec felt faint. He pulled the paper quest close to his chest in case Bethany and Jam had not caught what he had said. But it was too late. Jam choked, his face purple. He shot upward, coughing and sputtering in the air under the large white commode of Al's Well. Bethany looked stunned. She gasped and grabbed her neck as if she did not have Instagills implanted in her skin, and then she closed her eyes and fainted in the dark waters.

CHAPTER FIVE
Robbing People Blind

EREC LOOKED FIRST up and then down, not sure who needed more help. Jam grasped the toilet's edge, coughing hard, but he seemed to be okay. So Erec swam down and scooped Bethany into his arms. Her face looked so soft and vulnerable. He could not believe that she had passed out because she had heard his seventh quest—even though it was beyond horrible. He had to give up his life?

He pushed Bethany past Jam and out of the water. Jam helped him lift her through the sparkling porcelain opening above them until she tumbled forward onto the grass. Erec climbed out after her, feeling his Instagills close and air rush into his lungs again. Bethany was breathing, but her eyes stayed shut. She looked so peaceful that Erec was tempted to just let her lie there.

Jam felt Bethany's forehead. "Oh, dear. She's had a shock, I think." His black dinner jacket was drenched, but when he checked through the insides of its many pockets, Erec noticed that they were amazingly dry. "Let's try this."

He pulled out a small vial and took its top off, waving it under Bethany's nose. Her eyes instantly flew open and she bolted upright to a sitting position, crashing into Erec.

"Ow." They both rubbed their heads, laughing for a second until Bethany's smile faded. "What was this last quest? You have to go somewhere and give your life up—to save some strangers?" Her forehead wrinkled and she crossed her arms. "You just won't do it, then. This has gone too far. Your last quest ended up with you dying. The only reason you're here today is that you got lucky. I doubt that you'd be brought back to life again! Anything could go wrong." She stared at Erec, and when he didn't answer, she added, "This would probably be the end for you."

"It will be the end for me." Erec knew that he should tell Bethany the rest of the bad news, that he would be turning evil and doing awful things, but he felt sick saying the words. If the Fates wanted him to go this way, at least maybe Trevor would be saved, somehow. It might be what had to happen. "I guess this *will* be my last quest. I won't be coming back again." He closed his eyes. It was too much to absorb. How could his life be over already? But at the same time, he was a goner anyway, unless he could get his soul back. And that obviously wasn't going to happen.

Bethany's face turned red. "What do you mean, you won't be coming back? You're not actually considering this, are you?"

Erec tried to stay calm. "What choice do I have? Listening to the Fates was the only thing that saved you from Baskania. How can I not save Trevor?" He looked around. "The only reason that all of us are alive today is because I did what the Fates said. Otherwise the three Furies would have killed everyone. How can I *not* do this?"

"But you don't have to, Erec! Just stop all of this craziness and go home. We'll go find Trevor ourselves, with Rosco's help. Then we can figure out how to get him away from that bull creature. I'm sure there is a way. And it will be easier than that quest."

Erec turned away. It was too hard to look at her face as he said, "The Fates said the only way to save Trevor is this. My days are numbered anyway, okay? The Furies took my soul, and they still have it. Any day now I'm going to turn evil. I mean *really* evil, Bethany. I've seen the stuff that I'm going to do—and it's not pretty. I'm going to turn into a whole different person. That's why Tarvos called me to him. He was going to turn me into a Golem so I'm not a danger to everyone." Even speaking the words made him sick. How could he actually walk into his death? But at the same time, what else was there to do? Not save Trevor and instead become an evil maniac?

Bethany stared at him, mouth open. Finally, she said, "But you can get your soul back from the Furies, remember?" She thought a moment and then gasped. "Wait a minute. . . . You need to do this quest before you can talk to the Furies? This is horrible! You have to die before you can even talk to them about getting your soul back? There has to be another way. . . ."

"Bethany, I saw into the future with my dragon eyes, and no other way will work."

She squinted at him, eyes red, and covered her ears with her hands. "I don't want to hear this."

"I'm sorry." Erec gave her a hug and gently pulled a hand off her ear. "If I do this quest—even if I die—I might still be able to talk to the Furies after. If I die, maybe they'll give me my life back. That's what I have to keep thinking about."

He didn't feel too confident. But there really were no other options. Thinking about Trevor helped him focus. At least now he wasn't keeping all of his worries inside. Plus, he would be saving five people that were about to be killed by Baskania, wouldn't he? If he had to go, better that way than become a Golem . . .

Jam looked sick. "Young sir, Modom Bethany might be correct. Let's think first of another way to save Trevor. I'm sure your father would agree."

"There *is* no other way. Didn't you hear the Fates?" Erec shook his head. "Both of you have to promise never to say a word about this to my parents. They would try to do something stupid to stop me." He looked from Jam to Bethany. "I need all the help I can get to have the guts to go through with this. Do you think it's easy? It's going to be nearly impossible, but it's the only logical choice."

Bethany's voice sounded strangled. "Please, Erec. Just give it a chance. We'll try to save Trevor ourselves. We've done a lot harder things than that before! And I promise you—if I see you changing, turning into something . . . bad, I'll tell you right away, okay? I won't let you go on like that."

Jam nodded solemnly. "Young sir, I, too, will watch you like a hawk. And I will be prepared to restrain you if you start doing things that you shouldn't. Plus, I shall wait until that time to say anything to your parents, just in case you never turn evil at all. There is no need to worry them yet. But Bethany is correct. Do not even think about giving your life in this quest tomorrow. I must beg you to reconsider. Please, young sir."

Erec took a breath. They would never understand, he was sure. They had not been with him when Tarvos told him what his fate was. They had not seen the visions of Erec destroying families and hurting children. They did not understand that the Fates knew the only way he could save his brother. Erec's future was hopeless, no matter what he did at this point. Finally, he pretended to agree, so they didn't get in his way. He had to free Trevor. And he would save five innocent victims of Baskania as well.

Or at least he hoped he would have the guts to do it. Thinking about what might happen to him made him physically sick. But he was literally doomed either way, with no soul. And what about all of those other poor souls kept hostage with the Furies? That wasn't fair either. Erec tried to push them out of his mind.

He would go to the Diamond Mines of Argos—no, it was the Diamond Minds, whatever they were. Tomorrow, before noon, he would sneak away and do whatever he had to do.

"What is that look on your face?" Bethany stared at him suspiciously. "Something is up with you. I can tell."

Erec shook his head, the picture of innocence. "No, I'm just thinking about what to do." He forced a smile on his face. "Let's go home."

The paper with the quest on it was missing from his night table when Erec awoke the next morning. He guessed that either Jam or Bethany had taken it, hoping that he would not be able to do the quest without remembering its details. But its words were etched into Erec's mind: *Trade your life for the next five people to be killed by Baskania at noon tomorrow in the Diamond Minds of Argos.* The *next* five people to be killed? What was Baskania up to now? How many people was he killing? The idea made him sick.

Jam stuck his head into Erec's room and nodded with a smile. "Ah, you're awake. Splendid. Let me know if you need anything, young sir. And I'm so sorry. I hope you don't mind the . . . inconvenience."

"What inconvenience?" Erec didn't see anything unusual, but

when he tried to sit up he was yanked back onto his bed. He realized thin cords were stretched around his wrists and ankles. The bands were tight but not uncomfortable. Strangely, there were no ties anywhere, so he could not take them off. "Jam! Get me out of this thing."

"So sorry, young sir." He cleared his throat, embarrassed. "I didn't put those on. And I'm not able to undo its spell. I'm afraid that Bethany had a . . . um, talk with your mother this morning." He raised a hand and smiled sympathetically. "Don't be angry, young sir. They both care about you a great deal, and they just wanted to make sure that you would be okay today. Ring that bell by your bed if you need anything. And I am sure that someone will take those off this afternoon, of course. Oh, and you received this snail mail this morning."

Jam handed him a letter, then backed out of the room, apologizing. Erec tried to sit up and was again thrown back onto his mattress. The more he struggled against the cords, the angrier he got. Who were Bethany and his mother to make this decision for him? They were ruining everything. Now he would end up turning evil and losing his life anyway . . . all for nothing. The people dying today would not be saved. Trevor would never be rescued. He would never talk to the Furies and try to get his soul back.

Angrily, he tore open the letter Jam gave to him, able to raise his wrists high enough to read.

Erec,

I hope this finds you well. It has been a while since I've heard from you, so I thought I should give you some updates about what has been going on. Don't worry about this snail being intercepted. I found a spell to charm the paper so it can be read only by you and me.

Baskania is putting together a team of his top people to find Bethany's younger brother—the boy that is supposed to know the secret of the Final Magic he wants so badly. He's going to find that kid before long. His servants are looking under every stone in the Kingdoms of the Keepers. And when he does find the kid, it's going to be nasty. Remember how Bethany was chained to that desk while he rooted through her mind, and then he planned to take her brain out? That's what her little brother will go through too. I'm going to keep tabs, and I'll let you know as soon as they find him, whoever he is.

The Stain triplets are going to take over as kings of Alypium, Ashona, and Aorth soon. There's nothing we can do about that, except hope that they don't make too much of a mess of things. I wanted to tell you—you've got to finish your quests fast. Things are going to get ugly around here until you force them out as the new king with your scepter.

I'm still trying to find out exactly where Tarvos is located. As soon as I know, we'll round up a big group to get Trevor. Do that next quest—I'm sure the Fates know what they're talking about. Let me know if you need anything, ever.

Your friend always,

Rosco

Erec crumpled the letter in his fist. He wanted to do his next quest right now—but here he was chained to his bed. Resting was the last thing he wanted to do. His whole life was being ruined, and everybody else's, too, because he was stuck here. Locked up by his mother, sabotaged by his best friend.

He banged the wall behind the bed and shouted for Bethany, and then his mother. Neither came—they probably didn't want to argue with him when they had no intention of changing their minds. This was ridiculous. All they had to do was keep him a prisoner here until after noon and he would never get to do his quest.

He eventually stopped trying to call them, and examined the cords holding him down. They definitely had some sort of magic in them. He couldn't stretch or break them, even though they were small and soft. So he flopped back onto his bed and tried to resign himself to his new fate. A short life ended by turning evil and then into a Golem.

Erec must have shut his eyes for a moment, because he almost jumped a mile when he heard laughter right next to him. He turned to see who was there, but couldn't find anybody. Anger filled him again. Was it Bethany, stupidly trying to cheer him up?

Then laughs erupted from the other side of the room, startling him again. Nobody was there. Soon chuckles echoed off and on from different corners of the room. Nervous, Erec called his mother and Bethany again.

They did not come. But out of nowhere, a small, dark man appeared, standing in front of Erec right on his bed. He laughed a sillier version of the more ominous laughter that had been filling his room before. "Are you ready to go? Because you look ready to me. What's holding you up, boy? Afraid of the dark?"

It was the Hermit, the strange little guy assigned by King Piter to watch over Erec during his quests. He had a mysterious way of appearing right when Erec was ready to start or end his next quest. Erec had never been happier to see him than right now.

Today the Hermit was wearing a puffy pink and blue polka-dotted nightgown that was far too big on him. It was bunched up around his ankles, and the sleeves hung past his hands. On his head was something that looked like a bright orange diaper. He crossed his arms and tapped his feet impatiently. "Is your life tying you down, Erec Rex? Find you can't go all the places you want to go?" He giggled.

Erec held his hands up. "Can you get these things off me? I need to make it to the Diamond Minds of Argos—wherever that is—by noon."

The Hermit pursed his lips, hopping off the bed. "Hmm. So I take it that you want to do this quest after all, even though you have gone to all this trouble to keep yourself here?"

"I do want to go! My mom did this to me. Can you get these off?"

The Hermit reached under the orange diaper and scratched his bald head. "I don't know. Let me see." He whistled a moment, inspecting the cords and tapping them. "Silly boy. All you have to do is blow on these things. Give it a try."

Erec blew on one of the cords just as the Hermit snapped it off. "Wow! I didn't know I could do that." He blew on the other three in turn, even though he was sure that the Hermit was doing his own magic on the cords before he even blew.

Soon he climbed out of the bed, exhilarated that he was free. But a moment later he remembered what he had to do next. He was about to go give his life up. How could he do it? Was he really ready?

"Hermit, am I making the right choice?"

The Hermit eyed him skeptically. "Do you really think that there is a right choice, Erec Rex? There is no right answer, only what is right for you. You already have your answer. There are no other answers, only questions. Now it is up to you to pick the right questions."

That didn't help at all. "Am I going to survive this quest? What should I do?"

Erec's questions made the Hermit burst out laughing. He did a silly dance in a circle, singing, "What should I do? What should I do?" until Erec got angry.

"Cut it out! I might die if I try to finish this quest."

"Not true!" the Hermit exclaimed. "You *will* die. And you're not even enjoying it!" The Hermit seemed to take great pleasure in Erec's situation.

In his overwhelmed state, Erec went from being angry at the Hermit to confused to almost laughing with him. Finally he shouted, "Just tell me what to do!"

The Hermit said, dead serious. "Stay here. Skip the quest."

"But . . . but . . ." That was not at all what he expected the Hermit to say. "I can't. What would happen to Trevor . . . and to those people who would die? And my chances of ever getting my soul back?"

The Hermit winked at him with a grin. "I told you, you already had your answer. Now you're just asking the right questions." He held a finger to his lips, shushing Erec, and led him to the closet. "I brought you a present." When he opened the closet door, Erec saw a new Port-O-Door had been set into the wall. "Ta-da! Are you ready to visit the Diamond Minds of Argos?"

Erec nodded. He had to do this now before fear completely overcame him. He would just go and see what lay waiting for him there, not what would happen around the corner. Maybe there would be a way to save himself. There had to be.

When the Hermit opened the Port-O-Door, Erec walked into its vestibule. He waited while the Hermit pulled up a map of Otherness and found a place called Argos, far on the edges of a desert with no civilization nearby.

In a moment, Erec and the Hermit were walking out the door into a place like none that Erec had ever seen. Giant holes riddled the ground, and between them huge towering columns of rock shot up to the sky. Small stone paths wound like mazes between the holes and the columns. Erec saw no houses, no animals, no people. Only hard rock as far as the eye could see. He followed the Hermit along a winding path, careful not to take a wrong step and plummet down one of the round holes in the ground. When he leaned over and looked down into one of them, he could see something glowing red near the bottom.

"Be careful not to slip into one of the pits. Would not be pleasant for you at the bottom."

"What is down there?" Erec asked, focusing on his footsteps. The path they walked on varied from a few feet wide to just a few inches across.

"Those are the famous Diamond Minds. Not very fun to visit." The Hermit shook his head.

"Are those like diamond mines? Where diamonds come from?"

"No, silly boy. These are not diamond mines. The Diamond *Minds* of Argos are the creatures that live at the bottoms of the pits. They are ancient and powerful. Those funny little Diamond Minds know everything that has ever happened, and they can tell you what will come to be, if you're foolish enough to want to know. Once they lived together in a great community, and were one of the rare groups allowed to speak with the Fates."

Erec glanced again into one of the pits. Whatever glowed red down there might know what the future had in store for his family. Wouldn't it be nice if he could just ask . . . ?

The Hermit giggled, seeming to know what Erec was thinking. "It is normal to want to know. Which was part of the problem. The Diamond Minds became too important for their little britches. People would come from all over to see them. And the Diamond Minds would tell people their futures, yes they would. But that is doing nobody a favor, right, Erec? Are you enjoying your visions of your future?"

Erec tried not to think of what the Hermit conjured up, and shook his head.

"No," the Hermit continued. "The Diamond Minds wanted to prove how smart they were. So they *would* tell the travelers their futures, and that was too bad. There was death in all stories—family members, people themselves. Disease. Heartbreak. Despair. And the Diamond Minds did not leave out one detail."

The Hermit paused to do a cartwheel, which seemed to Erec a little risky with the deep holes all around. He giggled a moment. "But the people kept coming. You know how silly people are—you're one of those crazy creatures! They kept wanting to hear what awful things lay waiting for them. And the Diamond Minds got full of themselves, and started asking people to pay a price. Whatever was most precious to them as a token for telling their futures. The Diamond Minds competed to see who would get the best prizes, as if they deserved them, as if they showed who was 'best.'

"And of course, what would happen next? The Minds started to hate one another. Before long there was a terrible war, but not one with only two sides. There were exactly twelve hundred and seventy-two factions in this war." The Hermit waved a finger in the air. "Each Diamond Mind was fighting against all of the others. Hate grew along with despair, death, and destruction. Outsiders would still visit, and the Diamond Minds became ruthless at extracting their most precious gifts, and often that was their lives."

The Hermit shrugged. "Finally, the Fates locked each of the Diamond Minds into its own little pit, to stop the whole crazy mess. Their small bodies wore away, leaving those glowing minds to live on for eternity. A funny joke, I think." He giggled.

Erec wasn't sure why the Hermit thought that was funny. "What are the columns here for?"

"Oh, they are posts that the little Diamond Minds once used to talk to the Fates. They threw away all the good cheese for one smelly bit."

Farther on, they reached a small hut in the midst of the holes and columns. It looked oddly new among the ruins. "What is this place?" Erec looked around, but the Hermit was no longer within sight.

He peeked through a window and saw a Port-O-Door appear in a wall of the hut's one room. A man wearing a suit stumbled out, and the Port-O-Door disappeared. The man stared into space, wandering aimlessly. Then he stopped, frozen, in the center of the room.

Next to him stood a woman in a dress, her dark hair up in a bun. She turned toward the man but stared past him in another direction, a blank look on her face. A small painting rested in her arms.

Two more Port-O-Doors appeared in rapid succession. First a young man with dark skin tripped into the room, barely righting himself before he fell. He carried a large white box. A gray-haired man then followed, hands in front of his face as if he was feeling his way in the dark. He bumped into the first man, and they both jumped in surprise.

Something was wrong. The people clearly could not see anything. Were they blind? Erec had no doubt that these were four of the five people that were supposed to be killed by Baskania. Then he heard a familiar voice. He darted away from the window before anybody could see him. Barely peeking again from the other side, he was surprised to find someone inside that he knew from the contests in Alypium: Balor Stain's friend Ward Gamin.

Why was Ward here? Shouldn't he be hanging out in Alypium learning magic with the other kids? He looked pale and shaky. A patch covered one of his eyes, and he was wearing a dark suit jacket that hung off of him, several sizes too large. "I'm glad that you could come here today," he announced to the room, no emotion in his voice. He cleared his throat uncomfortably. Erec realized he was reading off a piece of paper. "You have come to see . . . I mean, *experience* one of the last remaining great miracles of the modern . . . um, age. The modern age. You are going to each meet one of the famous Diamond Minds of the past. They have been made safe for your convenience. The wonders of what you are about to behold will stay with you for the rest of your lives. Be honored that you were chosen by our great leaders to be some of the first to learn the secrets of your futures. Nothing will be held back from you when you meet the amazing Diamond Minds."

The four people in the room leaned toward his voice, looking excited, even though they stared in random directions.

"I would like to thank you again on behalf of the Shadow Prince for the generous donations that you have made to come here. You are donating your most valued treasures to his cause. And all of your eyes will be well taken care of. As you were told, eyes must be removed temporarily in order to visit the Diamond Minds. Seeing them would be disastrous. But they will be returned to you safely after today. I will now take your additional gifts, which I understand are your most valued treasures."

Erec was so amazed at what he heard that he stepped into full view through the window. There was no danger of the four blind people seeing him, and Ward Gamin was facing the other way. Ward was taking gifts from them and the Shadow Prince had removed their eyes—so they would be "allowed" to meet the Diamond Minds? So they didn't know that would kill them?

The woman held out her small framed picture. "This has been passed down through our family for centuries. Rembrandt was a famous artist on my grandfather's side. This is the only one left to us. . . ." She paused, choked up. "But giving this to the cause is a small token for this opportunity. Thank you."

Ward removed the painting from her hands. The gray-haired man pulled a small box from his pocket. "This ten-carat diamond engagement ring was my mother's." His hand clenched the box rhythmically, not wanting to give it up. "I gave it to my wife. We don't have much else now, but I'm happy to trade it for this. The Shadow Prince said that we will all be rich from the information we'll get today, right? Maybe I can afford another one someday for my wife. Not one quite this big, but . . ." Ward struggled to take the box from him.

The first man that had come in held out a small keychain. "Here is the key to our chalet in the south of France. It's a beautiful place, right near the Alps. My parents saved their whole lives to buy it. I'll miss it." He shrugged. "But bigger and better things to come, right?"

The dark-skinned man held out his white box. "I just can't wait to get my eyes back again. I hate not seeing things." He sighed. "This is the most valuable thing I own. It's a magical wallet that keeps refilling itself with money. It never runs out. My wife about killed me when I said I was going to trade it in. She told me it was the end of our marriage." He bit his lip. "Maybe she'll change her mind when I come home richer in even more ways. I almost didn't come today, but Balor Stain himself paid me a visit to tell me how important this was. He said he would consider me for an adviser position when he becomes king." The man smiled with anticipation.

Erec could not believe what he was hearing. Balor and Baskania had conned these people into giving up their most valued possessions, as well as their eyes, in order to die? Wasn't it enough to kill people without robbing them blind—literally—first? How could Ward Gamin do this to these people? Erec wondered what they had done that made Baskania want them gone.

But where was the fifth person who he was supposed to save? Maybe whoever it was would arrive soon. Ward led the group outside, guiding them with his hands. When they were all standing on a wide ledge near the door, Ward told them to stop. He put his hands on the woman's shoulders and led her to the edge of one of the deep pits in the stone.

CHAPTER SIX
The Diamond Mind

EREC PANICKED. It was happening so fast. His quest was to save these people—or to trade his life for theirs, whatever that meant. What was he supposed to do? He took off running, hoping a cloudy thought would tell him what to do. None came to him.

Ward saw Erec and hesitated. Erec shouted as he ran, "*No!* Don't let him push you in there! You're going to die!"

The woman jumped back and spread her arms out, pushing hard against Ward. The other three people clutched one another, nervous.

Ward looked up in amazement. "Erec Rex? What are you doing here?"

"Saving these poor people from *you*, that's what." Erec grabbed the woman's arm and yanked her away from the pit. "How could you do this, Ward? How could you live with yourself?"

Ward's jaw dropped. "What are you talking about? You're nuts. Are you here to steal the gifts that these people brought? Because you can't have them."

"I just want to stop you from killing them, that's all."

Ward sneered. "Listen to this guy. He can't stop spouting lies. I keep hearing what a slimeball he's become, and now I get to see it for myself. Jerk."

"Ward, *you're* the one who's lying. How can you do this? These people are about to die, and you're okay with that?"

Ward crossed his arms. "I don't know what you think you're going to get from this game you're playing, but you're not pulling anything over on us. We all know that everyone is safe here. These people are lucky, and they've given a lot to get to this point. And if you think you're going to steal their stuff, don't for a second. I won't let you—and the Shadow Prince won't either. So get out of here. Beat it." When Erec didn't move, he added, "I hear the Green House is waiting for you to bring them your scepter. I wouldn't want to hold you up." Ward grabbed the woman's shoulders again, leading her back to the pit. She looked nervous but determined, not resisting him at all.

Was it possible that Ward really did not know what was going to happen to these people? Erec tried another tack, unsure what to say. "Wait a minute. Ward, just tell me, have you done this before?"

Ward looked happy to stop so that he could answer. Maybe Erec was actually giving him a few doubts about his job. "No, I haven't. This is a special privilege for me to be in service of the Shadow Prince like this. Don't be too jealous, Erec. I don't think you're going to get a turn to serve him—ever. Now get out of here."

"Ward, listen to me. You were told wrong. It was my quest to come here and save these people. If you really don't want to hurt anybody, just let them go right now."

The older man waved a fist in Erec's direction. "Get out of here, punk. Stop interfering. And stay away from my diamond ring."

"Don't you touch that keychain," the first man said.

Erec was going to have to save these people against their wills. "Look, please. Just trust me here. I don't want your gifts. I want you to take them all back home again with you. You are not safe here. How about this for a deal? Go home, spend time with your families, talk to them, and do some reading about the Diamond Minds. You'll see that they are really dangerous. They'll always be here if you really want to come back."

The four people seemed to care less about what he said. The woman announced, "Obviously I'm not listening to some kid over the Shadow Prince. I'm ready. Let's go."

But Ward could not stop staring at Erec. "You're just jealous. I mean, come on. I remember during those contests when I first met you, last summer in Alypium, you said something to me like this. You were trying to rattle me, make me stop trusting my friends."

Erec remembered exactly what Ward was talking about. "I told you that someone was planning to get rid of you before the final contest to make sure that you weren't in the way. You know, so Balor and Damon Stain and Rock Rayson would be the winners. And I was right."

Ward turned red. "You did not say that. I don't remember it, anyway." He looked confused. "You just twist what people are thinking for your own benefit. Nobody believes you. Give it up." He looked up at the sky. "Did you guys hear that? I think the Harpies are coming. They are supposed to watch us and make sure I get you all into the pits okay."

In moments, five Harpies appeared overhead, swooping down toward Ward and his guests. Thick taloned claws sprouted from their large black vulture bodies. Their black hair was pulled tight into buns, and thick black eyebrows arched over their beaked noses and black lips. One of them screeched, "Ward Gamin! You have still not followed your orders. Do you need help?"

Ward froze. "N-no, ma'am. I was just going to, um . . ." He turned to glare at Erec. "We're fine. Watch." He led the woman to the edge of the pit and started to push. Erec watched in shock, too far to run and save her before she fell. Ward's hands gripped the woman's shoulders tightly, but he waved her back and forth at the side of the hole as if unsure what he wanted to do. Right as he gave her a shove forward, his jacket seemed to stretch behind him and he stepped back again.

"What's wrong with you?" the woman said. "Let's do this!"

Ward's face was red and he bit his lip. "Wait a minute."

"What's going on here?" she said. "You're not listening to that thieving kid, are you?"

"No." Ward looked up at the Harpies, who were flapping closer. "It's just . . ."

Erec stepped forward. "Don't do it, Ward."

Ward looked at Erec with pure hatred. "Shut up! I don't care what you say, don't you get it? There's something else that's bothering me here. Not what you're spouting off about. All you're doing is making me want to throw her into this hole more. If you say another word I'm going to do it too." He stared at his feet, squeezing the woman's shoulders. "It's just something that Balor said. . . ." Ward was speaking to himself now. "What was it? What's wrong with me?"

Then his eyes flashed. "I know! It's just that Tutti Vespucci is here. And Balor was going on and on a few weeks ago about how

Tutti was busted for selling people's eyes back to them from the Shadow Prince's Leyebrary. The Shadow Prince was going to get revenge . . . but now Tutti is here getting this reward. That's just . . . making me wonder."

The older man's jaw dropped. He gripped his arms together tightly. "What did you say, boy? I was busted for . . ." He grew pale. "You know, I changed my mind. I'd better be going home now." Tutti turned around, hands ahead of him, and stumbled back toward the door of the hut.

The woman in front of Ward froze, eyes wide. "I . . . think I better go back too. I'm not sure I actually want to do this after all."

"What else did Balor say?" the dark-skinned man called out, voice shaky. "Did he talk about me at all?"

"No, it was something else. . . ." Ward's brow knit in concentration. "He was laughing the other day when we talked about this, and he said something like, 'In a few days you'll know everything.' When I asked him about it he kept joking that I was going to know my whole future. It didn't make sense. And then when I left today, he said, 'Nice knowing ya.' It kind of creeped me out, but I thought he was just trying to make me nervous, the way he always jokes around."

Ward stared into space. Then he shook his head, aware of the people around him. "I'm sure it's nothing. It has to be nothing." At the same time, he made no move to push the woman toward the hole.

The five Harpies began squawking and closed in. Each of them grabbed one of the four visitors by their shoulders and lifted them off of the ground. The fifth grabbed Ward.

The blinded group soared above the ground, struggling against strong claws and screaming to be let go. Ward yanked on the leg of the Harpy holding him. "Stop it! Put me down!"

Each of the Harpies flew over one of the holes, ready to drop their victims to their deaths—including Ward Gamin. *Five people to save.* Here they were. Erec looked around desperately, wondering what to do. The Harpies were well out of his reach. Then, suddenly, he felt dizzy. He reached to grab a column nearby him, but it was farther away than he thought, and he almost fell to the ground. His head was spinning—could this be . . . ?

Just a moment later he could feel his body change. His clothing ripped as he grew taller, muscles splitting his T-shirt. In a surge of energy, black silken wings sprouted from his back. When he looked down at himself, he could see green scales now covered his skin. In a blink, everything around him looked green too, so his dragon eyes were out. With them he could see the white ropy Substance hanging in the air around him which held all of the magic in the world.

It had been a little while since he had taken the form of a dragon, something that happened now when he got the cloudy thought commands that protected him. It felt good to have the extra energy and strength that came with the change. But then, as he watched the five people heading toward their deaths, anger overtook him. He let out an immense roar that shook the ground. The Harpies, hanging in the air, turned to stare at him.

Erec waited too, for directions from the cloudy thought he was having. Would he have a chance of saving everyone? He was ready to do whatever it took, pushing aside the troubling fact that he would be giving his life to do it.

No visions appeared to him with this cloudy thought, just commands.

Fly at the Harpies.

Before Erec knew what he was doing, he was in the air. One wing stretched out and scooped a Harpy out of the way. His leg side-swiped another one, throwing her off balance.

Breathe Fire.

In a rage, flames burst from Erec's lips. He reached his neck forward and his limbs out, swinging around to push the bird creatures back. They flapped away, not over the holes in the ground anymore.

Attack!

With this command, every ounce of anger that Erec had inside of him was released. He sprang forward and clawed at one of the Harpies, tore his teeth into another. They fought back the best they could, bashing him with their wings while still clinging on to their victims. He kept coming at them, pushing them farther from the holes in the ground. First one and then another Harpy set down the older man and the woman, so they could attack Erec with their claws.

Shoot fire at their feet.

Erec breathed a stream of fire at the claws of the two Harpies who had set the people down. They moaned and hovered in the air, rubbing their feet together. Shooting Erec dirty looks, they flew back to pick up their victims. But as soon as they tried to touch them, the Harpies snarled in pain from their sore feet.

Two more Harpies set down the men that they were carrying and dove at Erec, swinging huge, sharp claws. Erec knocked them away just as the first two returned. They banged against him with their sides, stabbing him with their beaks.

Erec fought back, pummeling them with his legs and strong tail. He saw the fifth Harpy centering a terrified Ward Gamin over one of the holes in the ground. He sailed toward them just as the Harpy that was holding Ward let go.

Dive.

Erec took a sharp turn in the air and dove into the hole, pumping his wings and tail against the air. He grabbed Ward, then turned and flew up just before he hit the glowing mass at the bottom of the pit. Erec sailed out of the pit and set Ward down with the others. All of the Harpies chased him, diving at Erec with their beaks and talons. It was too much at once. A sharp stab deep in his side felt wet, and soon blood poured down his leg. Erec struggled to fight back, ripping at the feathered creatures with his claws and teeth. But weakness was overtaking him. Each time he turned to attack, another Harpy flew at him from behind.

Why wasn't he getting any more commands?

Erec heard Ward whisper to the other people around him, "There's a Port-O-Door inside. Let me help you guys out of here."

Erec's breath caught. They were all going to leave safely! He roared, hoping to distract the Harpies in case they might have heard Ward. It seemed to work—they came at Erec harder now. But his roar only drained him further.

That is when Erec realized why no more cloudy thoughts were telling him what to do. He had already accomplished his task. He wasn't supposed to live through this.

As Ward and the others snuck into the hut, Erec tore and slashed at the Harpies, hoping against hope that he might save himself. One of the creatures faltered as he ripped off most of its wing, and it spun toward the ground. But two of them evaded his attacks, staying over the top of him and jabbing down at him in turns. His head ached, and his side was on fire.

Erec's energy was gone. The bird women were forcing him down into one of the holes. He tried to escape between them, but another hard jab from one and a shove from another pushed him deeper in.

Erec desperately fought, thinking what he could try next. Several hard claws gripped his aching head. A Harpy shook him, batting his weak body against the stone walls of the pit.

Erec watched the green color drain from his skin. His vision returned to normal, and the scales on his skin disappeared. So this was it, then. His cloudy thought was over. He would drop to his death. Just as his wings disappeared, he grabbed one of the Harpy's claws, hanging on for dear life.

Why did it have to end this way? Erec did not see the purpose. He was glad that the others were safe, but couldn't his cloudy thought have lasted longer to protect himself, too?

Maybe his mother and Bethany were right. Here he was hanging over a deadly Diamond Mind, wishing that he was anywhere else. How stupid had he been to come here? Was it really too late to save his own life? There had to be a way. . . .

The Harpy flew lower and smashed her claw against the wall of the pit. Erec's knuckles hit stone again and again until, exhausted and in pain, he fell thirty feet, banging against the hard rock on the way down.

When he awoke, everything was dark. A few stars glowed through the top of the pit. Underneath him was a squishy pillow that must have caught his fall. It glowed red, bathing the space around him with a dim ruby light. His side still ached, and when he pressed his hand to it he discovered blood still oozing out. Something was dripping down his head as well—a swipe of his finger showed that he was bleeding all over.

Dizzy, he tried to get comfortable on the pillow. It moved under him like a fluid gel.

"Do you *mind*?" The voice seemed to come from the glowing pillow.

Erec looked around. Nobody else was down here. He supposed that the Diamond Mind was talking. "Where are you?"

"Under your rear end." The thing sounded disgusted. "Such poor planning by the Fates. This happens every time I get a visitor."

"I'm sorry." Erec scooted off of the squishy thing. "Is that better?"

"Quite. Now, let me see here, before I bother to use my supreme intellect to answer all of your questions, read your past, and successfully predict your future, let me have at least a modicum of fun by playing a guessing game. Hmm. I suppose you are here because you want your future told. Your life has been dull and meaningless, but you are pathetically sure that your future holds something extraordinary. You are but a tiny peon who has brought nothing original or interesting into this world, and you will continue to drain it of valuable resources until you are finally disposed of." The cushionlike creature yawned, although Erec could not see its mouth. "Your life is undoubtedly so boring that it would have been more interesting for me to be lost in my own thoughts rather than have to deal with your dreary ones."

After a pause, the thing sounded annoyed. "All right, let's go on, then. First, before I do the 'exciting' future read for you, I get to take from you the most valuable thing that you own. Give me a moment to conduct my search."

A warm wave of air swept through the space Erec sat in. There was silence for a moment, and then the creature said, "Well, well, then. What do we have here? This *is* a surprise. Finally I have a visitor worth thinking about. One of value. I actually can't wait to read your past, boy. Just look at the valuables you have in you! Many things of worth. Royal blood. Dragon eyes. Convertible parts. A small piece of a genuine soul. A true friendship that has sparks of a true love in it—so rare. All of those things mean quite a bit to you, I see."

"Convertible parts? What do you mean?"

"All of your parts have become something new—they can convert to a dragon state, it seems."

Erec nodded. He understood the rest of what the Diamond Mind said, including the true friendship. It hurt the most that he wouldn't see Bethany again.

"Very interesting. It is too bad for me, though, that the thing that is most valuable to you, out of all of these possessions, is your best friend. You do know, don't you, that she is your true love? If only she was here right now I would take her, no question. Shame that I'm missing that opportunity."

Erec breathed a sigh of relief. The creature was right. He would sacrifice any of the rest of it—his life included—to save Bethany. Thank goodness that this thing wasn't able to get at her. Thinking about how she was safe now made him feel better. "What do you want from me, then? My dragon eyes are pretty cool." Even though his quest had said that he would not live—that he would be trading his life—he still had hope that there might be a way out. If this thing took his eyes instead of his life, then he would stand a chance.

"Oh, no, no." The Diamond Mind brushed this off quickly. "Your eyes are not the most valuable thing you have with you here. I'm going to take your life—which will include that small piece that you have left of your soul. It's not as good as a whole one, but given that you are special it will be worthwhile for me to keep. Thanks for stopping by. It's actually been nice to meet you."

"Wait a minute!" Fear rushed through Erec like a tidal wave. This was happening too soon. "Can't you take it later? I'm using that little bit of soul—and my life right now. I need to do a few things before I die. I'll come back and give it to you later. I promise."

The thing chuckled. "I think we both know that you would not come back later, given the chance. No, your problems are your problems, I'm afraid. I will do your future reading for you first, as a bargain is a bargain. After that I will collect that soul fragment and your life." It sighed contentedly. "You can rest assured that you have fallen into the hole of only the most amazingly brilliant and unsurpassed Diamond Mind, so your reading will be highly accurate."

This thing had no shortage of self-esteem, Erec thought. He wondered if there was any way that he could change its mind and talk it out of killing him. But then Erec thought about his quest. He had to give his life . . . so how could anything he said make a difference? But would the Fates really let him die?

"Let's see here . . ." More warmth filled the pit, and Erec relaxed against the wall. Reading his future seemed a bit of a joke. This thing was supposedly so smart—it would have to know that all of the futures it read would be simply, "You are going to die in a few minutes. That will be the end of you." His forecast would be no different.

"A-*maz*-ing!" the rubbery being exclaimed. "This is fun!" More warmth then seeped through the space while it thought more. A deep, satisfied hum echoed around him. "Do you know how much I have longed for this kind of stimulation? It's like an oasis in the desert. Pollen to the bee. Synachnotonic for chriallotsime sufferers. Oh, what pleasure! What delight!"

Erec chose not to ask what chriallotsime was, but he did know that he was reaching his limits. "This is fun for you? That's interesting. I'm about to die, and I'm sitting here with a talking mushy cushion that is completely in love with itself. And that doesn't care at all that it's going to ruin my life and a lot of other people's lives. Maybe you're thrilled, but I'm miserable. Understand?"

"Oh, but you shouldn't be miserable! This is a veritable font of delight for me, you see."

Erec shut his eyes. "Wonderful. I'm glad you're so happy about it."

The thing continued, excited. "I'm so used to the same old boring people coming here to learn their futures. They are born, fall in love, work, have children, live, and then die. What a waste of my precious time. You, on the other hand . . . well, you've already lived and died, and then come back to life again. You have saved lives and caused death for others. You have combined your life with a dragon who loves you. You have gone back in time. All of this actually makes it a *challenge* for me to predict your future!" It sighed with satisfaction.

It occurred to Erec that this creature was looking at his entire life just as a mental exercise. "So, what's the big challenge? I think we both know my future completely: I'm going to die in a few minutes, here, because of you. Congratulations." He closed his eyes, a wave of pain passing through him. As much as he tried not thinking about Bethany, his mother, and the siblings he was leaving behind, thoughts of them began to take hold. Pictures of them crying for him, miserable, began to fill his head. What would their lives be like from now on? They would think that Erec deserted them, that he snuck away willingly to die, stupidly, instead of letting them keep him safe like he should have done.

The Diamond Mind sounded gleeful. "Not so simple, though! As we both know, you are on a journey to meet the three Furies— something I am quite jealous about, if you must know. So, you are going to do it without the benefit of a living body, but what does that matter? Such a thing would only get in the way when you are there with them. And it is possible that the Furies might give you back your soul—or, then again, maybe not. I assume that they will give you the Master Shem so that you can free Trevor, your brother. Or maybe they will cause something else to happen that will save him. But the Fates have made it sound like Trevor will be okay.

"Beyond this, with your personal life, it is impossible to say whether you will carry on with a completely boring love life with your childhood sweetheart, Bethany. This is because it is unclear whether or not you will ever return to life again. It seems doubtful, of course, from the clues I have interpreted. I do believe that you will never live again. But there is evidence both ways, and I cannot be sure. . . ."

Erec crossed his arms and put his shoes against the mushy pillowlike thing. It shivered and pushed against him, and he took his feet off of it again. "So . . . you're saying that you can't predict my future, then?"

"Absolutely not, boy. Not completely, anyway. I have successfully predicted your future to some degree, better than anybody else could anywhere, I assure you."

"It doesn't sound like it." Erec thought a moment. "I didn't hear what would happen next. It was just a lot of guesswork. All that you said was that you know nothing. You can't tell if I will live again or not. You don't know whether I'll get my soul back, or if I will have a future with Bethany. You know nothing."

"Of course I know nothing." The thing sounded angry. "How can I? With any normal person I can make predictions based on human behavior, which is simple to understand. I can tell people whether their marriages will last or not, given both spouses' attitudes. I can tell when someone will die—for the most part—even if I am not the cause of their death, based on risk factors and their lifestyle. I can tell if they will stay in their jobs or take a new one, based on what goes on in their minds and what is around them in society. But now I am faced with predicting the unpredictable: supernatural decisions of the Furies and their sisters the Fates. Nobody, even with supreme, perfect intelligence, can know how those beings will choose to act. They hold limitless knowledge that is unknowable to me. It is a very different situation."

"Okay, then," Erec said. "You cannot predict what would happen like you normally would. So you should not be able to take your price for making the prediction. You can't have the last bit of my soul. No deal."

There was a hush, and then an irritated snarling sound. "Don't try to play games with me, boy. I exacted that toll from you in order to do your prediction, not with any certainty about the outcome."

"But you didn't tell my future, did you?"

The voice sounded uncomfortable. "Of course I did. Well, as much as possible." There was a soft humming noise, and then a sigh. "I'll tell you what. Normally I would never offer this . . . but then again, normally there is nothing interesting to find out from anybody. I'm going to take the last bit of your soul. You won't need it anyway. But if for some reason the Furies give you your original soul back, and if they bring you back to life, then you may come back here to me. I will return this piece of your soul to you in exchange for finding out from you what happened. If the Furies don't give your soul back, you will have no need for this, anyway. I know that you do not want to live on if you are going to turn into an evil being."

As bad as it sounded, the Diamond Mind's offer seemed the best Erec could do. At least there was a chance he might someday be whole again. And the thing was right—Erec did not want to turn into something awful. "How do I know that you won't take my whole soul away from me if I come back here?"

The thing sounded indignant. "I never go back on my word. Of course I will do as I say. I will even keep your body intact for you here, at least for a while. Now, here we go. . . ."

Before he could say another word, Erec felt himself crumble and hit the floor in a heap. Something inside tugged hard against his chest. It felt like his heart was trying to leave his body. Every limb was numb, heavy. He could feel his pulse slow, its beats softening. The pulling inside of him worsened like it would rip his chest in two.

Then, with a *pop*, it all felt better. No more pain was left, only a lightness, an airy feeling. It felt like a breeze was blowing through his body . . . or maybe *he* was the breeze. It was a sensation Erec had never felt before, could never have imagined. He lifted up and looked around, and he was still in the same place . . . but another person was there with him now, lying on the floor below him near the Diamond Mind. It was a boy with straight dark hair that was curly in the back, cold blue eyes staring up at the ceiling. Peering closer was like looking in a distorted mirror—the boy looked oddly just like he did, but somehow paler, almost glossy. . . . Erec did a double take. This was strange. Nobody except him was down here before. . . .

Erec grew alarmed as he stared down at the boy. The boy looked exactly like he did, except that Erec was looking from the outside instead of into a mirror. Reality did not sink in immediately, as the concept was too strange to grasp. How could this boy look so much like he did? How did he get here?

Cold fear grasped Erec as he looked into the boy's eyes. They stared uncomprehending, glassy. He was dead. It took another moment for him to put two and two together. It was *him* lying there, wasn't it? The Fates said that he would die from this quest. The Diamond Mind took the last bit of his soul—he was sure that was the pain that he had felt. And then it had taken Erec's life, too. Isn't that what it said that it would do? He was dead. . . .

But at the same time, Erec felt completely alive. He was floating, somehow, over his body. He reached down to it, trying to feel the chest for a heartbeat. His own arm, the one he was using now to reach, was perfectly visible to him, so he wasn't gone. He was still there. . . . There were two of him, then? When his hand touched the body's chest, he could feel clammy skin, hard bones, and warm, wet insides. Before Erec realized it, his hand had reached through the clothing and straight inside of the dead body.

Erec jumped, shuddering, whisking his hand out of his own corpse. He was surprised and relieved that there was no blood on his hand, but none of this made sense. Why was he able to pass his hand deep inside of the body? And why could he still see himself here if he was dead?

Just to make sure he wasn't imagining things, he tentatively reached toward the body again. Eyes closed, he felt inside its squishy wetness. There was nothing but stillness. No heart beating.

In fact, thinking of that, he could feel that his own heart was not beating either. There was a strange stillness inside of him now. No stomach rumbles. No pounding pulse, or rush of adrenaline, even though he was quite alarmed. The strangest thing of all was realizing that he wasn't breathing. It was disconcerting. The regular, rhythmic in and out through his chest had been comforting, even if he had never thought of it that way before. In fact, it felt as if he was there, but at the same time, he wasn't.

But there was something else, too. Being still a moment, Erec noticed something he had never felt before. It was a sense of knowledge or understanding that wasn't there when he was alive. Erec realized that he didn't have to feel inside of the body to know that it was dead. He could tell that just by sensing the space around him. It was as plain as day. All he had to do was pay attention and things seemed to spell themselves out for him. For one, he was a ghost. That is why two of him were together in that small space. The boy lying dead on the floor was his body, the shell of what he used to be.

But his new self was much better, smarter, and wiser. Like a newborn discovering himself for the first time in a new world, Erec looked around the pit in wonder. As a ghost, he had a sense of purpose that he had never felt before, a need to move forward and meet the three Furies as he had planned. And doing so no longer intimidated him. It was as if all of the knowledge in the world was now available to him if he wanted it. The Diamond Mind next to him was transparent—in this new state Erec could read its thoughts. In fact, the thing was staring at him in fear and shock.

Erec's mind functioned more sharply than before. Everything was crystal clear. The Diamond Mind had done him a favor—he would be able to meet the Furies now that he didn't have a human body to drag along. But, ironically, the Diamond Mind was feeling guilty now about killing him.

Erec was surprised—the creature was torn in conflict. Of all the people that it had killed, none had become a ghost before its eyes as Erec did. And seeing that frightened it. As much as it knew about people, it knew nothing at all about ghosts. Fearing that Erec would take revenge, the Diamond Mind began to feel bad that it had taken Erec's life to begin with. It was chastising itself for being selfish and stupid, then stopping and justifying what it had done so it felt better. It was odd for Erec to be able to hear the thing's thoughts as easily as if it were speaking out loud.

But just as Erec could hear the creature's thoughts, he also felt like he understood them, and he knew what the truth was. It was amazing—being a ghost gave him so much insight. He remembered talking to Spartacus Kilroy, his old friend and King Piter's AdviSeer, after he had become a ghost. It had seemed that he had known everything then. Now he understood. . . .

"You shouldn't worry about it," he told the Diamond Mind. "I don't want revenge. I'm not even angry—you've actually helped me to meet the Furies. And don't worry about being selfish. You're not—for a Diamond Mind, anyway. You are who you are, and you have tried to be the best at what you know. The Fates had to isolate all of you, taking away your freedom, but they could not help that either. You are stuck here in a bad situation. So cut yourself some slack, okay?"

The Diamond Mind sounded meek, its voice trembling. "Thank you. I guess I was blaming myself a bit. Are you sure you're not angry, g-ghost?"

THE SECRET OF ASHONA

Erec laughed. "Not at all. When I was alive I wouldn't have believed this, but being dead seems like no big deal."

"Of all of the people I have . . . killed here, I have never seen one become a ghost."

"I know. Most people just move on. Only the few with something important to take care of stay."

The Diamond Mind spoke with wonder. "Do you know what will happen when you meet the three Furies?"

Erec thought a moment. "No, I don't. I can't read into the future." He wondered if he still had his dragon eyes, but could not sense them. When he tried to roll his eyes back to see if they would come forward, nothing happened. It was slightly disappointing, but all of his dragon parts had stayed with his human body. In this new form, though, he was able to do different things. For one, he had a better connection to the Substance, so magic would be a lot easier. Erec pointed at his old body lying on the ground, and a blue haze immediately surrounded it. "That will protect it until I'm back again. Would you keep an eye on it here for me, then?"

"Oh, yes. I'd be honored. Sorry again for any problems caused by your . . . death."

"It's fine. I'll be back for that little bit of my soul that you are keeping too." Erec smiled. It was time to go find the Furies now. The Fates had said they were in the Gray Mist Valley, in Alsatia. He had to get there by falling into Mercy's Spike in Pinefort Jungle in Otherness. Erec was delighted to realize that instead of his old human cluelessness about where things were, he now had a perfect sense of direction. He knew he could find his way to Pinefort Jungle just using his senses. Not bad, he thought.

Now, to get out of this steep hole . . . There were no ladders, and the Diamond Mind would not make a very good trampoline. On a whim, he bent his knees and reached high, springing up into the air.

The slight push of his feet against the ground was enough to catapult him skyward. In fact, he continued to soar through the air well after he was out of the tunnel. Fifty feet up . . . one hundred . . . two hundred. As the holes and stone columns began to look small beneath him, he started to feel concerned. Would he ever stop?

Erec must have been two thousand feet up, and he was still going. He felt perfectly fine—breathing was not an issue anymore—and he knew there was no danger of hurting himself if he fell. But how would he turn and go back down? There was nothing to push off of.

In a moment of calm focus, the answer came to him. Experimenting, Erec did a few flips in the air, then used his arms and legs to push against the thin atmosphere as if he were in a pool. He stopped, and after doing it again, reversed directions and headed back to Earth slowly. Interesting, he thought. Apparently he needed only a tiny push to move far.

In a while he touched down again, close to the hole from which he had sprung. He could tell already that this was going to be a very interesting journey.

CHAPTER SEVEN

Alsatia

IT WAS EASY to remember the way back to the Port-O-Door. Erec turned the knob and it flew open, but then he realized it was easier to pass right through the wood. Once he was inside, he pulled up the map of Otherness. In moments he spotted Argquard in the northernmost part of Otherness, which he knew was the region he was looking for. Once he tapped the map there, Pinefort Jungle filled most of the upper part of Argquard. Zooming in closer, Erec scanned an area that he knew would house Mercy's Spike, and there it was. No problem.

Moments later, Erec was through the Port-O-Door in the dense forests of Argquard. Strange creatures trotted around the forest floor, springing up and flying overhead. They were Ligwiths—Erec knew all about them with his new ghostly insight. The tall red birds with long legs were able to crumple themselves into compact balls at will. Some whizzed by Erec's head in ball form, and others kicked and batted the ball-shaped ones around, playing some incomprehensible game.

Erec knew the way to Mercy's Spike. It was not far, as he had parked the Port-O-Door in the perfect spot in a large tree trunk nearby. It was a challenge at first to learn to walk without bounding too far forward or springing too high in the air, but it didn't take long to master. If he tapped his toes down softly and moved his legs back and forth he didn't even have to touch the ground most of the time. It wasn't too hard to stay close enough that nobody would notice— his aim had become nearly exact. Later, when he was around people, he would need to look like everyone else, not shooting twenty feet into the air.

Mercy's Spike was a sharp needle-shaped rock formation that projected ten feet into the air from the top of a plateau. Erec's senses told him that it had been used for ritual sacrifices by clans of the past. Above it was another plateau, about fifty feet higher, at the edge of a mountainside. When someone jumped off of the top plateau and fell straight down, they would land right on the spike, impaling themselves on it.

The ceremonies must have been pretty dramatic, Erec thought, watching people sacrifice themselves this way. It was a shame that people used to believe that angry gods wanted them to kill off their friends and neighbors. But something strange had happened to the people who died this way. Almost as if the ancient religions were true, instead of dying a normal death these people's spirits were transported to a place known as Alsatia.

Erec pushed his toes softly against the ground and flew into the air. When he reached the higher plateau he waved his arms gracefully against the air and landed again.

It was nice to know so many things now that he was a ghost. Like the fact that Alsatia was a land from before time, when the earth was still young. It was a place of strong power, a haven for those in need. The Furies used it now as their home, but it had been used by others before who were in need of protection. Living humans could never get there, only spirits and magical beings.

Erec had a brief moment of fright, looking at the sharp spike looming below him. But he realized that jumping would not propel him to the ground—he would have to work to make himself fall. And impaling himself would not hurt one bit. Even then, Erec hesitated a moment. It was hard to shake the human memory of what his body would feel like if it was speared down the middle. He passed his own arms through himself a few times for reassurance, then leaned forward, arms out. Waving slightly, he pushed himself toward the spike. As it came closer, he adjusted his position and direction so that it would pass through his midsection.

Mercy's Spike impaled Erec's chest right where his heart rested, and it tunneled through the shadow of his body. Unlike humans who had probably stopped from the friction of the rock by about this point, Erec continued to slide farther down the spike, slowing and stopping midway to the ground.

For a moment he waited to be whisked away to Alsatia. Nothing happened. He hoped that it was not only the living who were able to use this spike as a transport there . . . but then again the Fates had told him that this would work—and he could sense it himself as well. What Erec did not know, what seemed unknowable, was what the Furies would decide to do with him once he arrived. Their minds were out of his grasp.

There was a sudden motion, and everything was turning around him. In a minute Erec realized that it was he who was spinning around the axis of the spike. Faster and faster Erec whirled until the land around him became a blur. Faster. Faster. It was white and black, swirling lines of haze that encompassed him. There was a kind of lifting that happened as well. But he could not see exactly where he was going.

Erec did not feel dizzy, luckily, as he had no real body. But he could sense that he was moving now, heading into the air. It felt like he was a small helicopter, traveling into uncharted territory. It was not an unpleasant sensation, but definitely different from anything he had ever experienced. All he could do was wait, sure that eventually the spinning would end.

And it did. He began to slow, then came to a full stop lying flat on a grassy field. White fluffy clouds floated overhead, and huge oak and maple trees dotted the nearby hills. Bright sun streamed light across well-tended gardens of flowers and manicured shrubs. Erec sat up and saw a swing set not far away, and a sand pit. Nearby were tennis courts and a swimming pool, and in the distance he could see rows of beautiful mansions. Beyond these and wrapping around the horizon was a majestic shoreline with waves rolling in to a white sand beach.

A few people were within sight, skipping through flowery meadows and strolling through gardens. One lazed on a raft on her back in the pool. Everyone seemed relaxed and happy. Not a bad place, Erec thought. At least the people that had died on Mercy's Spike had a nice reward.

He would have to ask around to find the Furies—unlike on earth, he had no sense of what was going on here. There was some sort of block, he could tell, keeping everyone's thoughts guarded. He wandered toward the village and came across a boy about his age.

"Hi." Erec smiled. "I just got here, and I'm looking for the three Furies. Do you know where they stay?"

The boy nodded. "I haven't seen you around here before. Good to meet you. I hope you like it—it's a pretty nice place. Sure, I know where the Furies are. They won't see you, though. Just put that thought right out of your head. They don't want anything to do with us. We just stay clear of them."

"But that's why I'm here. Can you just tell me where they are?"

The boy looked at him strangely. "You came here just to talk to them? Bad choice. I mean, you'll be happy here, you won't regret being with us forever. It's a great place. But the Furies will destroy you if you bother them. It happens every now and then. One of us will get too close to their cave, and *poof!* They'll get evaporated. Or if a Fury flies somewhere and a ghost gets in her way, then the ghost is dissolved. Take my word, you don't want to see them."

That was not what Erec wanted to hear. No question, he had to talk to them. But he had to be careful. "Thanks for the info. My name is Erec, by the way. If you don't mind, just point out where their cave is. I'm going to have to figure something out."

The boy shrugged. "All right, but don't say I didn't warn you not to go. I'm Jox." He held out his hand and shook Erec's. "It's not going to look like a cave, though, when you see it. Nothing here is the way it appears. What do you see when you look around now?"

"Gardens, fields, beach out there." Erec pointed. "Mansions that way. Why?"

"The surroundings look different to everyone who comes here. It's part of the mind block that this place has. Whatever is the most beautiful setting to you is what you see. People look different to you as well, just appearing how you want them to look. And it changes, too, if you get tired of seeing things a certain way. I used to see a dense jungle all around me, with beautiful, bright animals. Some of

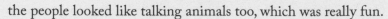

the people looked like talking animals too, which was really fun.

"But I guess I got tired of that, because now everything looks like it's part of a moving painting. I can stare forever at the trees, just watching the swirl of yellow and green oil pastels blending and reshaping. It's like being an artist in my mind. A friend of mine sees everything as being much smaller than he is, like he could step on any of us. But to us he looks normal size. I hear that the longer you are here the more unusual things can look to you. I guess you start to let go of the normal, earthly way of looking at things.

"Anyway, the Furies' cave might look like a beautiful house to you. To me it used to look like a giant stone fortress in a clearing in the woods. Now I see it as a massive scoop of cloud cream with swirling browns and blacks weaving around and around. It's amazing. But whatever you see it as, it will be big, and it's over that way." He pointed to the left of the village near some rounded hills.

"Thanks," Erec said. "You've been really helpful."

"You'll have to catch me up on what has been going on in the real world in the last five hundred years. I'm the last one who's come here, except for you, so I'm dying to know how things have changed."

"I'll tell you all about it . . . once I take care of a few things I need to do."

Erec headed toward the hilly area to the side of the mansions. The Fates had told him that the Furies would talk to him. They respected him—he was the one who had saved them. But if they didn't recognize him right away, they would dissolve him without paying attention.

Walking here was different from when he was a ghost on earth. It felt just as it had when he was alive, like he was subject to real gravity. Maybe that was because his image of this place was straight out of his own imagination. It wasn't hard scaling the hills though, and he was not tired at all after climbing up and down four of them.

On the other side was a clearing, and within it was a gorgeous glass castle that spiraled into the heavens. Spires shimmered with rainbow colors from the prism effect of the glass. Hundreds of birds circled the palace, diving in and out of openings in the roof and between flags made of a moving glass that rippled in the wind.

There was no doubt in Erec's mind that this was where the three Furies were living. He remembered them well—and it was hard to imagine the immense, ferocious-looking creatures living in such a delicate, breakable place. Red-haired Alecto, black-haired Tisiphone, and white-haired Megaera were seven feet tall, mostly because of their incredibly enormous heads which stuck out in front of them, hanging in the air and almost hiding their feather-covered, human-shaped bodies. Huge batlike wings shot behind them, and wild, silken, glowing hair flowed from behind them as well.

But the thing that Erec remembered most was how fierce they had been. The enormous amount of pure energy and hate that radiated from them was overwhelming. It was as if they were far larger than their bodies, larger than the entire world, even. Next to them Erec had felt tiny, like a crumb. Completely insignificant. Later, after he opened the Awen of Harmony from around his neck, the Furies finally had been able to let go of their hatred. After that, they had become so different, soft and understanding.

He wondered what they would be like now that the Awen of Harmony had worn off. At least they had kept their word not to wipe all human beings off of the planet. Erec hoped that was a good sign, and maybe they would decide not to wage war on their sisters, the Fates.

Was there a way to send a message to them that he was coming? Maybe they already knew he was here. He was standing close to their castle, wasn't he? And he wasn't disintegrated yet.

Some cats ran around on the ground, and one began to rub against

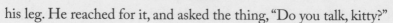

his leg. He reached for it, and asked the thing, "Do you talk, kitty?"

"Mew." The kitten looked at him when it made the noise, almost as if it understood.

"Can you give a message to the Furies for me? Tell them Erec Rex has come to visit and would like to speak to them."

"Mew."

He put the cat down, and it ran straight into the glass castle. In a minute it ran back out to him again. It took a few steps toward the castle and looked back at Erec over its shoulder.

"All right, I'm coming." When Erec started to follow it, the cat continued on toward the castle. Huge glass doors swung wide open, and they went inside, boy ghost following cat. The interior of the castle was blindingly brilliant, sparkling like a many-faceted diamond. Above, flocks of birds darted around the glass segments, soaring up through the open ceiling into the blue sky overhead. It was impossible to make out rooms or hallways amid the glittering lights, so Erec followed the cat's steady pace around sharp corners and past other meandering cats.

Suddenly, in an opening, three beautiful women appeared. Erec was sure who they were, but the Furies looked nothing like they had before. Alecto still had red hair, Tisiphone black, and Megaera white. But they wore long, shimmering dresses and tiaras in their curls, and appeared human now. No, better than human, actually. There was an intensity in their eyes that reminded Erec of the first time he had met them. It was hard to decipher whether they were angry or just merely interested, but Erec felt spellbound just looking at them. Their stares made him dizzy, unstable. Unable to keep standing, he sat on the floor before them.

Alecto smiled. "Look who it is, sisters. The only human that I would bother speaking to. It's our savior, the little prince. The Erec Rex child. And he's come all this way to speak to us."

Megaera put a finger beside her ruby lips. "Looks rather good, doesn't he? He'd make a lovely specimen to keep in amber for my collection. Well . . . I suppose we are going to spare him, aren't we? We do owe him, right?"

Tisiphone stared at Erec coldly. "Yes. Enjoy it, human. We're sparing you, and glad to do it. Why are you here?"

Erec was transfixed. It was hard for him to speak. "Can't you all read my mind and tell for yourself?" After saying this, he immediately worried that he had offended them.

Tisiphone laughed, thankfully not bothered at all. "Yes, we could. It's just a little harder to do here in Alsatia. There are some protective properties here that keep your thoughts safe. At least somewhat safe. I can tell that you came here to get something from us, right? A thing that will save your brother, and something else to save yourself? I suppose if I bothered to try I'd be able to read more." She yawned.

"You're right. I do need two things from you. One of them is a Master Shem—that is something I need to give to Tarvos so that he will let Trevor, my brother, go free. Also . . . I would like to have my soul back. I mean, now that you three are free . . ." As he asked, he had a sinking feeling that he knew exactly what their answer would be. "I'd really like to come back to life again. I mean, if it's okay with you."

The three incredibly beautiful women looked at him with eyes so intense that it seemed they saw right through him. If he were still alive, he was sure he would have forgotten to breathe. Their palace sparkled behind them, creating an effect he would never forget.

Alecto's long red curls flowed in the air around her as if they had a life of their own. "There is not much that I would deny you, Erec Rex. Understand that my sisters and I will be eternally grateful to you. You freed us from our prison of your own free will. You sacrificed yourself just to help us, getting nothing out of it yourself, and even losing your life. Not only did you do this, but you also gave us another gift. For no other reason than to help us, because you cared about us, you showed us happiness, peace, and love with your Awen of Harmony. You could have tried to do something different, to try to save yourself, but instead you helped us again.

"And, as disturbing as it is to say this, we learned something from you, a mere human. Moments before you came to us, we were ready to wage full-scale warfare on our sisters the Fates, and also to destroy the human race that has preoccupied them for so long. We were jealous of their attention to you. But your selflessness, and the Awen of Harmony, showed us that there was something that we were forgetting. Love, forgiveness, and peace were a gift to ourselves as well as to the rest of the world."

Erec reached to his neck to see if the Twrch Trwyth still hung there. Even as a ghost, he found the small glass vial shaped like a boar around his neck. He had acquired it, along with its five tremendously powerful crystal balls, during one of his prior quests. Each of the five different-colored balls imparted a special kind of magical aid that Erec could use if he was in need, but he tried to save them for emergencies. Two of them had been used up, leaving the Awens of Knowledge, Beauty, and Creation. Knowing that the Awen of Knowledge was still there was reassuring. That one, if he cracked it open, should let him know everything about any situation he was in. If worse came to worst he would be able to know exactly what to do.

Next to the Twrch Trwyth, Erec's Amulet of Virtues still dangled from his neck. He looked at it with curiosity. Still, only six of its twelve segments glowed with color. Shouldn't it have been seven now? He did follow the instructions of his last quest, didn't he? "Trade your life for the next five people to be killed by Baskania at noon tomorrow in the Diamond Minds of Argos." Obviously, there was something else that he was supposed to do.

Alecto continued, "I am agreeable to giving you the Master Shem. That is a small thing for us. But as far as returning your soul to you—you should understand that we need to keep all three thousand here in order to stay out of that terrible prison that you rescued us from. Unfortunately we cannot give it back."

"Unless . . ." Tisiphone raised a finger. "If you find another person's soul for us to keep, we would be more than happy to take that one and give you your own back. That would be our pleasure. And I would make sure that you were restored into your old body perfectly. We would even give you an extra long life, lots of riches, and anything else your heart desired."

That promise sounded wonderful. For a moment Erec got excited—what a perfect solution! The Furies would be happy and free, he would be alive again and restored to normal, and Erec would even have the Furies on his side to help fight against Baskania. The Stain brothers would have nothing on him then. How ironic—Baskania had been trying to use the Furies' release for his own benefit, and now they would be helping Erec against him.

But then another reality sank in. Who would donate their soul to the Furies? Who would give up their life, and let Tarvos turn them into a Golem? The more he thought about it, the more the idea seemed hopeless. Anyone giving up their soul would be sacrificing themselves just so that Erec could live. He could never ask someone to do that.

"Thanks. I'll . . . see what I can do. For now I'll just take the Master Shem so I can rescue my brother."

A small scroll fluttered out of the air and landed on the glass floor in front of Erec. He picked it up. The writing on it was strange—he could not identify it.

"There you go. You should know that thing you are holding is very powerful," Megaera said. "Tarvos wants it to activate his army of Golems and wage war. They are lethal fighters, and would wipe out any enemy. So your decision to give this to him will not be a small one."

Erec held the scroll away from him. Why did they have to tell him that? He would rather not know what would happen once he gave it to Tarvos. He couldn't even let himself think about it as a choice—Trevor had to be freed. "Thank you again. I hope I am able to come back here with another soul."

First Megaera, then Alecto, raised their arms, then soared upward, straight up through the roofless opening above into the sky. In moments they were back again, each sailing up and down over and over. Tisiphone watched Erec stumble out of the room, following one cat and then another so that he didn't crash into a glass wall. Before long he had found his way out of the dazzling palace.

The Master Shem, a small scroll the size of his finger, felt heavy in Erec's hands. This thing would control all of those Golem creatures that Tarvos had made out of the living soulless beings? Erec had come close to being one of them himself. Now that he was no longer alive, at least he didn't have to worry about that anymore, although he had plenty of other things to worry about.

What would he do now, though? Save Trevor, of course. But then what? Finishing the quests and becoming king of Alypium was out of the question if he was no longer alive. His existence as a ghost would only continue as long as he had a mission on earth, something supremely important to him. And for now that was saving Trevor . . . and then, he supposed, getting his soul back from the Furies.

Some of the ghosts that lived in Alsatia waved to him as he walked by. It was amazing that they were able to stay here forever. Coming back to this place could be another option for him when he was done with his missions, then. But a thought struck him. These people here did not need souls—they were already dead. Maybe one of them wouldn't mind donating theirs to the Furies for him!

As he sprang down the last rounded hill, Erec saw Jox sitting on the grass against a tree.

Jox sprang up and did a few cartwheels toward him and a flip in the air, then bowed low. "Erec! You survived! Glad to see that you made it back. How close were you able to get to the Furies? Did you see them?"

"I spoke with them." Erec was excited. Things might work out after all. "They talked to me because I was the one who saved them. They have my soul—and they said that they would give it back to me if I could find another soul to replace it. I could return to life again! And I have so much to do on earth still. So, I was wondering—it seems like you all don't need souls in order to live here as ghosts. If you're not using yours, would it be possible for the Furies to use it? They need another one if they are going to give me mine back."

Jox's jaw dropped. "Give my *soul* to the three Furies? You have to be kidding. I mean, we just met, and you're asking me to give up my *soul*?"

"I'm sorry." Erec tried to explain. "You see, it would mean a lot to me. And as long as you're not really using it—"

"Not *using* it?" Jox shook his head. "No, I'm using it all right. You do know what would happen to me if I didn't have my soul, don't you?"

Erec shook his head. "What?"

"I'd turn evil, that's what! It wouldn't take too long, either. I mean, longer than it would take for a living person. But give it a few months and I'd start to do all kinds of nasty things. Last thing anyone needs in this place is a bad egg. I heard that it happened one other time, some jerk without a soul snuck into this place. Luckily the good folks here were able to kick that piece of dirt out to deal with his own nasty afterlife by himself."

Chills ran through Erec. He would *still* turn evil without a soul, even as a ghost? There was no way that he could let himself go on like this, then. An evil ghost could do far worse things than an evil person. And what kind of nasty afterlife was Jox talking about? This was terrible.

There had to be a way to get his soul back. But, at the same time, who would give their own soul to save him? They would have the same awful fate that he had. Maybe it would have been better if he let Tarvos turn him into a Golem after all. The Furies could bring him back to life, and he could give himself up when he went to save Trevor. Then he wouldn't have to worry about any of this. . . .

"I'm sorry. I didn't know." Erec shook his head, backing away. "I have to go take care of my brother now. Maybe I'll come back another time."

"Not if you don't have a soul, you won't." Jox crossed his arms and stepped forward threateningly. "At least not for long. This isn't the place for you, all right?"

"Okay. I understand." It seemed that there was no place anymore where he would be safe.

CHAPTER EIGHT

An Unfair Trade

FINDING HIS WAY out was no problem. The spot where Erec had entered Alsatia looked like a window of wavy ripples hanging in the air. He pushed his head through and there was Mercy's Spike on the other side, just as he thought, surrounded by the beautiful Pinefort Jungle. He jumped out of the entryway, landing on top of the spiked rock formation. For a moment, Erec held it, grasping the needle with his hands, until he remembered he didn't have to worry about falling. Instead, he lightly pushed on the rock and sailed to the ground.

The Port-O-Door was just where he had left it. Erec wondered where his little friend the Hermit was. It would be interesting to talk to him now that Erec had so much knowledge. Oh, well. There wasn't much that the strange man could tell him that Erec didn't already now know. The Fates had been right, as usual—Erec now had just what he needed to save Trevor. It was time to find the passage-way that Tarvos had left open for his return. Erec easily remembered the spot that the bull had mentioned—it was in the giant Bubble Boulder of Racks Rocks. With his great new sense of direction, he knew the way to the part of Otherness called Quiet. He tapped the map of Aorth and found the spot that would lead straight there.

The Port-O-Door swung out of the side of a cliff onto barren, rocky soil. In the center of the huge pebble-covered ground was a circle of larger stones. Within that, in concentric rings, sat larger and larger rocks leading to an inner circle of giant boulders. And in the very center, towering above the rest, was a massive stony sphere that reflected sunlight in every color of the rainbow. This was the Bubble Boulder that Tarvos had referred to. Erec floated straight to it, glad that he did not have to climb and scoot through small openings as he would have in his old human form.

As he sailed around the Bubble Boulder he found a glowing red doorway. Tarvos had said that it would be apparent only to him, but that seemed hard to believe—it was so bright. He passed through the door, which felt like it was made of some kind of wood, and found himself in the middle of a desert.

Dunes of black sand were the only sight for as far as he could see. Misty wind whipped through a bloodred sky, and sand catapulted right through his body. He was in the underworld, he knew. And the entrance to Tarvos's cave was nearby. Not here, but just over the next dune.

He tapped lightly with his feet against the sand and shot upward, waving himself down on the other side of the dune. Quicksand swirled in a damp pit. This was it. Erec centered himself over it and waved his arms against the air, pushing down into the quicksand. Dense sand pressed hard enough to enter every bit of him. It felt awful to have his space invaded so completely.

After waving himself downward through the pit, he soon came out the other end into the same corner where he had once followed the small white bullfighter toy. There was no need to dust himself off—the sand stayed where it had been, above him. Erec walked to the corridor on the other end. It was impossible to believe that he had been here just days before—it seemed like a lifetime ago. He shook his head, realizing that it actually *was* a lifetime ago for him.

Tarvos grinned when Erec walked in, and Trevor sprang to his feet and ran to throw his arms around Erec.

"Wait!" Erec stepped back and held a hand out. If Trevor's hands passed through him, then he would have to tell him all that had happened—and he didn't want to worry Trevor and his family sick. Why should they grieve for him when he was still here? There was a chance he would be okay, and he wanted to focus on that. "I'm sorry, Trev. I'll hug you later, kid. Don't get close, I'm feeling sick."

Trevor backed away, and Erec gave him a big grin. "I'm so glad to see you! I got the thing Tarvos wanted. Now you'll be free!"

Trevor smiled back, but Erec could see how tired he was. "You got the Master Shem? I can get out of here, then?"

"You bet!" Erec grinned. He could read Trevor's mind and knew that he had been horrified by the endless stream of people he had watched turn into Golems. It would be a while before Trevor forgot those images.

Trevor was hungry, too. Tarvos had made sure he stayed alive, but the boy had not eaten a thing. "Time to go home. I know just where that Serving Tray is. We'll figure out the perfect meal for you. I bet you're going to want a triple cheese pizza with bacon and black olives, all to yourself, a huge grilled hamburger with tomato, French fries, and a hot fudge sundae with a cherry on top. I bet you'll want to eat them all at once!"

"How did you know—I was just thinking that!" Trevor's eyes widened. "Let's go!"

Erec held the Master Shem toward Tarvos, who knew full well that Erec had become a ghost. Erec was glad that Tarvos didn't mention it out loud, and hoped that Trevor didn't ask so that it would come out. Let Trevor assume that Erec had his soul back, and that's why they both were free now.

Erec read a little more of Tarvos's mind, but immediately wished he wasn't able to. The Furies were right. He was planning a full-scale war. If Tarvos were human, Erec would know all of the details. But he could read enough to see that the bull planned massive death and destruction. Erec was giving him the key to activate his entire army that he had been building for thousands of years. The number of Golems that he had waiting to be activated was nearly endless.

The Master Shem was the key. Tarvos would use it to command each and every Golem to become a fighting machine, stopping at nothing to carry out his orders. How could Erec just hand it to him and walk away?

Yet, he looked at Trevor, starving and excited to go home again. He couldn't just leave him here to die.

"Let me make it easy for you." Tarvos nodded toward Erec, and the three cranes that perched on his back swooped down toward the Master Shem in Erec's hands. In a moment they had it, and it was in Tarvos's giant claws. "Thank you, Erec Rex. You deserve your reward. And it looks like you won't need to worry about me anymore, either."

Trevor's eyes lit up. "Did you hear that, Erec? We're both free now!"

Erec smiled, hoping to mask his sadness. "That's great, Trev. Let's get out of here." He would have to get the Master Shem back again before long. He was so connected to the Substance now, he had powers that he had never tried using before—he could figure out a way. But not until his brother was safely home again.

His mission had been to bring his brother home, so that is what he would do. And as a ghost, he had to stick to his mission in order to stay on earth. Changing that messed up his whole reason for existence.

"I'm glad that you're back!" Bethany grinned and hugged June, who also looked like she could faint from happiness. Luckily Erec, with his new mind-reading skills, was able to convince all of them that he was feeling too bad to be touched.

"We were so worried about you." June reached for Erec again, but thought better of it. "Where were you? With the Furies?"

Erec nodded, but before he could talk Bethany added, "What happened? We were afraid that you went and did that stupid quest." She pointed to the Amulet of Virtues on his chest. "Nope. Still only six done."

"I got the Master Shem that Tarvos wanted. Then I gave it to him so we could have Trevor back."

Bethany looked torn between being thrilled and upset. "Why didn't you wait for me to go with you?" Erec could hear her thoughts as clearly as her words. She had been crying since the morning they had found him missing—and two days had passed here since then. She thought that she would never see him again. Her best friend was dead. And probably the love of her life.

It made Erec sick to think that she had been right, after all. He was dead now, and she had no clue. It seemed too cruel to let them know that he was a ghost. Let them all be happy for a while. If he could figure out a way to get his soul back, maybe he would never have to put them through that misery. . . .

"How did you get the Master Shem, Erec?" his mother asked.

"The Furies. I talked to them." He smiled, hoping they wouldn't ask much more. He did not want to lie, but would have to avoid the details.

Bethany looked excited, and started bouncing on her toes. "Did they give you your soul back?"

How to answer that one? "Not yet."

"Not yet?" His mother peered into his face. "So, do you think that they will give it to you, then?"

He forced a smile. "They said that they would."

If only it were that easy. Here he was, stuck without a soul and heading toward becoming evil. How would he be able to find someone that would give up their own soul for him? And was it even fair to ask anyone? Not really. What could he do?

An idea occurred to him. There was another ghost who was wiser than he would ever be, but it was not one who had lived a human life in the past. This was a golden ghost, by the name of Homer, who lived in the catacombs under King Piter's house where the castle used to stand. Homer guarded one of King Piter's most priceless possessions—the Novikov Time Bender, a time machine that Erec had used before. Homer had a great knowledge of the world of spirits, and had been alive for an eternity. Maybe he would know where Erec could find a soul to spare.

"Where's that Serving Tray?" Erec whizzed past his mother so fast that her head spun. He would have to remember to tap the ground more slowly so nobody would notice that he wasn't really walking. "It's time for Trevor's feast."

Trevor ate exactly what Erec predicted he would. It wasn't until

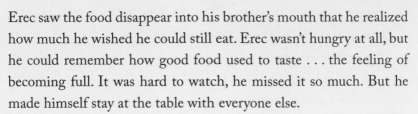

Erec saw the food disappear into his brother's mouth that he realized how much he wished he could still eat. Erec wasn't hungry at all, but he could remember how good food used to taste . . . the feeling of becoming full. It was hard to watch, he missed it so much. But he made himself stay at the table with everyone else.

"Aren't you going to eat?" his mother asked.

"I just did." He smiled. "Later."

It became harder acting like everything was normal when Jam insisted upon appearing at Erec's side every hour or so with meals and snacks for him. "Really," he kept insisting, "I'm just not hungry yet. I'll help myself."

It was also difficult to stay in the house at all. Now that Erec had the thought of visiting Homer, he was driven to go find him right away. He could not relax as a ghost, and just enjoy being around his loved ones. He still cared for them, but it was clear that he was here only for a purpose—to get his soul back, and maybe also to get the Master Shem back from Tarvos. Once he gave those ideas up he would be gone. It was like living one long, never-ending cloudy thought.

Until now, being a ghost had seemed easier than being human. But being home made everything completely different. There was nothing he wanted more than to give his family big hugs, and even give Bethany a kiss. Simple things, like eating, breathing, and sleeping seemed amazing. Most of all, he wished he could just relax and enjoy life without being driven like a slave to continue a mission.

If things went right, maybe he would be able to do all of those things again someday. But if they went wrong he might do awful things, hurt people, and have a horrifying afterlife. . . . He couldn't let that happen. One way or another, he had to fix this. It was time to go.

"Hey, look everyone. I have a chance to get my soul back, but I have to take care of a few things to do that. It won't take long, but it's really something I need to do by myself."

"What?" Erec could see that Bethany was hurt. She had felt rejected when he told her not to hug him, and now even more that he was about to head off on another adventure without her. It was supposed to be the two of them together, he knew.

"Can I talk to you a minute alone, Bethany?"

He led her into his room. One nice thing about being a ghost was that he knew exactly what she was thinking, and how to make her feel better. She sat on his bed and looked into his eyes, not seeing that he was any different.

Erec stroked her hair lightly with his fingers. It certainly wasn't something he would have done before he was a ghost, but he knew it was the right thing at the moment. "Sorry I didn't want you to touch me before. Something happened to me when I was gone, and you'll just have to trust that I'm going to try and make it better. But I'm not feeling good, and if anyone touches me it would be . . . bad." He rushed ahead, cutting her off. "And I want you to know something else. No matter what happens to me from this point on, I love you."

Bethany's face turned bright red, but Erec could see that she was glowing inside. He knew that it was not at all the kind of thing that he would have said when he was alive. But given that he was about to leave her again, possibly forever, it was what he needed to say now.

"I . . . you know, I . . ." Bethany was struggling, not sure how she wanted to reply.

"Hey. It's okay. Don't answer me. You're my best friend, that's all that has ever mattered. I'm really sorry that I have to do this alone. There is nothing on earth—nothing—that I would rather do than just spend time with you and my family. But all I can tell you is that I'm having something like a big, long cloudy thought. I just have to go take care of this. I will come back to you afterward,

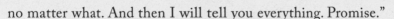

no matter what. And then I will tell you everything. Promise."

He could tell that she still was worried, but she felt much better about him leaving. "Okay, Erec. If it's like a cloudy thought, then I understand. Just be careful. I'd hate to lose you. Okay?"

Erec nodded, knowing that he was already lost.

Before anyone else could stop him, Erec darted into the Port-O-Door and shut it behind him. In a flash he had tapped the spot on the Alypium map where King Piter's castle once stood. The door opened into the house where he had recently lived with his father. In a flash, he whisked away the swatch of carpet that lay over the opening to the catacombs, and pulled the trapdoor open. Down a flight of stairs, around one corner then the next, Erec glided faster than he used to be able to run. He had known the way to this room even as a human; now there was no question. But this was the first time that he had come here to see Homer himself, not the Novikov Time Bender.

In moments, he stood before the glimmering cloudlike being. "Welcome back, Erec." Homer beamed. "It's so good to see you here again." Homer did not seem at all surprised that Erec was now a ghost. It was almost as if he had expected it all along. "I'm glad that you chose me to help you."

That sounded reassuring. Erec was not able to read Homer's mind, so he said, "I guess you understand why I am here. I need to get my soul back so I don't turn into some kind of evil spirit. Can you help me?"

"Don't worry, boy. There is a way for you." He sighed. "I wish I could help you more, but my kind has made a vow not to interfere with humans. I can get around that a bit, I suppose, because you are not exactly human at this point. You're a bit more like me. So I'll help you a little. But you're going to need to do most of the work yourself.

"You have a few choices. There are other spirits like you who occupy different regions. Some of them may help you, others won't. In order to get your soul back, you need to find a true friend. And he exists out there, but nowhere you would ever normally go. You need to discover places beyond in order to find what you seek—somewhere where there are lots of ghosts just like you. There are others in need of help, too. Those three thousand souls in bondage with the Furies all have the same sad story to tell that you do.

"Right now, you know better than to force a living person to give their soul for you. But if you don't act soon, you will become evil. And then you will likely do exactly that—bring an innocent human to the Furies, and take their soul from them. So take heed, and proceed with speed and caution."

"I'm trying—if I only knew what to do. Since I've become a ghost I can't stop being on the move, anyway."

"I know. Your type of ghost is always in motion—unless what they have to do involves waiting. Ghosts in that situation usually become very unhappy. They are quite impatient."

Erec realized that Homer must be incredibly patient. He was always here, in this same spot. Erec thought about what Homer had told him. "You're saying that I need to go somewhere where I can find other spirits, like me. Can you tell me where that is?"

Homer paused. "I cannot tell you where to go. That is meddling too much." He thought a moment, and smiled. "I suppose, however, that I could tell you where *not* to go. You should *not* look anywhere except for a place that is controlled by your worst enemy. That is the best that I can do."

It was time to move on. Erec sensed that Homer had said all that he would say.

CHAPTER NINE
Fire and Destruction

Erec's drive to get his soul back bordered on obsession. He had never felt this focused on anything when he had been alive. There was no need for sleep anymore, nor conversations, or anything else that would take him away from his goal.

A place controlled by his worst enemy. That was easy—Thanatos Baskania, the Shadow Prince, was obviously the person who had been against him from the start. All of the others: the Stain triplets, the armies of Alypium and Aorth, even President Washington

Inkle, all were mobilized under Baskania. The question was—what would Baskania have to do with spirits and ghosts?

Maybe he had some stashed in his fortress in Jakarta—the place where Bethany had been held captive in the spring? A thought occurred to Erec—one that was very appealing. If he found Baskania now and spoke to him, Erec would be able to read his mind completely. He would be able to find out exactly where any spirits were being held. And, on top of that, he could actually see what his archenemy was planning. Maybe Erec could interfere with his strategies.

That seemed to be the perfect answer. Erec had no fear of Baskania now—what could he do to Erec? Kill him? Seeing Baskania would actually be entertaining. Erec glided up the catacomb stairs back into the Port-O-Door. Straight to Jakarta, Indonesia. He knew where to park the door, nearby the cross streets of Jalan Kemang Raya and Jalan Bangka. Once there, he concentrated on tapping his toes against the ground to glide at a normal speed so he would not stand out in the crowd. The city was packed with people gathering at cafés and galleries, so he wasn't too worried about strangers paying him too much attention.

He was focusing on avoiding a group of people gathered around a food stall, and didn't notice that a young man in a business suit was walking fast right toward him. They normally would have bumped shoulders, but the man was walking forcefully enough that he passed right through Erec. He turned around, in shock, to get a better look at Erec, so Erec bolted ahead faster to get out of his view. *Oops.* He would have to pay closer attention next time.

Around the corner on Jalan Bangka, a signpost was perched on a neatly manicured lawn, reading WINDOWS TO THE SOUL—ONE STOP EYE CARE SHOP. It looked so quaint and innocent . . . how ironic that it was the portal to a horrifying fortress. Erec went inside. No longer would he have to worry about finding the right pair of glasses to show him where the doorway was to pass through to the fortress. As a ghost the way would be quite clear.

The man working in the shop had medium brown hair, was medium height, average weight, and had average features. The only thing that stood out about him were the simple, plain glasses on his face. Even though Erec had seen him before, it took a minute to identify him—he was so unnoticeable that he seemed to even disappear behind his own glasses, blending in to the rows of glasses behind him.

But the man recognized Erec immediately, and his face turned bright red. "Erec Rex! How dare you come back here again. Just because you got away the last time, don't think you're going to be so lucky now. I'm calling security!"

Erec shrugged. "Go ahead. I'm going straight in to find Baskania anyway, so I don't care." He could tell that the man was terrified. Reading his mind, he could see that he had gotten in trouble, as had many other people, for letting Erec escape before.

There was nothing Erec could do for him now. He looked around at the shelves of glasses, and spotted a hidden door in the wall behind a rack of glasses. He knew that it would not be visible to human eyes. This was obviously the way to get to the fortress.

"Pardon me." Erec smiled. He twisted open the doorknob, which was icy cold. Freezing wind flung the door back, blasting into the shop, and revealing a dark hallway.

The man's mouth hung open in shock. "I . . . how did you . . . ?"

"See you later." Erec winked, darting into the tunnel, slamming the door shut behind him. He swept through the long hallway at lightning speed into the light at the end. There was the beach that he remembered. It had seemed so hard to find a way across it the first time, with the ferocious phantom piranhas ready to devour any living thing. But Erec could fly himself now, so that would be no problem.

Even if he did touch the water, no phantom piranhas could hurt him.

When they had flown across before, there had been other horrible things to deal with. Erec remembered them now. Some of them would be no problem for him: the living things such as minotaurs, manticores, werewolves and wenwolves, lions, and tigers would pass right through him if they attacked. But Baskania was a fan of using the undead to guard his palace as well. He wondered if creatures like the zombies or the Vetalas—the horrific monsters that commanded and also ate the hordes of zombies—would be able to hurt him in any way. It seemed not. He already had lost his life and soul, what more was there to lose?

There were other things as well that guarded the fortress: Specters were pure evil spirits; spirit warriors were once-human ghosts that had been trained to serve in Baskania's army. And of course Shadow Demons, whose powers surpassed all of the others. Erec wondered if any of the spirit creatures could stop him now, but it didn't seem that there was much they could do.

He thought a moment about the specters. The ghostly creatures' whole existence was evil. Was that what he was destined to become if he didn't get his soul back? And the spirit warriors . . . they were ghosts like him. Why were they helping Baskania as their mission on earth? Had he worked a spell on them? Just to be safe, Erec would make sure that Baskania didn't find out that he was a ghost.

Suddenly Erec's eyes flung wide open. Spirit warriors—weren't they exactly what he was looking for? The golden ghost had said, "There are other spirits like you who occupy different regions. You need to look to places beyond in order to find what you seek." Well, this fortress was a different region of the world. Were there other places that Erec needed to go to find more spirit warriors, or other kinds of spirits who might be able to help him?

It was time to find out. Erec pushed against the sandy beach and sprung into the air. He soared over the dark, rippling waters, straight into the clouds. Turning a somersault in the air, he angled himself toward the other shore. It felt great to fly, even if the wind was blowing right through his body instead of against his skin. He touched down on the other side of a huge stone wall, in the midst of a pride of lions. Spotting him, a manticore rushed over with a growl. The thing raced straight through him several times until it lost interest.

The black iron fortress looked surreal, like Baskania wanted it to be as intimidating as possible. Dark spikes covered every turret, post, and crooked Gothic roof peak. Terrifying gargoyles wagged their tongues at the creatures below. Towers jutted all over, each looking as if it held hostages, and creatures of all types swarmed through the air between them.

Rows of zombies marched, unthinking, in circles around the palace, but Erec flew through them, untouched. He spied a disgusting Vetala, three rotting heads stacked atop one another under its black hooded cape. No problem to him now. He glided, untroubled, toward the front door of the fortress. As he grew closer, he knew that Baskania was inside. Before he talked to the Spirit Warriors, he had to get a glimpse into the mind of his enemy.

He bounded up the outer steps to the pointed gothic stone archway that led to the huge wooden castle doors. Two black-cloaked Vetalas stood in front, talking. Erec recognized one as Master Vetu, the Vetala in charge of the rest.

Master Vetu did not recognize him; however, he was delighted. "Well, well!" His middle head spoke to Erec, staring into him with piercing eyes. His low voice sounded slick and cold. "Look what we have here—fresh meat. How lovely. I was in need of a new head, this bottom one has seen its day." The eyes in the Vetala's top head spun wildly, giving it a crazed look. Its lower head was caving in, tongue sticking out and eyes darting around suspiciously.

"I'll take his hands," the other Vetala said in a husky whisper. "Mine keep falling to bits. I want one of his legs, too, to eat."

Master Vetu nodded, looking at Erec appraisingly. "That will be fine. We seem to be the only ones to have spotted this boy. No reason to share with the rest. We'll each take a leg, then." His lower face began to drool all over its chin.

Then Erec heard a sound that was more horrifying than anything else. It was a tiny baby crying. He looked around, as did the excited Vetalas. Lying on the stone ground next to them was an infant wrapped in a blue blanket. Erec could read the Vetala's thoughts—each wanted to tear into the child with its teeth before the other could get a bite. But the child seemed to have no thoughts at all—likely it was too young. How had it gotten here?

Master Vetu held up a hand. "The baby will be mine. You can start with this boy. Just make sure not to ruin his head."

The other Vetala swiped at Erec with a craggy clawed hand, but it passed right through him. The baby continued to cry, unnerving Erec completely. He had to get the poor thing to safety.

Both Vetalas stared at him now, realizing that he was a ghost. Master Vetu, to make sure, shot a bolt of red lightning out of his bony hand, aimed at Erec. The red beam diverted and was absorbed straight into the Amulet of Virtues that hung around Erec's neck. Not that Erec would have been hurt by the blast, but it was nice to know that his Amulet was still in working order.

The creatures then turned their attention to the baby. In one bound, Erec swooped the poor thing up into his arms and leaped onto the roof. The Vetalas looked up at him, shaking their fists and drooling.

The infant batted his blue eyes coyly at Erec and smiled. "Thanks, Erec, dear," it said.

Erec was so shocked he almost dropped the thing. This baby

could talk? It looked like a newborn. How was that possible?

"Oh, my, my, little Erec," it said in a squeaky little voice. "You'll never learn, will you?"

"H-how did you know my name? Who are you?" This was the first time that Erec felt fear, as a ghost.

"I'm your old friend. We met the last time that you were here, although I looked a little different then."

Erec immediately realized what he was holding. It was a Shadow Demon. The last time he was here—and the time he had met one in King Pluto's dungeons—the thing had chosen to look like a mirror image of Erec himself. It could also, at will, look like any vicious or gruesome being it chose.

The thing felt tingly in his fingers and he dropped it onto the roof tiles. "That wasn't funny."

"Ouch," the thing said, even though Erec knew that it felt no pain. "Don't you know that it's impolite to throw babies?"

"You're no baby. Do you think you're going to stop me from talking to Baskania? Because I'm on a mission."

"I know exactly what mission you are on," the Shadow Demon said. "I can read your little mind just as well as I could the last time. You never fail to amuse me, you know."

Erec remembered that the way to disarm a Shadow Demon was to simply walk right through the thing. The only way it tried to keep people from doing that was by frightening them, by making itself look like a Vetala or something awful. Well, nothing like that would frighten Erec as a ghost. Just to get it over with, he glided over the rooftop straight through the baby.

The Shadow Demon did not even try to alter its appearance to frighten Erec away. Maybe it knew that Erec was past that now.

Instead, the baby just laughed. "You are too much. Really." It cackled harder, which sounded strange coming from a baby, giving

Erec the chills. "What, do you think you can make me go away if you pass through me? Like you're still human or something? That would only keep me from *eating* a human. But you don't have much to eat, now, do you?"

"So, you can't do anything to me now, then?"

"Oh, I didn't say that." The baby winked.

Erec was confused. If only he could read the thoughts of this thing like he could read humans. "I'm going to go find Baskania now. Have a good day."

"Oh, I will. I'm going to have an excellent day. It's always fun when you visit. Feel free to speak to the Shadow Prince. I'll be going with you, if you don't mind. Kind of part of my job, you know."

Part of his job? What was his job? Erec remembered that the Shadow Demon alerted Baskania that intruders were there. That was no issue now—Erec wasn't hiding.

But there was one problem that occurred to him. The Shadow Demon knew something that he was hiding from Baskania—that Erec was a ghost.

"Bingo," the baby said. "It doesn't take you too long, does it? I mean, for a human at least."

"Hey, could you not mention that to Baskania? I mean, he doesn't need to know that I'm dead. I'd just like to find out a few things from him, and keep that to myself, okay?"

The baby opened its mouth and a snake tongue darted out. It stretched its jaws wider, and a fat snake with red and black stripes oozed out. After about six feet of snake had appeared, the rest of the baby morphed into a pale rattle at the end of its tail. The snake hissed, "You want me to keep your sssssecret, then? Why should I do that? I have made an agreement with the Ssssshadow Princsssss, you know."

"I understand. But you are your own boss. Why help that guy out when you can help a fellow ghost?"

"You're not a fellow anything to me," the snake hissed. "A deal is a deal, and fun is fun, you know."

"Please. I'll trade you for anything I have. Do you want this Amulet of Virtues?" Erec had no need for the amulet. As a ghost he could never be king. And if he ever became human again he'd be happy to give quests up forever if he could get his soul back.

"Thanks for offering me ssssomething entirely usssselessss. I will make a trade, though, for that lovely Twrch Trwyth, and the three Awen that are left in it."

Erec did not have to read the Shadow Demon's mind to know that the Twrch Trwyth would give the thing far too much power. The Awen were strong enough to have an effect on even the three Furies.

"Have it your way, then." The snake sprouted wings and flew in circles through the air around Erec's head.

Erec tried to ignore it and go on his way to find Baskania. It really didn't matter if the snake blew his cover, anyway. It wasn't like the human Baskania could do anything to hurt him now that he was already dead. He had to find out where Baskania was keeping all of the spirits, and also what his plans were. That was the only important thing. That was why he had to come here, after all.

Erec could hear the snake laughing as he sailed down to the fortress gate.

It was easy to find Baskania—Erec could sense exactly where to go. He leaped to the front door of the castle, the Vetalas swinging around in a fury. Ignoring them, he passed right through the wooden door.

Inside, he glided down hallways and up staircases with no effort. He tried to keep his pace within the norm for a human, just in case he could keep his cover. Around corners and down hallways—Erec could not wait to face his enemy now that he was the one with all of the power.

The flying snake hovered right behind his shoulder the whole way. Erec finally flung open the wooden doorway to the room where Baskania was. Hundreds of candles glittered through the huge gold leaf–painted room. Ornate paintings and tapestries decorated the walls. Baskania sat behind a polished wooden desk, carved with gargoyles and Minotaurs. His face had stretched wide to fit twenty-six eyes, all of which gazed at Erec with surprise.

After a moment, his face began to morph. Eyes in the lower half sunk into his skin, forming deep pits. It was nauseating, like his face had become a sick version of Swiss cheese. Then his skin flattened over the pits to create a smooth expanse of skin. A wide area caved in, cracking across the lower part, until it broke into a sharp, thin-lipped mouth, stretching into a cruel smile.

"What a welcome surprise! I am delighted to see you here, Erec. I'm curious how you made it through my fortress, but I'm sure that I'll find out soon. What can I do for you?"

Erec glanced at the Shadow Demon, wondering if he was going to tell Baskania right away that Erec was a ghost. But the floating snake seemed content to wait and watch. "I wanted to talk to you, that's all."

Erec felt something pushing against his mind, his thoughts. The sensation was coming from Baskania, he was sure, but he couldn't tell what it was. It was almost as if his enemy was trying to enter his space without even moving—probably trying to read his mind. Whatever he was doing, though, Erec could tell that it wasn't working very well.

When he focused on Baskania's thoughts, he had a harder time reading them compared to other humans. It was as if Baskania had a shield around him. But he was able to make out a few things. Baskania was confused as to why he could not read Erec's mind. He was guessing that Erec had learned some magic to protect himself, or was wearing an amulet or charm. He was also hoping that Erec had come to hand over his scepter. He wanted that badly. And he also planned to take Erec's dragon eyes before Erec left.

Erec laughed, thinking how disappointed Baskania would be if he learned that Erec had no dragon eyes at all now.

Baskania looked surprised that Erec laughed. "I see that things are different with you now, my friend. Why don't you sit and talk to me a while. I'm sure we have a lot to learn from each other." His lips curved in a tight smile.

Erec nodded and sat down. "Just so you know, I'm not going to be giving you my scepter." Erec could sense Baskania's crushing frustration. It felt good to be able to upset his enemy with no fear of what might happen.

Baskania seemed to realize Erec's lack of fear, which added to his anger. He tried to suppress it until he learned more. "We'll worry about that scepter later. I'd like to hear what you've been up to. It's obvious you have changed a bit since we saw each other last."

"I suppose so." Erec shrugged. He could feel the pushing again from Baskania trying to read his mind, and then sense more of his frustration when it didn't work. "I've gone through some interesting things lately. You can say I've learned a lot. I just visited my friends, the Furies. They gave me a pretty powerful gift." He paused, letting Baskania's curiosity and excitement build. Erec enjoyed rubbing in that the Furies were not under Baskania's control. More than that, they were helping Erec now—and it was driving Baskania wild with jealousy. Everything that Erec had said was true, but Baskania had no idea what he was referring to.

It was not a feeling that the Shadow Prince was used to. Erec could hear his voice crack. "What was the gift, Erec?"

"Their last gift?" He shrugged, watching all of Baskania's eyes widen with envy and resentment. "That's between me and them."

"So . . . the Furies are beholden to you now? You gave your soul to release them from Tartarus, right? And now they owe you." A look of realization hit him. "That should have been *me* they owed their freedom to. I had thought you would never make it out of there alive. I mean . . . I'm happy for you." Baskania revolved between bitterness and real excitement—thinking of how he could use Erec for even more things now. Erec wished he could read Baskania's mind easier so he could see everything that he was planning.

"Thanks." Erec shrugged, trying to look bored. As interesting as this was, he needed to find out the answers to his own questions, so he'd have to be more direct. Even if Baskania didn't answer, Erec could read his mind and find out what he needed to know. "So, where do you keep your ghosts and spirits?"

"Where do I *what*?" Baskania was truly confused. Erec could see an answer shape in his mind, along with the fact that he wasn't going to tell Erec anything. "What ghosts and spirits are you talking about?"

Erec concentrated and could see that there was indeed a place where countless ghosts like him were kept by Baskania. They were being trained to fight, and turned into spirit warriors. Baskania was thinking about them silently, and his thoughts were clear enough. A number of the spirits had been humans who were sacrificed to the three Furies, and this group had no souls anymore: These unfortunates were in the process of turning into evil specters—Erec was right. That was exactly what he was bound to turn into if he did not get his soul back soon.

But where exactly were they kept? Erec had to try to keep Baskania's mind focused on them. "You know the spirits I'm talking about. What are you doing with them? Where are you keeping them?"

He got a flash of an answer, but it wasn't complete. Somewhere in another realm. That's what the golden ghost had been alluding to. It was someplace they could not escape from. Where was it?

Baskania squinted with all of his eyes. "Why are you asking me this? Did the Furies send you? Do they want the spirits for themselves?"

That seemed the perfect answer to give to Baskania. Maybe it would frighten him into letting those poor ghosts go. So he nodded. "Yes, the Furies want them all. You have to let them go, and give them all to me."

Baskania just stared at him, probing. Erec knew that he was suspicious. If only Erec could tell exactly where the spirits were . . .

"Where are you holding them?" he asked. "How far away are they?"

That did the trick. The answer entered Baskania's mind—the spirits were housed in a zone in the Earth's atmosphere that was separated from the rest of our world. Baskania himself had created it to trap these beings—it was inescapable to them. It amazed Erec when he saw the place in the Shadow Prince's mind. Baskania had a complete understanding of spirits—and so many other things as well. He would have been wise, were he not so twisted from greed and power.

The spirit zone was called the Hinternom, and it was accessible only through a trapdoor here at the fortress in Jakarta. Innocent spirits were led to the door and sucked through by its special magic. Once inside the Hinternom, the only way for the spirits to ever leave was to learn to fight, and to accept Baskania as their master.

Well, now Erec knew not to go to the room with the trapdoor. If he didn't choose to go there on his own, there was no way that any human could force him. He wondered how the other spirits had been misled. Wouldn't they have been able to read the mind of the human who was planning to trick them? Maybe Baskania was the one that did it. He could hide some of his thoughts.

Baskania tapped a sharp fingernail against his desk. "I don't think the Furies want those spirits, Erec. I don't think they have any need for them at all. In fact, I feel that you are lying to me. You have met with the Furies, and they are beholden to you. But you are lying about the ghosts." Erec could feel the pushing from Baskania harder now. Some of his probes were actually entering Erec's space, although nowhere close to working. Erec cleared his mind and Baskania's efforts failed completely.

Since Baskania used his mind-reading skills to intimidate people, Erec decided to turn the tables. "I see that you keep the spirits in the Hinternom. You created that place yourself. Congratulations. It must have been hard work."

Erec's comments worked better than he had expected. Fear flooded his enemy. Baskania was convinced that Erec had developed powers and connections with the Substance that were far beyond his own abilities for the first few hundred years of his life. He thought he would be no match for Erec now, that it was too late to dispose of him, and that his plans were foiled.

It was satisfying to hear those thoughts, so Erec smiled, increasing Baskania's fear even more. Then a slick smile took over the Shadow Prince's face. "Erec, I'm impressed with you. Really. I admit—as you know, I once felt at odds with you. I wanted things that you had— your scepter, your dragon eyes. But you have gained so much power. You are a bright learner, obviously, and a worthy ally. As you can see, it would be best for us to be friends, rather than waste our time and efforts trying to destroy each other. I hope you agree." He folded his hands peacefully before him.

Erec could tell that all traces of fear had left Baskania. He was doing a good job at hiding his thoughts now that he knew Erec was listening to them. "I don't know." Erec tapped his chin. "Why don't you tell me what you're planning and I'll decide."

"Of course." Baskania nodded. "Well, my plans are changing as I'm getting a chance to know the new you. Up until now I had planned on using the triplets, Balor, Damon, and Dollick, to rule the Kingdoms of the Keepers. As you know, this is a natural progression as I myself created these worlds. Of course my three cloned sons should be the crown princes. But, of course, those boys are not me—not nearly. Two of the three are atrocious failures. The cloning job was awful, to say the least. Needless to say, the doctor that did the procedure has been disposed of. He used laser slices from me to create the boys—the slice for Damon obviously went through too much bone. Dollick was cut from my stomach—I had just eaten lamb for dinner.

"But why waste my time with those three when you and I could rule together? You will keep your own scepter, and wield it as you like. Together we will make sure that the world works the way that it should. It will be ours to command. Just think . . . you would have everything you ever wanted."

As Baskania said that, images entered Erec's mind that filled him with delight. The scepter would be his! Even as a ghost, Baskania's words were able to lead his mind like a dog on a leash. He did want those things. And maybe Baskania would be a good friend to him after all.

A small bit of reason in the back of Erec's head tried to push those thoughts away, but it was difficult. He tried to remember his reasons for not liking Baskania. He had lied to Erec before. But it was hard not to trust him now. Erec could see it perfectly: the Shadow Prince and himself, the Moon Prince, ruling the world. Wasn't that what the Hermit had called Erec once—the Moon Prince? He had said Erec was "Reflecting the light of the Sun King, and held by the gravity of the Fates," whatever that meant.

Thinking about the Hermit brought a little sense into his mind.

What would the Hermit say about this idea? Probably that Erec was crazy. He tried to fight off the temptations that Baskania had put into his head, but it was becoming harder. The Shadow Prince's words were so appealing. . . .

"Erec," Baskania said, softly. "I don't want to harm you. I want to work with you. But I'd like you to help me with a few things first, if that's okay with you."

Erec nodded. "Of course, anything would be okay." He could tell that Baskania was trying to control his thoughts, but even though he could see it clearly, it was still working.

Baskania smiled. "Let's start with those dragon eyes. I need them to help get us where we want to go. More power for the two of us, you know."

Erec did know. It was what he wanted too. Power to use his scepter, power to rule, power to make people see how great he really was. Giving Baskania his dragon eyes was a small thing, really. "I don't have them here, though," Erec said. They're . . . somewhere else."

"Not here?" Baskania looked confused. All at once, Erec's good feelings screeched to a halt. "I don't understand. They are not attached to your eyes anymore? Where are you keeping them?"

Groggy, coming out of a haze, it was hard for Erec to remember why he was here. Should he tell Baskania the truth? It seemed safer not to, but he wasn't sure why. "I . . . don't know." He reached up to rub his eyes, then set his hands back down again when he realized that his eyes felt nothing. "I don't need them right now."

Erec could feel the pushing again of Baskania trying to read his mind, and he started to come back to his senses. Baskania had brainwashed him. A mere human had so much control over the Substance that he was able to overpower a ghost. Then again, Baskania had created the Hinternom, and even the entire Kingdoms of the Keepers, by using the Substance.

But there were still some things he could not do, and one of them was to read Erec's mind right now. Which was good, because Erec was starting to worry. He had to figure out what to do about the Hinternom and get out of here before Baskania pulled any more tricks. No wonder the giggling Shadow Demon behind him was having so much fun watching them—Erec had learned a lesson.

At least his dragon eyes and scepter were far away, safe. His dragon eyes were protected in his dead body, and he had sent the scepter away with a spell designed to make sure that he could not call it back on his own.

The pushing got harder, and Erec could feel a ray pierce through his thoughts. "It's hard to tell what you are thinking, Erec. But I can see that it has to do with your scepter. Where are you keeping it?"

Erec shrugged. "I don't know. It's gone." He cleared his mind to stop Baskania's probing.

"There are ways of making you talk." Baskania stroked a silver eye sitting on his desk, its pupil a hole with black coal inside. It looked like it was staring at Erec. "But I'd rather you just told me on your own, friend."

The good feelings about Baskania started to return. Erec tried to fight them, but it was hard. Maybe he *should* tell Baskania how to call Erec's scepter back. It wasn't hard to do. Erec just needed help from someone else, and Baskania would be glad to do it.

He remembered the command that he had given his scepter months ago. King Piter and he both had a hard time resisting its temptation, and it was starting to destroy them. He had to send it away and make sure that he could not bring it back on his own. So he had told it, *Scepter, I want you to get lost. Stay far away from human beings, and don't come back to me until* someone else *tells me I am ready for you.* Baskania could do that for him, now, if Erec just told him what to say. . . .

"I can see that you're thinking about the scepter, why you sent it away . . ." Baskania was concentrating.

Erec tried to make his mind blank, but he wasn't sure why. Oh, yes. It was the scepter. He had to keep it away. But why? He wished that he had it now. It would feel so good to hold it again, feel its power again. Wielding it would make him stronger than the Shadow Prince. Maybe he would show Baskania a thing or two. Then they could rule together—but with Erec in charge. Yes. That was it.

Wait! His common sense fought back. He wasn't ready for the scepter. It would destroy him. What was he thinking?

Baskania got a glint in some of his eyes. "You are telling yourself that you are not ready to handle the scepter yet. But that is not true, Erec. You are ready. You are ready to use your scepter right now."

That was exactly what had to be said to bring it back—did Baskania know? In a flash, the golden scepter appeared in Erec's hands. Its power instantly overwhelmed him. As a human, touching the thing gave him a feeling of warmth and security. Using it created electric waves of power. But as a ghost, holding it was exhilarating. He could feel his own power amplify by multitudes. It was as if he and the scepter were one, it had become a part of his being. There was nothing he could not do now.

Baskania's eyes widened in shock, and then greed. "That's a good boy, Erec. You listened to me, then, and called your scepter here." Baskania had no idea that it was he himself who called the scepter to Erec. With his magnified power, Erec could see through Baskania easily. He had all kinds of plots and ideas, and he was so obsessed with them that he was always in a kind of pain. From where Erec sat now, holding all of the power in the world in his hands, Baskania seemed like a lost little boy.

The Shadow Prince frowned. "I can't see what you are thinking

THE SECRET OF ASHONA

at all now, Erec. But I'd like to hold that scepter for a minute, okay? I really admire it."

"*No!*" Erec pulled it close to his chest. "I just got it back. I need to keep it for a while." He knew that he would never let it part from him again. Why had he given it up before? It was rightfully his. Of course he was ready for it. Why not? They had things to do together. So many things . . .

"I see." Baskania looked thoughtful. "Would you like to show me what you can do with that beautiful piece of gold? I think I'm a good audience."

"Sure." Erec wanted to try something impressive. "Watch this."

Fire, he thought. Fire was striking. He would turn himself into a blazing fire. *Scepter, do as I command!*

Before Baskania's eyes, Erec burst into flames. He grew larger and larger, orange, yellow, and red melding together into an inferno that was roughly the shape of his body. The ceiling was not an obstacle in his way—he burned right through it and up several other floors of the fortress, making people run, screaming. It felt so good to be back again, he thought. This is what he was meant to be—free and on top of the world.

Erec tilted his head back and laughed, fire streaming from his mouth. It shot out of his fingertips, and he slashed at the building around him. The destruction felt wonderful—a release of all of his tensions. Why hadn't he tried this before? It took a moment to realize that he felt so good that he might never return to his normal form again. Why not stay a permanent blaze of fire? But that didn't seem right, somehow, so he forced himself to appear as a boy again, and made the fire stop.

Seated again, Erec looked around in amazement at the devastation. Had he really done this? It hadn't seemed to matter when he was made of fire, but he felt concerned. He should fix it again.

But with the whirl of a finger, Baskania had already restored the fortress to its original appearance. His eyes were gleaming. "Did you see that? I can't believe the power I will have." He closed his eyes and took a breath.

An intense feeling of trust for Baskania took over Erec. They were best friends. There was nobody who cared about him except for the Shadow Prince. It would always be the two of them together. The sentiments that he had had before paled in comparison to what he felt now. Baskania and Erec would be together, against the rest of the world, forever. And it felt so *right*. So much more right now that the scepter was back with him again.

Erec could feel something change inside of him. This feeling was too good, too intense, to ever forget. This was what he would always want now. To rule, with Baskania, his ally, at his side. Together, they would never be stopped.

CHAPTER TEN
The Hinternom

"THAT WAS WONDERFUL." Baskania was rubbing his palms together. Erec could tell that he was practically drooling for the scepter. "Can I try something with it now?"

"No, you can't." Erec caressed the gem-studded gold. "It's only for me. But I can do things for you if you want my help."

"That's nice." Baskania cocked an eyebrow. "I like to hear that, friend. I could use a helper like you. It would also be nice to try using it myself—just once. How about that, Erec? Would you share it with me one time?"

A wave of kindness and trust overwhelmed Erec, and he felt happier than he could remember. He was here with his two best friends ever—Baskania and his scepter. It was like a big, happy family. Because of how he felt, he was even moved to be generous. "I will share it with you. Once. But not now. It might be a few weeks before I am ready."

Baskania looked questioningly at the Shadow Demon who was still hovering in the air as a snake behind Erec.

Erec did not care anymore what the Shadow Demon said to Baskania. He was stronger than both of them put together. He could see that Baskania was asking for help, that he wanted Erec's scepter for himself. Well, who wouldn't? Erec wasn't angry with him. As powerful and connected with the Substance as he was, Baskania was still only human. Erec had far surpassed that now.

Poor Baskania. Just like a child, Erec thought. Baskania was ashamed to have to rely on the Shadow Demon; he wanted to be in control by himself. But Erec was too powerful. Erec wanted to take Baskania under his wing and help him feel better. He would give him anything that he could, really. Just not the scepter. Not yet.

The Shadow Demon snake did a few somersaults in the air, and then morphed into a replica of Baskania, wearing the identical black cape and business suit. "Well, you see, it's like this," the Shadow Demon Baskania said to the other who was seated behind the desk. "Things are not as they seem. The reason that this . . . thing in front of you does not have dragon eyes is—"

"—It's not Erec!" Baskania shouted. "How could I not have seen that? Erec Rex would never be this powerful. But who could it be, then? And how did it get Erec's scepter?"

The new Baskania shook his head. "Not so simple. This is not someone else. It is still Erec, in a sense. But not in the sense that you think." The Shadow Demon seemed to enjoy playing with Baskania.

"What do you mean?" Baskania was getting impatient, but did not want to raise his voice to the Shadow Demon.

"Simple." The Shadow Demon laughed. "This is his ghost. Erec Rex is dead."

Baskania's eyes widened. "Of course! How could I not have seen this before?" He looked Erec over in wonder. "This is amazing. Perfect! Where is the body?"

"Right here." Before Erec could read Baskania's mind, his own body appeared on the floor before him, perfectly preserved. In his arms lay the scepter—an identical version to the one in Erec's hands. Erec was confused for a moment. Two scepters? But it seemed like they were the same one. . . .

In a flash, the scepter was out of the arms of his dead body on the ground and in Baskania's grasp. At the same time, the one in Erec's hands disappeared.

Baskania held the gold scepter, stroking it and gazing at it with wonder. "This is wonderful. Much better than Pluto's scepter. We are going to be such good friends, you and I."

Erec's jaw hung open. How did that happen? He was holding his scepter tight—how could it disappear from his grasp like that? Baskania's mind was completely unreadable now—although Erec was sure he knew what his enemy was thinking. He would be reveling in the same power that Erec had felt just moments before. Except with Baskania's strength, the power of the scepter would be magnified even more.

What had he done? He had handed the most powerful object in the world to someone who would use it for destruction. If only Erec still had it . . . he would use it for good. In fact, right now he would lock Baskania up in a place he could never escape from.

But a horrible thought occurred to Erec. When he did have the scepter, he hadn't used it for good at all—had he? What had he done with it? Not create food for the hungry, or even rescue the spirits locked away in the Hinternom. Instead he turned himself into fire and ruined the fortress. And he enjoyed it too.

The scepter was going to make Baskania far more destructive than he already was. And Erec was helpless now to stop it.

Baskania tore his eyes from his prize and walked to Erec's body on the floor. "Where did you find this thing?"

The Shadow Demon Baskania yawned. "It was in one of the Diamond Minds' pits in Argos. Erec had been keeping it there, in case he ever made it back alive again."

Baskania giggled with delight. "How perfect! I'll take those dragon eyes now. Then I'll have everything!"

There was a tugging feeling, and then everything in the room got a little darker. Erec could still see—but he realized that was only because he was a ghost. The eyes that had been in his dead body were now gone. Baskania pulled an eye patch off of his face, revealing a deep pit. "I've kept this waiting, because I just knew I would get what I wanted some day. Now is the time!" He pushed the dragon eye into the hole, and looked around the room with it. "Wonderful! It's attaching already. I can feel the power in it—and it's even stronger because I have the scepter. Nothing can stop me now!"

Erec was horrified. He had made this happen by coming here. How stupid had he been? What conceit! In a single swipe, Erec had ruined—no, ended—the whole world. Baskania would surely devastate everything now.

As Erec watched in horror, Baskania grew larger, at least a foot taller and wider. Erec had a bad feeling that it was not something he was trying to do—he could have easily changed his size before. More likely it was a side effect of the enormous strength coursing through his body now.

Baskania's voice reverberated through the room. "Thank you, Erec Rex. I could not have asked more of you."

Baskania kicked Erec's dead body. Something jiggled around its neck, and Baskania stooped over it. "Wait a minute, here. What's this?" He held up the Amulet of Virtues. "This annoying thing has got in my way one time too many. It will be mine now." Baskania tried to remove the Amulet without success. At least that was one thing that he would not be able to take—a powerful spell kept it on its wearer.

Baskania snarled. "This thing is no match for us!" He tipped the scepter toward it and in a moment Erec's Amulet of Virtues was in his hand. "And look at this." He poked at the Twrch Trwyth—the small glass boar-shaped vial with the three Awen left hanging on it. "This is my lucky day! How many more gifts will I receive?" In a moment, both the Amulet and the Trwyth vial hung around his neck.

Erec's heart sank. This was the worst mistake he had ever made. As a spirit he was no wiser than he had been when he was alive. In fact, he felt like a complete idiot. He deserved something horrible to happen to him.

There had to be some way to fix things. Was there anyone else who could get the scepter, dragon eyes, and Twrch Trwyth away from Baskania? No—there was no match for the Shadow Prince. Erec would have to warn his family that they had to go into hiding. Not that there was anywhere to hide now.

The damage was done, and there was no fixing it. He had to move on and find the Hinternom in the atmosphere—even though he had completely messed up, he still had a mission. He would search for a way into the thing, and maybe even crack it open so he could save the poor, trapped spirits inside.

Baskania laughed with glee. "I don't think so, Erec Rex. You will never escape. You are my guest now. I owe you so much for all of these wonderful gifts that you have given to me today. I'll repay the favor by putting you somewhere safe, where nothing will ever harm you again. In fact, it's exactly where you want to go."

He cackled, pointing in the air. A fine silver net dropped over Erec. Erec tried to move, but the net held him still. It seemed ghost-proof. Was this how Baskania had forced the other spirits into the trapdoor that led to the Hinternom?

"On your way, then, Erec." Snickering, Baskania pointed his scepter at Erec. Erec jumped to his feet. On their own, his knees shot up high, one at a time, and he marched himself out of the room, the net still around him. Leaving behind Baskania and the Shadow Demon who looked like him, Erec marched like a puppet down the hall and up several flights of stairs. He knew where he was heading—and there was nothing at all that he could do about it.

Down another hallway, he moved as commanded to the destined room. His hand shot up, opened the door, and he walked inside and shut it behind him. Erec could feel the suction from the trapdoor even before he opened it. *Please,* he thought. *Let there be a way to escape. If I'm trapped, I won't even be able to warn my family of Baskania's new power. I'll never be able to say good-bye.*

But his own hand reached down and yanked the trapdoor open. In a second, his entire being was sucked inside, and the door slammed shut behind him.

Spirits surrounded him. Some were walking on a surface that seemed like the ground, although Erec knew that they were far above the clouds. Most of the others, like Erec, floated, adrift. This was the end, then. He would be trapped with them forever. He remembered from reading Baskania's thoughts—the only way for a spirit to ever leave the Hinternom was to learn to fight and accept Baskania as their master. Erec would never do either of those things. His time was done.

It was a small consolation that he would be locked away here forever. At least when he turned evil—and that would probably be sooner than later after that experience with the scepter—he wouldn't cause people harm. How could he have come to this end? It seemed so awful, so unfair. But he knew deep down that he deserved his fate. Everyone else here was an innocent victim. Only Erec should be imprisoned for eternity.

Floating.
Floating.
Floating.

Floating.

Floating.

It was impossible to say how much time had gone by. Erec didn't even care. All around him, spirits were floating, drifting aimlessly and depressed. A few occasionally tried to break through the barrier of the Hinternom, beating themselves tirelessly against the borders. Others decided to take the only real route out—warfare training with the generals. These spirits were learning to use weapons, as well as fighting techniques and magic. Erec barely cared to watch or listen to what was going on. He would never swear allegiance to Baskania—or leave this place again.

As far as he knew, life on Earth had already ended. King Piter had told him once that if Baskania got ahold of the scepter—or Erec's dragon eyes—he would destroy the world with them. If that was the case, everything might already be gone. It was too upsetting to think about.

Floating.

Erec overheard spirits talk about how they were required to take a pill before being allowed to leave. It was a kind of assignment module that linked them into a gigantic structure commanded by Baskania. The pill made it impossible for any of the spirits to disobey. *What a nightmare,* Erec thought. *Baskania's completely tied things up. What a mess.*

Floating.

Specters whizzed through the crowd of spirits. Erec cringed when he saw them. They were what he was destined to become. Unlike the spirit trainees, the specters did their own thing, knocking crowds of spirits on their sides and banging heads together. At one point he saw a specter destroy a bunch of weapons in the hands of Spirit Warriors just as they were leaving the Hinternom. One pulled a few finished trainees back through the door just as they were about to be set free. The specters were released at odd times out from the Hinternom. Even though they were untrained, they were still given a pill so that they would be forced to follow commands. Erec hoped that he would be able to resist that pill when the time came. Ending his life as an evil specter in the servitude of his worst enemy was the worst fate he could have.

Floating.

It was getting harder to think. Erec was stuck in a deep haze of sadness and regret. But something was making him look around. What was it? He heard something. . . .

"Erec! Erec Rex!"

Someone was calling him? Who would know him here? Maybe one of the ghosts had lived in Alypium and had seen him walking around. They probably hated him. Wasn't worth paying attention to . . .

"Erec—I know that's you. What are you doing here?"

The voice sounded familiar. Erec looked around again. Spirits floated in all directions, looking human in form but having no substance.

One of them drifted in front of his face. "I know that's you, Erec. It is, isn't it? Can you answer me?"

It was somebody that Erec did know . . . it was Spartacus Kilroy! His old friend, and his father's prior AdviSeer. Spartacus might not have been the best AdviSeer, but he would do anything for the people he cared about. It had been awful when Spartacus died—Baskania had made it happen. He tried to give Spartacus's soul to the Furies in trade for favors. Luckily Erec had stopped that from happening, but he wasn't able to save Spartacus's life.

Erec nodded, and Spartacus threw an arm around him. "I thought that was you. It was hard to tell without your eyes. . . ."

Erec forgot that he would look eyeless now that Baskania had taken them from his body. But he tried not to think about it. It was great to see a familiar face, even in this awful place. "What are *you* doing here? I thought you would be wherever spirits normally go. . . ."

Spartacus shrugged sadly. "I did too. After I saw you last, I returned to my farm and helped Artie and Kyron get squared away taking care of the mess there." He laughed. "That was a little crazy. But I finished my goal, to get the farm taken care of. And then I just waited to go wherever spirits go. I had no idea what would happen to me next. Soon I felt someone calling me. I figured that I should follow it. And you can guess where that led me—right to Baskania's fortress.

"When I got there, there was a long line of ghosts that had heard the summons as well. We all still thought it must be the next step in passing from this world. Why else would so many of us be called there? So we waited patiently for our turn, with no idea that Baskania was sending us through that trapdoor into this place. He did a good job at hiding his thoughts—I didn't know what was going on. Later, in here, I heard that a few spirits who caught on and tried to escape were captured with a silver net and dragged here anyway. Every now and then another huge dump of spirits pours in here, and I know that Baskania's put another call out."

Erec shook his head. "At least you have a good excuse for being here. I was stupid—I practically walked here of my own free will." Erec told Spartacus how he had lost his soul, and then his life. "So it's hopeless now. I've given Baskania everything . . . and I'm doomed to become a specter. I've failed completely."

Spartacus looked overwhelmed. "I can't believe it, Erec. I just can't. . . ." He searched Erec's face. "We have to figure a way out of here. I thought it was hopeless. You know how I feel about Baskania—I'll never be his servant again. I was sure that I'd stay in here forever, until I saw you."

"What?" Erec raised an eyebrow. "Why do you think seeing me changes that? It's even more hopeless now . . . if that's possible."

"But it's not." Spartacus looked excited. "There are two of us. I was all alone before, but having someone on my side—now there's hope. One thing I've learned from you, Erec, is that anything is possible."

"I wish I felt that way." Even though Erec felt terrible, he was glad to have found a connection to his past life. Kilroy was right, it seemed to give him some kind of hope. But he didn't want to fool himself. There was no way out of this place.

Erec and Spartacus spent most of their time watching Spirit Warriors train and eventually leave the Hinternom. Talking about the past was too painful. But even if they had nothing to share, Erec had to admit that it was nice to have a friend.

The longer they watched the others leave, the more tempting it became to do the same thing so that they could get out. Staying in the Hinternom was not just boring, it was excruciating. Every ounce of Erec wanted to continue with his mission to regain his soul. Spartacus, too, was drawn to leave and find his final resting place.

"Do you think we could fake it?" Spartacus asked. "I mean, we could do the training, learn how to use the weapons and the magic. There has to be a way to avoid swallowing that pill. If we get out of here without it, we'd be free."

It sounded good, but how could they do it? "We have to watch exactly how the Spirit Warriors leave here, and what happens when they take the pills. Maybe we can figure out a way!" All of a sudden, it felt like the weight of the world was lifted off of Erec. Yes, he had ruined everything, even given Baskania ultimate power. But if he was released, maybe he could find a way to undo his mistake. What if he could get the scepter back somehow, and then get rid of it for good before it made him go power-mad? Then he could take the Twrch Trwyth and his eyes back, get his soul, and finish the quests. . . .

It sounded insane, and inside Erec was sure that it could never happen. Baskania was far too powerful now, and he would have the scepter with him all the time. But even if he could just escape and get his soul back . . . even if he could just say good-bye to his family . . . it would be all worthwhile.

It happened so suddenly that Erec had no time to prepare or brace himself. Instant, unbidden rage filled him to the point of explosion. He and Spartacus had been watching a training session, and for no reason at all anger hit him so intensely that he dove at one of the ghosts holding a machine gun, grabbed it, and shot round after round through the spirit's body. Then he broke the gun over his knee, at the same time amazed that even a ghost would have the strength to do such a thing.

Of course the bullets did not harm the spirit, but he stared at Erec in shock. The general who was instructing the group looked Erec up and down appraisingly.

Erec waited to be yelled at for interrupting a session, terrified that now he might be not allowed to train. But the general seemed oddly pleased. "What do we have here? Someone who is ready to get out and fight, I see. You'll be a good warrior, I can tell. What is your name, spirit?"

Erec knew better than to alert anyone who he really was. A fake name was on the tip of his tongue—the one he had used in Alypium before. "It's Rick Ross, sir. Sorry to interrupt."

"Oh, and he's obedient, too. Perfect. Rick, when are you going to start training?"

"Anytime, sir. My friend and I are ready to go." He waved toward Spartacus, who saluted.

"Very good. I'll see you both here for the next session, then."

Erec and Spartacus drifted away. Erec was in shock. What had happened back there? Obviously this was the first step on his way to becoming an evil specter. Soon it would be out of his control completely. He had to get out of here and finish his mission before it was too late. Once he became a specter, he would serve Baskania and stay evil forever.

Spartacus looked worried, but he wisely held his tongue and changed the subject. "I'm ready to do this. And I have an idea about avoiding the pill. Take a look." He led Erec to the bottom of the Hinternom where Spirit Warriors were leaving. They waited in line, then took turns going up to the general in charge. The general would check them off of a list, and then give each one a pill. Once it was swallowed, the general draped a red sash over the spirit's shoulder. The spirit would then get in a second line and wait to be discharged through the heavily guarded exit.

"What happens if a spirit sneaks through the guards and darts out of the exit?" Erec asked. "I doubt that they could stop me if I really tried."

"Don't do it. I've seen it happen again and again. One of us breaks through, and surprise—nobody stops him. But instead of escaping through the tunnel, they scream and melt away into nothing. They say it's the red sashes that let us get through unharmed."

They watched a while longer. Spartacus said, "The pills enter spirits and stick in them, making them follow commands forever. I was thinking—there are pipes that go into the generals' quarters. All of the supplies come out of those pipes, like the guns and the pills. I've watched them a long time to see if the sashes come out of there too, in case I might be able to steal one. But I can't find them any-where. But I think the pipes themselves could help us, though. We could take bits and push them into our throats and out our backs. If we drop the pill straight into the pipe, it would slide through and out without even touching us. I don't know if it would work, but it's the best I can come up with."

"That's fantastic!" Erec was amazed. "That sounds like a great idea! We'd have to make sure the pill went right into the pipe and didn't touch our mouth. What a great idea, Spartacus. Let's try it."

Neither of them could wait one more second. They flew straight to the generals' quarters, and Spartacus showed Erec where pipes of different sizes emptied into the Supply Building. "Here they are. I'm not sure how hard the pipe will be to rip off."

Erec remembered how easily he had just torn a machine gun in two. "Let me try it." In a moment he had broken off two segments of pipe, each about five inches wide and a foot long. He handed one to Spartacus. Even though he knew that solid objects could not hurt him, the idea of sticking that huge thing through his neck and back seemed awful.

But Spartacus had already done it. "Look, it's easy!" His voice was not affected by the huge piece of metal wedged behind his mouth. "Just push it through, and move it where you want it. I can hold this thing still inside of me—it feels the same as if I was holding it with my hand."

Erec positioned the pipe so that the end just barely stuck out of his back, under his shirt. "Wow! It's not hard to make it stay there at all. Let's see, here . . ." He dropped the thing with his body, and it clattered to the ground. "Interesting." Erec put the pipe back through his face and hid it under his skin. "Looks like there is still gravity here. It's hard to tell, since we're always floating."

"Same as on Earth." Spartacus nodded.

"It just seems different here. I guess it's because there is nothing but a platform where the Spirit Warriors train, and everyone else is floating."

Spartacus fished a bullet out of his pocket and opened his mouth. He dropped it straight into the pipe and then smiled. A moment later, he lifted the back of his shirt up, and the bullet dropped out onto the clear force-field floor of the Hinternom. "Looks to me like it works!"

Erec felt optimistic for the first time in what seemed like forever. He was going to get out of here—and very likely without becoming a lifelong prisoner of his worst enemy. They kept the pipes inside of them so they'd be prepared at any time, then found the general who had talked to Erec. Before long he finished with the group of trainees. More spirits rushed forward than could be in the next group, and the general turned them away.

Erec caught the general's eye. He stood perfectly straight and saluted. "My friend and I reporting for duty, sir. As you asked, sir."

The general saluted back, a glint in his eye. "At ease, soldier. What a pleasure to see this attitude in a recruit. I remember you . . . Rick, right?"

"Yes, sir. Rick Ross, sir."

"Pleasure to have you, Rick Ross. I'm General Guff." He pointed at two spirits in the training group. "You two—out of here. You'll take the course later." He nodded to Erec. "Hop on in, you two. Let's see what we can do with you here."

The trainees stood in a line. General Guff handed each an immense crossbow and explained how to use it. Each ghost shot at tiny specks on a wall—Erec's pierced right through his mark. After going through several weapons, Erec realized that the training was easier for some than others. He only had to be shown things once or twice before getting them near perfect. General Guff kept an eye on him and seemed pleased with how well he was performing. After trying out various weapons, they listened to strategy sessions where the general taught them how to handle various situations. Since spirits had no need for food or sleep, there were no breaks.

"Tell me," General Guff thundered. "You're alone in a desert town. You have been commanded to kidnap a man wanted by the Shadow Prince. Thirty spirits descend on you—they are here on earth to do nothing but protect this man. And let's throw in a few specters, too. They're all coming after you, and they know how to grab you and stop you. What do you do?"

The general paced a while, disturbed that nobody had an answer. "Here is a clue. As a ghost, you can hold anything that is around you. If a large crowd of humans are in your way, grab the air and spin, like this." At once the general was spinning in place so fast that his features were no longer visible. The air around him whirled fast, turning into a visible cyclone. Erec could feel the wind rushing through his body—strong enough to devastate a village.

At once General Guff stopped and the tornado disappeared. "A perfect strategy for clearing out human crowds. But how would you get rid of spirits that are in your way? Any ideas?"

Nothing that Erec could think of would work. Objects would pass right through them, unless they wanted to hold on to something. The only things that Erec had seen destroy spirits were the tunnel that led out of here, and the three Furies—neither of which would be at his disposal.

The general paced some more, and then stopped. "This is important for you to know. It's a technique devised by our leader himself, the Shadow Prince. There is something else that can be held on to that can tie spirits up into knots. No ideas at all?"

Everyone shook their heads.

"The Substance. Ever hear of it?" General Guff looked disgusted, as if each one of them was pathetic. "It's all around us. Doesn't matter if you can't see it—just feel for it and you know that it's there. You can hold onto the Substance all around you and spin, just like you do when you create a whirlwind. The Substance network will bind up the spirits, and it will be a long time before they can get loose. Watch this." He proceeded to spin again, fast.

This time Erec was blown back into the mass of other spirits. In moments he could not move at all. It was as if a giant net was binding them all tightly together. The general moved his fingers in the air a few times and soon they all fell apart again.

"And that's the next thing I need to teach you. How to get out of a Substance net. You need to know finger magic. Who here can do that?"

Erec and one other spirit raised their hands. Erec had not even thought about finger magic since he had died. Was he able to use it as a spirit, then? That was good to know. . . .

THE SECRET OF ASHONA

The general sighed. "The rest of you will be worthless if this happens to you. I'd suggest that you stay far away if you see a ghost start to spin. Probably would be too late, though. But you two—Rick Ross and Velma Patterson? Step forward."

Erec stepped forward alongside a young woman spirit.

"It's just like all other finger magic," General Guff said. "Except that you have to make a snipping motion with your hand. Picture the Substance that is holding you, and imagine that you are cutting it. At the same time, you have to *ask* the Substance to open up for you. Time to try it now. Step back, everyone else." He motioned for the rest of the spirits to move away from Erec and Velma. Then he spun again, just long enough to tie those two up together. "Okay, now see what you can do."

The Substance was so tight around Erec that it was hard to even move his fingers. He concentrated, feeling the bands around him, and imagining how they looked. *Cut*, he thought. He pictured the strands being chopped apart by his scissorlike fingers. As he moved them, he focused his thoughts on the Substance. *Would you open for me, Substance? Will you let me out, please?*

His movements allowed the magic inside of him to gather together and course out through his fingers. Power surged through him, reminding him slightly of how his scepter had felt. As he cut the space around him with his fingers, he could feel his body free up. In moments he was able to move again.

Velma had a harder time, but she soon freed herself through the hole that Erec had made. The general did not seem too concerned. "Good enough. You'll have to deal with this on your own if it happens to you."

General Guff taught the group how to survey a large area and find a small object using a kind of ghost radar, but Erec already knew that he could do that. They talked about a few other situations, until one in particular made Erec perk up.

"Any ideas about how to deal with specters that get in your way?" The general gazed around, a snarl on his face.

Everyone shook their heads. At least nobody here knew that Erec was headed toward becoming a specter. The general might not let him train, then.

"It's simple, actually. Of course you could spin a Substance Web and trap them—but not too many of you would be able to do that. Specters aren't the brightest candles in the bunch. They go into destruction mode—which can be great if positioned in a strategic place at the right time. But all of them want one thing desperately: their soul back. All you have to do is tell them that you know where their soul is, and they'll stop whatever it is that they're doing. Make up some place far away, and assure them that they can get it back when they go there. They'll be off in a flash." He laughed. "Dumb things won't even remember you the next time they see you, so no worries about revenge."

This stunned Erec. Not only was he doomed to become evil, but he was going to lose his mind, too? Great.

The general mused to himself. "Souls. Interesting things, those. Ever seen one by itself, separated from its spirit?"

None of the group had.

"Slimy." General Guff looked revolted. "They attach on to anything that they find—objects, each other, spirits. If you already have a soul, and a loose one gloms onto you it can feel nasty. Just keep flicking at it until it goes away."

That sounded awful. Erec wanted his own soul back so much, but it seemed to sink in more when the general talked about it. After all of this time, Erec could actually start to feel a part of himself missing. No wonder he was turning evil. . . .

Something sparked inside of him—maybe it was the sad thoughts he was having. In a moment, though, he was furious—then

THE SECRET OF ASHONA

raging. The only thing that he could think of that would damage the others was to spin, hard. He grabbed the Substance tightly in his being and twisted. Then he whirled faster than the general had. With each turn, Erec cried out in fury. Why was he here? Why was all of this happening to him?

He kept spinning and spinning until his rage finally evaporated. The entire group of soldiers in training, along with the general and every spirit in sight, were lumped in a huge pile in front of him. Erec wondered if he had managed to tie up the entire Hinternom. If the tunnel that led out of here would not have disintegrated him, he would have made a run for it right now.

It was horrifying, however, to realize that he had gone completely out of control again. It was happening. He was becoming a specter. Would General Guff know? What if he kicked Erec out of the group? Erec had to calm down and finish this training before he lost it again—if it wasn't too late.

He concentrated on cutting with his fingers, summoning all his power into his hand. *Substance, it's me again. I'm so sorry. I didn't mean to do this. Please open for me—help me let these people go.*

There was other slicing of the Substance in a few more places, where several generals were tangled. Before long everyone was free again, drifting off to where they had been before. General Guff called Erec over. "You!"

Erec was terrified. If he had ruined his chances of escape, he would be miserable forever.

"That's right. You!" General Guff slapped Erec on the back— something only another spirit could do to him. "Show-off. You like to stand out in a crowd, don't you?" He was grinning ear to ear. "We both know that not a lot of spirits could pull that off. Not bad at all. So, are you angling for one of the master weapons, then?"

Erec nodded, as if he knew what the general was talking about.

"We'll see about that." He slapped Erec on the back again. "Seems like you just might be able to handle one."

The training session ended with each spirit receiving a weapon and practicing with it. Most of them sported rifles, and as many were terrible aims as good shots. One particularly uncoordinated spirit was given a slingshot. General Guff led a small group, including Erec and Spartacus, into a floating enclosure that looked like it was made out of cloud. He gestured toward a few rows of weapons resting in the rippled white substance.

"Here you have your special weapons. Your Speed Shooter, your Jolly Gun, your Rapid Transitator, your Stun Breeze. Take your pick." He winked at Erec. "I have something special for you, kid. I think you've earned this." General Guff pulled a long stick with a red ball on the end of it from the back and handed it to Erec. "A master weapon for you. It's called a Calamitizer. Enjoy this one."

The master weapon looked like a toy drumstick. "What does this do?"

"Just what the name says." The general winked. "Causes calamities. If you don't mind, just practice with it once—and not inside here. I'd like to see what you can do with that thing."

Spartacus picked a Rapid Transitator—a weapon that moved both humans and spirits from one place to another in a second, as long as both places were within sight. He practiced shooting it, making spirits disappear and reappear where he wanted. It was fun to watch the faces of those who all of a sudden were someplace different from where they had just been.

After a while, Erec decided to try his Calamitizer. He took a breath and waved it. . . .

Power rocketed through his arm and out of the stick. In moments, the spirits around him tumbled through the air, spinning wildly. Substance was flung around, creating nets and capturing everyone in

THE SECRET OF ASHONA

its wake, and weapons fired on their own accord. Gravity shifted this way and that, and objects tumbled up sideways in the air. Thunder cracked and lightning shot through the Hinternom. Cyclones spiraled out in all directions—if this had happened in a city Erec wondered if any of it would be left standing.

Finally, the devastation settled down. Other than destroying a few Substance nets, there was not much damage that could be done in the Hinternom. But waving this on Earth would be another story. . . .

General Guff slowly clapped his hands. "Bravo! What a great demonstration of the equipment. I can see that we have a top-notch fighter on our hands here."

Great, Erec thought. *A Calamitizer to destroy everything around me . . . I'll have to get rid of it before I change much more. It's just what I'll need when I'm an uncontrollable evil specter.*

CHAPTER ELEVEN

The Storage Facility

I T WAS HARDER THAN EVER for Erec to relax as he stood in line with Spartacus. He was so close now. If only he could get out of here safely!

General Guff stood at the front of the group, and handed out red sashes and pills to each Spirit Warrior, one at a time. Erec was able to keep his Calamitizer in a pocket—Spartacus's Rapid Transitator was slung around his shoulder.

"Next!" It was Erec's turn. He smiled bravely at General Guff, hoping that no surges of anger would come out and ruin anything before he left.

"My star pupil." The general smiled. "It's my pleasure to give this to you." He draped a red sash around Erec's arm and neck. "This will keep you safe when you go through the tunnel. And here is your pill, to make sure that you stay obedient."

Erec nodded and took the small black pill from the general. *Here goes nothing!* He opened his mouth wide and reached far enough back to feel metal around his fingers. With a small clink, the pill dropped into the pipe and shot straight out of his back into Erec's tucked-in shirt.

He had done it! Erec turned and winked at Spartacus with a grin. Spartacus lit up with a smile right back at him. They were about to be free!

Moments later, they were in the next line ready to leave the Hinternom. Everything was perfect. The Spirit Warrior in front of Erec shouldered her rifle and approached the tunnel. A guard said something to her, and then she jumped into the opening. In a moment, she was swallowed up and shot through to freedom.

Erec's turn. A large, hairy spirit guard nodded to him. "You got your sash. Check. Your name?"

"Rick Ross."

"Check. And open your mouth."

Erec was not sure if he should make a dash for the tunnel, but he decided not to make anyone suspicious. He opened his mouth, ready to run . . .

The guard laughed. "Looks like the pill didn't take. No problem. It happens sometimes. Here—"

Before Erec knew what was happening, the guard shoved another black pill through Erec's skin in his neck. "That'll work for ya. Now yer off!" The guard shoved him into the tunnel before he could turn around and warn Spartacus.

It was the guard's shove, not gravity, that sent Erec plummeting through the dark tunnel back to Earth. He was released about fifty feet in the air, and continued shooting toward the ground until he hit, painlessly. He lay there a moment, eyes closed. It didn't matter where he was now. After that pill he would be a prisoner of Baskania's forever.

Spartacus dropped from the sky and landed on top of Erec . . . actually taking up the same space that Erec was in. It was an awkward feeling, so both of them moved out of the other's way. The other spirits that had landed had already vanished, happy to be free.

"Did you get away without a pill?" Erec asked.

Spartacus shook his head, in shock. "I'm sorry. My plan was a flop. Now we're both doomed."

"It wasn't your fault." They slid away together aimlessly, taking in their new reality. "I wonder how we'll get called to his service."

"Who knows."

It wasn't long before both of them began to feel their own callings as well. "This stinks." Erec looked around as if an extra soul would appear to him out of the blue. "How am I going to get my soul back before I turn into a specter? I don't even know where to start."

"I'm just as clueless. All I want is to go where I'm supposed to be now—wherever that is. But that pill is holding me here. I can feel it."

"What would we do if we were alive?" Erec wondered. "I don't have my dragon eyes anymore. That would be the best thing right now. I'd see what the future holds, and then try different ways to change it until I found out what worked." *What else might help?* "I know! We can go talk to the three Fates. . . ." But that wouldn't work either. The only way that he had been able to talk to them was by using his dragon eyes first. They would only come out for people who could read the future.

Spartacus laughed. "Sounds like those eyes really did you

well—when you had them. Too bad you can't get some more of those things."

"Yeah. I don't think there are a lot of dragons ready to hand over their own eyes. Aoquesth was special. . . ." Erec wished that he could see him again. It made him think . . . where was Aoquesth now? Probably in some special place that dragons go when they die. If only he could see him again. Was there a way, maybe, now that Erec was dead as well?

The only way that Erec knew how to contact dragons was with a dragon call—and that also involved using his dragon eyes. He couldn't do anything now. "I just wish I could talk to him. Do you know of any way?"

Spartacus shook his head. "The same way you called dragons when you were alive?"

"I can't now." For having so much ghostly power and a master weapon in his pocket, Erec felt completely powerless.

"Just try. It can't hurt." Spartacus shrugged.

"I don't even know how to try." He sighed. "Stop looking at me like that. All right—I'll wing it. But don't hold your breath." Erec sat on the grass and looked up at the sky. There were no dragon eyes to bring out, so he just stared with his own. . . . "Oh, wait a minute." He slapped his forehead. "I don't even have any eyes in my sockets anymore. This will never work."

"You can still see, can't you?" Spartacus asked gently.

"I guess. Not that that matters." Erec gazed upward and thought about Aoquesth. *Aoquesth . . . can you hear me calling you? It's your old friend, Erec Rex. I need your help, badly. I'm not alive anymore either. Can you come here and see me? Aoquesth? Please . . . ?*

Erec fell back into the grass. "That was hopeless." He laughed. "But as long as you're happy now that's good."

"You'll feel better, knowing that you tried."

"Sure. Whatever you say." Erec thought about going home to talk to his family before continuing his search—they must be worried sick by now. He also wanted to see what had happened now that Baskania had all that power . . . and how much time had passed. . . .

A dark speck grew in the sky, widening like a black hole whizzing toward them from space. It came at them so fast it was breathtaking. And it wasn't until it was close that Erec could make out features. . . .

Dragon features. It was Aoquesth.

Erec could not believe it. He recognized the dragon immediately, with his dark reddish-purple scales and sharp black spines down his back and tail. If possible, Aoquesth was more beautiful now than he had been alive. He arched his back and reared his head up into the sky, stretching his wings to what seemed like an impossible thirty-foot span. Then he gazed at Erec.

A connection sizzled between them, even stronger than in life. Both looked into the spaces where the other's eyes had been, the eyes they had once shared. Aoquesth had given Erec so much of himself. And Erec realized that Aoquesth had never really left him. Erec had been carrying a part of him around—even a part that wasn't recently stolen by Baskania.

"I'm so sorry. . . ." Erec felt horrible losing both of Aoquesth's eyes—it was such an important gift. He must have let Aoquesth down.

"Erec." The dragon shook his head. "There is nothing you could have done. I'm just glad that you are okay. I've been thinking about you, you know."

Erec laughed bitterly. "I'm not actually okay. I died, and I'm just a ghost now. It's all really awful, and it's mostly my own fault."

"I already know that you are a spirit, Erec. That is not what I meant about being okay. You're still you, and that's what is important."

He tossed his head into the air. "Believe me, there is a lot more to 'life' after life itself is over. It has been wonderful being reunited with my dear Nylyra again."

That only made Erec feel worse. "I'm still not okay, though. The Furies have my soul, and I'm going to turn into a specter before long. I can already tell that it's starting to happen."

Aoquesth sighed, but Erec noticed steam did not come out of his nose like it had when he was alive. "I know this too, Erec. I know a little more than you might, as a human spirit, you know. Even without my eyes."

Erec felt another stab of guilt. Then he could not resist anymore, and threw both arms around the dragon's neck. Apart from the fact that neither was breathing, it felt the same as when the two had been alive. Aoquesth wrapped his neck around Erec's back in a kind of a hug. They stayed like that for a long while. Erec wished that he could bury himself somewhere where nobody would ever find him again . . . where all of his problems would disappear. He was locked into a future of torture and there was nothing he could do about it. He was so glad that he had called Aoquesth, just so he could see him again. But how would the dragon spirit possibly be able to help him now?

Aoquesth pulled back and looked at him. "I'm glad that you called me too. And maybe I can help. I really don't know yet. Neither of us is able to look into the future anymore, of course."

Of course. Because of Erec's bad decisions, they had both lost the eyes that let them do that. "Do you really think you might be able to help me?" Erec tentatively began to cling on to that idea. The longer he went without his soul, the more uncomfortable he felt. It was starting to eat away at him, almost like a pain inside. He wanted it back so much, to feel whole again. And if anyone in the world could help him, Aoquesth seemed the most likely. "What should I do?"

The dragon sighed again, deeply. "I wish I knew, Erec. But my dragon sense tells me that you need to follow the path to which the Fates have you assigned. It might seem that you have failed. And maybe you have. Maybe you deviated far enough away from what they wanted that there is no going back again. But you never know. This may all be a part of their master plan."

That made Erec think. Had he followed the advice of the Fates? Oddly, as much as he faulted himself for everything that had happened, it seemed that he really did do what he was told. Instead of listening to his mother and Bethany, he did what his seventh quest instructed him to do—sacrifice his life for the five people who would have died in Argos with the Diamond Minds. Dying wasn't the wrong choice, then. His sixth quest had led the Furies to take his soul away. So the Fates had put him in this position too—a spirit without a soul. So, he was supposed to be like this?

He thought further, remembering what else had led him here. After he died he had to visit the Furies to get the Master Shem to free Trevor, which he did. He also had to try to get his soul back. It was the only thing that was keeping him going as a ghost. And how did he decide what to do? The best adviser he could think of was Homer, the golden ghost in the catacombs under King Piter's house. Homer had told him to look in "other regions" and "places beyond," where his worst enemy kept spirits. Where else could that have been other than the Hinternom?

Erec had thought that he had completely messed up by walking in to talk to Baskania. And maybe he had. He had figured that he would have to try to break through the Hinternom from the outside and free the captive spirits there, and one of them might give Erec his soul. But maybe that wasn't the way it was supposed to have worked at all. Maybe he was supposed to have done exactly this.

But this didn't seem right either, because things were hopeless now. He must have messed up somewhere along the way. . . .

"I don't know either, Erec," Aoquesth said. "I wish that I did. I am able to travel most places, even into Alsatia, but I cannot enter the cave of the Furies. They would demolish me just as they would anyone else—except for you. But I am here for you, any time that you need me. You know how to call me now, as a spirit. But if you ever do regain your human form I will give you another way to reach me."

Aoquesth broke the tip of a small spine off of his tail. Holding it in his claws, he pushed it through Erec's chest, straight into his heart. "That will stay inside of you forever, whether you are living or not. And even if you are alive again someday, all you will ever have to do to call me now is to say my name."

"Thank you, Aoquesth." It felt so good to know that his old friend was back, in any form.

"There is one thing I would be able to do for you, if you should need it in the future."

Erec immediately knew what Aoquesth was going to say, and as much as he was glad to hear it, it gave him the chills. He needed to hear it said, though. "What is that?"

"If things don't work out, Erec, if you realize that you are going to become a specter forever and have no way out, you can call me. I can end things for you, if you need me to. I know how to obliterate you."

That is exactly what Erec thought he would say. It sounded awful, but at the same time made him feel relieved. "Thanks, Aoquesth. That's really good to know."

The dragon nodded. "It was nice to see you. I think you should continue on your mission. It will lead you somewhere where you may find there are few choices." He looked at Spartacus. "I can see that both of you are going to have a hand in what will happen. And I think you should both be proud of yourselves."

Proud? Erec wished that he felt that way. "It's hard to be proud when I've destroyed the world by giving everything to Baskania."

"But have you? Everything? You haven't given him yourself. Think about what you have done, though. Five people are alive right now because of you. You were selfless, Erec."

Erec smiled. Aoquesth was actually giving him a reason to feel better and stop beating himself up. The dragon's comments about the Fates sending him on this path also helped. "Thanks, Aoquesth. You've helped me already. I hope I see you again soon."

"I'm sure you will." The dragon stretched his wings and leaned back. "Good-bye, Erec." He pushed off lightly and soared into the air, disappearing into a cloud.

One thing that Erec was thankful for was that being a ghost kept him from crying—because he was sure he would have tears streaming down his face by now. He smiled at Spartacus. "You met Aoquesth before, didn't you?"

Spartacus laughed. "Just for a second. That dragon threw a blade at me, and it pinned my old blue cape to the wall of his cave. I kinda ran out of there. Never saw this side of him, though. What a great creature."

"Yes, he is. And a good friend." Erec's thoughts went back to his future, whatever that entailed. "I actually feel better now, even though I don't know why. We have no more idea what we need to do to get out of this mess."

"Oh, yes we do," Spartacus said. "We know exactly what to do now. Aoquesth very nicely reminded me of that."

"What?" Erec was confused, and tried not to get too hopeful that Spartacus had an answer.

"We're going back to see the Furies. I'm going to give them my soul for you."

❊ ❊ ❊

They must have stood there facing each other for an eternity. Erec was unable to respond. *No!* he wanted to shout. *I will not take your soul from you. I will not allow you to turn yourself into a specter for eternity for my sake. I cannot ask for that, or even let it happen. You deserve better!*

But another part of him wanted that so badly he could not stand it. To have his soul back! His living body, too! To run at Bethany and tackle her in that huge hug he couldn't give her before. To play on the grass with his dog, Wolfboy, and feel his wet tongue lick his face. To eat! Erec remembered with envy how wonderful it felt to bite into a thick, juicy hamburger. What joy! So a small voice in Erec argued, *Why not? Why shouldn't it be Spartacus dealing with all of this, not me?*

But reason won out. "Thanks . . . Spartacus. That is more than kind of you to offer. I really . . . really wish that I could say yes. But I can't do that to you. I couldn't do it to anyone, now that I think about it. Especially you."

Spartacus smiled. "Too bad it's not your choice, then. I'm going to go visit the Furies with or without you. If you want to go spend time with your family now, then go ahead. When you're done, the Furies will already have their extra soul, and you can get yours back from them at any time."

"No!" Erec fought his excitement. "I can't let you do this! It's crazy. You matter just as much as I do. And how could I live—how could I enjoy a day of my life—knowing that you were out here suffering? Thank you so much, but no."

"Remember? I said that you had no choice. That's how you can live with yourself." Spartacus dusted himself off, looking satisfied. "Anyway, I have a plan. Give me a little credit here. I'm actually looking forward to this."

"A plan? What are you talking about?"

"Here's the deal. If things stay as they are right now, we both will stay dead. I'll go on forever stuck as a Spirit Warrior for Baskania—a fate worse than death for me. And you'll become a specter, with the best option being that Aoquesth obliterates you. Right?"

Erec paused. Spartacus was starting to make sense. "Yeah."

If I give my soul to the Furies you get everything back—your life, *your* soul. You will be in perfect shape. I'll never be alive again anyway. There is no chance of that."

"But your soul . . ."

"That's the point. I don't need to worry about that anymore. Because after I give up my soul, I'm going to ask the Furies to obliterate me. And if for some reason they object, we can ask Aoquesth to do for me what he offered to you. I'll be free. My life as a Spirit Warrior will be over before it's even begun."

Erec was amazed at the logic of what Spartacus said. As things were, one of them would become a specter—and soon be gone altogether—and the other one would become a Spirit Warrior. If they did as Spartacus said, one of them would be gone altogether, and the other one would be fully human again. He was right. It was the only thing that made sense.

At the same time, it seemed so selfish to think that way. Maybe everything sounded so perfect because he just wanted it so much.

"So, what's it going to be, friend?" Spartacus asked. "Are you going to the Furies with me, or am I going to do this by myself?"

"You're really going? I mean . . . really? For sure?"

"I'm really going." Spartacus grinned and slapped Erec on the back. "I'm doing myself a favor too. It's such a relief to know that I won't be doing horrible things for Baskania forever. I'm glad we haven't been called into service yet or this might have been much harder to pull off. So I better get this done before it's too late. You coming?"

The words were slowly sinking in. Joy was beginning to seep through every pore, every ounce of his body. He shook his head in

disbelief. "I have to go with you. The Furies would destroy you immediately if you got too close to them unless I was there. And then your soul would be gone along with your spirit."

"That answers that, then. Let's go!"

In a haze, Erec glided with his friend in a direction that led them up a few hills and then to a river, which they bounded across with ease. Even though they had no idea where they were, it was easy to have a sense of how to get anywhere on Earth. This was the right way to Pinefort Jungle in Otherness, which would lead them to Alsatia. There was no need for a Port-O-Door. Traveling as a ghost was lightweight and simple. No matter how far they went they never tired, and gravity would not slow them down.

Even though they were moving fast, it felt like a meandering stroll. Erec understood that this was because Spartacus was scared about what lay ahead, and he did not blame him. Being so close to his goal made Erec want to zoom to the Furies at full speed, but he controlled himself. They would get there soon enough.

Finally Spartacus said, "There's no use putting this off. If we wait too long Baskania will order us to go somewhere and it will be too late."

Relieved, Erec nodded. At once, he and Spartacus bounded high into the air. One thousand feet . . . two thousand . . . three . . . They soared higher and higher like helium balloons. Before long, instinctually, Erec pointed his feet in the direction that he knew they had to land, and Spartacus followed. They waved arms against the thin air, slowly picked up speed, and headed toward the wilds of Otherness. Soon the ground approached them, and mountains and trees grew larger. Before long they sailed straight to the floor of Pinefort Jungle.

Both of them were going so fast that they sank deep into the dirt, then pulled themselves back out onto the ground. Erec could not get used to the feeling of sharing his space with other things.

"It's this way. A big rock formation called Mercy's Spike. Pretty nasty-looking if you ask me. Humans used to impale themselves on that thing—that's why there are a bunch of spirits living in Alsatia."

When Spartacus saw the needle formation he shuddered. "They must have been awfully brave. That would hurt, if you were alive."

Erec nodded. "They wouldn't stay alive for long. Glad it's not a problem for us. Are you ready?" He pushed up, and then over onto the short plateau that overhung the spike.

Spartacus followed him up, with a grave look on his face. "Ready as ever."

Erec leaned forward and waved his arms against the air to propel himself downward. Spartacus immediately followed. Mercy's Spike flew through both of their hearts, one after the next. Eventually they stopped, midway down.

"Is this it, then?" Spartacus asked. "What happens now?"

"Just give it a minute." Before long the two of them began to spin. Soon they whirled like tops around the axis of the rock through their midsections. They accelerated faster and faster, until all around them looked like a blur of color, and then a murky, moving gray.

Erec could feel himself lifting, and he knew that he was moving somewhere. The spike in his middle grew smaller, then disappeared altogether as he sailed into the sky. As he was spinning so rapidly, his sense of direction was completely gone. Soon they began to slow down, and finally stopped, resting flat on the ground.

What Erec saw around him made him start with surprise. Gone were the fields of rippling grasses, swimming pools, and sandy beaches. Instead he was sitting upon a giant treetop. Its leafy branches spread for nearly fifty feet, and other treetops were nearby. Monkeys swung on branches, popping their heads up to get a glimpse of Erec and Spartacus, and darting back down again. A few people sunned themselves on woven pads of sticks and leaves, and one person in the distance was riding a unicycle from branch to branch.

"This place is amazing," he said, awestruck.

"It sure is. Look at that." Spartacus pointed, and Erec saw a tall man holding on to a branch with his toes, hanging upside down and eating a banana.

Erec laughed. "Good thing we can't get hurt if we fall, huh?"

"Fall?" Spartacus looked confused. "You'd be worried about falling off of a bench?"

"A bench?" Then Erec remembered. "We're seeing different things. The last time I was here, this place looked like a beautiful little town with mansions and a huge beach. Now we're on treetops, really high up."

"Seriously?" Spartacus looked amazed. "I thought this looked the same to everyone. We're in a massive library that stretches all the way to the sky. It's beautiful, with oak and teak shelves, gorgeous patterns in the wood, and beautiful books. There's endless amounts to read and look at. Wow! And over there"—he pointed again—"is a little guy looking at a book that is at least twenty feet tall! This place is amazing."

"They say if you stay here then things start to look different once you get tired of seeing it this way." Erec began to walk in the direction of the Furies' castle. He figured that this time it would not look like a sparkling, diamond palace. Spartacus rushed after him. "Are you sure that you really want to do this? It's not too late, you know."

Spartacus nodded. "I'm positive. I feel great about it."

Bounding over the leafy treetops, Erec stopped when a familiar face waved him down. He recognized Jox, but was surprised by the angry look on his face.

"What are you doing back here?" Jox put his hands on his hips. "You won't be able to stay, you know. I'll get you thrown right out."

"What's going on?" Spartacus looked confused. "Erec's a good kid."

"He might have been a good kid," Jox said. "But he's on his way to becoming a specter. And we don't want his kind ruining our nice little world."

Erec started to respond, but Spartacus held a hand up. "It's okay. I'm giving Erec my soul today, so he can get his own soul back. And I promise that I won't stick around here and bother you after that."

"Really?" Jox looked shocked. "You don't want to do that. I mean, you're going to ruin your afterlife."

"It's already ruined." Spartacus laughed. "This is my only hope. Let's go, Erec."

The two went farther, over what looked like a few taller rounded treetops, to what appeared to Erec as a gigantic bird nest with sticks covering the top like a roof.

"That's it." Erec pointed.

"Wow . . . a huge turret, spiraled with gold and gems. It's amazing."

Erec laughed. "Looks like an intricate pile of twigs to me. But that's where we're headed. I'd better go in first. Wait here, okay?"

He bounded into a hole in the side of the nest. Birds fluttered everywhere, and he followed a few of them around corners, under and over huge sticks and feathers. Around a final corner perched three immense birds: one red, one black, and one white. They preened themselves and picked at their feathers with their beaks.

"Good to see you again, Erec," the red one, Alecto, said, with a voice that sounded fluttery and light.

Erec was not fooled for a second by the delicate sound of the Fury. He knew that she could tear his being to shreds in the blink of an eye.

The black one, Tisiphone, purred, "We see that you have brought a soul to exchange for your own. Good for you. Let's bring that young man in here now."

In a blink, Spartacus stood at Erec's side. He gazed around him in wonder. "Wow. This is amazing."

Erec wondered what Spartacus was seeing. It must have been completely different from Erec's view, although Erec was sure he'd prefer his own.

"So," Megaera, the white bird, said. "Are you donating your soul to us, so that Erec Rex will be able to get his own back?"

"I am."

Erec could see Spartacus shivering, and he put a hand on his shoulder.

"Both of you may go into the soul storage facility, then," Alecto said. "I will loosen your soul now, Spartacus, so that you can give it willingly when you get inside. Only after yours is gone will Erec be able to take his own back again. Our storage facility knows what is going on inside of it. It will not allow either of you back out again until the correct number of souls are left behind."

"Lead them there, Agathea," Tisiphone said to a tiny hummingbird buzzing above her head. She winked at Erec. "Agathea is my favorite Harpy."

The bird circled in the air a few times and dove in front of Erec. It looked nothing at all like a Harpy. Then again, nothing here was as it looked. Anyway, it was just as well, as far as Erec was concerned, that Agathea looked like a bird. He had enough bad associations with Harpies. Agathea led them around a few corridors in the nest and then down a ladder made of twigs that seemed endless. They went farther and farther down, until they were at the underside of the nest.

Spartacus had a gleam in his eye. "Can you believe that spiral staircase, inlaid with gold? I've never seen anything so beautiful!"

At the bottom was a large room that looked to Erec like a vast, curved root cellar, shaped like a giant saucer. In the center was a round trapdoor that had no handles or other way to open it. Erec could not tell what the door was made out of—it looked like a shiny, glittery substance.

The little hummingbird twittered, "The storage facility is alive. The Fury sisters gave it life so that it can serve them. It knows that you have access, so all you have to do is knock to get in, and knock when you are ready to come out. But like Tisiphone said, you are going in with one soul between the two of you—you won't be able to leave with more than one. So don't think about trying anything funny. One word from the storage facility and the Furies might not be so friendly anymore."

That was a veiled threat if Erec had ever heard one. But they didn't have anything to worry about—there were no plans to steal souls. He asked Spartacus one last time, "Are you sure about this?"

"Definitely."

Erec knocked on the round door. There was a rumbling sound, and then the door lifted into the air, hovering next to them. Inside, the storage facility was deep and dark.

"Let's do this." There was no need to worry about ladders or how far down the floor was. In fact, as foreboding as the place looked, Erec was overjoyed to go inside. His soul was in there! He might become whole again. It was impossible to wait a second longer or think of anything else. Erec pushed against the air and propelled himself into the darkness of the storage facility.

CHAPTER TWELVE

Spartacus's Gift

NSIDE WAS BLACKNESS. Soft slimy things surrounded him,
touching him and fixing themselves onto him. They were
souls, Erec knew, and each of them was looking for a home.
In a sense it was a disgusting feeling, but to Erec who had
been pining for his soul more and more, it felt wonderful.
Each one wanted to be his, and they all seemed like they might be
good substitutes. *Why not have many souls?* he wondered. *Give all of
these poor guys a place to live.*

Even though Erec was in heaven, floating through a sea of

exactly what he had been missing, there was still something wrong. He had all that he wanted and more . . . but at the same time what he really craved was his *own* soul. It seemed selfish, to want something so perfect when there were so many others here needing a place to go. But he knew that his was in here somewhere. Would he be able to find it? Would he even recognize it after all this time?

Sticky, gelatinous beings glommed onto him left and right, and he pulled them off in search of the one that was his. He felt like the luckiest person on the planet—like someone that would be given everything he wanted for the rest of his life, and still decided to be picky, turning down the best of everything and getting even better.

Which reminded him—hadn't the Furies promised him that if he came back to claim his own soul, they would not only return him to life, but also give him everything he ever wanted? This was all too good to be true. The best gift in the world!

And then it happened. It found him. Erec knew it immediately, and his soul knew him as well. It just took a moment, and the thing slipped inside of him like it had never left.

The feeling was amazing. He was whole again! There were no cravings—there was no more loss. He was united completely, and soon he would have his body back as well. There would never be another day where he would not appreciate this gift that he had been given.

But then it hit him—Spartacus had given that gift up, for him. Spartacus should have been whole and well right now. It was not his fault that he had been killed by Baskania. And now he had given up his soul as well. Soon, on top of it, he would be sacrificing his spirit, too. There would be nothing left of him. Erec felt horrible thinking about it. Although he understood that it made sense, and that Spartacus could not have it any other way—he would not go on as a slave to Baskania—it was still hard to take.

Even though Erec had his own soul back again, other souls kept latching on to him, hoping to be saved. Erec felt terrible for them.

If only there was something that he could do for them. It seemed wrong to leave them here, prisoners to the Furies. . . .

He began to make his way toward the door, wondering if Spartacus had parted with his soul yet. The door would not let them out until that happened. But Spartacus was waiting at the entry, a sad look on his face. Erec knew that the deed had been done.

Erec put a hand on his back. "Thank you so much. Are you feeling okay?"

"Not as bad as I thought. I mean, I can tell that it's missing. It wasn't easy to let go of, I'll tell you that. Knowing that it would be sitting in here, missing me. The other ones are desperate by now—the whole thing is upsetting."

"I know. It doesn't seem right, just leaving them all here." He pulled off a few more of the sticky creatures and another bunch clung on to him. Now that he felt so good, inside and out, it seemed even worse that all of these souls would be caged up here for an eternity. It was as if he had taken a part in their pain. He was fine now—how was he supposed to just go on and live a happy life knowing what suffering was going on here? Never in the past had Erec just walked away from others that were in need. So how could he start now?

"Ready to go, then?" Spartacus looked sick. "I'd just as soon get this over with. Maybe I'll just come right out and ask the Furies for the favor of destroying my spirit. Or you could ask them for me. It sounds like they want to help you. Would you do that for me?"

"No! I mean . . . yes, of course. But wait, let's just think about this for a minute. . . ."

"There's nothing to think about. That's the next part of the plan, and the whole reason that I am doing this. I don't want to go on as a Spirit Warrior for Baskania. I want out."

"I know. I understand . . . but I have an idea. At least, I want to have an idea. We can't just leave these souls in here to rot, can we? Isn't there a way that we can sneak them out somehow?"

Spartacus perked up. "I hadn't really thought about that. I mean, the Furies are so powerful, how would we ever get anything past them?"

"Maybe we couldn't. But shouldn't we at least try?"

"What if they're reading our thoughts right now? That would be the end of you. All this for nothing."

"That's one thing on our side here in Alsatia. This place is like a shield. It blocks others from reading your mind. I mean, they still could do it if they tried. They showed me that. But they generally don't bother. The Furies are used to everyone's thoughts being laid out for them. They don't care enough about humans to really probe unless they have a reason."

"I hope you're right. But how could we even try to get souls out of here? This storage facility room is alive, and knows the numbers inside of it. We'd have to trick it as well."

"I know. I wonder how smart the room is, though. I mean, maybe there is a way to put in something that the room thinks is a soul, and then take one out."

"Good luck with that. We'd have to figure out a way to break into this thing too."

"I don't know," Erec said, "We've been given passes into this place. The room knows that we're allowed in and out."

"Can you imagine rounding all of these guys up, though? They're all over the place, swarming around. It would take forever to fish around in here and make sure there were none left. Plus, they're greasy and sticky—it would be a mess."

Erec thought a moment. There had to be a way to get them all out quickly. If only he could catch them in something . . .

"I've got it! At least, I think this might work. Stay here, far away from me, and hold on to this as tight as you can." Erec tapped the wall. Spartacus pushed his fingers through the metal-like substance and gripped it hard.

Erec floated into the middle of the room, pulling souls off of himself left and right. But the moment that he took one off another glommed right onto him. He had to make them all stay away if this was to work. . . .

"Stop it!" Erec jerked a few souls away from him and put his hand out. He hoped that they understood him. "Stay away from me. I'm trying to help you, but you have to give me room."

Most of the souls moved back, but a few more could not help themselves and rushed up to grab him.

"All of you! I mean it." He plucked them off and kicked in the air toward another that approached. "Stay away! I'm trying to help you. Give me space!"

A few souls approached, trembling, but then backed off again. Erec finally had room to work. He closed his eyes and concentrated. The Substance. He could feel it in here just like he had in the Hinternom. With every ounce of his being, he grabbed every strand of it that he could hold, with every cell of his body. *Got it*. Now it was time to spin.

The whirling that Erec had done on his way into Alsatia, and the spinning that he had done when he was possessed as a specter, was nothing compared to what he did now. He twirled so fast, gripping the Substance so hard, that he felt shock ripples wave around him. Then he slowed and stopped, hoping that the disturbance was not enough to attract the attention of the Furies.

It worked. The souls in the room were all bunched together now, tight, in a Substance Web. He floated around the edges of the room, checking to see if any wayward souls were loose, but there were none. He had done it!

The souls whimpered and moaned. "I'm sorry, little guys. I did this to try and help you escape. Can you wait awhile like this, do you think?"

There was no answer, and he was not sure how much they

understood. But at least they would be easier to rescue—that is if Erec could figure out a way to get them out of this room.

Spartacus's hands were still dug into the wall, but his body seemed to stretch impossibly across the room with his legs and feet tangled in Erec's Substance Web. "Um, can you help me, here?"

"Oops! Sorry! Let me fix that."

Erec remembered how he had been taught by General Guff to cut the Substance Web. He made a cutting motion with his fingers, concentrating on the magic that was inside of him and sending it into his hand. Then he thought about the Substance that he had just tangled so completely. *Focus on it. Talk to it.*

Substance, I need your help. I'm trying to rescue these souls, but my friend Spartacus got stuck in your web. Would you open for me and let him go?

He made a cutting motion with his fingers, and could actually feel some of the knots in the Substance melting away when he sliced. In a minute, Spartacus was free. He snapped back into his normal shape.

"Thanks." He looked down at himself. "I didn't know I could stretch like that. But I didn't let go." He laughed. "That's pretty impressive. Now they're all stuck in a bunch. Perfect!"

"If only there was a way to get them out of here."

"But there is." Kilroy had a gleam in his eye. "Thanks to you, now that these things are all in a bunch." He patted the weapon that was hanging around his neck—the Rapid Transitator.

Erec's jaw dropped. "You mean . . . do you think that would work?"

Kilroy shrugged. "Only one way to find out."

"Wait—let's think this through. Your Rapid Transitator can move things from any one spot to another, as long as they're both in sight, right?"

"Yeah. So once the storage facility door is open I can use it and—boom! That bunch of souls will be out of here."

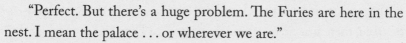

"Perfect. But there's a huge problem. The Furies are here in the nest. I mean the palace . . . or wherever we are."

"The library."

"Okay, whatever. But this storage facility is going to alert them right away. All of the souls are going to be bound up together inside of here. You can't send them anywhere that you can't see. So it would be easy for the Furies to put them back in again, and destroy the two of us. We have to figure out a way to trick the room, so the Furies don't know what's happening until it's too late."

Spartacus nodded. "That makes sense. But how do we do that?"

"I have no idea." Erec thought about what to do. If he only had his dragon eyes again he could consult the Fates at the Oracle. . . . But he was going to have his dragon eyes back again, as soon as the Furies put him back in his body.

Erec thought about that a moment, confused. The Furies had said that they would restore him as he was. Did that mean that they would give him back the eyes that Baskania had stolen? There was nothing he could do but ask them. It seemed like it would be a small task for the Furies to do that.

"I don't think there is anything that we can do right now," Erec said. "We need to be careful and plan this right—we're only going to get one shot."

"Is there someone that could help us? Maybe Aoquesth?"

"That's not a bad idea. I want to ask the Fates what to do, but I need my body back first. We'll have to come back here when it's time."

"There's only one problem." Spartacus frowned. "If you come back to Alsatia, you won't survive Mercy's Spike again. I'm going to have to do it on my own."

Erec had not thought about that. Once he was alive, getting here would be a whole different story. "I don't know . . . you might not be able to free these souls by yourself. I'll have to find another way. Or . . .

if I have to come back then I will, I guess...." All of those souls had to be freed, there was no question about it. And Erec had the feeling that it was a part of his quest, and he had to do it. But how could he risk death again? Was that really what he was supposed to do? The thought made him shudder....

Spartacus smiled. "You're a good man, Erec Rex. Brave, too."

"Not so much, really. We'll just do what we have to do. I'm sure you feel the same."

"I think so." Spartacus smiled. "Let's get out of here. I'll stick around you for as long as I can. Hope I don't get called into service by Baskania soon."

They left the souls tied up, and knocked on the sparkly door. It levitated into the air, and Erec and Spartacus passed through. The two of them did not need directions to know the way back to the Furies.

"Clear your mind," Erec said. "Don't think about the souls at all. I don't want the Furies to catch onto our ideas."

"I'll just pay attention to the details in the library. It's so beautiful, that's more than enough to fill my mind."

Even though the birds' nest that Erec was seeing was not what he would call beautiful, it was really cool. The passageways were built out of sticks and straw, making the whole thing look like a massive play hut. Up the long flight of stairs made of sticks, then around a few corners, and they were back with the Furies again.

Erec thought about his surroundings, like Spartacus was planning to. The branches were woven so tightly in the walls. And there were curtains made of spun leaves....

Alecto preened her scarlet feathers. "I see you have your soul back, Erec Rex. Congratulations. Would you like to be restored into your body now?"

Think about the cushions made of sticks. Would those be comfortable? he wondered. "Um ... yes! I would like my body back. Thank you!"

Alecto began to raise a claw, and Erec shouted, "Wait! Could I also have the things that were mine again with it? Like my eyes—they were combined with Aoquesth's dragon eyes. Baskania stole them from me after I died. And the Twrch Trwyth, and my Amulet of Virtues—he took those too. Oh, and my scepter!"

Erec waited, hopeful, trying to control his thoughts. *Cushions. Concentrate on the cushions.*

"Of course you can have all of those things," Alecto said. "It will be my additional pleasure to take them away from Baskania. What a selfish mortal."

Erec jumped with glee. Everything would be fixed now! All of his horrible mistakes would be corrected! He looked at Spartacus with delight, and the ghost gave him a smile.

"That reminds me," Tisiphone said. "We promised that you would have everything you could want. Money, fame, a palace. Would you like to be king, Erec? It's the least that we could do."

It was hard to turn down having everything handed to him. It all sounded so good. Wouldn't it be nice not to have to do any more quests? He would rule right away and do everything that he wanted to do. Even use the scepter . . .

But that would not work. Erec wasn't ready to use the scepter yet—that had been proven to him. And if the Fates hadn't allowed it themselves yet, he must not be ready to rule.

Plus, how could he accept favors from the Furies who were living in freedom because of the souls in their basement . . . *Stop!* He froze his thoughts. *Cushions. Think about the cushions. They look so comfortable, even though spiky sticks are popping out of them.* Spartacus looked at him curiously when he didn't answer.

Megaera, the white bird, asked, "Would you like one, then?"

One what? Erec couldn't figure it out. "A palace?"

"No." She giggled. "One of the cushions you keep thinking about.

I read into your mind to see what you wanted to do about becoming king, but it seems you are much more interested in cushions!"

All three of the Furies laughed in the way adults would chuckle about a wayward toddler. Megaera said, "You do know, don't you, that what you are looking at aren't really cushions? Those are granite rocks, part of our cave here. But I can make you a cushion to keep that looks just like the one you keep thinking about."

Erec nodded, trying to stay focused on the cushions. She had read his mind. He was nervous that she might probe deeper, or that he would slip and think the wrong thing. "That would be great. Those cushions look so . . . interesting. But I don't know about being king. At least not yet. I have to do some other things first." *Cushions. Cushions. Cushions.*

"Money? Power?" Tisiphone said. "Surely you want something."

What did he want? Some new magical ability sounded good. But what? Trying hard to keep his mind off of the souls, he considered what would protect him if he ran into Baskania again. It had been annoying that Baskania had been able to read his mind so easily, even when Erec was a ghost. "Okay. I know. I'd like it if nobody was able to read my mind anymore—ever."

The Furies considered that for a moment, and then Tisiphone said, suspiciously, "Anybody? Or just any human?"

Erec immediately realized that she was suspicious of him trying to hide things from them. "Just humans is fine! I mean, Spartacus should be able to read my mind. I'm thinking about Baskania in particular. He's very powerful, and can read my mind even when I'm a spirit. Can you make it so that he cannot read my mind ever again?"

"No problem." Tisiphone smiled.

"Anything else?" Megaera asked.

The more help the better, Erec thought. Spartacus would be helping him until he got called into service from Baskania. . . . "Spartacus

THE SECRET OF ASHONA

swallowed a pill that put him under the complete control of Baskania. Can you remove that spell so that he is free now?"

Spartacus gave Erec a smile and a nod.

Alecto said, "We can do that, of course. But Baskania will know. And there will be consequences. But we are not the Fates, and do not predict outcomes of events like they do."

Megaera added, "Not that we couldn't if we wanted to, of course. Their power does not surpass ours."

Erec wondered if that was the case.

"Of course it's true," Tisiphone said with a smile. "But it's not something we have chosen to develop. So I cannot tell you what will happen, only that something definitely will happen. If I remove Spartacus's servitude pill—and if I remove yours—Baskania will know. This is the nature of the magic. And all I can say for sure is that you don't want Baskania knowing that much about you and Spartacus right now. Something tells me that."

Spartacus shrugged. "I won't be around long anyway, so it doesn't matter for me."

Erec tried to change the subject quickly before either of them thought about the souls. "Well . . . I guess we won't do that, then. Will the servitude pill that I took still affect me when I become human again?"

"I don't see why not," Tisiphone said. "It should not affect you in the same way, though. Your spirit might be under Baskania's command, but your body and soul will not, as they were not there when you took the pill. So you'll likely be able to fight it off."

Erec had not thought about the pill still affecting him. He had hoped he would be returned completely to normal. It was bad news, but compared to all of the great news it really didn't matter. He tried to think if there was anything else that he could ask the Furies for. Maybe if he was invisible he could get around easier. But then again, the thing he wanted the most was to be completely normal, and enjoy being with his family, so that wouldn't work.

What if Spartacus was invisible, though? That might help both of them. He turned to Spartacus. "What do you think about being invisible? You might be able to sneak out of Baskania's assignments easier, or show up and not get told to do anything. And if you're around me, you'll have the element of surprise if you're helping me."

"That makes a lot of sense." Spartacus frowned. "But wouldn't it be hard if you couldn't see me?"

"What if I'm the only one that can see or hear you? It's not like—" Erec almost said that Spartacus did not have a long time left to live, but he quickly cut that thought out of his mind, in case it led somewhere else. "It's not like you have a lot of friends around to talk to."

Spartacus laughed. "Correct as well. Sounds like a plan."

Alecto yawned. "Silly human ideas. Well, it's fine with us. Of course, we will always be able to see and hear you, ourselves. There you go."

Spartacus did not look any different to Erec at all. He wondered if his invisibility had already taken effect.

"Visit any time you like." Alecto seemed bored. "And Spartacus? Would you like anything else? To be brought back to life, maybe?"

Erec looked at Spartacus, who seemed distracted.

Megaera laughed. "Look, he just wants all of those books that he thinks he is looking at. I can hear it in his head—*books, books, books.* Such simple creatures, really."

"Would you like those books, Spartacus?"

He nodded. "Yes, thank you. I don't need to be alive again. Sounds good, but without a soul . . ."

"Yes," Megaera nodded absently. "You would get taken by Tarvos right away. I don't blame you on that one."

"All right, then." Alecto swished her wings. "Erec, I'll put you right where you were when you lost your life, and you'll have everything back again. As well as the power to see and speak to Spartacus. And nobody will be able to read your mind anymore—except for us, if we choose. Anything else?"

Cushions. Cushions. "Cushions?" It popped out of Erec's mouth by accident.

Megaera laughed. "You shall have the cushions, too. And books for you."

"Oh—can you put my scepter near me, but not touching me? Thanks."

Alecto nodded lightly. "Here you go."

In a flash, Erec's surroundings narrowed tightly around him. It happened so fast that it took a minute for him to realize that he was in another place entirely. Sitting on a dirt floor, steep walls of earth around him. Nearby were several of the intricately woven stick cushions that he had seen when he was with the Furies, just like they promised him.

The pit. He was in the pit of the Diamond Mind. Where he had died.

Things were definitely different now. This was a feeling that Erec recognized as if it was from a distant memory. Movement. He could feel his body as it moved. Things were happening inside of him—and they felt so wonderful! Breathing . . . and a heartbeat. Because he had not experienced those for so long they seemed breathtaking . . . overwhelming. It was all so beautiful.

Other things, too. When he closed his eyes, he stopped seeing. And when he opened them light came in again. As a spirit he had sight even with missing eyes. And his skin felt pressure where it rested back against the wall. He was alive!

Erec rubbed his hands over himself to make sure, and he could feel

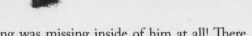

warmth, and touch. Nothing was missing inside of him at all! There was no aching for a missing soul. He was back, completely in one piece!

How lucky. Erec was overwhelmed with happiness. He would be able to go home again, live a normal life. Do quests! Even difficult quests seemed like nothing after what he just went through—as long as they didn't involve dying again. He was so overcome that he stood and jumped in the air, arms up like a prizefighter who had won the world championship.

But all at once he sat back down. Spartacus would be suffering for him. And the souls were still locked away in Alsatia. His life could not be truly his until he did his best to help them.

"Erec Rex?" a gleeful voice echoed in the pit, making him jump. "You're back. I can't believe it! I was keeping your body for you, as you asked. But then it disappeared and I figured that things had gone badly. I was sure that we would never meet again. And now here you are!"

It was the Diamond Mind. Erec had almost forgotten he would be here. "I made it. I can't believe it either."

"I saved the last bit of your soul. Would you like that back?"

"Yes." Erec had forgotten about it completely. It was such a small piece he had not even noticed that it was missing. That had been all he was living with before?

"Take it. I told you I keep my word."

Something sparkled before him, and then Erec could feel it enter his chest. He felt no different from before. "Thanks."

"Wonderful. Now I want to hear everything."

Erec smiled at the creature. First he felt on his neck for the Twrch Trwyth. It hung there, all three remaining Awen untouched. Baskania must have been saving them—Erec was thankful that they were still intact. He looked at the Amulet of Virtues that was once again around his neck. Only six segments were lit with colors.

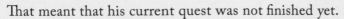

That meant that his current quest was not finished yet.

Which did not surprise him. How could he be done when all of those souls were still prisoners? One thing he had learned from doing quests was that there was a greater goal to accomplish beyond just following the simple orders. Now he knew that saving the souls was what he was meant to do all along. If only he could figure out how . . .

"Tell me," the Diamond Mind insisted. "I must know what happened to you."

Erec wanted nothing more than to leave and see his family again. But he spent a few minutes recounting his adventures for the Diamond Mind. As he was talking, however, he felt something strange, as if there was a kind of energy in the air. It bothered him, made him itch in a way, feel uncomfortable. But it wasn't until he reached the part of his story when Baskania took his scepter that he remembered to look—

And there it was behind him, against the wall of the pit, surrounded by some cushions made out of sticks. He had not even noticed that it was there, but could definitely feel its presence. The Furies had done as he asked and placed it away from him.

But now that he saw it, he felt desperate to touch it one more time. Holding back, he stared at it with a possessive fear. More than anything, he never wanted to part from it again, he wanted to use it more than ever . . . but he also wanted it to be gone. It horrified him to think of what he had done with it before. And he was sure that given the chance, he would do that again, or worse.

No, he had to command it to go away again. But there was one thing that he wanted to see first. It was a small thing, and he hoped that he could use the scepter this way without it possessing him again. Maybe he could command it without touching it. . . .

Scepter, I want to see what Baskania used you for when he had you. Show me what happened.

A white screen appeared in the air. Erec was relieved that, as he was not touching it, the scepter did not create the same mad desire in him. But a feeling of power still rushed through his body. The screen proceeded to show Erec a movie that contained everything Baskania had done with his scepter. It was horrifying.

For fun, Baskania made seven men split into a thousand pieces each and then reassembled them, mixing parts, so that they all appeared strangely put together and oddly related to one another.

He turned a general that he was bored of into a giant pudding, and then commanded his soldiers to eat him for dessert.

He shot multiple bolts of power at the moon to remove it from the night sky. The great ball of rock shattered into five pieces, the largest of which turned red.

He gave a talk and made the audience laugh hysterically when he told a joke, to the point where none of them could breathe. One officer died of asphyxiation before he released the spell.

He made himself grow larger than he had been before so that he could fit more eyes in his face and body.

He pointed the scepter around the library and had an instant input of all of the books that were there into his brain, as if he had read them all at once.

The list went on and on. Baskania had used the scepter continuously, and mostly for things that he could have done without it. But Erec knew why—using it felt so good, and gave the user such a sense of power, that he would want to do everything with it. Watching how Baskania abused the magic made Erec want to stay away from the thing even more. It disgusted him.

Baskania also had spent a lot of time talking to the scepter as well. It advised him, and prodded him into using it more, although Baskania would have done so anyway. Luckily the thing also seemed to preoccupy him and distract him from the dragon eyes and the Twrch Trwyth. The scepter wanted Baskania's full attention.

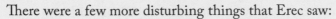

There were a few more disturbing things that Erec saw:

Baskania used the scepter to create a huge crowd at the coronation ceremony for the Stain triplets. Balor, Damon, and Dollick were crowned the kings of Alypium, Aorth, and Ashona. He then used the scepter to create huge castles for the three boys, as well as ornate crowns that he affixed to their heads.

He created massive statues of himself that erupted straight out of the ground in Alypium and in Americorth North, and from the sea bed near Ashona. These towered over all of the buildings. The statues had moving eyes, and watched all that happened within their sight, reporting everything to Baskania.

He placed Fear Essences into the air of both Upper Earth and the Kingdoms of the Keepers. It created an atmosphere that increased stress and made people prone to anger and greed. It also made them more subject to being ruled, as they would be less likely to communicate with one another.

He created a new group called the Special Tax Service. Countless men and women were enslaved by the scepter, and made to go door to door collecting valuables for him. People were required to give up their most valuable possessions on a monthly basis "for the good of the people."

He put a spell on his name, so that it could not be spoken without saying, "I worship the Shadow Prince" three times.

And with a particularly powerful swipe of the scepter, he put an idea in the head of every person in the world. Baskania made them all believe that he was born the one true ruler, that nobody should ever defy him, and that they were all there only to serve his needs.

Erec sat a moment in disbelief after the screen vanished. The Diamond Mind was silent too—it obviously was as stunned as he was. Thank goodness that Erec had taken the scepter back from Baskania. King Piter had been right—Baskania would surely have destroyed the world with it if he had it for much longer. He wondered how much time that would have taken.

"How long was I gone?" he asked the Diamond Mind.

The creature spoke quietly. "Three weeks, to the day. I suppose I wish that I hadn't asked you what happened. I really was happier not knowing all of this."

Erec shook his head. "I want to send this scepter away again, but first I'm going to have to reverse some of the things that Baskania's done." He thought about it for a while. "I have to be careful, though. It's too dangerous for me to use the scepter for one more thing than I need to. So let's pick and choose."

"Are you asking for my help?" the thing asked.

"I guess I am. You saw the movies with me. I don't know what to do."

"It seems like you should reverse the false idea he implanted in every human that they are here only to serve him, and that he is the one true ruler."

"Definitely. And fix the moon! I also need to get rid of those Fear Essences. I'm so happy to get my body back that I can barely notice them . . . but I can sense that they're there."

"The spell on his name should go. That is a horrid abuse of power."

Erec nodded. "And the Special Tax Service. Disgusting." He sighed. "I should probably leave the rest as is. I'm afraid doing all of that will take far too much out of me as it is, and leave me too vulnerable to the scepter. I don't see a choice though."

"Another problem," the Diamond Mind added, "is that Baskania can redo some of those spells on his own, even without the scepter. He is quite powerful, and extremely connected with the Substance."

"I know. The scepter feels so good to use that even Baskania ended up doing much crazier things than he would have otherwise. But he might like those things now that he's tried them." Erec was quiet, and closed his eyes. Then it became clear. "I might have to stay here a while after this. I'm not sure how long it will take me to recover. . . ."

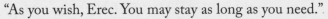

"As you wish, Erec. You may stay as long as you need."

"Okay. Here goes." He concentrated. *Scepter, do as I command you. First, reverse Baskania's spell on his name. Free the slaves from the Special Tax Service and disband it. Get rid of the Fear Essences that Baskania put into the air. Remove the false ideas that he implanted into everyone's minds. And then make it impossible for him to repeat any of those spells again. Never go to Baskania again. Never work for him. And after you have done all of this, disappear and stay far away from me until I am ready for you. This time, you must disappear until both I* and *somebody else say that I am ready to use you. Do these things now, and nothing else.*

Erec watched as the scepter lifted off of the ground, shaking. It rose into the air, red and gold sparks flying from it. Loud snaps in the air around it sounded like miniature thunder cracks. Erec wondered if the amount of magic that he had just commanded the scepter to do was more than it had ever done at one time. If he had been holding it right now he surely would have gone insane from the power running through it.

But even from a distance, Erec could feel an enormous pull on his body and insides from the massive spells that were being performed. Lightning erupted out of his skin, and some of the sparks entered the Diamond Mind. Huge waves of pressure billowed from inside of Erec through the pit, throwing him against a wall. If he had still been a ghost he would have been blown straight into the dirt. The scepter pulled every ounce of magic from him and used it, as well as from the Substance around them. Erec's mind was electrified from the surges all around him.

For a while it felt like a nightmare that would never end. But then, all of a sudden, the scepter vanished.

Within the same second, Erec and the Diamond Mind fell straight into a deep sleep.

CHAPTER THIRTEEN
A Scary Future

HOURS LATER, Erec's eyes opened. Sunlight streamed into the pit. The Diamond Mind was awake and humming.

Erec immediately felt even happier than before. The air seemed lighter, and the world more peaceful. Now that the Fear Essences were gone, everything seemed wonderful. He had done it. Fixed things. What a relief!

At the same time, however, his body felt drained and sick. The energy that the scepter had taken out of him had left him reeling. Every inch of him ached, and he was overcome with exhaustion. In his core, there was also an intense craving for the scepter that was so overpowering that it made him dizzy.

In a normal situation, experiencing all of this would have made him miserable. But he was so happy to be alive, body and soul, that he didn't care. He was back—and the world was back. It had been saved from his horrible mistake as well. Erec wondered what Baskania must be thinking about the scepter and his dragon eyes disappearing. He would have no clue what had happened to them—thinking about it made Erec laugh. But he knew that Baskania would be feeling even more of a craving for the scepter than Erec did, and he would do anything to get it back.

It took most of the day before Erec felt ready to move. The Diamond Mind did not speak, also recovering from the shock. Finally, when Erec was ready to go home, he realized that there was one thing that he needed to do first. He was whole again—soul and all—so there was no reason for him to be evil anymore. He had to look into his future again, just to know that everything would be okay, that those old visions no longer were going to happen. . . .

Erec closed his eyes and pictured himself going into a dark room inside of his head. It was peaceful inside. He took a moment to relax there and feel the triumph of the day. Everything was right in the world again. He could not wait to see what his future held now. Inside of the room was a second room, darker and quieter.

When Erec entered this one he felt completely at peace. There was the black box on the table, humming and vibrating. It seemed to call out his name and to hold all of the good things in the world that were to come. He touched it, and felt better than he ever had in his whole life. He had taken a big risk, and been through a lot. But now it was all perfect. . . .

It was time to pull the cord and open the shades on the two windows. No longer did he fear seeing himself do evil deeds.

Trevor looked up at Erec with big brown eyes, confused. "Why are you doing this? Let me go."

Erec gripped Trevor's wrist harder. "That's enough from you. Come with me." His mouth winced into a fake smile. "I would never do anything to hurt you. Remember that."

Trevor shook from head to toe as Erec dragged him down the hallway. Erec knocked on the tall wooden doors of the Inner Sanctum. When they swung open, he shoved Trevor inside and followed behind him.

"Look what I have for you." Erec grinned at Baskania.

"Wonderful!" Baskania beamed. "What a treat."

"Enjoy him." Erec dusted his hands off with a grin. "Thanks again for letting me serve you. It's my pleasure."

Baskania laughed with glee. A silver cage fell out of the air and over Trevor. Trevor put his little hands on the bars and gazed through at Erec with sad eyes. Erec felt a twinge of grief, but he pushed it aside. He had done what he needed, and that was all that mattered.

"How about a dragon?" Erec suggested. "I know one that I can deliver here. I thought that would be a nice next gift for you."

Baskania strode over and patted Erec's head with his hand. "Boy, you have turned out to be a pleasure for me. I'm so glad *that we've gotten to know each other better and moved past that bad time we used to have."*

Erec was pleased. Baskania was happy now, and that's what was important.

Erec dropped the shades shut in horror. This made no sense at all. He was going to be evil still? Or at least completely stupid and beholden to Baskania? How in the world could he hand over his precious brother? And a dragon? Erec loved dragons. He would never deliver one to Baskania to be chopped up for parts.

The black box was supposed to know everything, but it must have been wrong. He had his soul back! There was nothing that could force him to do such awful things. He just wouldn't do it! Nothing could make him hurt Trevor like that. Erec would keep his eyes open, and he would make big changes as soon as he figured out what would affect him like that.

It took a few deep breaths to get his perspective back again. Nothing bad had happened yet—and he would make sure that it didn't. For now, things were great. He stood and stretched, ready to leave and go home. So he bounded up lightly on his toes . . . and nothing happened. It was a surprise—Erec had forgotten that gravity would affect him again. So . . . how was he supposed to get out of this steep pit, then?

The Diamond Mind seemed to know what he was thinking. It cleared its throat. "I've been thinking about this too. For a long time now, people only fall down the pit, but never climb back out again. They used to bring roll ladders, and climb in and out that way. But I'm not sure how to get you up there now."

The walls were too far apart to scale, and there was nothing to grasp on to to climb. What a ridiculous irony, he thought, if he was to be restored completely to health and then stuck down in this pit until he starved to death.

"Help!" he shouted, looking at the sky far above. "Is anyone out there?"

"Only me," a familiar voice answered. At the edge of the pit above, Spartacus was lying on his stomach, looking down at him. Stacks of books surrounded him, just as the Furies had promised to give to him. In a moment the spirit was at Erec's side, and then Erec felt himself whiz into the air alongside him.

"Thank you! You saved me. How long have you been here, Spartacus?"

"Since you've been down there. I watched those awful movies about what Baskania did—unbelievable! You did the right thing, reversing everything, you know. And asking the Furies to let only you see and talk to me. That's perfect."

"Yeah." Erec grinned. "So, you gonna hang out with me until we figure out how to save those souls?"

"You bet. I have nothing else to do, until Baskania calls me into service. We better save those souls before then, because that's when my time is up."

"What do you mean, your time is up?" Erec knew full well that Spartacus planned on asking the Furies to destroy him when that happened, but he didn't want to accept that yet. "Maybe you'll do something for Baskania, then get out again and be free—it might not last forever."

"I'll never find that out. Because I'm not serving him. The minute I get the call from him, I'll make a pit stop in Alsatia and try to rescue the souls on my own. Then I'll let the Furies obliterate me, no matter what happens. That'll end things the right way."

Erec did not want to imagine that. But he understood. "I have to let you know what I saw when I looked into my future. You're the only one I can tell this to—it's just too awful to admit to anyone at home." Erec recounted his vision of giving Trevor to Baskania.

Spartacus winced. "That's awful. Was I in the vision?"

"No."

"That's it, then. I'll make sure that I stick around you at all times. I won't let that happen, okay?"

"Thanks." Erec felt relieved. He looked around. "I lost my sense of where things are now that I'm not a ghost. There was a Port-O-Door somewhere around that brought me here, but I forget where it was."

Spartacus laughed. "Glad to help. But you won't need a Port-O-Door if you're with me."

In a moment, Erec was flying in the air. It was a strange feeling, soaring forward in a standing position. Because he could see him, he could tell that Spartacus was holding his shoulders—even though to others he would have looked very odd. They flew forward, over the treetops.

Now that Erec was alive again, he was terrified of the height and the speed, especially as he did not feel tightly secured. "D-don't drop me!"

"Of course not." Spartacus laughed. "It's not like this is hard to do. Have you forgotten already? You might want to close your eyes for this part."

All of a sudden, they sailed straight up into the air at rocket speed. At about five thousand feet, he sailed right by the window of an airplane. A woman looked out at him in shock, and Erec stared right back, equally amazed. The woman probably thought she was seeing things.

"S-stop." He could barely get the words out of his mouth. "I c-can't breathe. It's too c-cold here. It's too fast."

Spartacus stopped, hanging in the air. "Oh, I'm so sorry. We just were here the other day—I forgot it's different when you're a human.

Guess there's no way you'd make it to the top of the atmosphere now."

"No!" Erec choked thinking about it. "Go down slow, okay? And no higher, either."

"Sure. I just wanted to get some good distance so we can shoot across the ocean quicker. You know."

Erec wished he could not see that Spartacus now held him with just one hand, and was using the other to change their direction. Soon they were blowing sideways, and slightly downward. Erec could not stop shaking. It was freezing, even with Spartacus going slower.

Eventually the sun warmed him a little, and he could enjoy the view. Before long, the coast of America came into sight, and then houses got bigger around his mother's apartment in New Jersey. He laughed, wondering if anyone would see him drop out of the sky.

But nobody did. He landed gently on the grass outside of the apartment building, then caught his breath and ran inside. He could not wait to see everyone.

"Bethany! Mom! I'm back!"

There was a commotion, and then all of a sudden Erec was bombarded with hugs from all sides. It felt so good to see everybody and so amazing to be hugged, Erec could not believe it. Tears streamed down his face, and he didn't even try to hide them. He swung Zoey in circles and threw her into the air, bowed a few times to Jam in response to his profuse bowing, tickled Bethany, and laughed when she got him back until he cried again.

"You were gone for so long!" Bethany was out of breath, tears in her eyes. "I thought . . . I thought we'd never see you again! Every day things seemed worse. I was sure that you were dead—I don't know why I thought that, but I was convinced! And now you're fine!"

June shook her head. "I'll never let you disappear like that again. It was torture. Like the whole world was destroyed. We could barely function."

Even Trevor spoke. "It feels like life is starting over again." He smiled. "Thanks for rescuing me, Erec."

"Don't be silly, Trev. Anytime." Sadness and fear welled inside Erec when he hugged his brother. The images he had just seen of Trevor in his future filled his head. He would never let anything bad happen to Trevor again—and Erec would never, ever put him in danger. He would have to be on alert at all times.

A horrible thought occurred to Erec then. If he saw himself giving Trevor to Baskania, and about to give him a dragon, what else had he done for him? Had he handed over Bethany . . . and his mother? It was too terrible to think about. He would have to look into his future again soon and try to get clues.

There was a strange smell, and it was making Erec hungry even though it was not appetizing at all. He looked around to see what was making the odor, and then he froze. . . .

There it was! His scepter—leaning up against the wall of the apartment! How could it be here with him now? Was it following him? Maybe he wasn't able to get rid of it anymore. What if it wouldn't go away?

If he had been relaxed before, every ounce of contentment fled from his body. There was nothing in the room except for the scepter and him. He had to touch it. He knew that he couldn't—it would be the end of him. But he had no choice. After the amount of power that the thing had pulled from his body just recently, there was no way that he could resist it this time. It was too much.

Slowly, he walked closer to the patterned gold, studded with gems. It was his, wasn't it? Maybe he *was* ready for it, otherwise it wouldn't be here. *No!* he shouted to himself. He should not touch it. Not yet. But he couldn't help it. Desire overwhelmed him.

Only one finger . . . just one finger wouldn't hurt anything, would it? He would just give it a small tap. Barely moving, his hand closed in. Just one little touch . . .

He squeezed his eyes shut, knowing that he was doing something very wrong. But at the same time he was filled with a wild excitement for what was about to happen. . . .

Nothing. Erec didn't understand. There was no feeling to the gold other than a slight coolness. He grabbed it with both hands now. Absolutely no electricity at all. What had happened? Had it stopped working? Was Erec immune to the thing now?

Not able to help himself, Erec picked the scepter up and pointed it at a wall. *Make an apple pie appear.* It was the first thing he could think of.

Nothing happened.

Bethany laughed. "Remember that thing?"

Erec looked at her blankly. "My scepter? What happened to it?"

"That's not your scepter, silly. It looks like it though, remember? That's the pretend one that I got from the druids as a present. You know, with the fake Lia Fail stone? That's when they gave you the fake Serving Tray—the one that made only disgusting food, and Jack got the map that would always take him home again?"

Erec set the fake scepter down, embarrassed. "I remember now. It just fooled me." He could feel his face turn red. "Stupid thing. What's that I'm smelling?"

She laughed. "It turns out the fake scepter isn't totally useless after all. I found it when I was going through the things that I took to Ashona. The druids had told me how to activate it to make it work for someone, but I never bothered trying it. Everything else they gave us turned out to be a joke. So just for fun, playing around I assigned it to Cutie Pie."

Hearing her name, the fluffy pink kitten, Cutie Pie, leaped into the room and up onto Bethany's shoulder. The cat bounded down and jumped on the scepter a few times as if demonstrating what Bethany was talking about.

THE SECRET OF ASHONA

"I kind of forgot I even did it, and Cutie Pie didn't notice that the scepter was programmed to her for a few days. But it made some kind of connection with her I guess. Because before you know it, one of the bedrooms was full of sardines. I mean, top-to-bottom stuffed with the little fish. And there was Cutie Pie, happily munching her way in at the doorway. It took a while to get rid of them all, but we never got the smell out of there." Bethany laughed.

Erec didn't find it so funny. "That thing *works*? You need to keep it away from everyone, okay? Don't use it for anything! How do you program it to . . . never mind. Don't tell me. Whatever you do, never tell me. Even if it's just a shadow of what the other one can do, I don't want to know. . . ."

He realized that he was starving when Jam brought the Serving Tray back in. How long had it been since he had eaten? He had no idea—and could not believe how excited he was to taste food again. "I'll have a thick, juicy hamburger with tomato, lettuce, and ketchup. And French fries, a chocolate milkshake, and a cheese omelet. And fried chicken. Oh, wait—I'll have some homemade chocolate chip cookies too. And fresh baked brownies. And peaches. And mashed potatoes." He kept swiping food off of the tray to make room for more. When he could wait no longer, he picked up the dripping hamburger and took a huge bite. . . .

Heaven. He hoped that Spartacus wasn't watching, it would make him jealous, he was sure. But for now the ghost remained hidden.

"So, what were you up to?" Bethany asked. "Did you get rid of that skin thing, or whatever was stopping you from hugging us before?"

He laughed. "I did. Now that I'm okay I can tell you what happened, and you won't get too upset, I hope. I wasn't alive when I was here last. If any of you touched me you'd be able to tell that I was a ghost."

There was a stunned silence, and then his mother chided him. "Not funny, Erec. Don't joke about things like that."

"I'm not joking! It really happened." He told everyone his entire story from the moment the Hermit let him escape the cords on his bed.

Bethany's eyes widened. "Baskania had put Fear Essences into the air? No wonder we were all so miserable when you were gone. I mean—of course we'd be upset that you weren't here anyway. But we were fighting all of the time, and nobody would help anyone feel better. How could the Shadow Prince have done that? And we all thought he was such a good guy."

"A good guy?" Erec could not believe his ears. "You know better than that . . . all of you. What are you talking about?"

There was a silence, and then June said in a low tone, "We did know better than that. It's just sinking in now, Erec, but Baskania's spell must have worked on us, too."

Erec thought about the spells that he had reversed with the scepter. "Do you mean that you all believed that Baskania was the true ruler and you should all serve him? You have to be kidding."

June shook her head. "I don't know. It just seemed obvious—" She plunked into a chair with a hand over her heart. "This is crazy. I can't believe what we gave up last week."

"What?" Erec wasn't sure he wanted to hear this.

"The Special Tax Service came by—and the most valuable thing I could think of was the Seeing Eyeglasses. None of us could get them to work so that we could see you, which was another reason I thought that you had died. . . ." She looked stunned. "And you *had* died. And now you're here." She hugged him again, for a long time.

Erec's heart sank. "You gave up the Seeing Eyeglasses to Baskania? I can't believe it. Well . . . it wasn't your fault. You were under a spell."

June looked down. "I thought I was doing the right thing to help the Shadow Prince, the 'best guy on the planet.' This is disgusting."

"Don't feel bad. It was all my fault that Baskania got that scepter to begin with. Now he's even crazier."

After eating more than he had ever put away in his life, Erec took a long nap. It felt amazing to sleep after so much time had gone by. And waking up without the driven feeling of being a ghost was incredible too. Erec could happily spend the rest of his life doing nothing at all except for eating, sleeping, and being with his family.

Except . . . those souls were still prisoner in the storage facility under the Furies' nest. How could he go on enjoying his own life and letting them all rot in a prison? He knew that saving them had something to do with completing his quest. He would think about it and figure some way, he hoped. Once that was done, he would spend the rest of his life at home relaxing, which was all he really wanted to do.

It wasn't hard to make excuses so that he could be alone in his room. Everyone knew that he was exhausted. But Erec wasn't just tired. He was frightened. Seeing himself giving Trevor to Baskania had horrified him. If he looked into his future again he might get a clue so he could keep it from happening.

At least he had his soul back, so he had control over himself. And, thank goodness, he hadn't seen himself as a raving maniac in the future, as he had before. . . .

But he wanted to find out for sure that those things would be different now. Not seeing them in the last vision wasn't enough. He could not possibly be that soulless evil jerk who was tormenting families and stealing from kids, but he still had to see it for himself. He knew he could ask specifically to see certain things when he looked through his dragon eyes.

He tried to relax on the bed, but all of his muscles were tight. At first it was hard to envision the dark room in his mind, but soon he pictured himself entering it. As usual, it was warm inside, calming. The second room inside of the first one was even more relaxing. Erec hung on to the assurance that he felt from being inside of it. Maybe everything would be okay. He would soon see that he would be a nice person again in the future. And he would figure out how to protect Trevor from anything Erec might do.

Show me the time in my future that I had seen before . . . where I was threatening to rob that innocent family. Let me see what I'm doing now during that same time, how things have changed.

Erec ran fast, holding on to an ax and swinging it wildly. He was sweaty and out of breath. Anger and hate surged through him. Before long he came to a small house made of logs. He had to break into it. Erec raised the ax above his head and brought it down onto the door, splitting the wood. He yanked it out, then did it again and again. Pieces clattered to the ground as he kept chopping.

In a rage, he reached inside and unlocked the knob, then flung the door open with a growl. Before him, a family trembled. The mother held a young child tight, his arms wrapped around her neck. An older girl clung to her knee, crying.

The father stepped in front of them, arms out in a gesture of protection, but his hands shook badly. "Leave us alone. You can take anything you want from here. I don't care what happens to me, but stay away from my family."

"Jewels. Necklaces. Watches." Erec squinted around the room. "Where do you keep them?"

The man stuttered, upset. "D-don't take those. Please. Anything in the whole house is yours—but don't steal our jewels."

Erec swung the ax back over his shoulder, aiming at the man's neck.

THE SECRET OF ASHONA

"Sorry!" The man stepped back in shock. "I'm sorry. Go ahead. They're upstairs in my wife's dresser. But we don't have much. T-take what you want."

Erec shoved past them and went upstairs. He rooted through drawers, dumping out piles of clothing and old notebooks. . . .

Erec slammed the shades shut. So, nothing in his future was different at all, then? His old dragon friend, Aoquesth, had shown him that the future he saw could be changed. He had even changed it himself before. So why was this still the same? He had his soul back now—but was it too late and would he still turn evil anyway? He didn't want to see what would happen with the kids in the park, but he had to know. . . .

Show me what will happen now during the next vision I had. The one where I took candy from all of those kids. Let me see how things will be different now, at that same time. . . .

Kids ran all around a playground, handing out candy. Anger seared through Erec, making him shake. "Give that to me!" He dove at the kids with a snarl. A low growl escaped from his throat as he grabbed candy from their hands. People stared at him with wide eyes, as if he were a maniac. But there was no time to stop— so many kids, so much candy. And he had to take it all!

Mothers darted toward their children, trying to save them. But Erec could run faster than they could. One of the toddlers was surprisingly strong, and Erec struggled a while before yanking the sweets out of his hand. His mother looked equally confused and terrified. Right behind her was a kid about to put an opened lollipop right into her mouth. Not when Erec was there—he'd get it first! Shoving the mother out of his way, he snatched the sucker out of the little girl's fist, leaving her crying and rubbing her hand. . . .

He shut the shades again, dumbfounded. Nothing was different at all. He thought about searching his vision of handing Trevor over to Baskania for clues, but it was too depressing. What was going to happen to him? Losing his soul even for a short while must have been too much for him. He would have to talk to Bethany again and make sure there was a way to stop him the minute he started to turn bad. With a heavy heart, Erec left the dark rooms in his mind. He lay still on the bed for a long while, wishing that time would stop moving forward, and that he would be able to stay right there forever.

Erec's entire family—June, Trevor, Nell, and Zoe, as well as Jam and Bethany, all wanted to go with him to visit the Oracle. That was fine with Erec. He wasn't ready to part from them, either. So after he dragged himself out of bed the next morning, they went into the Port-O-Door and found Delphi on the map of Greece.

Erec hoped that the Fates didn't mind that he was bothering them again so soon. Normally he would only visit the Oracle if he badly needed advice. The Fates had made it obvious that they wanted him to think for himself. But he had followed their directions, and now he was stuck. Erec did not know who else to turn to.

The weather was warm, and sun streamed through an impossibly blue sky, lighting the crests and currents in the river with sparkles. They walked a short distance to the old stone well that sat by the water. It occurred to Erec that he would once again have to look through his dragon eyes in order to call the Fates. It was almost too much. He could not bear to see himself being so horrible in the future. What would he see this time? Himself shooting Bethany?

No. He had to ask to see something positive. There had to be a time when he was doing something good. He had turned Trevor over to Baskania, right? Well, maybe he would rescue him later. That was it! Erec had to ask to see that . . . and maybe it would be the case. *Please*, he thought, *show me a time when I am helping Trevor escape from Baskania.*

His family, Bethany, and Jam hung back while Erec leaned over the stone well. Soon, he imagined that he opened a door and entered a quiet, dark room inside of his head. It was so familiar now, so easy to do. It was nice inside there, comforting—and he tried to find solace in that feeling. He found the second door inside of that room and opened it. Going inside felt even better. It was darker, warmer, and so peaceful. . . .

Just being here, and close to the box of knowledge that sat on the table beside him, he again had the feeling that he could do anything he wanted to do. If only he was right! Here were all of the answers in the world. He just had to open his eyes and use well what it told him. Inside he knew everything. Erec rested a hand on the humming box and felt its wisdom. He was ready now to see what it would show. So he found the silken cord that dangled between the two dark windows and pulled. The window shades opened.

Trevor was crouching, arms around his knees, and shaking head to toe. Erec laughed cruelly, and gave him a kick. "Worthless piece of garbage."

Trevor stared at him with big eyes, in disbelief. Tears rolled down his cheeks.

"Look at that. He's useless." Erec smirked, then kicked Trevor into a large box that was on its side on the floor. He looked up at Baskania and laughed. "Let's throw him in that trash compactor to be crushed. Trash is all he is, anyway."

"That's fine." Baskania looked at Erec greedily. "Now, let's see what else you have for me today."

"This." Erec held the scepter out to him. "It's yours again. I got it from the Furies for you. This time nobody will take it away. Why don't you take my dragon eyes first, so you don't forget? Once you are using the scepter, you'll be thinking of other things."

"Good thinking, boy." Baskania's whisper was tight with greed. "Here we go."

The room went black. Erec felt the scepter lift out of his grip.

"This is it!" Baskania's voice echoed. "Oh, it's so good to have you back in my hands again. I've missed you, lovely. Let's see what we can make you do now!"

Erec could feel the electricity spark in the room. Screams echoed from outside. What was Baskania doing with the scepter? He could not even imagine. . . .

Erec dropped the shades on the windows, disgusted. This was impossible. Things were far worse than he could have imagined. He would not save Trevor. On the contrary, he would destroy him, throw him away to die in a trash compactor—and think it was funny. Erec would return to Baskania on his own and give him back everything that he had before—the scepter and Erec's dragon eyes. And let him ruin the world again. This was impossible!

It didn't make sense. He had asked to see something good, him rescuing Trevor. But there was nothing good in his future. Nothing at all.

So . . . he was still going to turn evil. Maybe Baskania was going to put another spell on everyone, and it would convince Erec that he had to serve him. If only there was a way to avoid that. . . .

He had to find a way out of it. He would change his future, stop all of this, and free the imprisoned souls . . . but how would Erec ever know what to do?

Maybe the Fates would tell him. At least he could ask. He leaned over the dark still waters of the well and called to them. "Fates? Are you there? It's Erec Rex. Can you help me?"

In a moment, the waters of the well began to swirl into a wild whirlpool, rippling with colors. Rose- and violet-colored drops splashed into Erec's face. And then, at once, it was still.

"Like, o-m-g! He's back! Can you believe it, girls?"

"Unh—ya. He's like a live-in, almost. Wow."

"Practically. Should we ask him to pay rent?"

The three Fates giggled. "Pass me another Cosmos Ripple, Nona. I can tell this is going to be a fun one."

"Sorry to bother you," Erec said. "I really need your help. All of these souls are locked up in the Furies' storage facility, and there's no way to get them out without the Furies finding out. Unless I can figure out a way to trick the storage room. Can you tell me what to do?"

"Listen to that boy, girls! He's, like, stopped using his own brain, like, completely! He only wants to follow orders—I mean, gag me!"

"Unh, I know. Tell me about it. Like, duh."

"I'm sorry," Erec said. "I'll try to think about it. Can you just give me a hint?" He felt desperate.

The Fates seemed to think this was hysterical. "Do you think you can outsmart our sisters, little human boy? You can just, like, pop up and sneak away the souls that are keeping them free?" Her voice sang, "I don't think so!"

That made sense to Erec. "I don't think so either. But the last time I talked to you, you said that maybe I should free all of the souls and send the Furies back to Tartarus. Were you just joking then?"

"Like, doesn't he even know what is a joke and what isn't? What are we going to do with him, girls?"

All of them replied in chorus, "Laugh at him!" And they all cracked up.

Erec tried not to feel frustrated. "Please. I just want to check. There is nothing I can do to help those souls, then?"

"How many people have to tell you, Erec? You make your own choices! I think the Hermit has said that to you, like, fifty times. Like, wow."

Now Erec was really confused. "So I *can* save the souls, then? But I can't trick the Furies. So they'll know I'm trying to rescue the souls, and they'll put them right back again. And that won't help anything."

The Fate that answered sounded sarcastic. "Like congratulations, Erec. You are sooo smart. What are we going to do with you?"

Another one said, "So, yeah. I mean, you can't fool the Furies and release the trapped souls the way things are *now*. You will have to decide on what is right and wrong before then. Ob-vi-ous!"

"Totally!" another added.

Erec thought out loud. "Right and wrong? It's wrong for the souls to be stuck there for sure. Maybe I could get the Furies to leave their nest . . . or cave or whatever it is. Then they wouldn't know what I was doing. . . ."

A voice sung back, "He doesn't lea-rn, does he?"

"No-oo, he does-n't."

"I have to think of a way?" Panic was overtaking him. He needed to know what to do! "Something might make them leave? I could tell them you wanted to talk to them! That would do it!"

"If they wanted to talk they would be here, duh. Think again, doofus."

"I don't know. Maybe they would chase after someone who they thought did something bad to them. Baskania—they don't seem to like him much. What could he have of theirs that they want?" An idea was starting to form in his head. There was no way that he could fool the Furies if they were in their cave, that was for sure. "What about the Hinternom? Maybe they'd like to use that to store their souls, or keep more for later, in case the ones they have died?" That was it! Erec could try and see if they'd go for it.

Erec heard a few yawns. "Bo-ring! Nothing like hearing someone think to themselves. Nice talking to you, Erec baby! Ciao!"

"Wait! I have another question. This is really important. How can I avoid Baskania putting a spell on me? I keep seeing what I'm going to do in my future and I can't let it happen!"

More yawns. "Anything else? We have 'really important' things to do . . . like chat and laugh at you behind your back."

"No!" Erec panicked. "Stop! Tell me anything. Will I find my lost siblings soon? Would that help me? What should I do to keep from going bad?"

One of the Fates sounded frustrated. "The *only* thing I will tell you to do is to stop asking us so many questions! If you start to bug us we'll never talk to you again! Now, like, go turn into a dragon or something!"

The waters in the well grew quiet and still.

CHAPTER FOURTEEN

Bad News from a Pen

VOICES ECHOED and crashes resounded on the other side of the Port-O-Door when Erec and his family returned from the Oracle. They stood in the vestibule, afraid to go into the house.

"What's that?" Erec put a hand in front of the doorknob to stop Zoey from opening it. "Somebody's in there."

June looked worried. "I left the doors locked. Who could it be?"

They listened for a minute. Something was dumped onto the floor, and then something else. It was obvious that the apartment was being searched.

"Let's see who it is!" Bethany looked angry, and wanted to march in the room and see what was going on. "We're not going to let them get away with this!"

"Let's be safe. I'm sure it's Baskania's soldiers. They're probably searching for the scepter. After all I've been through lately, I've learned not to rush in."

"But I thought your apartment was protected by the chalk King Piter gave your mom!"

Erec thought a moment. "I guess Baskania did something when he had the scepter—located us or something. It won't be safe here anymore."

Spartacus stuck his head into the vestibule of the Port-O-Door through the wall. "You're right, Erec. Alypium and Aorth soldiers are all over the place, searching for your scepter. Guess who sent them."

"I thought so," Erec said. "How long are they going to stay?"

Everyone looked at Erec funny, like he wasn't making sense.

"Who knows?" Spartacus said. "I've been having fun with them, though. If you want to come out it's okay—I'll protect you all."

Erec laughed, imagining what Spartacus had been doing to the soldiers. "Are you sure we'll be okay? I mean, can you watch all seven of us at once?"

Now Erec's family, Jam, and Bethany were all staring as if Erec had gone crazy. "Are you talking to yourself?" June asked.

But at the same time, Spartacus was saying, "No problem, kiddo. Piece of cake."

Erec remembered what it had been like to be a ghost, and agreed that Spartacus would be able to handle the soldiers. Plus, it would be fun to see what happened. So, to the surprise of everyone in the Port-O-Door, Erec opened it up and walked out.

"There he is!" one of the soldiers shouted. A few pointed guns at him.

"Nice and slow, Erec Rex. Put your hands over your head. No funny stuff."

Erec put his hands over his head. His family walked out behind him, stunned. June tried to reason with a soldier, and Zoey started bawling. But then the windows flew open. One at a time, guns popped out of the soldiers' hands and flew out, disappearing in the distance.

"Quit that! Stop!" One of the officers still carrying a rifle pulled the trigger. The bullet shot out, but stopped in the air midway to Erec, its target. It then began to perform loop-de-loops in the air, and ended up flying back to the officer and wedging itself up his nose.

"How is he doing that?" The soldiers were obviously frightened, but trying not to show it.

One officer sounded like he was in charge. "Erec Rex. We have a warrant to obtain any magical items that you have in your possession, including a golden scepter, and any objects that you might be wearing around your neck. Please hand those over, tell us where the scepter is, and we will leave you in peace. We saw it here when we first came in, then it seemed to vanish."

Erec laughed. "That wasn't the real scepter. I wish I could help you. I can't give you anything, though. You'll have to go tell your boss he's a big loser."

This didn't go over well—probably because the soldiers were terrified of coming back empty-handed.

"See here." A tall, brutish soldier with chest hair popping out from under his uniform stalked over and looked down on Erec, thick hands on his hips. "You better not mess with us, or you're going to be sorry, kid." He stuck a finger out and poked Erec hard in the shoulder.

In a moment, the soldier was flying overhead in circles, shouting in horror. "Put me down! Stop it! Please—I'm sorry, okay?" After a few circles near the ceiling, the guy flew out the window and landed on the lawn.

Erec looked around with a smirk, as if he had done that himself. "Anyone else want a ride?"

Most of the soldiers fled the apartment, and the few that remained were tossed out of the window by Spartacus. Erec dusted his hands.

Bethany looked at him with amazement. "How did you do that? You've gotten amazing at finger magic!"

Erec laughed. Why not let her think he had done it? It wasn't like Spartacus could rat him out—nobody could hear him.

Except for Erec. "Oh, that's a good one," Spartacus said. "Take all the credit for my hard work."

"I'm sorry," Erec laughed. "It's not like anyone here could pat *you* on the back, anyway."

Bethany's face turned red, thinking that Erec was talking to her. "Well, we can't all be superheroes, I guess." She stuck her chin in the air and crossed her arms.

"I'm sorry!" Erec caught up to her. "I wasn't talking to you."

"It sure sounded like it." Bethany obviously didn't believe him. "Who could you be talking to, then?"

There was obviously no more keeping this secret. "Spartacus Kilroy. Remember we did things together as ghosts? Well, he's here now. He's the one who took care of the soldiers, not me."

Everyone looked around the room as if they might be able to see him.

"Where is he?" Zoey asked.

A chair bounced up and down in response.

"Thanks, Spartacus!" June exclaimed.

"It's good to see you again!" Bethany said. "I mean . . . be with you . . ."

"He says hello," Erec said. Then he winked. "Spartacus says that he couldn't have done anything without me, even as a ghost, and that he someday wishes that he could be as powerful as I am."

"Oh, yeah?" Spartacus knew that only Erec could hear him, but he grinned. "Time to do a little dance, Erec." He picked Erec up and turned him upside down in the air, then bounced him all around the room.

Zoey screeched laughing, and Bethany pointed, eyebrows up. "Look what Spartacus is doing to him! Looks like he doesn't agree with you, Erec!"

"What?" Erec played innocent, still floating upside down. "I'm doing all of this myself, of course."

Spartacus carried Erec to the kitchen table, head down and feet up. He produced a banana cream pie with the Serving Platter and in a minute pushed the pie into Erec's face.

Now everyone was laughing.

Erec swiped a finger full of pie off of his cheek and ate it. "Not bad."

Spartacus said to him, "Tell them that you were joking. Say that you're a mere mortal weakling. Go on."

"Never."

A blueberry pie got produced, and hung in the air in front of Erec's face. "Say it . . ."

"Oh, all right." Erec announced to the room, "I am a mere mortal weakling. Spartacus is the one who can do everything."

The pie drifted back to the table, and Erec was put back on his feet.

He ate a little more pie and then washed his face off. "We're going to have to get out of here soon. If Baskania's armies found us here, they're going to be back with more powerful people. He's not going to stop until he gets that scepter again." Erec cringed, thinking about his vision of the future where he handed it to Baskania.

"I agree," June said. "King Piter has been asking us all to go to Ashona with him and Queen Posey. I'm starting to think that's a good idea."

"I've never been to Ashona," Erec said.

"It's amazing!" Bethany jumped up and down, rubbing her hands together. "It's so pretty there. And Queen Posey gave me my own little bungalow that's attached to her castle. It overlooks a coral reef—we can watch the fish play outside. And there's a porthole that we can go through to swim outside when we want, with our Instagills. We can even talk to the fish!"

"Awesome!" Zoey looked excited. "I want to go! Mommy—can we go?"

June smiled. "Let's do it! Everyone gets to pack one light bag, quickly. Then we'll pay King Piter a visit."

Erec stuffed some clothes into a bag. In the back of his closet he found a pair of shoes that he had not used in a while: his magical Sneakers. They let him move soundlessly and smoothly, no matter how fast he ran. If he stamped them on the ground they threw sound elsewhere to distract anyone looking for him. He put the shoes on, and also threw his MagicLight into the bag. It had been a prize when he was in the contests in Alypium last summer. Similar to a flashlight, it left beams of light hanging in the air until it was shut off.

Bethany told him that he didn't need much because they had everything he could want at the castle. Zoey took her favorite dolls. Only Jam brought a lot of things—he loaded a huge duffel full of supplies. He also brought a bag for the lifelike objects that June had bought from a Vulcan store online: a toothbrush that walked, with little arms and legs, an alarm clock that used to like to wake Erec up by throwing things at him—and its female companion clock that Erec had found in Baskania's fortress, as well as a toaster oven that liked to shoot burnt toast at people. June put an arm around the final animated object—a walking, juggling coat rack. They all walked into the Port-O-Door, including the coat rack, and shut the door behind them. Erec doubted they would ever come back again.

Erec had never even looked at the Ashona map in the Port-O-Door. He was surprised that it was not one continuous area like a large city, but rather was a network of underwater islands connected by tunnels and long slides. It was located on the ocean floor, but an elevated part contained coral reefs and plateaus. The largest area in the middle was Ashona Central, and this was where Queen Posey's castle was located. June tapped the castle on the map. The only place accessible from the outside was the front entryway.

The Port-O-Door opened into a huge arched stone entryway. Before them thirty-foot-tall oak doors stood wide open. Behind them a clear barrier showed straight through into the ocean.

"Look!" Zoey ran over to see it up close, and Bethany and Erec chased after her. Nell followed slower, with her walker, along with Trevor.

"There's an octopus!" Bethany pointed. "Did you see it going into that cave? We can go out there later and swim around. They have scuba equipment here for anyone who doesn't have Instagills."

"I would love that!" Nell looked excited "This is like a family vacation!"

Bethany looked wistful. "I'm glad you're like my family. I wish I had one of my own to go on vacation with. Pi is always traveling with the Springball team, and he's it."

"You have another brother." Erec immediately regretted reminding her of that.

"I know. I think about him all the time. Doesn't help that I don't know where he is."

Erec completely understood what it was like to have missing siblings, but he thought it best not to mention it.

"This seems like a safe place to stay." Jam looked around approvingly.

A guard in the doorway took information and approved entry into the castle. June walked over and he cleared his throat. "Can I help you, ma'am?"

"Yes. This is Erec Rex, King Piter's son, and his family. We'd like to see King Piter and Queen Posey, and stay here awhile."

The guard sat up straighter. "Oh, yes. Of course, ma'am. Well, just a second." He tapped a screen in front of him and a woman's face appeared. "Yes ... they claim that they are related ... Erec Rex. I see."

Then he looked up with a smile. "No problem, the cameras have identified you all. Come on in."

If Erec had thought that the entryway to the Castle Ashona was beautiful, he could not believe how amazing the inside of the castle was. The tall walls of the rooms and hallways were wavy instead of straight, with bright blue moving lights giving them the look of waves. Delicate aqua curtains fluttered around giant windows that looked everywhere onto the underwater reef.

Artists' renderings of fish of all sizes hung all over the walls, darting around on occasion to sit in other places. Perfect, huge seashells were strewn along the edges of the rooms, along with small piles of sand. Blue skies and rainbows lit the ceiling, fluffy white clouds moving through on occasion. The entire castle gave the impression of a movable piece of art.

But nothing was more impressive than the far end of the huge entry room. Instead of a wall, the massive atrium opened into a giant beach covered in sand and coral. Fish flickered through the air as if they were flying, and turtles cruised through the room without touching the bottom. Starfish crept around the sand on the floor.

There was an unusual blue tint to the atmosphere in the room, as if coloring had been sprayed into the air for effect.

Erec's group slowly made their way toward the large opening. It was amazing. A squid wiggled into the space. Erec walked right up to the creature, and it looked him in the eye and puffed ink. The black stuff hung as if suspended feet above the floor, slowly spreading in curlicues into the space around it.

Nell, in particular, was captivated by the sea life. She stood quietly and watched, a smile spreading over her face. While everyone else pointed and talked, she gazed in rapt silence all around her.

"Why are the fish flying?" Zoey asked.

"I don't know, honey," June said, looking as amazed as everyone else.

Bethany asked a uniformed man who was rearranging rows of white rocks on the ground in patterns. "How come the fish are up in the air?"

The man chuckled. "They're n'aint actually flying, missy. This here's a sea room. Queen Posey put wat-air in here. It works both like water an' air, so the fish can swim in it and you can breathe too. If you try to jump up, you'll see you can swim, too."

"Queen Posey did that with her scepter?" Bethany looked amazed.

"With a little help from the Secret of Ashona." The man winked. Then he whispered, "None of us would be able to live here at all without the Secret. Not even the Queen and her scepter could keep it safe to live this far underwater all by herself." He squinted at Bethany. "You all have family here. Can you keep the Secret?"

She nodded with wonder.

"This place is not just a set of watertight rooms, dearie. She's a living, breathing organism. All of the parts of Ashona are connected into one gigantic creature. She lets the people live safely, and makes sure that we get what we need. And she responds to Queen Posey, alone, as her ruler. The Secret of Ashona lies deep under the city, and she controls everything that happens here. We couldn't live without her—she helps us with everything: oxygen, food, and water."

"Why is she a secret?"

The man looked around furtively. "A lot of people know about her, so she's not a secret, really, anymore. But how she works, well, that's something that very few know."

Bethany flapped her arms in the wat-air and lifted off the ground. "It works! Try it, Erec!"

Erec jumped up, out of curiosity. Slight pressure around his body kept him floating. In a moment, he, Bethany, and his siblings were flipping themselves around the wat-air in the room like dolphins, but breathing all the time. It reminded Erec of being a ghost.

Bethany laughed. "This is what it's like to have Instagills! Now everyone can do it."

"What are Instagills?" a sea horse asked, right by Erec's ear.

His eyes flew open. "Did you talk to me?"

The sea horse looked around. "I don't see anyone else having a conversation with me, big guy. So, you going to tell me what Instagills are? Is this some new device you humans are using to go into the water? Never happy where you are, are you people?"

Erec laughed, and pointed to the closed Instagills in his wrists. "Nah. Only me and my friend Bethany have these. They were gifts from Queen Posey."

"Oh." The sea horse darted around suddenly, excited. "I see, then. They must be something quite wonderful if they're a gift from the queen. Quite wonderful, indeed."

On the other side of the huge sea room was a clear barrier that looked into a busy coral reef. Erec put his hands against it, noticing that he could not pass through, although the fish were able to swim in and out with ease.

Trevor pointed to the entry room. "Just like the other side. We can go through there into the castle, but the fish can't cross."

June began to gather the kids. "Time to find King Piter, everyone."

A servant was waiting for them when they crossed back into the huge entry room. "Are you ready to visit with the Queen, ma'am?"

June nodded. They walked through the busy area, servants scurrying about. It was just like it had been in King Piter's castle—however, here they did an excellent job keeping the place tidy. People in shimmering aqua uniforms handed out sushi, scallop cups, and tuna sandwiches as they passed by.

The hallways that led away from the giant entry room were rounded and cozy, the walls rippling and the pathways curved instead of straight. It seemed that they had been walking forever before they entered a beautiful room. It was round, with a high domed ceiling, and walls that shifted between blues and greens. A large pool filled the center of the room, its border inlaid with giant pearls. Directly above it in the ceiling was carved a huge round skylight that was the same size as the pool, surrounded by a beautiful painted fresco of octopuses, stingrays, starfish, serpents, and eels. Dolphins leaped in and out of the water, playing with one another.

Erec had been here before. Last year, when he was doing contests in Alypium, Queen Posey brought him to this room with her scepter. The thought made him pine for his scepter for a moment. Where was it now? Floating around where no humans were, no doubt.

Queen Posey looked just as beautiful as Erec remembered her. Long, dark hair waved around her tired face. But she probably wasn't tired—it was her Instagills, three dark lines under each of her eyes, which made her look that way. Silver fish scales adorned her shimmering dress, making it ripple with colors. She perched on a huge oyster-shell chair on a pedestal, as did King Piter.

THE SECRET OF ASHONA

"June! Erec! So good of you to come!" The queen stood. "Please, all of you, make yourselves comfortable."

Jam darted to King Piter's side and dusted him off, offering him snacks and a footrest that he had thought to pack.

The king smiled. "Ah, Jam. Nobody could replace you." Then he strode over and put his arms around Bethany and Erec. "How are you two? It's great to see you! Bethany, I'm glad you're back. And you, too, kids." He gave hugs to Trevor, Nell, and Zoey, then asked June hopefully, "Will you all stay awhile, I hope?"

June looked overwhelmed. She began to bow a few times to the king and queen, then stammered, "Y-yes, your majesty. We were . . . um, hoping to stay here for safety. You had said that would be okay—"

"Of course it's okay," King Piter boomed, grinning. "We're all family here, right? So, Erec, tell me what's been going on."

It was good to hear strength in King Piter's voice again. As long as he was near Queen Posey's scepter, he could stay alive and well.

Erec told the king and queen everything that had happened to him. Both of their faces paled, as did June's again, as he recounted his experiences as a spirit on his way to becoming a specter. The room remained quiet for a while.

Then the king laughed halfheartedly. "Well, thank goodness you're all right now. I guess it's a good thing that you did all of that. Even though you had to . . . die." He choked on the word. "Well, it sounds like you're done, at least. You're on your way to becoming the next King of Alypium. I just wish that was finished and you didn't have any more of those crazy quests to go through. I'm ready for you to have that scepter of yours safely under your control. Especially since Posey's here is acting up now, for some strange reason."

"What's wrong with it?"

His sister, Posey, answered, "It's not responding to me at all anymore. And I'm out of touch with the Secret of Ashona who is underneath my kingdom and keeping us all safe in here. It's very concerning."

Erec immediately froze. "I think I know what's going on. Baskania had sent me a letter telling me to hand my scepter over to the Green House. Of course I didn't—but the letter said something about having your scepter soon as well. Baskania must have come up with a way to take it over."

Posey frowned. "I can't imagine how. It's still here with me. But it's true, I can't do anything with it."

King Piter said, "Maybe when Baskania was using Erec's scepter—maybe he asked to control yours. I'm not sure that would even work, though. Well, at least the thing is still here and keeping both of us alive." Erec knew the five-hundred-year-old king and queen would die without its power nearby. The king tried to hide his concern and gave Erec a smile. "And you have your soul back again. So you can take it easy now, right?"

"I have to find a way to free those souls that the Furies are keeping prisoner, Dad. It's part of my quest—and it's the right thing to do."

Everyone looked uncomfortable. Erec knew that they all disapproved and were afraid for him. But at the same time, they had to realize that he owed his life to the Fates from this very quest that they gave him. Who was he to walk away now? On top of that, Erec knew something that they did not. There were horrible things that he would do in the future, including killing Trevor, terrorizing strangers, and giving Baskania his scepter and his dragon eyes. He had to do good things now to make up for all that. If the Fates wanted him to risk his life, maybe it was for a reason, to stop him from turning evil.

The king gave a quick shrug. "I can't advise you to do that, Erec. Why don't you leave things be as they are? Just forget about those souls. You are safe now, and that is what is important."

The chair that King Piter had been sitting in suddenly toppled onto its side. Erec grinned. Only he could see that Spartacus was making a statement.

The King grew even paler. "I . . . I'm sorry, whoever is here. I know, other people count in this world besides my own son. It's just that you have an important path." He put a hand over his face. "I don't know what to do."

"You don't have to do anything, Dad. I've already talked to the Fates about this. They said that I need to figure out what's right and wrong by myself." He looked around. "I thought it would help to get the Furies to leave their cave so I can sneak in when they aren't there. Any ideas?"

Queen Posey smirked. "It's not like they're going to just up and leave those souls behind, are they?"

"Maybe we could make the room holding the souls come away on its own," Bethany said. "It is alive, right?"

Erec nodded. "It is. I wonder if we could find a way to control it, make it think that we're the Furies."

The king shook his head. "You have to be careful. None of these ideas sounds possible, and I don't know if there is a way at all." He scratched his chin. "The Fates once gave me a pen that will write out answers to any question I ask. I save it for emergencies. Overusing it can make you dependent on it, like the scepter." Erec knew what he meant immediately. "But I think that this qualifies." His brow furrowed. "I hope I'm strong enough to use it now." A glint surfaced in the king's eye as he fished through his long, black robe. "It's always with me. The Aitherpoint quill. Ah, yes. Here it is."

The quill was a simple feather with its tip carved into a point. The feather was a glossy, deep, shiny black, with a red flourish on the end. The king cradled it in his hands. "Jam, do you have some paper I could use?"

Within a second, Jam had produced a pad from one of his vest pockets. "Of course, sire."

"Thank you." The king set his chair upright and sat back down. He set the pad in his lap and poised the pen over top of it. "Quill— my son, Erec, needs to set free three thousand souls who are held captive by Alecto, Tisiphone, and Megaera, the three Furies. How should he proceed?"

The pen broke free from the king's hand and began to scribble on the paper furiously. The king strained to look at its writing around the moving quill. Suddenly, it dropped into his lap. The king gently placed it back in his pocket and read what was written:

"Erec Rex must pledge his services to his worst enemy. Only after he gives himself over completely will he find a way to set all three thousand souls free."

A cold clammy feeling spread through Erec. This could not be. Serve Baskania? This might be the step in the wrong direction that would lead him to turn evil. In fact, he was sure that would happen. If he gave himself over to his worst enemy, he truly might do things like hand Trevor over to him, and give him his scepter and his eyes.

Only . . . Erec was confused. The Fates had never steered him wrong before. And the Aitherpoint Quill was a direct link to them. Erec had always listened to what they told him to do . . . but now he felt sure that he should not. Then again, a small voice inside of him asked, maybe *not* listening to the Fates now might be what would lead him to do those terrible things. How could he know what to do?

King Piter looked just as stunned. "This can't be correct. No, Erec. I forbid you to do this. It would be more than just a personal sacrifice of yourself for all of those souls. If you give your services—and everything you have—to Baskania, our whole *world* would surely perish." He dropped his head, hopeless, but then looked up. "This is not a command, remember. It is not a quest. It is just a solution offered by the pen. There may be other solutions. Better ones." He tried to sound confident, although Erec could tell that he was not convinced of his own words.

"Much better ones," another voice added . . . and suddenly the Hermit was sitting in another of the oyster chairs next to the king. He wore a long black kimono with a red fan across the front, and a pair of bright pink boxer shorts on his head, splayed out to look like a jester's cap. His legs were crossed, and he tapped his chin with mock seriousness. "Maybe you, yourself, have a better solution to give to Erec. I'm sure you would have done a finer job saving his soul as well."

"Hermit!" The king looked relieved. "I'm so glad to see you. We're in a mess here."

"We're in a mess, my king? Oh, no, I don't think so. Look around—" The Hermit waved a skinny arm around the room. "Not a mess here at all. It is the *mess* that is in *you!*" He swung around to point at Erec. "And you!" Then he pointed at Bethany. "And you!" The strange little man pointed wildly at everyone in the room, and then crossed his arms triumphantly as if he had made an important point.

The king nodded impatiently. "Erec feels he has to free the souls that the three Furies are keeping captive. The Aitherpoint quill said that Erec should give himself to Baskania—pledge his services to him. That's crazy, though. What do you think, Hermit?"

The Hermit got up and danced around his chair in a circle. "Crazy quill. Crazy dance. Live your life like a fancy-pants."

If Erec did not know how amazingly wise the Hermit was, he would have thought everyone was nuts for asking such a goofball what they should be doing. But instead, everyone waited patiently, expectantly, for what the Hermit had to say.

Before long, the Hermit stared expectantly too, imitating each of their faces. He rubbed his hands together, excited. "What will he have to say? I can't wait to hear it! What a wise, wonderful man the Hermit is." He danced a little more, then said. "Everybody dance! To the beat of your own gong! Get up on your feet now—come on. You! You!" He pointed at Queen Posey, June, and everyone else. "You want answers? Then, be dancers!"

Zoey shouted, "Yeah!" and jumped up to dance with the Hermit, making everyone laugh.

Bethany grabbed his hand. "C'mon, Erec. How long has it been?"

It seemed ridiculous at first, but how could he turn down a dance with Bethany? Soon they whirled around the room to soundless music. Maybe the Hermit was right, it was better not to be so serious all of the time, even when life seemed impossible. Nell bounced a little in her walker, and Trevor got into the groove and spun around her a few times. Even King Piter and June bounced around a little in their seats, having fun watching the kids. And when it seemed that only Queen Posey was not part of the dance, all of a sudden she whirled out of her chair, jaw open in shock. Feet off the floor, she spun around the room, one arm out as if dancing with a ghost.

Which, only Erec could see, she was. Spartacus Kilroy, an arm around her waist and another hand holding hers, bounced and dipped the queen around the room, and then set her back in her oyster seat.

The Hermit clapped and whistled. "Bravo, your highness." He bowed low. "You surely did not want to be shown up by us, now did you, your majesty?" He giggled.

Queen Posey's face turned red. "I . . . I didn't do that." She looked around, uncomfortable.

"Now, now," the Hermit chided. "Don't be so shy."

King Piter's face crumpled, anxious again. "Can you tell us now, Hermit, what Erec should do?"

"Yes." Erec was surprised that the Hermit sounded so commanding. This was a change. "He should take a breath in. Then breathe out.

Just like that. Can you do that Erec? Very good! Now repeat it again and again, until you die again. Excellent!"

Erec rolled his eyes—typical Hermit humor. Nobody would make him spill the beans unless he wanted to, even though Erec was sure that the Hermit knew very well what Erec should do.

He decided to give it a try. "Hermit, I'm going to get those souls out of there, if it's the last thing I do. But I don't know how to sneak them out with the Furies in there. And the Aitherpoint quill says I have to dedicate myself to my worst enemy. But those things don't have anything to do with each other, do they? How do I know if the quill is right—I don't want to do something stupid just because the quill said to." He wanted to tell the Hermit more, about the terrible things that he saw himself doing in the future. But everybody else was listening, and he could not stand for them to know.

The Hermit smiled and put a hand on Erec's head. "Little Erec. I'm so proud of you!" He pinched Erec's cheek. "You care about the right things. I see you are learning well. You will be a great thing some day." It sounded to Erec like the Hermit meant to say, 'a great king,' but then again, he could never tell with the Hermit. "You ask if working for Baskania and freeing the souls in Alsatia have anything to do with each other. I will say, only as such things as brushing your teeth and finishing your schoolwork have something to do with each other—both have to be done before going to bed. Just think of your little tasks—outwitting the great Furies and donating yourself to Baskania—as small things you must do before going to bed. Does that help?"

The Hermit had a way of making things sound even worse than they were. "So, I'm really supposed to do this, then? Is there any other way for me to free those souls other than helping Baskania? Because I really don't want to do that."

"Erec, Erec." The Hermit shook his head, as if talking to a toddler. "Brushing your teeth might not be fun, but it will keep them from rotting out of your mouth. And I know the schoolwork is a chore. But if you want to be a good boy, and do all that you want when you grow up, you have to do it."

Erec understood the gist of what the Hermit was saying—just like every other time in his life, he had to follow the path that the Fates had laid out for him. It was never easy, but it was the right way to go.

But giving himself over as a servant to Baskania . . . ?

"Ready?" Spartacus clapped his hands together. "Let's get this show on the road!"

Erec remembered how driven he had been as a ghost, so he knew why Spartacus was in a hurry. But the last thing that he wanted to do was leave this comfortable place with his family and Bethany, to depart from love, safety, and comfort, and jump into danger and misery. "Give me a day, Spartacus. One day to spend with everyone here—in case I don't come back."

June clapped her hands over her mouth and looked at King Piter.

King Piter sat in stunned silence. He looked back and forth between June, Erec, and the Hermit. Finally he shook his head. "No. I understand, believe me. I know as well as you do that you were put here for a purpose. But as your father, I have to say no."

June sighed in relief and rushed to put an arm around Erec. "How are we going to keep him here? The last time I used magic to tie him in his room he managed to get out—and that's when he died!"

Saying this seemed to reinforce to everybody that there was nothing they could do . . . and also that even his dying had not been so bad.

Erec tried to ease her mind—but he didn't want to lie. "It's okay, Mom. I'm going to be fine. You can't stop me from going, so just don't worry—"

THE SECRET OF ASHONA

"Don't worry?" June began to pace, growing angry. "Don't worry? Of course I'm stopping you. I'm . . . stopping you! Okay?"

"Mom—you can't do anything about it."

"Oh, yes I can! Do you want to watch me? King Piter said no, and I said no. I'm not letting you out of my sight. Do you hear me?"

"That won't work, Mom."

"Just wait!" June shouted. "I'm not losing complete control of you. I'm still your mother. Don't underestimate me, buddy. You're not going to be left alone for a second."

Everyone in the room stared at him, wondering what he was going to say. Erec himself had no idea. He wanted her to feel better, but she couldn't stop him from leaving when the Hermit was here to help him. Would she be following him into the bathroom?

The Hermit winked with sparkling eyes. "Madam, I promise you that I will make sure this boy doesn't go anywhere he is not supposed to go." He bowed so low that the neon pink boxer shorts that served as his hat touched the ground, and remained there once he stood up.

Erec had no doubt what the Hermit meant by that—Erec was supposed to go to Baskania as the Fates wanted him to.

June shot the Hermit a strange look, as if trying to read more into what he said. Then she relaxed. "Okay," she said. "Thank you, Hermit." Then her eyes darted to Erec.

He gave June a smile. "Okay, Mom. If the hermit says to stay, I'll stay."

Even though Erec knew that was not what the Hermit was saying, June looked relieved. Erec supposed she was clinging on to her only hope that he would be okay. He wished there were some other way—and that he himself had hope to cling on to.

CHAPTER FIFTEEN

A Trip to La Place des Yeux du Monde

EREC AND BETHANY went for a swim through the porthole attached to her room. With their Instagills there was no need for scuba equipment. It was the first time that Erec had been in a deep reef, and he was amazed at how beautiful it was. Glowing red anthias and orangeback bass shimmied around the patchwork of rock, pastel corals, and wiggling bright-red, blue, and white anemones. Brilliant blue tang fish with shocking yellow spines darted in and out of rocks in huge clusters. Erec could hear them discussing the huge pink octopuses hanging out in their reef, and it took a while before he realized that they were referring to him and Bethany.

"So, are you really going to stay here with us?" Bethany looked excited but nervous. "You can tell me the truth."

"I can? I guess I should be mad that you told my mom where I was going last time, and tried to chain me into my room."

Her face grew pink. "I'm sorry. I only did it because I cared. I just couldn't lose you."

"I know. I'm not angry at either of you." He shrugged, hoping to leave it at that.

"But really—this time, are you going? Were you just trying to make your mom happy?"

Erec did a somersault in the water. If he told her, she probably wouldn't take it well. She might even go worry June again, and it wouldn't change anything. "I don't want to talk about it. Can we just have a good time here now?"

Bethany seemed to know what that meant. "Erec, I'm so worried about you. Would you promise to take me with you if you go anywhere?"

"Not this time, Bethany. Any other time. Think about it—what if I had taken you with me before, when I went to see the Furies? You would be dead now. It's the only way that you can get to Alsatia to see them. And the Furies might not have brought you back to life." He thought about that a moment. Would they have? They had offered to make Spartacus alive again. But how could he have risked Bethany like that? And there was no way that he would bring her back to Baskania, after she had been his prisoner so recently.

"You know"—Bethany twirled a curl between her fingers in thought—"if you really were going to follow what the quill said, if you really became Baskania's servant, you'd have to bring me along to give to him as a prisoner. A real follower of his would do that, you know."

"Are you crazy?" Erec tried to calm himself down. "Suicidal or something? If I have to become a servant of that guy, it's bad enough. I'll never really want to help him."

She shrugged. "Just saying. I mean, I'd rather be there than waiting here wondering how long you'll be alive this time."

Erec understood. "After I do this, Bethany . . . if I can save those imprisoned souls, I'll never do anything without you again. I was a spirit without a soul or body, and it stinks. It's like being a broken piece of a whole—just like they are. I have to try to do something for them. I wish you could come with me." Erec tried not to think about the risks involved in getting back into Alsatia. What if he really had to die to get back? Would he really give up his own life to save three thousand souls? He hoped that he could make himself go through with whatever he had to do. This time, after turning against the Furies, they would not bring him back to life again.

Of course, before he even got to that point, he would have to give himself to Baskania as a servant. . . .

Luckily Bethany had no idea what he was thinking about, and she lit up with a smile. "Okay, it's a deal. Just be careful, whatever you do."

"Deal."

"I may be able to see us together in the future, and that will help me too. I've been working with a tutor here on becoming a seer. And it's been awesome."

Erec got nervous. If she could see into the future, what would she find out? Erec cringed at what he had seen himself doing: ruining the world. Giving everything to Baskania. Bethany would never see a happy future, even if Erec did miraculously survive. "That's cool. Maybe just don't look into the future too much, okay? I mean, it's not worth it. You could get upset for nothing."

Bethany looked suspicious. "Upset for nothing? What do you think I'll see?"

THE SECRET OF ASHONA

"I don't know." He backed off. "Nothing. It's just . . . you know how looking into the future is."

"No, I don't know. And speaking of that, every time I asked you about what you saw at the Oracle, you seemed to change the subject. What's going on?"

Erec closed his eyes. All of his secrets had become too much. If he couldn't tell his best friend, then who could he tell? "Promise not to say anything to anybody this time?"

"I won't. Believe me, I regretted making June so upset. It was all for nothing, too. You can trust me, really."

"Okay." He paused. "I saw myself giving the scepter to Baskania. And . . . my dragon eyes." He could not bring himself to tell her that he had also given Trevor over and then thrown him in a trash compactor to die. It was just too horrible. "I could see him start to use the scepter for awful things, right away, too."

Her eyes widened. "You're kidding!" She thought a moment. "Well, it's no problem, right? You can change the future. You know that. Now when you get into that situation, you'll know not to give the scepter to him. If you're the one holding it, the power will still be yours. It will be your choice." She sounded satisfied.

"We'll see." Erec was doubtful that would work. Some spell had obviously been cast on him in the future, or he would never have given the scepter to Baskania in the first place.

"I'll be working on reading the future while you're gone," Bethany said, arms crossed. "It will make me feel like I'm with you, I think. At least it will give me something to do. I'm getting good at the close stuff, but that's really easy. Like I can see you doing a somersault in one minute."

Erec waited to see what would happen, and had no urge to do a somersault at all. He raised an eyebrow. "Are you sure about that?"

"Oops." She giggled. "Okay, so it doesn't always work. I think when I told you, it changed things. Let me try again." She put a finger against her cheek in thought, and waited.

Erec still felt no urge to do a somersault. Instead he scooped up a pink coral fragment near his foot and tried to throw it in the water. It sank down a foot away from them.

"There!" Bethany sounded triumphant. "I saw you doing that!"

Erec laughed. "That's kind of hard to prove, isn't it? You can't tell me I'll do anything in advance, so I just have to take your word that you read it in my future after the fact."

"I guess." She shrugged. "But I also saw that two blue fish started nibbling at the coral in a minute." They waited, and sure enough two fish found a meal in the coral piece nearby.

"Cool. How do you see that kind of thing? Is it by imagining something in your mind?"

"No—it works totally different from your dragon eyes. It's all math, which is why I love it so much. There are patterns everywhere, in everything that happens. And the future can be predicted using those patterns. Most people couldn't do it." She shrugged, turning a little pink. "Not to brag or anything."

Erec laughed. "No worries. I know you're slightly good at math."

Her eyes grew dreamy. "I love it. It's like I was born to do this. All I have to do is pay attention to everything around me. I watch the patterns in what happens, and sometimes they start to fit together in waveforms, or three-dimensional structures like crystals. It's so cool. Everything that happens is part of a giant plan, I think. All of the events are woven together into a massive math problem that has spinning and moving parts, worlds within worlds within worlds. . . . Sorry. I get a little carried away." Her face turned pink again.

"It sounds amazing."

"I'm really bad at it so far. But I love the challenge. The more that I look, the more I can see what's coming. But right now it's only a few minutes in advance. Once I get better, I might be able to look years into the future."

"Sounds like you'll be the perfect AdviSeer for some lucky king of Alypium one day."

"I hope so."

Erec fought the urge to give her a hug right there. *Maybe even more than an AdviSeer*, he thought. *Maybe a queen.*

Spartacus paced in Erec's room, banging into things on purpose to keep him from sleeping.

"I know!" Erec finally shouted. "We're going. In the morning, okay? I'm not just putting it off, I need some rest! I'll be too tired to do anything if you don't leave me alone awhile."

Spartacus sighed impatiently. "All right. Fine. Shall I wake you at seven?"

"You're more annoying than my old alarm clock. No, let me wake up on my own. And then eat breakfast. And then say good-bye to Bethany. Then we'll go."

Spartacus threw his hands into the air, but he walked out and left Erec to sleep.

Not that Erec could relax. For hours he thought about what he was giving up, questioning if he was doing the right thing. He was walking away from everything he loved—his whole life. And working for Baskania was the worst thing that he could think of. It was the opposite of everything that made sense. He must really trust those Fates.

Erec's good-bye with Bethany lasted a lot longer than Spartacus liked, but finally Erec gave the nod. Spartacus placed his hands on Erec's shoulders, and in a minute they were flying through the sea. Erec was glad that he had Instagills. In Spartacus's impatience, he may have forgotten that Erec could not breathe underwater.

As nice as the water felt, Erec shook like a leaf when he was whizzing through the air afterward, soaking wet. "C-can't we take a break? Or go slower?"

Spartacus set him down until he dried a little. He was all smiles again now that they were traveling. "I'll stay with you as long as I can when you're with Baskania. Just because you're his servant doesn't mean that I will be. I'll be watching out for you, kid."

That made Erec feel a little better. But not much. Because he was heading closer and closer to the fortress in Jakarta. The last time he had been there was a disaster.

A thought hit him—there was one person where he was headed that was on his side. Rosco Kroc, his old friend, still worked for Baskania, even though he was secretly against him. Erec had to contact Rosco and tell him he was coming. Rosco would be able to help him for sure.

Erec fished a snail out of his pocket. He began to look for paper to write on, but then remembered that Rosco told him to just send an empty snail and he would find Erec. Erec told the snail to go to Rosco Kroc and dropped it into the grass.

"We need to camp out here awhile," he told Spartacus. "Rosco is going to meet us. I need to talk to him before seeing the Shadow Prince."

Spartacus asked, "Why didn't you just ask me to get him? I'll be right back." The ghost disappeared.

Erec wondered who would make it back first—Rosco alone or with Spartacus. It didn't take long to find out. Within a few minutes, a stunned and freezing Rosco Kroc dropped out of the sky in front of him.

"Rosco!" Erec grinned. "That was fast. Did you get my snail?"

"What snail?" He looked annoyed. "Why bother with that if

you were going to bring me here by magic? Just so you know, it's not considered the way to do things. I was in the middle of something, and . . . you nearly gave me a heart attack. How did you send me so high in the air? It felt like I was being held by something."

"You were—by a ghost. It wasn't me that brought you here. It was Spartacus Kilroy. He was the AdviSeer of King Piter—"

"S-Spartacus Kilroy? He came to get me? D-does he think I'm responsible for his death?" Rosco's green-scaled face registered shock, and his teeth began to chatter.

Spartacus shook his head. "Look how he talks in front of me like I'm not even here. Pathetic."

Erec laughed. "No, Rosco. It's nothing to worry about. Spartacus was just trying to help me. I told him that I needed to talk to you."

"You're commanding ghosts now?" He looked around him in fear. "What kind of ghosts would that be? I should be able to see Spartacus if he's a spirit."

Erec shrugged. "Not this time. But I'm not commanding him, anyway. He's helping me because he's my friend."

Rosco calmed down a little. "I'm glad he's helping you. . . . Tell me what's going on. What did you need me for?"

"I'm on my way to visit Baskania and offer my services to him." Erec told Rosco the entire story that had led him here.

"I thought that I'd heard everything," Rosco said. "But this tops it all. I can't believe that you are going to help the Shadow Prince. And you saw into the future that you are going to give him your scepter and your dragon eyes? You *can't* do that, Erec."

"No kidding. I don't want to. It's just that . . . I don't exactly know how to stop it. I'm guessing that Baskania might put a spell on me to make me completely brainwashed. He did it before." Erec shuddered.

"Well, I'll be on the lookout so I can stop it. We have to be really careful. Baskania can't have any clue that I'm aware of all of this. I'll have to be with you the whole time—maybe I can get you assigned to me somehow."

"I'll be with you too," Spartacus said. "And I'll make sure that scepter doesn't get into Baskania's hands. At least, as long as I'm not called away."

"Thanks, Spartacus."

Rosco looked creeped out. "What did the ghost say?"

"He's going to help me too."

"You mean he's going to stay here?" Rosco sounded disturbed.

In a moment, Rosco was hanging in the air upside down. "Something has my feet! Is it him?" He sounded terrified.

"Spartacus, put Rosco down! He didn't mean anything by that. Rosco's just nervous, that's all."

Rosco was set back onto his feet, trembling. "I'm sorry, Spartacus. I'll try not to say anything bad. . . ." He closed his eyes for a moment and refocused. "Okay, let me help you, Erec. I'll go tell the Shadow Prince that I need assistance with something. . . . I'll figure out what. You can show up when I'm there. That way I can help if things go wrong. And I'll try to work it out so that you get the job of helping me."

It was a relief to have a friend looking out for him. "That's great. Even if I give myself to Baskania—which I'm supposed to do—you can make sure I don't do anything bad."

Rosco cringed. "Wait a minute. This will never work. What was I thinking? The Shadow Prince can read minds. He'll know exactly why you are coming to him, and that you aren't really there to help. He'll never trust you to serve him."

"Don't worry—Baskania can't read my thoughts anymore! Nobody can, except for ghosts. So I'll be safe. That was a gift from the Furies."

"You're kidding! That's perfect. Oh, he's not going to like that."

Rosco chuckled. "He can't read mine, either, remember, so we're set. After I traveled back in time something happened, so I'll always be a mystery to him. We're the only two that will know what's going on."

Spartacus put his head in his hand. "Once again, it's like I don't exist." He picked a stunned Rosco up by his ankles and lifted him high in the air. "This'll help him remember there's more than just two of us."

"Put Rosco down!"

Spartacus set Rosco onto the ground, a little more roughly this time.

"S-sorry. I'm sorry, Spartacus. I'll try to remember that you're here. Always here . . ." He shook his head. "I need to think of a project to present to the Shadow Prince. Something we can work on together. He's been obsessed lately with finding Bethany's brother— the one who is supposed to be able to give him the secret to learning the Final Magic. That prophecy is obsessing him. I'll tell him I have a lead and need someone to go undercover with me. Someone that can pose as a kid."

"We really *should* track down Bethany's brother!" Erec lit with excitement. There was nothing he'd rather do with his time working for the Shadow Prince. "Only, we'll tell Bethany who he is, not Baskania."

Rosco nodded. "Again—we need to be very careful. No information can fall into the wrong hands. I know who is heading up the team that's researching her brother. We'll see what they've learned so far."

Erec nodded. "Sounds like a plan."

Rosco dusted himself off. "I'd better head back." He held a hand up. "And I don't need help, thank you, Spartacus. Not that the rocket-like ride thousands of feet into the sky wasn't a blast—if you like having early heart attacks and that sort of thing. But I'm perfectly capable of using my own magic. The Shadow Prince is in his Paris megacorp complex today. It's the first time he's been in Upper Earth for a while, though. Seems like he's been busy at the Jakarta fortress, which means that he might be planning some kind of battle or war. I've been listening for information, but he doesn't like to share unless it's necessary."

Battle or war? "I hope it's not all about getting my scepter from me. I'm sure he wants it like crazy now."

"He wants everything like crazy. But having that scepter taken away made him go ballistic. You are lucky you weren't on the same continent; he was smashing mountains. But you gotta know that guy—as angry as he was, he didn't slow down one bit. If anything, it only sped him up. He's got so many plans, a battle or war is nothing to him."

That sounded worse than Erec thought. And he had to go help this guy? "Thanks, Rosco. I'll see you in Paris, then. Good thing you told us—we were headed to Jakarta. What time should we be there?"

Rosco pursed his lips in thought. "It will take me an hour to show up and get ready. I usually get in to see him right away, but since I'm not sure, let's give it two. That will give me time to warm him up to my idea about needing a kid to find Bethany's brother—and also a little time to talk to the team that's working on it."

"What if you're done talking to him before I show up?"

"No problem. I can always pop back in for something once you are there. But I'll time it right at two hours. I'm pretty good at sticking around and discussing things, anyway. I know how to keep him interested."

Rosco raised his arms and flew into the air. "Much better this way, Spartacus. I'll see you guys soon in Paris. *La Place des Yeux du Monde*, on the Champs-Élysées. You can't miss it."

"Spartacus can get me anywhere. We'll see you soon."

✳ ✳ ✳

THE SECRET OF ASHONA

Erec had never been to Paris, so Spartacus took him early. The Champs-Élysées was beautiful. Tall, manicured trees and beautiful parks lined the wide street, which led into spacious areas of upscale shops and restaurants. Erec didn't realize that he was hungry until he looked through the window of a pastry shop at the éclairs and intricately shaped tarts. They looked too beautiful to eat. He reached into his pocket only to remember that he had no money at all. He hadn't even brought his magical Serving Tray for food. Of course, as a ghost it had not been an issue.

Reading his mind, Spartacus managed to find a fat chocolate éclair which appeared in Erec's hand as he was walking. After almost two hours of sightseeing, Erec arrived in front of the biggest building in the city, one that rivaled Notre Dame in its splendor. It was *La Place des Yeux du Monde*—or Eyes of the World Place, Baskania's headquarters for his United Nations–based global political party and its campaign for world peace.

A street vendor outside of its tall carved wood doors flipped crepes on wide metal disks. He cut bananas and sprinkled powdered sugar and chocolate over the tops of the light fluffy desserts. Erec's mouth watered—he grew hungrier by the minute—so he walked closer. The smell was wonderful. But the voice of the vendor caught him off guard. It was definitely not Parisian—in fact the man had a distinct New York accent. And his voice sounded familiar.

"Next!" he shouted in English. "Get yer crepes here. Real Paris-type crepes, perfect for all youse French types. Come and get it."

Erec moved closer to get a look at the vendor. He was short and balding, with oiled black hair. For a moment he stared at Erec and then a look of recognition popped onto his wide face. "Erec Rex! Unbelievable. What are you doing in front of . . . dis place?"

Erec saw the man's fingers graze a small metal lever under a cloth on the cart. Then his memory clicked. This was the hot dog vendor who had worked in front of Grand Central Station in New York. Erec remembered his name at once—Gerard. He was the one who had let Erec and Bethany into the underground F.E.S. station that led them to Alypium for the first time.

"I don't know." Gerard was working for Baskania, that was clear. But Erec didn't have to be afraid of getting turned in. He was on his way to go offer his services to the Shadow Prince anyhow. Gerard's hand began to pull back on the lever. "I mean, I'm here to help the Shadow Prince. I've learned a few things and I want to talk to him."

Gerard frowned. "Hmm. So you're going in dere, then? On yer own? I could . . ." He looked around. "Announce you. I think I will. Just to be safe, ya know."

"Go ahead." Erec smiled. "Whatever you like."

Spartacus said, "It's been two hours since we saw Rosco, so we should go in now."

Gerard spoke into a speaker, stating that Erec Rex was entering Baskania's headquarters. Erec, feeling like a fly walking straight into a spiderweb, pulled open one of the big ornate doors of *La Place des Yeux du Monde*.

La Place des Yeux du Monde was beautiful and somber at the same time. Stone and dark wood covered the walls, ornate tapestries hung in deep colors, and heavy velvet curtains swathed the windows. Erec recognized Baskania's blind servants scurrying in and out. They wore black cloaks with hoods over their heads, following orders day and night.

"This way." Spartacus led Erec through a few dark corridors to a bank of elevators. "Top floor."

Erec tried pressing the button that led to the penthouse office suite, but it was locked. "We can't get up there."

Spartacus cracked a grin. "You're with me, kid. You can go anywhere."

THE SECRET OF ASHONA

They took the elevator to the highest floor, then walked into a lush hallway connecting multiple business suites. People in designer suits bustled by, sporting leather briefcases and gold watches. They all looked important and busy; no blind servants were anywhere to be seen in this area.

"Ready?" Spartacus took hold of Erec's shoulders.

"I—" Before Erec could respond, he was whizzing down the hallway to a locked door. A few people glanced at Erec, surprised, as he sped by, floating. Erec grinned apologetically.

Spartacus popped through the door and unlocked it from the other side, opening it for Erec. "Right this way."

Erec followed him up five flights of steps to another locked door on top. Spartacus slid right through it, and then back again. "Hmm. Just a moment."

While Erec waited, his stress level grew until his stomach began to burn. He felt like he was ready to jump out of his skin. What was he doing here? This was insane. Every time he saw Baskania, the man tried to kill him. The last time he was with him it was clear that he would stop at nothing for Erec's eyes and his scepter. Which— Erec shuddered to remember—he very well might end up giving to Baskania. He had regretted doing this before, why did he think it would be any different now?

The Fates, he kept telling himself. The Aitherpoint quill. It couldn't have given him the wrong advice, could it? What if it did? Erec panicked. Was it too late? Suddenly it seemed this was clearly the wrong thing to do. He turned around, stomach in knots, and ran down the steps.

Moments later, he was sailing right back up again.

"Spartacus! Put me down. I changed my mind."

"Not on my watch. We haven't come all this way just for you to chicken out."

"This is crazy, though! What was I thinking? I have to get out of here, fast, before it's too late."

"It *is* too late. I've given you my soul. . . ."

Erec thought a moment about what Spartacus was saying. He had forgotten why he was here. He was free for only one reason, and he wasn't done with his quest yet. All of those souls were apart from their spirits and suffering. Erec was lucky to be breathing now—this was not the time to be selfish. "You're right. I'm sorry. Let's do this."

Spartacus had found the keys to the stairwell. Erec strode through, following the ghost to an enormous door at the end of a long hallway.

"This is it." Spartacus pointed. "It's unlocked. You better walk in first. It's less likely I'll be noticed then."

"Okay." Erec tried to put together what he would say to Baskania. He was terrified. Anything that came out of his mouth would sound ridiculous. Like, "Hey, it's me again. I've changed my mind, and now I think you're the best. Want my eyes now?" He would have to think of a reason for him to change—maybe visiting the Furies . . .

Well, it was too late to go back, no matter what would happen. "Here goes." He pushed open the heavy door and walked inside.

THE SECRET OF ASHONA

CHAPTER SIXTEEN

A Visit to the Enemy

CANDLELIGHT FLICKERED ALL around the huge room, along with hundreds more candles in chandeliers hanging from the ceiling. Burnished gold covered the walls, which were decorated with ornate paintings taken from museums. Baskania sat behind a huge mahogany desk. A man in a business suit was speaking to him about marketing Eye of the World. Two others nervously shifted in their shoes as he spoke. A pair of blind followers waited patiently at the side of the room. Rosco stood next to Baskania's desk, arms crossed, listening to the marketing presentation. He tapped his toe impatiently.

As the consultant continued to speak, oblivious to Erec's presence, Baskania slowly rose. All of the five eyes across his forehead bored into Erec's. When Erec had been a spirit he could sense when Baskania had tried to read his mind. Now he could not feel it, but it was easy to tell that's what Baskania was trying to do. He wanted to know why Erec was back.

Two eye patches now rested on Baskania's face. He had obviously removed both his original eyes for Erec's dragon eyes. Erec cringed. How would he ever get out of here without giving them right back to Baskania? This vision may be the last he ever had.

"Erec Rex." Baskania smiled pleasantly, a sharp tinge in his voice. "Fancy seeing you here. I rather thought you were in my Hinternom, learning how to be a good Spirit Warrior for your new master. But it seems that every time I think you are taken care of, you surprise me." His five eyes narrowed. "And look at that. You have your dragon eyes back again as well. How lucky. I assume you have my scepter, too? Well, it's kind of you to come return them to me." He waved an arm and a silver net fell over Erec. He recognized it as the one that captured ghosts.

Now was time for the best acting job of Erec's life. "I'm not a spirit anymore." Well, that much was true at least.

Baskania frowned. "Good try, little Erec. But unfortunately for you I'm not a simpleton. You obviously think I'll just remove the net and let you fly away."

"Why would I fly away if I just got here? I came to see you on my own, didn't I? And I'm alive again. See for yourself."

"If you were alive I'd be able to read your mind. So that's not the case." But he got up and touched Erec's head, felt the pulse in his neck. "What is this? How did you come back to life again?"

Erec detected a note of fear in Baskania's voice and he congratu-
lated himself. "The Furies helped me. I got my life back, but they
warned me that I would become a completely different person than I
was before. I agreed, but it was true. Now I look at things in a whole
new way."

"Good job!" Spartacus slapped him on the back. Even though
Erec knew nobody else could hear Spartacus, it was hard not to feel
shaken, like others might notice. Erec wished that he would stay
quiet.

"Go on." Baskania waited, interested.

"I'm here to work with you. I hope you'll take me after what
happened between us before. I'm happy to do whatever you want. It
would be great if you don't kill me, because I have some powers that
could really help you now. I'd like to do the best for you that I can."

The Shadow Prince's eyes bored into him. "Why can't I read your
mind anymore?"

"I don't know. I think it has to do with being a spirit and coming
back to life. Or something that the Furies did. I'm not sure." He tried
to look innocent. "Sorry for barging in. I just wanted you to know
that things are going to be very different now."

Baskania's words resounded fierce, uncontrollable. "Where is the
scepter? I need it back."

Erec had no idea what he was supposed to do. The quill had told
him to serve Baskania. Wouldn't that mean giving the scepter to him?
He had even seen a vision of himself doing just that . . . but there was
no way he could ever let that happen. Was he supposed to, though?
He couldn't! Erec froze in indecision, then he made a choice. He was
here, like he was supposed to be. But he would never hand over his
scepter. Never. "The Furies took it. It was part of my trade to come
back to life again."

Baskania slammed his fists down on the table and screamed,

"You *idiot*! You have ruined everything. That scepter was the most powerful of all three, and I *want it back*!"

Erec lowered his head, secretly glad. "I'm sorry, master. I'll do everything I can to get it back for you."

Baskania perked up. "Do you know a way?"

"No. But I might be able to find one. The Furies seem to like me enough to make trades for things." He wasn't sure where this track would lead him, but he wouldn't mind taking some of Baskania's precious possessions. It would serve him right after taking so much from other people.

"Get out of here." Baskania waved the men in suits from the room. His blind followers loped out behind them.

"Mind if I stay?" Rosco cocked an eyebrow. "I'm not so sure I believe this kid. I think he's faking."

"What?" Spartacus was incredulous. "Is Rosco turning on us now?" He gave Rosco a hard slap on the back. Rosco bounced forward, and coughed hard to cover up his sudden motion. Erec gave Spartacus a dirty look.

"I agree," Baskania said. "Something is fishy here. But I do like what I'm hearing." He thought a moment. "So, you're willing to give me your dragon eyes, then?"

"I am." Erec smiled. "That's why I came. To help you in any way. I figured you'd want my eyes, to start. But if it's okay with you, I'd like to keep them a little longer."

Baskania laughed, and Rosco joined in, chuckling. "That's a good one. You'd like to keep your eyes, just like everybody else. What you want doesn't count, though. Remember?"

"That's not it." Erec tried not to sound desperate. "I need them for a while so I can help you more. To do things I couldn't do for you if I was blind."

"What would that be?" Baskania sounded amused. "I can't

imagine what you could do that anyone else working here could not."

Erec thought hard. "The Furies. I need to use my dragon eyes to be able to see them. And if you wanted me to try to trade things to get your scepter back . . ." He hoped that Baskania could not tell that he was completely lying.

Baskania rubbed his chin. "You need your dragon eyes in order to speak with the Furies again? What if I just talked to them myself?"

"They don't like you. Pardon me, master, for I think they are fools. But they believe that you were trying to take advantage of them in the past. You were going to release them from Tartarus, but only if they gave you what you wanted. They do not want to talk to you. In fact, if you approach them, they will destroy you."

"Well, then." Baskania looked alarmed, and then excited. He rubbed his hands together and sat down at his desk. "It looks like I have a few choices to make. If I kill you now, I get both of your dragon eyes. I may never see the scepter again. If I trust you to serve me, I may get the scepter back and the dragon eyes. Or you may escape and I will end up with neither."

"Why would I escape if I came here on my own?"

"That is another question I ask myself. You may be here to steal something."

"What would I want? If I was going to steal from you, I can't imagine I'd come offer you my eyes, anyway. It's up to you if you want to take them now or wait and let me try to get your scepter first."

"One thing will make it easy to trust you. I'll allow you to keep your eyes for a short while, until you attempt to get my scepter back from the Furies. But you must sign them away to me now. That will guarantee that I will get them, one way or the other. Will you do that?"

"Of course." Erec gulped. This was terrible. Was this really what he was supposed to do?

"Okay, then." The Shadow Prince produced a sheet of paper by waving his fingers over his desk. He tapped it a few times with a quill, and then signaled Erec to come over. "Sign here." He pointed to a line at the bottom of the page.

Erec reached for the quill, and the thing jerked back in the air and stabbed his index finger.

"Sign it with your blood, Erec."

Erec trembled inside. He tried not to show his feelings. Was this blood oath going to be the end of him? Was this going to brainwash him to become the person he saw in his future?

But he set his finger over the page and signed his name with his dripping blood.

"Good." Baskania patted the page, satisfied.

Erec assessed himself. *Have I changed? Do I want Baskania to have my scepter, now?* He was relieved that he did not feel any different. "How does this work?"

"It's simple. You've given your eyes to me. All I have to do is claim them and they will be with me immediately."

"Will that . . . hurt? Will they just get yanked out?"

"Hmm . . . I never really thought about that. I guess we'll have to see."

Spartacus growled, "He's thinking that it will hurt you more this way, and he's glad about it. I'm half tempted to dump one of those flower pots over his head."

"Don't!" Erec shook his head. Baskania looked at him, suspicious, and Erec's heart started thumping. He thought fast. "Don't take my eyes that way, by claiming them like that. Just let me know when you want them and I'll come to you."

"That depends, I suppose," Baskania mused. "How soon can you get the scepter to me? Can you go see the Furies tomorrow?"

Erec did not know the reason for his being here, but it seemed that one day was not enough time. Plus, now he had a chance to find Bethany's brother, with Rosco's help.

Rosco was silent, but watched Erec intently. Erec wished that he would say something, to try to fix things. But he understood that Rosco needed to appear like a bystander, and not raise suspicion.

"I can't go tomorrow." Erec cleared his throat, thinking. "The Furies won't talk to me again that soon. They said I could come back in a week." As soon as he said that he cringed. Why hadn't he given himself longer to find Bethany's brother, and do whatever the Fates wanted him to do? At the same time, he did not want to stay here at all. A week would feel like forever with Baskania breathing down his neck.

Rosco looked surprised, but then frowned suspiciously. "I don't know about this. I'm not sure I would trust this kid for a second unsupervised around here. We should find someone to watch him like a hawk, make sure that he doesn't get into anything."

Baskania's mouth curved into a smile. "Good idea, Rosco. I take that as an offer. Erec, you are to remain at Rosco's side for the entire week. One week from today you shall return to the Furies with whatever objects I decide to give you as a fair trade, and reclaim my scepter for me. After that, I will take your dragon eyes, and you may remain on as a servant here, or in Jakarta."

That sounded horrendous. Erec was glad that Baskania could not read his mind. He had one week left—at least he would be with Rosco during that time. If only he knew what he was supposed to be doing that would help him free those captured souls. That was the reason he was here to begin with. . . .

Rosco sighed. "No problem, sire. I suppose I could use him while he's here. I'm going to crack down on those fools that are trying to find Bethany Cleary's brother. Erec here can do some of the work. Wouldn't it be a nice irony for him to hand his girlfriend's brother over to you."

Baskania nodded. "Nice touch, Rosco, as usual. Make sure he

doesn't leave your sight until next week." He turned his attention to a stack of papers on his desk.

In a second, Erec's surroundings changed to a spacious room with an overstuffed couch and ornate chairs. Beautiful framed paintings covered the walls and woven rugs were underfoot. Erec recognized the place as Rosco's apartment. With relief, he sank into the cushions on the couch and hugged a pillow to his chest.

Rosco sat next to him. "You going to be okay? That was pretty rough."

"I think so. I don't have much time here, though, and I don't even know what I'm supposed to be doing."

"Let's assume that the Fates know better than we do. It seems they like to put you in the right place, at the right time, so the right things will happen."

"Yeah, but that's what is so confusing. Say they wanted me to be alone in Baskania's fortress with him now? What if I wasn't supposed to have called you?"

"It's too late to worry about that now. But the Fates know how you handle things, so it's probably not a mistake." He shrugged. "Well, you have a week. Why don't you rest up today. Tomorrow morning we'll talk to the group searching for Bethany's brother."

Erec nodded, trying not to think about what the end of the week held in store for him.

After a breakfast of cheese omelets and toast, magically made by Rosco, Erec felt like a new person. Sure, things were bad, but they could be worse, right? Even if Baskania took both of his dragon eyes, there must be a way, through some spell, that Erec could regain his sight again. Everything seemed possible in the Kingdoms of the Keepers. It would be scary if Baskania was able to see into the future, but at least he would never have the scepter. Nothing could make Erec give that to Baskania, and even if he became hypnotized somehow, Rosco and Spartacus would make sure it didn't happen. During this week he would figure things out. . . .

"So, are you ready to go to Jakarta? That's where the Erec Rex headquarters is."

"Erec Rex headquarters? Wow, that makes me feel important."

"Oh, you are very important to the Shadow Prince. You know, by sauntering into his office and offering him everything he's always wanted, you've made him a very happy guy."

"I'll meet you there. Nice to tell me where you're going this time," Spartacus said, even though Rosco couldn't hear him.

Rosco snapped his fingers, and the setting around Erec and him changed again in a flash. Erec had been standing in Rosco's kitchen popping raisins into his mouth, and all of a sudden he was in a busy hallway with soldiers rushing past.

"Sorry about that." Rosco noticed Erec's shock. "It's a lot easier to get around this way than using a Port-O-Door."

"I can't believe how good you are at magic now." Erec remembered when Oscar could not do the simplest things. That is until his tutor, Rosco—his future self—taught him everything he knew.

Rosco shrugged. "I've had a lot of time to practice. Follow me— this is the way to the E.R.H.Q: the headquarters all about you and Bethany. I used to spend a lot of time here."

Erec did not want to think about what Rosco might have been doing in the past, before he considered Erec a friend again. They went down a short side hall into a large room with high ceilings and oak paneling. Shelves of books lined the walls. Researchers and typists occupied rows of tables, and agents in long cloaks wandered in and out.

"May I help you?" A woman glanced up from a glass desk by the door. "Oh, hello, Rosco, and . . ." She looked at Erec in shock. "You brought . . ." She held a hand out and stood. "I can't believe it.

Stay right there." She picked up a phone. "You need to come down immediately. Rosco is here with *Erec Rex*. . . . No, the real Erec Rex—the boy, himself . . . I'm not joking, he's standing in front of me, right here. . . . No, he's not doing anything. He's just waiting with Rosco. . . . Yes . . . Yes . . . Thank you."

A tall man with short-cropped brown hair dashed into the room. His sparkling green eyes grew wide when he saw Erec. "I . . . Why are you . . ." He turned to Rosco in shock. "Did you bring him here?"

"No," Rosco cracked, "he brought me. Erec Rex decided to offer himself up to us, just to help a bit. Isn't that nice?"

The man looked back and forth between Rosco and Erec, not believing his ears. "Are you . . . serious? I don't understand. Does the Shadow Prince know that he is here? I mean, we have to alert him, *now*."

"Of course he knows, Noj. This is our new project, here. We only get to keep him for one week. Then the Shadow Prince has other plans for him. But I wasn't joking. Erec Rex has changed his mind about things . . . with a little help." He chuckled wickedly.

Noj looked too nice to be working for Baskania. "Um . . . that's great. Wow. I, uh . . . come on in and sit down. Can you talk a minute? I never thought I'd have this opportunity. Can I hear what made you decide to help us?"

Erec and Rosco followed Noj into a comfortable study. Noj gave Erec a soft drink and pulled out a tray of cheese and crackers. He sounded excited. "This is a huge treat. I mean, I've been leading our teams here, studying about you for years. And with all that's happened lately we've made a lot of headway against the enemy." He looked embarrassed. "I mean . . . I guess you're not the enemy anymore. I don't know. . . . How did it happen? This seems so unlikely. I mean great—but unlikely."

Erec laughed. "I agree. Believe me, helping Baskania destroy the world is the last thing I could see myself doing."

A look of recognition crossed Noj's face, and he looked at Rosco with a smile. "Okay, so he's not perfect. I always heard that he twists things around like that. I can see how he could con people who didn't have their guard up." Noj looked at Erec with suspicion.

"Great job, Erec." Spartacus laughed. "You better keep your ideas to yourself here."

"Tell me about it." Rosco grimaced at Noj, rolling his eyes. "Kid's a barrel of laughs. He got his soul back from the three Furies—you know he gave it to them last spring. And now he's a different person. He's sensible. But you can't tell all the time from talking to him." Rosco winked. "We thought it would be perfect if he brings his girlfriend's lost brother to us. Maybe he'll have some information. Where are you at with that now?"

"Spinning our wheels, I'm afraid." Noj shifted in his chair. "We've found out that Ruth Cleary, Bethany's mother, did indeed have another baby after Pi and Bethany. This was not too long before the Shadow Prince cleaned out all the evil influences from King Piter's castle."

Evil influences? Erec wondered if Noj truly believed that killing Bethany's parents and the palace guards was "cleaning out evil influences." And also putting King Piter under a spell, and making Erec, his mother, and his triplet siblings disappear.

"So," Rosco pressed on, "the baby was born about eleven years ago, then. What happened to him?"

"Unknown. His parents were disposed of during the cleanout, Pi Cleary was raised by an aunt, and Bethany was watched by Early Evirly, raised as his niece. The Shadow Prince planned to use her as a seer, like her mother was, once she was older. Erec here messed that plan up. But nobody knows what happened to the baby. The Clearys did not have a lot of close friends. They spent most of their time in the castle. And even the people who knew the baby then have no idea what happened to it that day."

"Hmm." Rosco rubbed his chin. "Any leads?"

"Only one." Noj pointed to Erec. "Him."

For a moment Erec's fists clenched in panic. *He* was Bethany's brother? That wasn't possible. He had kissed her—

Then he realized that it couldn't be him—he was fourteen, not eleven. They had different fathers.

Rosco frowned. "What do you mean? You think he knows something? Or he's hiding the brother?"

"Nope. But he might remember something."

Erec shook his head. "Sorry to disappoint you, but I have no memories at all from that time of my life. I found out that my memory was removed—" He instantly shut his mouth before saying any more. The last thing he wanted this group to find out was that he had a memory floating around out there somewhere. . . .

"Exactly." Noj slapped his hand on the table. "Your memory was removed when you were young, as was Bethany's. We haven't been able to locate hers anywhere, but we do have a strong lead now on yours."

A lead on his memory? A mix of excitement and fear welled up in him. If anyone else found his memory, they would know about his missing siblings. Maybe they would find clues about where they were now. Erec needed to get it back first. He tried to look casual. "Where do you think it is?"

"We traced the Memory Mogul's records. Unfortunately they're messy and incomplete. But he took notes sometimes on the people he sold to. Yours went to a boy about your age. We don't have an address or any other identification—the Memory Mogul just jotted down what interested him about certain sales—but it narrows the search a bit. We're scouring high schools throughout the Kingdoms, as well as checking sporting teams, boys' magic clubs, or anything else that a kid might be involved in. Our team is checking every-where to see if anyone heard of a kid who remembers things about Erec Rex. It's amazing the ground we've covered. . . ."

Erec was stunned. How could he beat those efforts? "How many people are tracking my memory down?"

"There are about seventy detectives out there now. It's going to take time, but we're confident that we'll find something."

Rosco asked, "What about Bethany's memory?"

"No luck at all with those sales records. We're still asking around all of the high schools, just in case. But it could have gone to a boy or girl of any age—someone that might be in college or older now. It's going to be a lot harder to track without a starting point."

"I had a small piece of Bethany's memory," Erec said. "It was only a few hours long, after most of it was already taken out. Nothing much was in it." He knew there was nothing in that memory that would be of importance.

"You have some of her memory?" Noj lit up, excited.

"Not anymore. The Nightmare King took it."

Noj shuddered. "Is that guy for real? I thought that was just a story to scare kids." He bit his lip. "Well, I hate to do it, but I guess we'll have to send a few of our people out to talk to the Nightmare King. I'm sure the Shadow Prince can get us in." He looked at Erec skeptically. "If the guy exists."

"He does, but I wouldn't send people there. It was just a tiny memory."

Noj marked a few things on his paper, looking tired. Rosco appeared bored. "So, that's the plan, Noj? Just keep searching high schools? Is there anywhere else that kids his age might have gone? Especially someone who remembers what it's like being Erec Rex when he's little?"

An alarm sounded in Erec's head. He wanted to jump up, shout, dance around. It was all clear to him at once. There *was* someplace where a lot of kids his age got together once. The contests, last summer in Alypium. Kids from all three Kingdoms were there. Only that wasn't all. Something stood out to him now. He was amazed that he had not thought of it before. When he was there, he had not asked if any boy had his old memory. However . . . there was a kid who basically told him that he did. Someone who walked around telling everyone that he was the real Erec Rex, that he remembered everything. Erec, and everybody else, had thought that the boy was a crackpot. But now it made sense. This must be the kid who had his memory.

Rosco and Erec exchanged a glance. Erec signaled toward the door. He wanted to grab Rosco and run out of there, find this kid. What had the boy looked like? What was his name?

"Well." Rosco stretched his arms, then yawned. "I'm going to grill this kid some more, see if I can get anything out of him."

Noj laughed. "I'm sure the Shadow Prince read his mind already, so there won't be much good to that."

Rosco snapped his fingers. He and Erec appeared back in his apartment again. Erec fell back onto the same couch and spilled his thoughts to Rosco.

"I think I remember that guy, too, now that you mention him," said Rosco. "The one who went around telling everyone he was Erec Rex. He was a strange one. His name was Connor, right? White hair and dark eyes?"

Connor! "That's it! I saw him around a few times after the contest. He worked in a pet store for a while . . . and then I saw him at Paisley Park once."

Rosco nodded. "He hung out around Alypium, too, when I was sneaking around as Oscar Felix. We better find him quick, before anyone else does."

Spartacus flew through the wall of Rosco's apartment. He

THE SECRET OF ASHONA

hung himself by his collar off of a hook on the fireplace mantel and crossed his arms. "Don't bother taking me along when you go. I'm just supposed to protect and watch out for you, but it's not worth your effort to actually be considerate or include me when you go somewhere."

"I'm sorry—I'm sure Rosco just forgot you were there. But I'm glad you came." Erec wondered if Spartacus was really annoyed at traveling by himself, or more jealous that he wasn't involved in what was going on.

Rosco appeared confused, then a look of recognition and then fear crossed his face. He started to speak, but before words came out, he clutched his chest. His head bent, face squeezed into a knot. With a look of pain, his hands shot to his ears as if his head was about to burst. Then he leaned his head back, mouth open, and made a sound as if he was gargling liquid. Erec was terrified that something horrible was happening to him. Rosco's eyes looked like they would pop out of his head, and the gargle noise turned into a scream and then finally a long, earsplitting howl.

When Rosco howled, Erec felt a tugging in his chest. He needed to move, to go see Baskania right away. It wasn't clear why, but there seemed to be no choice. Something inside was calling him. . . .

"Sorry." Rosco looked embarrassed. "I try to resist howling back when Baskania calls. I've been practicing, but so far I can't stop it." He looked intently at the floor, gathering himself together. "I have to see the Shadow Prince right now. He wants me."

"I do too." Erec stood. "He's commanded me to come to him."

Rosco looked confused. "I don't understand. He hasn't given you the howl—only his most trusted inner circle is that connected to him. And he can't transport you to him if he can't see you. He can't make you want to come, either. I don't get it. . . . Has he found some way to influence you?"

Erec paced the room, antsy to see Baskania as he was commanded. As the feeling grew, he remembered the pill that he took in the Hinternom, and he told the story to Rosco. "He must be calling me to his service."

"The Shadow Prince is playing with you," Rosco said. "That's his style. He asked me to bring you anyway—that would have been good enough. But he likes to remind people what power he wields over them, so he commanded you this way also. He's probably testing, too, to see how well it works. . . ."

"I don't want him to know that he had any effect on me at all. Then he'll do it again and again."

"Exactly." Rosco thought a moment. "How bad is it? I mean, you're still standing here. I admit, after the howl I'm going nuts needing to get to him. It gets worse the longer I wait—but I'm pretty good at resisting. I've timed myself and gone a full ten minutes once before I couldn't take it anymore."

"I have no idea how long I could last. It's not as bad as a cloudy thought, though. With those I pretty much just do what I'm commanded without thinking about it. The Furies said the pill would only affect my spirit, but not my body or soul. I'm dying to do what he says, but I could fight it off—at least for now."

"We can't let him know he has any control at all over you." Rosco rubbed his hands together. "I've got it. I'm going there now—alone. I'll tell him that I was going to bring you, but you were resting, trying to remember things to help us. I'll say that we agreed that I would come back and get you in a while."

Erec nodded. "Make it quick, though. If I have to wait too long I just might start walking to Baskania from here."

"Don't worry. I'll keep an eye on you," Spartacus said. "Look." He hopped down, pulled one of his eyes out, and rested it on Erec's head.

"Ugh! I didn't know you could do that. Put it back."

Rosco looked at him strangely. "Do what?"

"Nothing. Just Spartacus."

Rosco shuddered. "I'll be back soon."

It was hard for Erec to hold still. The craving to see Baskania was overwhelming, like resisting food if he was about to die of starvation.

"You're doing great," Spartacus said. "I get the feeling that if I was commanded by Baskania I would have no choice at all but to follow orders."

Rosco appeared, midstride, and walked across the room as if he had been there all along. "Success. The Shadow Prince wasn't happy that his pill didn't work on you. You shouldn't have had any choice at all." Rosco clapped his hands together. "I bet he's not going to bother using it now. But he wants us for a dinner meeting in the Inner Sanctum. Lucky you—you're getting taken into the group."

Erec rolled his eyes. "Just what I've always wanted. Should Spartacus come?"

At the same time, Rosco answered, "Probably not," and Spartacus said, "You couldn't keep me away if you tried."

Erec decided to let Spartacus do as he chose and stay out of it.

CHAPTER SEVENTEEN

The Spider Boy

GLEAMING GOLD plates and thick silver cutlery adorned the long, polished oak table. Gems in the table were inlayed in intricate designs, and its legs were carved into ornate scrolls and gargoyles. Heavy pewter mugs beaten into waffle patterns sat beside thick-cut crystal goblets that thinned to impossibly delicate tops.

Seated at the table, in a room lit by hundreds of candles, were generals, business executives, and politicians. Erec recognized Jesper Konungsson, the president of the United Nations, from a news story about a horrible accident that his wife and daughter had gotten in. At the head of the table sat Baskania, King Pluto, and Washington Inkle—the president of Alypium. Two seats beside him were for Rosco and Erec.

Erec could not believe that he was in the Inner Sanctum, Baskania's headquarters in the Green House in Alypium. Was it possible that Baskania truly trusted him now? Probably not completely. But Erec was getting the respect Baskania gave to his closest advisors. He knew it was this kind of attention from Baskania that turned his friend Oscar into the Rosco Kroc who ended up doing so many horrible things before realizing the truth.

Baskania waved them into the empty chairs. Instantly, blind servants rushed to each seat and placed more soups, salads, and appetizers on the table than could possibly be eaten.

"So glad you are joining us." Baskania tilted his head to Erec cordially. "I have some good news. After thinking it over, I've decided to bring you in at a higher level than I originally planned. Although I admit it would be greatly pleasing to see the famous Erec Rex as one of my blind servants, it strikes me that you have more to offer. The courage and strength that you have shown so far in coming here is not to be taken lightly. No, you will be far more to me than just a trophy. I have offered you power before, and now I'm going to give it to you.

"First of all, you will keep your sight. It won't be hard to remove the dragon eyes from the backs of your own. This way I will be able to give you back one of your eyes, for you to use. Of course, as with all of my followers, I will keep the other so that I can see what you are seeing and thinking if I need to."

Erec bit his tongue, suddenly afraid. If Baskania had his eye and could read his mind he would be in immediate danger. But, then again, the Furies had made that impossible.

Baskania looked pleased. "Second—and you may like this even

better than keeping your eyesight—I plan to give you a scepter to use. It will be Queen Posey's, not the one that you will be returning to me from the Furies. But I liked what I saw when you wielded it before. I believe that its power will make you become a stronger person. More like me."

Erec nodded. He was sure that a scepter would make him more like Baskania—he would instantly be a selfish, power-hungry maniac. But still, Erec could not help feeling honored. Of all the people here, *he* was the one that Baskania chose to give Queen Posey's scepter to? Not Balor Stain? Looking around, Erec realized that the Stain triplets had not even been invited here. They were just pawns, he realized. Erec was more than that, though. Baskania seemed to look up to him. Erec wondered if Baskania had Posey's scepter already, or if it was still in Ashona and he was controlling it from here.

"Thank you." Erec was not sure how much he was acting, and how much he truly felt appreciative. "I am honored to serve you, master." He bowed his head.

"Excellent. Now, let's hear the reports on the battle preparations."

A heavily decorated general with bushy gray eyebrows and whiskers stood. "Sire. Events are progressing as planned. Our army has tripled, and we continue to add Spirit Warriors and monsters into our reserves, waiting to be called into action. We are gearing up for the attack. And, I'm pleased to say, more good news has surfaced—Tarvos has managed to activate his Golem warriors. I have no idea how he did it, but he found a Master Shem. The deal you offered to release him from captivity if he used his military for you is a go. His Golems will decimate Otherness, and then Upper Earth, once you are ready to unleash them."

Erec's heart stopped. This was why Tarvos needed the Master Shem? And Erec had been the one to hand it to him?

What a fool he had been. If only he had thought things through. There might have been another way for him to rescue Trevor. He had not even bothered to find out what Tarvos's plan was. But then again the Fates had told him it was the only way to save his brother. . . .

A man in a long white lab coat stood and dusted himself off. His hair fluffed out in all directions, and his wire glasses were as thick as soda bottles. "May I speak, your specialness?"

"Yes, Swerdley. I'm looking forward to your research. Please go ahead."

Swerdley bowed multiple times, upon the last of which he hit his head against the wooden table. "Oops! Um . . . sorry there. Anyhoo, I've perfected the mind-control concoction, Your Princeliness. And I've created five delicious flavors for it. Bubble gum, watermelon, fried snake, raspberry, and chocolate. So many treats we can make with this—and feed it to all the people!" He rubbed his hands together in anticipation. "Nobody will be able to resist its flavors. And once they eat, they will be yours to command forever!"

Erec's stomach dropped. Baskania was now planning to mind-control people all over the place by feeding them magic-injected foods? That was disgusting!

Baskania rubbed his hands together. "Wonderful news. Everything is coming together now." He turned to Erec. "I do believe I have you to thank for most of it—especially getting my scepter back for me."

Erec felt sick. Baskania owed him even more than that, down to handing Tarvos the Master Shem. "Thank you, master."

Baskania took a sip of tea. Erec noticed that he did not eat much. "I have decided what you can give to the Furies for me, in exchange for the scepter. There is something I have that they would want. The Furies can do anything—almost. But they, too, have their limits." He pulled out a thick book bound in black leather. "This will give them the power to do more. It is an ancient spell book. Nothing fancy. Many of its incantations are for things so simple that Washington here could do them." He gestured to President Inkle, who blushed uncomfortably.

"But there are a few special spells in this book. One of them will be of great interest to the Furies."

Everyone at the table leaned forward in their seats, anticipating what kind of spell the Shadow Prince might be referring to. But instead of explaining, he simply handed Erec the book and said, "Page four hundred twenty-two."

"Thank you." Erec rested the book on his lap, under a napkin. What could page four hundred twenty-two offer that the Furies could not already achieve? Erec was dying to find out.

"Woo-hoo-hoo!" Spartacus danced above the table. "I can't wait to get a load of that one! Good job, Erec. Hey, do you think I should dump one of those thick, pink drinks on Baskania's head? That would be a lot of fun. . . ."

Erec glared at the ghost and shook his head. He was in no mood for Spartacus's jokes now. Baskania looked at him with interest. "I wish I could read your mind, boy. Tell me what you are thinking."

Erec gulped. Darn that Spartacus! "I was just wondering what I'm going to do if the Furies tell me that the spell book isn't enough to trade for the scepter."

"I see. That is possible, I suppose, although I can't imagine what else they could want. . . ." He thought a moment, finger to his lips. Then a smile crossed his face. "I know. The Furies like to collect souls. How about if I give them a few spares? You'll bring fifty spirits with you from the Hinternom, and we'll let the Furies enjoy them."

Erec was horrified. Make more spirits lose their souls like he had? Erec knew how horrible it was to go through, how doomed each of those spirits would feel. "Actually I think the book will be fine. Let's wait on those spirits and see."

"I don't want to wait." Baskania slapped his hand on the table. "Never second-guess me again, Erec. I will have the souls prepared for you next week when you go."

"Good one." Spartacus slapped Erec on the back at Rosco's house. "You've created fifty more specters, with just a few words to Baskania."

THE SECRET OF ASHONA

"Don't remind me. I feel awful about it," Erec said. "But I won't let that happen to those spirits. I'm the one who will be bringing them to see the Furies. I just won't tell the Furies that the souls are for them."

Rosco looked around in the air, wondering where Spartacus was. "The Furies aren't dumb, Erec. Just because it's not as easy for them to read your mind in Alsatia doesn't mean they won't figure things out."

Erec had not thought of what he would say to the Furies when he went back—or even how he would get there. He didn't want to lose his life entering Alsatia. Maybe he'd fake that he went to see them, make up something. Of course, one of these days he would have to find a way to really visit them, when he was ready to release the souls.

Rosco took the book out of Erec's hands and laughed. "This is perfect. Of course Baskania wants to give this book to the Furies—he hates the thing. It reminds him of the one spell inside that I can do and he can't. Drives him crazy."

"You can do a spell that Baskania can't?" Erec was intrigued. "What is it?"

"It's the same one that the Furies can't do. Look on page four hundred twenty-two."

Erec flipped open the heavy, leather-bound book. Handwritten script embellished the yellowed and fraying pages. Some of the spells looked simple, such as splitting logs in two and burning twigs. Others were interesting, like conjuring spirits and persuading people to do things.

"This looks a little easy for Baskania," Erec said.

"Most of it is. He's a collector, though. And he's compulsive about it—every time he finds a spell book he makes sure that he can do everything inside of it. If not, then he learns the next trick quickly, so nobody has anything on him. Imagine—hundreds of years of constant learning. It's truly amazing."

Spartacus shoved a vase aside on a table and sat next to it, making Rosco jump. "Tell Rosco it sounds like he still looks up to the guy."

Erec repeated what Spartacus said, and Rosco nodded. "Of course I do. Nobody has dedicated themselves more to the study of magic than that sorcerer. He was born with a gift, and he didn't waste one shred of it. Of course, how he went about things was terrible. He's become completely corrupted. But there is no overlooking the eons he spent building his power and skills."

Erec found page four hundred twenty-two. On it, a detailed method was described about how to stop time. It involved mental preparation and an incantation. Erec remembered when Rosco had stopped time to save Erec from some snakelike police officers. He had probably also done it when he escaped from Balthazar Ugry. "Baskania can't do this?"

"Nope." A pleased smile spread over Rosco's face.

"So you're more talented than he is?"

"Not really." Rosco laughed. "This would be simple for the Shadow Prince normally. But it turns out that the Substance won't let him do it. The guy can get away with almost anything, but the Substance seems to have drawn a line in the sand with him there."

"Wow. I didn't know that the Substance was able to make decisions. Can it think by itself?"

"It seems so. People who are able to communicate with it—absorbent people—can actually ask it to do things for them."

"That's true. I've asked the Substance to tear apart and open up to make holes or cut a Substance Web open."

"Well, there you go. It knows what is going on. And for whatever reason, the Substance won't allow Baskania to stop time. Probably it realizes what havoc he'd create with that power."

"And the Furies can't stop time either? I thought they knew everything."

"Pretty much everything. Most things are simple to them. But they cannot stop time on their own, like their sisters, the Fates, can. It is possible that if they learn this incantation they could do it, though. The Furies have never had a need for incantations. But why should this work for a human and not someone as powerful as them? They don't even know they're missing this."

Everyone thought about what the Furies might do if they could stop time. Would they wipe out their sisters—the three Fates—completely?

Rosco walked into the kitchen to get a drink while Erec flipped through the book. "Look at this." He pointed to a page while Spartacus looked over his shoulder. "A body-morphing spell. How cool is that?"

The scrawled ink at the top of the page read:

Body Morphing—unlimited

You can change your form into anything you can imagine. Have you ever wanted to see life through the eyes of an orangutan? Be a fly on the wall during a conversation? Or maybe just spend some time recuperating as a stately oak tree on top of a hill? This simple incantation will let you be all you ever wanted to be. Many enjoy revisiting a second childhood or becoming exquisitely beautiful. Others take to the trail as a wild horse or soar over the wilderness in the form of an eagle.

The beauty of this spell is that it can be temporary or permanent, and you can change multiple times. But be careful! It is possible to die when you are in the form of any of these objects. If you become a worm, and you are stepped on, your death will be permanent. But injuries, while they will last in your altered state, will not carry over into your human form. Be careful what you choose to become!

Warning: Morphing into an inanimate object is possible, but will be irreversible.

"Is this true? . . . I could become anything at all?"

"It sounds like it." Spartacus pointed. "It says 'unlimited.'"

Erec grinned. "I've got it, then! I can use the spell to become a spirit. That way I'll be able to get in and out of Alsatia without dying on Mercy's Spike."

"Brilliant!" Spartacus jumped onto Rosco's table lamp and danced a jig. "I thought I was going to have to go there alone."

"I'll just learn this spell and change myself back and forth. Let's see if I can do it."

The lower part of the page read:

The following incantation should be memorized, and can be performed silently, in one's thoughts. After it is recited, simply think of whatever thing you want to become. Before you know it, you will see life in a whole new way!

ASARDEN HOLLOTO BEELTEN BOND
MEELIFRYING SOLBOTTO NACHTRHAND SORD
TIMLIN STARCHETSU NAGRATHWAY TIMRAND
WESTFAIL TIM LUM BEETRAND SORDV

To reverse the spell, simply recite the word "Nuiay"

At the bottom of the page were a number of provisos and explanations. This seemed perfect. "I'm going to try it out, and see if I can do it. What should I try to turn into?"

Spartacus shrugged. "I've always liked spiders. I guess it doesn't matter what you become since you can reverse it right away anyway."

"As long as I don't turn into a worm and get stepped on. No worms. And no inanimate objects." Erec hoped that he could pronounce the words correctly. "All I have to remember is how to reverse this, in case I can't read the spelling in my next form. That word is hard to say— would you call that 'nee-way'?"

"I suppose. It would be amazing if this works."

Erec took a breath and read from the book, *"Asarden holloto beelten bond, Meelifrying solbotto nachtrhand sord, Timlin starchetsu nagrathway timrand, Westfail tim lum beetrand sord."* A strange feeling filled the core of his body, as if something deep inside had melted and was bubbling like lava. What did he want to become again? Spartacus mentioned a *spider. . . .*

The ceiling above Erec shot toward the sky, and the room around him grew to massive proportions. Even Spartacus was huge now, bending onto his knee and searching for Erec on the floor. A strange feeling filled him, like a kind of a deep itch that was everywhere all at once. Could he move still? He tested an arm, but it didn't go in the right direction anymore.

When he looked down at himself, he jumped. Huge hairy steel-like legs shot out in all directions. They seemed hinged, as if he was a robotic contraption of some kind. He tried to walk. At first he fell onto his face—which was oddly attached to his back. But in a moment he got the hang of it. All of his extensions moved at once to transport him around.

So, this was what it was like to be a spider? Would he be able to spin a web? It was amazing how different spiders looked up close, from the right size. He was pretty fascinating. Erec would have to be careful never to step on one again. . . .

Spartacus tapped the ground in front of him with an enormous finger—one that could crush him in a heartbeat—and panic raced through Erec's small frame. Even though he knew that Spartacus would not hurt him, he could not stop himself from running in the other direction.

"It's okay, little buddy! I'm your old friend, Spartacus!"

Heavy footsteps fell, one after the other, heading in Erec's direction. A huge voice boomed, "Erec? Where did you go? I made us some snacks."

It was Rosco, and he was heading straight toward where Erec stood, exposed, in the middle of the floor.

"Wait!" Spartacus shouted at Rosco, forgetting that he could not be heard. "Don't step on that spider!"

Rosco stopped a foot away from Erec and glanced around the room. Electric fear raced through Erec's limbs, and he ran as fast as he could. Rosco noticed him then. "Darn spiders." He raised a foot and aimed at Erec.

Erec eyes moved upward and saw exactly what was about to happen. *No!* He tried to scream at Rosco to stop, but he could not make words form in his new shape.

"Stop!" Spartacus screamed, also unheard. He dove toward Erec, but Rosco was already in motion.

Erec darted sideways just as Rosco's foot smacked down on the floor, crashing into the wood next to him. It was all happening too fast. He ran one way and then the other, back and forth. Maybe that way he could throw Rosco off. One of his eyes shifted down to check out the wall. There was a crack not too far away, but he'd have to run as fast as he could . . .

Rosco's foot shot toward him, but Spartacus was ready. He

shoved Rosco back hard. Rosco tripped and fell onto the floor.

"Who . . . what?" Rosco looked around. "Was that you, Spartacus?"

Erec tried to get his wits about him. He had to turn back into himself fast before Rosco tried to crush him. What was the word again? All Erec had to do was say it in his head and it should work. . . . But how did he pronounce it? He tried thinking, *Nee-way.*

As soon as he thought the word, he felt a funny tingling inside of him again, just as when he first read the spell. This must be it, then! As bad as it had been as a spider, at least he had not turned into a *worm.* . . .

He could feel himself changing, but the room size did not shrink back to normal. What was wrong? Was he turning into a tiny version of his original self? This was horrible.

But then something worse happened—his vision disappeared completely. He could sense that there was light around him but could not make out any shapes. Had he accidentally turned into an inanimate object? That would be permanent!

He tried to move, hoping he could at least do something. With relief, he could feel himself stir, but it was not like anything he had ever experienced before. The floor was hard under his body, and he could sense every inch of himself turning and twisting on it. At least he wasn't frozen, but things were terribly wrong. He must have morphed into a blob—a formless object that wasn't able to function anymore.

With great effort, he pushed himself forward. Somehow the whole front of his body expanded, catapulting his head forward and leaving his back parts behind. When he could no longer stretch more, he pulled back in, this time bringing his behind in closer to his head. If he repeated this again and again he was actually able to move forward.

But how grotesque he must look! Like some kind of freakish, nasty flesh pile. Now how would he free the captive souls, finish his quests, or do anything at all? Even if he lived like this, what would Bethany think of him? He would never even be able to see her—and didn't want her seeing him like this. He felt like kicking himself, if he only had feet under control to do it with. Why had he tried using the spell book without asking Rosco? He obviously had not been ready.

Footsteps echoed louder now, and shook his whole body with the hard wood floor under it. "Spartacus, I don't know what you're up to, but you'd better not push me around like that. I'm trying to help Erec just like you are." The steps grew closer. "Where did that spider go?"

Erec was amazed that Rosco had not seen him yet. Even Spartacus didn't make any comments on his unusual shape.

Rosco said, "I'll be darned. The spider's gone, and now there's an earthworm here. What is this, the wilderness in here?"

There was shuffling, and then something heavy crushed hard into Erec's back end. It felt horrible—very wrong—though not exactly painful. When he tried to move, his hind parts were connected to the floor, as if he was stuck.

No . . . not just stuck. Smushed. He was the earthworm Rosco was talking about, and Rosco had just stepped on him.

With all of his energy, Erec flipped himself back and forth trying to set himself free. It was not working.

Spartacus's voice said, "Is that you, Erec . . . ? *No!* Stop, Rosco!"

Rosco was about to smash him again? Finish him off? There was nothing Erec could do. But he heard a crash, and Rosco said, "I mean it, Spartacus. Leave me alone!"

How had Erec turned into a worm? It didn't make sense. Had he thought of a worm before saying the spell word? But it was supposed to reverse the spell. Well, he thought, he better try it again. Things couldn't get much worse. *Nee-way,* he thought.

Nothing happened. This was crazy. Would he stay this way? It would have been worthwhile if he could have used the spell to become a *soul* so he could get into Alsatia. . . .

The room shrank, and Erec could see again. Spartacus was pacing, searching on the floor for him. Rosco was rubbing his head and getting up. "Where is that worm?"

But Erec still did not feel normal. He was cold, and lonely. Very alone. Fragile, like the air in the room was blowing through him. Not nice. It seemed as though he was all insides, missing his outer shell. Spartacus and Rosco seemed completely different now too. They both looked wonderful.

He rushed to Rosco first, grabbing him around the shoulders. Even though Erec's arms passed right through him, Erec was able to hold on somehow. He could not stand to be alone anymore. The feeling was too awful, like living without a skin.

Spartacus stared at him in shock. Rosco couldn't see him, but Spartacus was completely aware now. But Erec could see something in Spartacus that he had never noticed before. There was a hole inside of him. That was a space that was hurting him, Erec could tell. It needed something. . . . It needed . . . a soul.

Erec could help. He could fix it, and being there would take care of all of his problems too, cover him, warm his essence, and make him whole again. He had to go. . . .

In a second he glommed on to Spartacus. Spartacus must have felt as relieved as he did, because he clasped his hands over his heart and sighed. Erec felt so much better that it was a while before he could even think again.

But when he did, he had a vague idea what was going on. Spartacus needed a soul . . . and that's exactly what Erec had turned into. Now they were both happy. Maybe he should stay this way forever—it would solve Spartacus's problems. Maybe Erec didn't even have any choice in the matter. So far he had morphed into a spider, then a worm, and now a soul. Thinking, he realized that those were the exact things he had thought about after he said the incantation word.

Erec's heart sank. He had no idea what he was getting into with this spell. Maybe if he thought the word one more time, and then imagined turning back into his old self . . . but he hated leaving Spartacus soulless and miserable again. It was a horrible feeling—Erec remembered it well. And it would only get worse.

Maybe later, he told himself, he would return to help Spartacus like this. But he had too many things to do. It was time to try again. To be safe, he forced himself to move away from Spartacus, even though doing so was painful. *Nee-way. Think about my old self. Erec Rex.*

Erec appeared next to Spartacus. Rosco looked at him in shock. "Where did you go? I'm supposed to be keeping an eye on you, Erec. Don't scare me like that!"

"You almost killed me!" Erec realized he was panting, and tried to calm down. "That spider on the floor? It was me! And the worm, too! I almost died. . . ."

Spartacus added wistfully, "And the soul. Don't forget that."

It was hard to even think about being a soul—Spartacus's soul. Even though it had seemed so right at the time, it was completely strange. And now he felt a little guilty about leaving Spartacus as a specter again.

"I don't get it." Rosco walked over to the open spell book on the table and his jaw dropped. "You tried this morphing spell? And you made it work?" He shook his head in shock. "You must have some power in you, then. Connection to the Substance. Because this won't work for just anybody."

"Could you do it?" Erec asked.

"Sure, I could. There's not much I can't do. But I'm lucky—and I had a great teacher."

"Baskania?"

"Well, him too—but he wasn't the one I was thinking of. My first tutor seemed to know the right way to teach me everything."

Erec laughed, because Rosco's tutor was himself. He had gone back in time and found himself when he was young, become his own

THE SECRET OF ASHONA

tutor. "I wish you were my tutor too. The Hermit's okay, I guess, but he hasn't spent a lot of time with me, or taught me fun things—except for finger magic." He sighed. "I guess I shouldn't use spell books like this. It didn't work like it was supposed to. At the end when I thought, *Nee-way,* it was supposed to reverse the spell. But it didn't."

Rosco looked the handwritten page over, confused. "Nee-way?"

"Nee-way."

"That's not right. How were you saying that again?"

"Nee-way."

Rosco shook his head and scanned the page. Then he jumped, and screamed, *"No!"* He froze in terror, staring at Erec. "Don't say anything. Don't move. Just . . . stop." He waited, watching Erec expectantly.

Now Erec was confused. What was Rosco watching him for? It didn't make sense.

Rosco put his hands up. "Maybe you're okay. Maybe that last time—or the first time—it didn't take. . . ."

Before Erec could ask Rosco what he was talking about, a strange feeling filled his insides. It was the same gummy, bubbly feeling that he had when he morphed before, but this time it was stronger. What was happening now?

The room shot up around him, becoming huge again. Although he could not feel his body changing, he could see giant hairy jointed limbs jutting out from his sides again. How could this be happening—he was a spider again now? He looked up to see Rosco and Spartacus bent over him with amazement on their huge faces.

Erec tested out his legs and walked a few steps. Was he going to be stuck forever this way now? But then the bubbly feeling came back again and the room went dark. . . .

He was a blob again. An earthworm. And he could feel that his back end was still smushed. It was broken free from the floor now, though, so he could drag it along. Sitting still seemed worse than

stretching, moving. He was too exposed here . . . a moving target . . .
Someone might step on him. . . .

The feeling was back inside of him, and the room shrank again.
He was a soul—and there was Spartacus, an empty spirit needing a
soul. Without thinking, he rushed to Spartacus and became his soul,
made him a whole person again. It was a relief.

"Where did you go?" Rosco was looking all over the floor. Spartacus
did not bother answering, knowing that Rosco could not hear him.

But then the bubbly feeling returned and Erec was his normal
self again. He had not left Spartacus, but as the ghost was made of
vapor, he simply stepped out of Erec's space.

"What's happening to me?" Erec was terrified. "That spell really
messed me up. What if it happens again?"

"You said the wrong words." Rosco's hand was clapped over his
mouth.

Before he could say anything else, Erec morphed into a spider
again, then a smashed worm, and then a soul. It happened faster this
time, and was more disorienting. When he turned back into himself,
he started to speak, but then he crashed toward the floor as a spider
again. Spider—worm—soul—self—spider—worm—soul—self. The
changes flickered faster and faster until his parts seemed to be everywhere at once, blinking in and out of the room.

Finally, it stopped. Erec was himself again. Sick and exhausted, he
collapsed on Rosco's plush blue couch.

Rosco sat next to him. "I'm sorry, Erec. I should have been watching you, and warned you not to try any spells without my help. This is
my fault. And I'm going to find out a way to reverse this—don't worry."

Erec was very worried. He was so tired that it was hard to form
words. "What's happening to me?"

Rosco brought the spell book over and pointed to the bottom
of the page. "You said 'Nee-way,' and that wasn't the right thing to
reverse the spell. You should have said this." He tapped the word

THE SECRET OF ASHONA

"Nuiay." "That would be pronounced, 'Na-wee-I.' Subtle change, but all the difference in the world." He showed Erec the writing at the bottom of the paper. "'Nee-way' continues the spell, and lets you morph into the next thing that you think of. But the worst part is this." Rosco held up the book so Erec could read:

Be careful! Saying Nee-waye three times or more will make your series of changes permanent. This is an opportunity to enjoy many different forms throughout your future! And it will add an unexpected variety to your life. Surprise your friends—and yourself. You will never know when it will happen next. But think hard before you choose this path—it is irreversible!

"What! I can't believe it. But I didn't say . . . that word three times, did I?" Erec could not believe what he had read. He couldn't have done that, could he?

"You did. I'm sure you said it three times." Rosco put a hand over his eyes, then pointed at the word Erec was supposed to have said to end the spell. "You better say *this* one quick, to make sure you don't morph into something new. Say 'Na-wee-*I*.'"

"Na-wee-I." Erec felt no different. "This is awful! Do you think I'm really going to change into those things again? How will I know if it's going to happen?"

"Don't ask me. The book says you'll never know when you morph next. I've got to find a way to change this. If we have to, we'll see what the Shadow Prince can do. He's practically a miracle worker—I'm sure he can help in some way."

Erec did not want to owe anything to Baskania. He hoped that someone else could fix him instead.

CHAPTER EIGHTEEN

Old Memories

IT WAS EASY FOR SPARTACUS to locate Connor in Alypium. He carried Erec under one of his arms, and Rosco flew alongside following them. Connor still worked at the pet store, but today he was practicing magic with his tutor in Paisley Park. Spartacus discreetly set Erec down behind a tree. Rosco followed him to where Connor was trying to levitate twigs with a remote control.

"Look—I lifted that butterfly!"

Connor's tutor looked skeptical. "I think it was just flying away from you. Why don't you work on that stone again?"

"Excuse me." Erec smiled. "Connor, I'm Erec. We've seen each other around a few times, but I've never really said hello."

A look of recognition flashed across Connor's face. "You're that kid who likes to tell everyone that he's Erec Rex, aren't you? Well, I'd appreciate it if you stopped spreading those crazy rumors. I'm the real Erec Rex, not that anyone seems to believe me."

Erec bubbled with excitement. This kid had to have his old memories. Otherwise he was completely crazy. But it wasn't easy talking to him. "You know, I think I know what the problem is. I think you have some of my old memories. They're confusing you, so you think you used to be me. If it's okay, we can get rid of them. You'd probably be happier without them, and then I can have them back again."

"What?" Connor looked exasperated. "Now that you know who the real Erec Rex is"—he pointed to himself—"you want to take all of my old memories? Do you think that will turn you into me? Go get a life."

Erec had to take a deep breath. This kid was completely deluded. "You really think that you're the real Erec Rex?"

Connor sighed. "I get so much flack about this from everyone. How could I expect you, of all people, to understand? But, yes. I am Erec Rex."

"Don't you see? You feel this way because of those memories I'm talking about. Once they're out of you, then you can just be yourself again."

Connor was having none of it. "Nice try, but it's time for you to go away now."

"Please! Just come with us. It won't hurt at all."

Connor's black eyes flashed at Erec. "You don't take a hint, do you? You are crazy. Everyone is right about you." He pointed to himself. "You . . . you're giving Erec Rex a bad name!"

Rosco stepped in. "Listen, boys. It's okay. We're not going to worry about this now. But Erec here is right." He put a hand on Erec's shoulder.

"You did have a memory implanted in your brain when you were young. And the reason we came to find you now is that it's like a time bomb. It's going to go off soon. If you don't take it out then you'll start to go crazy—soon. Just think it over, and we'll check in with you later."

As they walked away, Erec said, "Why don't we just make him go to the Memory Mogul, and take my memory back, like it or not?"

"That won't work. The Memory Mogul will not take out or put in any memory by force if someone doesn't want it."

"Isn't there anyone else who could do it?"

"Baskania would be happy to, but then he would keep the memory, of course. I think we're just going to have to convince Connor that he wants that memory out—that it's starting to make him go nuts. . . . I have an idea."

Erec and Rosco walked around the Agora waiting for Connor's lesson to be finished. Spartacus went back to Baskania's headquarters in Paris to hunt for anything that might be helpful in releasing the captured souls, since Erec wasn't spending time there.

Erec spotted a candy shop he had been in once and remembered that they sold packets of chocolate rain from Cinnalim. Even though it would not be as fresh as the handfuls that Erec ate straight out of the Cinnalim sky, it still sounded good. He told Rosco he'd be back, and walked toward the shop. A tall man with a shaved head stepped in front of him, stopping him short.

The man's voice growled, slow and angry. "You're Erec Rex, aren't you?" He rubbed his fist with his hand. "You've got a price on your head, boy. Even if it wasn't for that, I'd love to put you in your place. You've done nothing but cause trouble in Alypium since you've been here. Telling lies, saying that you're the true king. I've heard all about your antics. I'd be thrilled to rough you up a bit for that alone. But now . . ." A crooked grin spread over his face. "Now I can get me some good money to hand you over to King Balor. There's all kinds of rewards from him lately. Prizes for hunting down clowns, firing my crossbow into dragons' caves, and the like. But this here is going to be the best reward of all." He laughed. "Too bad for you, I can't remember if you're wanted dead or alive. I'm kinda thinking it might just be dead."

Erec tensed. "Listen, you have it all wrong. I'm working with Baskania now—so I'm on your side. I'm on a mission for him, trying to find someone that he's looking for. So I wouldn't mess with me if I were you." He stuck his shoulders back and tried to look tough.

The bald man laughed. "You think I'm falling for that? Do I look like I was born yesterday?" He reached behind him and . . .

Erec felt dizzy for a moment, and then everything turned green. Huge ropes of Substance filled the air around him. It had been a while since he had seen the world through dragon eyes.

Jump.

Erec sprang into the air, growing so fast that he ripped through his clothing. The man fired a flaming arrow out of a small weapon. It passed below his feet, just missing Erec. The man swung around, obviously well trained with weapons. He aimed upward this time, straight at Erec's chest.

Dive and swing.

The next flaming arrow barely missed as Erec curved through the air. Now he hurtled back toward the ground, swerving at the last second to knock the man onto his side. A trained hunter, he rolled on the dirt. Two long shimmering poles extended from his shirt sleeves and into his hands. He aimed again.

Breathe fire.

Erec barely missed the man—on purpose. But the heat from the flames threw him off target. Small missiles shot from the rods and veered close to Erec's face and side. The fire was enough to send the man scrambling away, but before he got far another crossbow resurfaced and fired. . . .

Dive-bomb.

Something big was coming. Erec did not know what it was, but even in dragon form he would never survive it if it was launched. He had to attack fast. Pummeling through the air, he butted his head straight into the man's stomach. The bald man flew backward, the wind knocked out of him.

Erec walked slowly, morphing into his normal self again. He was afraid that the man would come after him, but instead he lay still, breathing slowly, hand over his stomach. People glared at Erec as he passed by as if he had done something horrible instead of just avoiding being shot. Someone threw a rock at him and it hit his neck, cutting into his skin.

Rosco watched from across the street. He tilted his head, signaling Erec to follow. They walked back to Paisley Park in silence.

After Connor finished with his tutor, he walked home. He passed through Paisley Park, and then onto a small street near the Agora. It was windy, and his white hair blew forward, whipping around his eyes. At first it was hard to hear, but when he listened carefully the wind was talking to him.

"Connor . . ." It tickled his ear. "This is your old memory speaking to you. I have come to haunt you. We will be together every day now. Let us dance!"

At this, the wind whipped Connor into the air, where he spun wildly. Connor looked at the ground, frantic. "Let me go! Stop!"

He fell to the earth hard, landing on his side. Connor winced, holding his hip.

Again, the wind whispered in his ear. "You don't want to dance with me? Well, maybe we can go for a walk, then."

Connor was scooped up and sailed forward, whizzing around corners and barely missing being hit on fence posts. He shook head to toe. "Put me down! Let go!"

At once he was thrown onto the dirt. "You don't like to walk with me either?" The voice in his ear sounded threatening. "We're not going to get along so well, then, you and I. I hope you like night-mares, because I'm going to give you those every night from now on. And in the daytime we're going to dance all the time. Dance and walk . . . maybe talk about the old days, when you were Erec Rex.

"Do you think you're going crazy? Is that it?" The voice paused, giving Connor time to wonder exactly that. "Well, maybe you are, then. Maybe we both are. It's time to enjoy that, I think. Don't you, Connor?"

"Stop!" Connor put his hands over his ears. "Go away!"

"But I can't go away, Connor. I'm a part of you. We're one, you and I. So from now on, it will be like this all of the time. Isn't that wonderful?"

Rosco, invisible, was playing the part well. He extended the word "wonderful," into a long, eerie, and theatrical grunt. He picked Connor up again and tossed him up and down in the air like a balloon.

Erec was watching from behind the corner of a cloud cream shop. He laughed at Rosco's antics, but then he felt strange inside. Bubbly. Then, shooting what seemed like miles downward within a second, he crashed into the ground.

Everything became dark. He tried to run for protection, but nothing happened. He was a worm again—he remembered the feeling well. But he was outside now, exposed like a piece of steak on the plate of a giant. He couldn't move . . . there were no legs. So he stretched himself forward.

How could this have happened so soon? His back parts were still flattened, and it was hard to drag them behind the rest of him. He had to get off of the sidewalk—keep moving until he felt grass underneath him. Even then, anybody might step on him, and that would be the end for him.

Why had he thought of a worm, of all things, when he was using the morphing spell? It would have been so much better if he had become a horse or an eagle. The thought of birds flying by gave him the chills. He knew he looked like a tasty morsel. . . .

Footsteps pounded around him. Erec clenched, tried to move out of the way. Luckily they passed without crushing him. If only he could call for help! Or if he could control his morphing and become something else before it was too late.

Something scratched the sidewalk next to him, then scraped it again. "Well, well. Look what we have here. The perfect lunch." It was close, just inches away. And even though he understood its words, the sounds were definitely not human. In fact, he was sure that they were bird chirps.

A sharp thing pinched around his middle, and he lifted into the air. He was going to become bird food! After all he had been though, how could it end like this? To die as a worm? His front and damaged rear half of his body hung limply as he bounced higher into the wind. The beak cinched tighter around his middle.

What was that word from the spell book that would change him into something else? Maybe thinking it would help. *Nee-way.*

He expanded, the bird's beak clamping shut through him as if he were not there. Erec floated with ease, looking down at Rosco and Connor. Spartacus was back now, and he was looking around for

Erec. *Poor Spartacus.* Erec was driven toward him, ready to become his soul. . . .

No. That was not why he was here. He had to become himself again, get his memory back. For now he would follow Connor and watch what happened.

Connor was running home. Rosco floated alongside of him, invisible, whispering "That's right. Run! Run!" in his ear. Spartacus was following, searching everywhere for Erec. Erec floated along, undetected.

They all entered Connor's house with him—Rosco still invisible and Erec still a soul. That's when Spartacus saw Erec. Relived, he joined in with Rosco's game, and picked up oranges and an apple. He juggled them until Connor's mother walked in.

"Well," she said. "Look at you! I'm glad to see you're finally picking up some magic now. Claiming that you're really King Piter's son was sounding pretty silly when you couldn't even make a leaf move."

"Yeah. Uh-huh." Connor's face was white. "I-I'm not feeling well, Mom."

"Well, go lie down, then. Get the door first, will you?"

Rosco had flown around and knocked on Connor's door, and now was visible again. The boy answered, trembling.

"I wanted to talk to you," Rosco said. "I found out that you got a bum memory a long time ago. We're trying to recall all of them before they cause permanent damage to their owners. You can't imagine how bad off some of those people are—I'd like to remove your problem before it gets worse."

"Okay!" Connor nodded, arms wrapped tightly around himself. "Let's do it now. I'm ready—anytime."

"Good kid." Rosco patted his head. "No time like the present, then." He snapped his fingers, and Connor and he disappeared.

Spartacus nodded for Erec to come outside, then asked him, "Why . . . how did you become a soul again?"

It was hard for Erec to put anything into words in this form. It was time to try changing again. . . . *Nee–way.*

And there he stood, his old, normal self. Spartacus stared at him in amazement. Then he grabbed Erec's shoulder and jumped into the air. . . . Moments later they were landing at the Memory Mogul's shop.

"Ouch!" Erec banged hard against the outside wall of the shop when Spartacus sailed him into it.

"Sorry. Oh, wow, I can't believe I did that. I completely forgot that you can't go through the wall with me."

Erec dusted himself off and walked in through the door. It was just as he remembered it: A long counter stretched across the room, and behind it rows of shelving hung on the walls. Each shelf was covered with tiny packets—memory chips that had been removed from countless visitors. A man leaned over the counter—the Memory Mogul—his white hair and beard standing on end all over his face like a puffy dandelion gone to seed.

Erec remembered how hard it had been to talk to the man. He had tried out so many other people's memories that his own memory was completely shot.

Connor looked nervous. "C-can you please take out an old memory that you put in me once? It's turned bad. Very bad."

The Memory Mogul chuckled. "An old memory, huh? Yes, I've seen quite a few of those in my day. Some of them do get tired after a while. I understand what you're saying. Reminds me of one time when I was using a certain memory here quite a bit—I almost forgot who I was for a while after that." He smiled fondly. "So . . . what is it that brings you here today?"

Erec waited at the back of the shop. If Connor was doing this willingly, he didn't want to interfere. But he began to brim with excitement about getting his lost memory back again.

"I need my memory out. The one that you put in me a long time ago." He thumbed at Rosco. "This guy says it was Erec Rex's old memory, but I still think that bit is really my own. Whatever you put in, just take out, though. Okay?"

The Memory Mogul's eyes glazed over and a smile lit his lips. "Erec Rex, you say? I still remember the day that I got the memory of Erec Rex. And I do admit my memory isn't exactly what it once was." He mused in silence a moment, then looked at Connor. "Can I help you?"

Connor looked at Rosco, frustrated. Rosco gestured toward the Memory Mogul with a smile.

"Take out the memory you once gave me."

"Memory? Do you remember what that memory was?"

"It might have been the memory of Erec Rex, but I'm not sure. . . ."

"Ah, Erec Rex. I still remember the day that he came in here, with his mother, that girl child, and a baby. What a day that was— I've played it over in my head plenty of times. I even tried out his memory a bunch of times. Shame I can't recall much about it anymore."

Connor looked surprised. "I do remember coming here to get my memory out—but it never made sense because I still had the memory even after it was supposed to be gone." He thought a while. "Could it really be someone else's memory then? Erec Rex's memory?" He looked sick. "All of my life I thought it was really me. Why would my parents give me someone else's memory?"

"I don't know." The Memory Mogul's hair waved back and forth in the air like thousands of white antennae. "Probably something bad happened to you that they wanted you to forget. Maybe you lost a sibling, or a close friend."

"That's awful. Can I get my original memory back again?"

"I suppose I could look for it. What's your name?"

"Connor Flannigan."

The Memory Mogul flipped through an ancient ledger and slapped a hand on a page. "Aha! Here you are. Connor Flannigan. Lucky for you, it's still here after all this time. Looks like nobody wanted this one. . . ." He searched on a high shelf and pulled a dusty packet off, reading his notes underneath it. "Oh, I see. Well, that explains it. Are you sure you want this back? It's not pleasant, I'm afraid."

"I do." Connor looked brave.

"Well, it's up to you. But I warned you—it's not a nice memory." He walked to the counter and leaned over, blinking at Connor and Rosco as if he had never seen or spoken to them before. "What can I do for you boys today?"

Rosco tapped the packet that was in the Memory Mogul's hand. "Take out the memory that you gave this boy, and put this old one of his back in."

"Okay. Okay. Lean forward, young man. Now sip this." He produced a small vial of pink liquid from a dusty shelf. Connor drank it and immediately fell face-first onto the counter. "Let's see what we have here, now." The Memory Mogul pulled a few rusty tools out and laid them next to Connor's head. Erec was horrified—what was he going to do with those?

The Memory Mogul inserted a long metal probe into Connor's ear. He shoved it in farther and farther until Erec was sure it must have been sticking into the center of his brain. It didn't seem like Connor would ever live through this. Then the Memory Mogul looked into the end of the probe as if it were some kind of scope. "Hmmm. Very interesting. It looks like there *is* a memory I put in there; must have been a long time ago looking at the technique." He looked up at Rosco, brow knit. "Do you think he wants that memory removed, then?"

"Sure does."

"All right. Let's take that specimen out of there." Another long metal contraption fit into the first one. The Memory Mogul inserted it carefully, frowning and eyeing the level of the two instruments. Right when he seemed happy with its position, he took a hammer and smashed both of them hard, deep into Connor's head.

Erec gasped. "No! What are you doing?"

"It's okay." Rosco held a hand up. "This guy knows his stuff."

Erec sure hoped so. It was not looking so good to him. The Memory Mogul grinned at Erec. "All in a day's work, boy. Don't interrupt the expert, now." He then picked up Connor's head and proceeded to smash it three times—hard—against the counter.

Conner remained asleep, luckily. Erec had no idea removing a memory would be so awful. Small bits of the metal rods now extended from both of Connor's ears—he was completely impaled. The Memory Mogul poured some kind of oil through the hole in his ear. Erec could hear it make a *glug, glug* sound as it seeped in. He lifted Connor off of the counter and the oil dripped out his other ear onto the table. Then the Memory Mogul took out a small hand blender and began to push it into Connor's head.

"Stop!" Erec ran over. "What are you doing—trying to kill him? We just need to get his memory out, not mix his brain up!"

"Boy!" The Memory Mogul looked annoyed. "Let me do my job. I've done this countless times. If you must know, I need to loosen the frenulum of the amygdala—a spot I myself discovered from which memory chips may be held and activated. This is standard procedure. Now stand back." He shoved hard and the blender entered Connor's ear.

It seemed there was no possible way that the Memory Mogul could have been exact about the area he was blending. Erec shuddered, wondering what was going to happen. When the Memory Mogul pulled the blender out, dripping with the dark oil, Erec almost threw up.

"Here it is!" The Memory Mogul lifted Connor's head and pulled a small thing out that looked like a wet potato chip. "The memory. Good as new. I wonder if this boy wanted another memory in there to take its place...."

"He does." Rosco tapped the other chip on the counter with Connor's name on it. "This was the one you took out for him."

"Oh. Of course." The Memory Mogul placed the chip on Connor's ear and blew lightly. It sailed easily into his head and disappeared. "Time to wakey-wakey." He shook Connor's shoulder.

Miraculously, the boy awoke. "Huh? What . . . I have a different memory now! I'm *not* Erec Rex." He turned to Erec. "You are. It wasn't my memory. I'm sure of that now." Then his face grew glum. "I had a sister." He sat on the floor, saying nothing else.

Erec eyed the chip containing his own memory that was sitting on the counter. "Can I have that, please?" He hoped that inserting it would not be as horrifying as removing a memory had been.

The Memory Mogul smiled pleasantly. "May I help you?"

"Yes. I'd like this memory, right here."

"Have you paid me yet, boy?"

"Um, no. How much is it?"

Rosco put three gold ring coins on the table, and the Memory Mogul lit up with delight. "Wonderful! Now, what can I do for you, sir?"

"Put this memory in that boy."

The Memory Mogul placed the wet chip on Erec's ear and blew it in. . . .

It had been a terrible day. His mother was busy, and she didn't see Erec and his brother and sister even once. June was playing with them, and she was always nice. But his brother tried to take Erec's favorite truck and they got in a fight. Then he didn't get as much ice cream as everyone else for dessert, and nobody even listened to him when he told them about it.

Erec was three and a half, and he was a big boy now. He got to sleep in a big bed all by himself in the nursery, and even had his own cup of water on his nightstand. But the best thing of all was getting to sit on his father's throne. Daddy said that Erec would get to be king of Alypium when he grew up, and he could not wait. . . .

Erec was little, in a stroller that fit three babies. It was sailing through the air over the Agora, pulled by a winged horse. June rode in a small carriage that bounced along behind them.

The Hermit was in the playroom again, and he was so silly. Erec always laughed when he did his dances. And the Hermit was the only grown-up who always made sense. Today he told Erec "Fun is for having. It is the one thing that is there forever." Erec agreed.

Erec tried not to react to all of the memories rushing through his mind. There was so much he never knew—that he had forgotten. His triplet brother and sister had shared so much with him: playing silly games, fighting, those names they had all made up for themselves.

Their names! He remembered them now. Princess Pretty Pony— her name was Elizabeth! And his brother, Prince Muck Muck. He was Edward. That's right: Erec, Elizabeth, and Edward. The three next rulers of the Kingdoms of the Keepers. Erec would be the future king of Alypium, Elizabeth would be queen of Ashona, and Edward the king of Aorth.

It was as clear as yesterday. They used to talk about it all of the time. Elizabeth had a special way in the water, he remembered that, too. But all of the details weren't there. Some parts were clearer than others.

Rosco returned Connor to his house and came back to meet Erec in front of the shop. "You look dazed. Are you okay?"

Erec nodded. "It's just weird, remembering everything. My brother and sister . . . I miss them now. A lot. I really need to find them. It's been hard doing all of these quests alone. I want to get to know them again, and catch up for lost time."

While they were in Alypium, Rosco and Erec each got a nectar fizz sundae from a cloud cream shop. Then they returned to Rosco's apartment at the snap of his fingers, Spartacus following close behind. Erec told Rosco how he changed into a worm and almost got eaten. "But at least I figured out how to change myself when it happens."

Rosco whistled. "You'd better be careful. If that happens at the wrong time, you're a goner."

That night, Erec could do nothing but sit on Rosco's couch hugging a pillow to his chest. It had been too much—changing into a worm and almost being eaten, then having a world of memories put back into his head. Before he had his old memories back he was sure he would do nothing but delve into them and learn as much as he could. But instead, the old times that he had lost just made him feel bad. He wanted his family back again, the way it once had been. Of course he would try out those memories again soon, but not this minute.

Right now, Erec was overwhelmed. Tarvos was building an army of Golems, and Erec had given him the key to command them. Baskania would take Erec's dragon eyes away from him at any minute. Erec saw himself giving his scepter to Baskania, and he was on a path to becoming evil and killing Trevor. Erec had to find Bethany's brother before Baskania did. And on top of everything, three thousand souls were still held captive—and trying to save them might not end well.

CHAPTER NINETEEN

A Talisman from a Living Foe

DISTRACTING HIMSELF from his problems, Erec flipped through the spell book that Baskania had given him. The time-stopping spell on page four hundred twenty-two was interesting:

This simple spell may not be usable by most—it is necessary for one to have a solid connection with the substance which holds all magic in order to perform it. But for those who are able to use this spell it can come in quite handy. Few situations are not fixable by the simple stopping of time. Even minor problems, such as being fired from a job, can be made pleasurable. Just use this spell, stand your boss up, put a few thumbtacks on his chair, and sit him back down. Once you start time again, you will feel far better than you did before.

Warning: Permanent stoppage of time is not recommended. If the user dies before starting time back up again, humanity will be on indefinite hold.

Erec laughed. "This would be great to know. Not that I need to risk trying another spell out of this book. I think I've learned my lesson."

"Wait a minute." Spartacus sat next to him. "This could help us a lot. We need to get the souls out of their prison. . . ."

Erec's eyes lit up. "You're right! If we went back to the Furies' storage facility and opened the door to go in . . . and then we stopped time . . . Maybe this was what I was meant to get from Baskania before going back to Alsatia."

"Hold up there," Rosco said. "You're talking to Spartacus? I'm not sure I like what I'm hearing."

Erec was impatient. "I have to learn that spell. This time I'll make sure I pronounce things right first. But it's the only way I'll get all of those souls out of their prison."

Rosco thought a minute. "I guess if you're careful . . . I'm going to help you, though. This spell is my specialty. But did you read the bottom of the page? It will only work if you have a talisman from a living foe. Someone you have fought. That can be hard—it has to be from a person or animal that has attacked you or tried to hurt you. Also, they have to have enough strength to power the spell, not a mosquito that bit you."

"The only enemy I can think of is Baskania. He has enough strength."

"That's not going to work. The Shadow Prince gave you the spell book—he'll know exactly what's going on if you swipe a lock of his hair. You have that book only because you're supposed to give it to the Furies. What about finding an ear of the manticore that attacked you, or some other creature . . . ?"

"That manticore got eaten up in the Nevervarld. And there's no other creature . . . wait! What about Tarvos? He tried to turn me into a Golem. I could take one of his horns."

"Good luck with that." Rosco laughed. "Do you think Tarvos is going to let you take his horn? That's where he keeps his source of power. Find a new foe. We'll go out into Otherness and corner a Minotaur. When it attacks you, I'll paralyze it, and you can take a lock of its hair. That should work for your talisman."

That made sense, but something bothered Erec. "You said that Tarvos stores the source of his power in one of his horns? Do you know which horn that is?"

"I don't know. I've heard one horn is for his power source and the other will be where he keeps the Master Shem. Why do you want to know? Don't worry about Tarvos anymore. There's nothing you can do about that."

"The thing is, I have to stop Tarvos. Soon. Didn't you hear that Baskania is about to use him to attack Otherness and then Upper Earth? *I* gave him that Master Shem. I've been waiting to figure out how to stop him, and all I have to do is to take his horn. It can't be that hard. There has to be a way."

"There is *no* way that you are going to disarm Tarvos. Even *I* wouldn't try that." Rosco threw his hands into the air. "Erec, you have to stop trying to save the world."

"I could help you," Spartacus said.

Erec grinned. "Good point—Spartacus can lend a hand. Listen, I'm in about as deep as I can get already. I was sent here to get what I need to free those souls. This could be it. I was going to have to fix my mistake with Tarvos anyway."

"But . . ." Rosco looked frustrated. "This can't be what you're supposed to do. You'll get hurt. Or not make it back at all. Think about that."

Erec did think about it. But he had sworn to himself that he would get that Master Shem back. Now he needed a talisman from an enemy—and getting it from Tarvos would disarm him. How could he not try? He winked at Rosco. "What are you talking about? It's Tarvos who needs to be worried. What's my track record, anyway? I mean, I've dealt with a lot worse. . . ."

Rosco laughed. "That's the old Erec I know. You don't like to take no for an answer." He shook his head. "I think it might be harder to change your mind than to steal Tarvos's horn. But it's not something you can rush into. We need to find out more about him. Maybe we could look him up online—"

"Or go to the library in Alypium. The one that used to be part of the castle." Erec had a surge of confidence. The Fates knew what they were doing. His last quest had sounded so simple, yet awful. Giving his life for five people who were slated to die at the Diamond Minds of Argos. But it had led him on a series of adventures straight up to this point. So, if he decided that he had to disarm Tarvos now, wouldn't they have predicted that? That meant it might be something that he had to do. It was impossible to know, but he had to try what seemed right. . . .

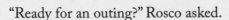

"Ready for an outing?" Rosco asked.

"Never more than now."

The librarian didn't blink when she saw Erec and Rosco appear before her eyes. "Oh, hi, Rosco. Glad to see you have this hoodlum under control. He's come in here so many times, disrupting everybody."

Erec could not believe his ears. "I have not—"

Rosco interrupted him. "I know. It's a good thing this rotten apple turned himself in. Hope I can reform him."

The librarian nodded sagely behind her long cat-eye glasses.

Looks like word about him traveled fast in Alypium. He wondered what the renegades from his fan club with Janus now thought of him.

Rosco winked at her. "Do you have any books here about Tarvos—the underworld creature who collects soulless humans?"

"Of course." She gleamed back at him. "Second floor to the right. In the section on bulls."

They walked upstairs and found the heading "Bulls" in the Animals section. Rosco pointed to a book on the shelf: *Minotaurs: The Misunderstood Breed*. "The only thing misunderstood about Minotaurs is how fast they can rip you into shreds."

"Look at this one." Erec looked at the cover of a book called *Congratulations! You Got a Bull's Eye—Now What Are You Going To Do With It?* "One hundred and one uses for the eye of a bull?"

"I think that's something Hecate Jekyll would have liked. Look over here; there are a few books about Tarvos."

Erec pulled out a book called *The Man Behind The Creature Behind The Shadow Behind The Myth. Tarvos Expert Unveiled*. "I wonder what this is about." The book talked about a scholar who knew everything about Tarvos. It described his childhood, how he lost a parent to the creature, and his life story. "This isn't about

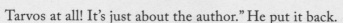

Tarvos at all! It's just about the author." He put it back.

"This one's better." Rosco shoved a book in front of Erec called *Wave Your Own Cape: Dispelling the Tarvos Myth and Regaining Control of Your Soulless Life.*

"But this makes it sound like Tarvos isn't real." Erec found a book called *The Total Loser's Guide to Getting Your Soul Back* and flipped it open. Spartacus looked over his shoulder with interest.

> *Reclaiming your soul is simple—don't let anybody tell you otherwise. Just as easily as it can slip through your fingers and disappear in a near-death experience, your soul can be found again and put back in place, giving you a full and complete existence. Keep Tarvos at bay with our three-step plan. Remember, any soul may be recovered for usage at any time.*

> *How do you find the thing once it's gone, you ask? Our book will go over the many techniques that can be used for each step, at any time frame you are in. Our proven steps are easy to do—even a newborn would have no trouble at all. First—the Recall. We will discuss methods such as séances, spirit nets, and the Tarvos Shuffle to bring your soul back to you. Second—the Cleaning. Although your soul can reenter your body at any time, a thorough scrubbing is always a good idea first. And third—the Attachment. This time, put your soul in to stick for good. Use our methods to ensure a complete joining that will never break again.*

The Tarvos Shuffle? Erec flipped through to find that section.

> *Tarvos is a creature that has the appearance of a gigantic bull, and was originally free-roaming in Otherness. His appetite was tremendous, and his size and strength allowed him to devour even*

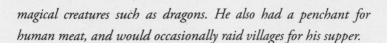

magical creatures such as dragons. He also had a penchant for human meat, and would occasionally raid villages for his supper.

Fear of Tarvos spread far and wide. Hunters pitted their strength against him, but none returned to tell the tale. On a fateful day, Tarvos broke into the home of a sorcerer who had been working on a portable source of magic. Before the bull pounced, the sorcerer thought quickly and used his new invention. He surprised the bull by calmly walking up and placing the portable power source on the bull's shoulder.

The sorcerer spoke—and, for the first time in its life, the bull understood. With the power source, Tarvos could also now speak, and he liked it. It is said that the sorcerer tried to make a deal to trade the power source for his life, but Tarvos simply destroyed the man. Before long he was doing magic the likes of which nobody had ever seen, creating bulls out of mud and melting houses in the village. Tarvos changed his horns into storage cones, and set the power source inside one to carry it with him always.

He became unstoppable. Nobody was safe in any village or town. He gave himself an impermeable coat so he could never be harmed. The Fates decided that, to protect humanity, he would be placed in a cave in the Underworld. To give him a purpose, they allowed him to rid the world of its soulless living beings. Using small toys to attract his mindless victims, Tarvos was able to gather masses of them and turn them into an army of Golem sand creatures.

In order to assure that no harm would come, the Fates gave the Master Shem, the only key to commanding Golems, to their sisters, the Furies, who are locked in Tartarus for eternity. This will assure that the Golem army is never used for destruction.

It is also thought that the Shadow Prince is working on inventing his own method of activating Tarvos's Golem army, and possibly even freeing and harnessing Tarvos himself. If that is the case we can all be assured that something originally terrible will be used for the greater good—a wonderful thought for humanity.

Erec felt sick, and had to put down the book a minute. *He* was the reason that the Furies were out of Tartarus. *He* was the reason that Tarvos had the Master Shem. And he had to take it away again and fix things as they were before.

Spartacus pointed at the page and laughed. "'Using small toys to attract his mindless victims.' Like you'd be dumb enough to go into the Underworld by chasing a toy."

Erec narrowed his eyes at him, remembering the wind-up bull-fighter. "Shut up. It's not like you're mister perfect."

He flipped ahead to find the part about the Tarvos Shuffle.

So, what do you do if you've waited too long to find your soul, and Tarvos has brought you to his lair? Hopefully you will have purchased this book before that happens! Unfortunately, most people do not know how to resist Tarvos. In moments, they become Golems, and will stay limp sand creatures until the day that the Master Shem finally mobilizes them. But there is a way out, even if you've come this far!

We like to call it the Tarvos Shuffle. Simply jump and swerve, back and forth, which will make Tarvos confused and throw off his aim. During this time, you must spit in your hands and rub them together well. With a deft move, jump high off the floor—it helps to wear gravity-defying shoes for this feat. Grab hold of one of the bull's great horns, and twist. Tarvos's horns are thick and tough,

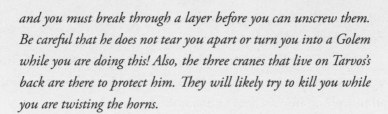

and you must break through a layer before you can unscrew them. Be careful that he does not tear you apart or turn you into a Golem while you are doing this! Also, the three cranes that live on Tarvos's back are there to protect him. They will likely try to kill you while you are twisting the horns.

Tarvos is known to keep his magical abilities in one of his horns, likely other important possessions in the other. Once you take his horns, you can use them to control him completely. Simply cut the sharp point off of one of his horns—its insides are hollow. Blow through it, and Tarvos will be under your spell. He will release you, if you ask him, and help you on your way. Then you may use our other just-as-easy techniques to regain your lost soul.

Erec could not believe his eyes. *This* was supposed to be so simple that a newborn baby could do it? It seemed doubtful that anyone could survive the Tarvos Shuffle. It was obvious that nobody had done this successfully yet, or Tarvos would no longer have horns.

But at the same time, Erec would have a ghost helping him. Taking one of Tarvos's horns would either let him have Tarvos's magical ability, or give him the Master Shem back—because Erec was sure that was where he was keeping it.

"We can do this." Spartacus pointed to the page.

"You'll never be able to do that," Rosco said, at the same time, looking over Erec's shoulder.

"Who knows? The book sounds a little crazy, but . . ." If Erec took the Master Shem back, that would save the world from invasion by those dreaded Golem creatures, and keep them out of Baskania's hands. He shrugged. "I need to give it a try, with Spartacus's help. I've been waiting to figure out a way. Then if I learn the spell to stop time, I might save the three thousand souls from the Furies. Who knows?"

As he spoke, Erec realized how crazy his plans sounded. But were they any more crazy than being brought back from the dead, and morphing into spiders and smashed worms?

At that thought, the room around Erec flew out on all sides, and he thunked, a fat worm, onto the book he had been reading. He looked around wildly, but Rosco had disappeared. His voice boomed, though, from down below. . . .

"It's okay, little buddy. I saw you run into that hole, Erec. I know you're a spider now, and I promise I'm not going to crush you. Just come back out and climb on my finger, and we'll look at the book together until you change back."

Erec wished that he was able to shout to Rosco, or even say anything. It was pretty funny that Rosco thought he was a fleeing spider. At least he wasn't hurting the poor thing. The room was blurry, and it was impossible to focus on anything around him. But there was a sound—"Eew!"—and a shadow approaching rapidly—

"Erec?" Rosco's booming voice was close now. "Ugh. I'm sorry, I guess that spider wasn't you. Um, can you hear me like that?"

Erec could not exactly nod or answer. He remembered what he had done before to change back fast. What was that word? *Nee-way.*

He morphed into his normal self, sitting on the book, then hopped off. "Sorry," he panted. "That's just weird."

Rosco looked stunned. "Yeah . . . It's okay. Glad you're all right."

Erec wiped the sweat off of his face. "I wish I could go back into the Underworld through that Bubble Boulder like last time. But Tarvos only left it open once. Let's look in these books and find the best way back."

"I can get you there. But read this." Spartacus waved pages in front of Erec's face. The book was called *Dream Vacations or Nightmares?*

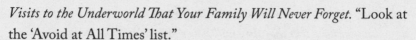

Visits to the Underworld That Your Family Will Never Forget. "Look at the 'Avoid at All Times' list."

The book described a multitude of places that a vacationing family would not want to see on a visit to the Underworld. It sounded like most of the Underworld was included in the list. Spartacus tapped one of the pages.

Again—don't forget to bring two gold coins to the Underworld— that is, if you want to get back out again! Although it is a stunning destination, there are a few tricky spots you will want to avoid. Many areas of the Underworld contain the word "swamp." Just for ease, we like to advise our readers to stay away from all of those places. Some of them include the Swamp Marsh of Disease, the Swamplands, the Never Ending Swamp Fields of Disaster, and the famous Chicken Swamp of Bruno. Also, stay away from any destination that includes the following words in its name: final, death, grim, swallow, sickness, craziness, scum, or toothbrush.

A number of Shadow Demons monitor the Underworld like police officers of the area. So if you run into one, don't despair! They will generally acquaint you with the place and make sure that everything is as it should be. One of their duties is to decide who gets to leave and who should stay on permanently. So you may have the wonderful surprise of becoming a permanent resident! Your vacation will go on forever. This is nice for the Shadow Demons as well, because the Underworld needs to stay populated. If you are bound and determined to return home again, it is advised to follow the Shadow Demon's directions wisely.

Another place to avoid while you are there are the lovely Suction Pits of Despair in the Desert of Eternal Heat. While the Desert

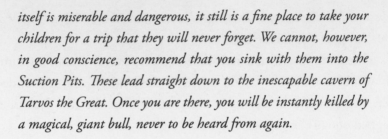

itself is miserable and dangerous, it still is a fine place to take your children for a trip that they will never forget. We cannot, however, in good conscience, recommend that you sink with them into the Suction Pits. These lead straight down to the inescapable cavern of Tarvos the Great. Once you are there, you will be instantly killed by a magical, giant bull, never to be heard from again.

"Do you have two gold coins on you?" Erec asked.

Rosco pulled two ring coins out of his pocket and gave them to Erec. "You going to hang on to these just in case?"

"Just in case?" Erec laughed. "I'm ready to go now. Spartacus has had it with waiting."

Rosco raised an eyebrow. "We're really going to do this? I don't know. I'm all for helping you learn to stop time. But why not get the talisman from another foe?"

"I need to stop Tarvos anyway." Erec waved a hand toward the book. "But you shouldn't come. It's not worth the risk. At least I could get a cloudy thought and turn into a dragon if things get bad."

"Tarvos eats dragons," Rosco reminded him. "You wouldn't be a match for him."

"I need to do this."

Rosco closed his eyes. "You've been lucky so far following your gut instincts and listening to the Fates. But do you think I can let you go to that awful place by yourself? I'm supposed to be watching you. You're still a kid!"

"What is it with the adults in my life trying to stop me from what I'm supposed to do? The Fates are why I got the book of spells from Baskania. I'm sure that they knew all of this would happen."

"But what if you're wrong?" Rosco raised his voice.

Erec paused a minute and thought. "I have to go with what I feel is right. The Hermit said that too."

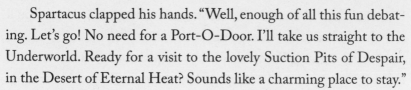

Spartacus clapped his hands. "Well, enough of all this fun debating. Let's go! No need for a Port-O-Door. I'll take us straight to the Underworld. Ready for a visit to the lovely Suction Pits of Despair, in the Desert of Eternal Heat? Sounds like a charming place to stay."

Erec nodded.

"You don't want to take Rosco, do you? I'm all for leaving him behind too. Just nod and we're out of here."

Erec nodded again. No use putting Rosco at risk. In a second, Spartacus's hands rested on Erec's shoulders, and they flew straight out the window.

Before Erec knew it, they had flown deep into a cave, and were turning this way and that in the darkness. He was glad that Spartacus had a good grip on his shoulders, because he could not see a thing. Every now and then there was a glimpse of the floor split apart in spots, and with subterranean streams rushing by. There was no way he could have found his way through here by himself.

Soon he was set down before a thin gap in a craggy, damp stone wall. Eerie red light seeped through the narrow rift in the rock. It seemed doubtful that any family would come here for a vacation. In fact, every part of him wanted to run away, even knowing that he had to go inside. There was a foreboding feeling about the place, like people were just not supposed to be here.

"Do you know what it's like in there?" he asked Spartacus.

"Nope. Never seen it. Do you want me to check it out first?"

As much as Erec did not want to be left alone here, he definitely wanted to know what lay ahead. "Thanks, Spartacus."

The ghost set him down and disappeared. The cave had an eerie feel. He could not get the idea out of his head that if Spartacus disappeared he would be stuck there forever.

But the spirit returned before long. "I found the way to the

Desert of Eternal Heat. It's harder to get my bearings in there. You'll see what I mean, it's a strange place."

Without giving Erec a chance to ask questions, Spartacus pulled him higher up the wall through a larger crack. Erec's arms scraped against the stone as he passed through. On the other side, bright red light glowed intensely. He had to squeeze his eyes shut for a minute to get used to it. A strange, bubbly feeling came over him, and when he opened them, the light seemed even brighter. He was suspended in the air over an immense river, eerily lit by an unseen, flickering source. Everything around him looked dark purple. Warm sulphur-smelling mists rose from the waters.

Erec's limbs jumped in shock, feeling like he was about to fall into the dark water. He flailed for a minute, hanging with no support or help from Spartacus. But after a moment he realized that he was clinging to some kind of rope. It was strange how easy it was to hold himself up—he wasn't tired one bit. In fact, it seemed he could go on forever hanging there, without exerting himself at all. He waved an arm or two around—or three? What was he holding on with . . . ?

Erec's thoughts stopped cold. Multiple arms? His eyes drifted over his own body, and there were the hairy jointed armor-type limbs again. He had turned into a spider so quickly when his eyes were closed that he had not even noticed it. So, what was he hanging on to, then? On closer inspection, the rope was a tall stick of dead grass that bent over the river.

He began to shake. What if he morphed back into his full-sized self now? He would fall into the water. But looking at the dark bubbles below him, he knew that there was something nasty about it that he should not touch.

Spartacus's voice seemed extra loud since he was small. "Sorry, Erec. It took me a minute to realize where you went. I could sense that you were still here, but I couldn't figure it out." He scooped

THE SECRET OF ASHONA

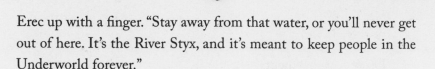

Erec up with a finger. "Stay away from that water, or you'll never get out of here. It's the River Styx, and it's meant to keep people in the Underworld forever."

Erec remembered the Waters of Oblivion that he had once crossed in order to go to Tartarus to find the three Furies the first time. One step in that stream guaranteed death. He had walked through it—and had died shortly after. Luckily for him, he was brought back to life. But the last thing he needed was to tempt fate again. Spartacus scooped him into the air, safely away from the edge of the River Styx. Erec thought the word *Nee-way* and about his normal form, and he morphed back.

"Phew. Thanks for saving me! Can you fly us over the river?"

"No. I checked it out before, but I couldn't take you there even if you were a spider. I can cross myself, but the atmosphere is crazy above the river. It squeezes me into tiny particles. Even as a spirit I can barely fit through it. There is no way you could go over in one piece. There's a boatman, though." Spartacus pointed into the distance.

A dark shadow on the water grew larger. Soon a man was visible standing on a wooden raft, pushing himself forward with a long pole. Waters lapped over the sides of the raft, and occasionally the man stopped to shove things off the wooden boards with his stick. Before long, he washed ashore near Erec and Spartacus. Thick white worms wriggled off the wood as it slid onto land.

The boatman wore a torn canvas coat, its heavily frayed hood over his head. His skin was wearing away in places, bits of bone popping through his cheeks and knuckles. A curly black beard covered most of his face, but his eyes shone with a sly gleam and his mouth curved into a grin. "Welcome to the Underworld." His accent was from North England, but he drew out his vowels in a way that made him sound a bit crazy.

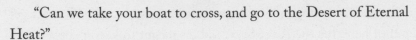

"Can we take your boat to cross, and go to the Desert of Eternal Heat?"

"Do ye have payment?"

"Payment?" It took Erec a moment to remember the two ring coins in his pocket. He pulled them out. "How much does it cost?"

The boatman eyed the gold. "That will do."

"Okay." One chair perched in the middle of the raft. Erec climbed on and sat down. "Can you take me straight to the Desert of Eternal Heat, then?"

The boatman shook his head. "I take you across the river. That is what I can do."

Erec climbed on and sat in the chair. "What about Spartacus?"

"Whooo?" It sounded like the boatman was trying to imitate an owl.

Erec remembered that Spartacus would be invisible to the boatman. "He's a spirit that is with me."

"Nooo." The boatman shook his head. "There is room for only one."

"It's okay, Erec. I'll squeeze through overhead again. You take the boat and I'll meet you on the other side."

Erec waited patiently, but the boatman did not move. Finally, he asked, "Are you waiting for something?"

"Payment."

Erec tried to put the two coins into the man's fingers. One slipped through his jutting finger bones and onto the strung-together logs of the raft. Erec grabbed the coin again before it was lost. The boatman remained immobile. He nodded, slowly. "Ye must put your payment into its mouth." He pointed down at a decaying body of a woman that was suddenly on the raft.

Spartacus held his nose. "She's dead."

"What? You're disgusted by that? Who are you to talk?" Erec

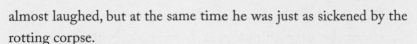

almost laughed, but at the same time he was just as sickened by the rotting corpse.

The dead woman turned her waxen eyes to look at Erec, and slowly opened her jaws. A few spiders ran out . . . and Erec immediately sympathized with them. How horrid it must have been for them inside of there! And he was supposed to put the coins into her mouth. . . .

Holding his breath and trying not to get sick, Erec lowered the gold ring coins to her black lips. Her lips opened wider into a broad, gaping grin, and a dark purple tongue wiggled out. Carefully, he brought the coins close and dropped them in. The dead woman gobbled them up as if they were pastry dough, sighed heavily, and belched. Her mouth opened again in a wavering wail, and she slid off of the raft and into the water.

The boatman pushed his pole against the shore and set off with Erec into the River Styx. The waters were rocky, and waves lapped over the boat edges coming close to Erec's shoes.

Erec pulled his feet closer to the chair. "I can't touch the water, right?"

"Ye can touch it."

Erec wasn't sure what the boatman meant by that. "Will it hurt me, though?"

"No, it doesn't hurt." The boatman pushed on, then beat away at something in the water with his stick. Erec noticed the white worms again, wriggling at the sides of the raft.

He had the feeling that the boatman was leaving out some important information about the water. "If I touch the water, will it kill me? Or make me have to stay in the Underworld forever?"

The boatman cackled. "It could do. Ye know what they say . . . that which doesn't kill ye makes ye stronger."

Erec thought about that for a moment. "Do you mean that the water here could help me, too?"

"Ye ask a lot of questions." He rowed some more, then beat something else away with his pole. There was a scuttling noise, and some of the worms wiggled closer to Erec. . . . It took him a minute to realize that they weren't worms at all. They were fingers, and some of them were attached to hands. People were hanging off of the boat, and now someone was trying to climb on. A decaying figure, half of its head an exposed skull, scrambled aboard. Its mouth hung open, gaping and snapping, and it crawled toward Erec as if it wanted to bite him.

Erec jumped, pulling his knees to his chest. "Get that thing off of here!"

The undead creature dripped flesh onto the logs of the raft as it crept closer, and the bits of skin wiggled away like worms. Its teeth looked sharp, and its head swung back and forth as it moved. The boatman put his pole squarely in the middle of the creature's face and pushed, flinging it into the water with a splash.

"Zombies," he huffed. "That's what'll happen to ye if ye decide to go for a swim in the Styx now."

"I'd turn into a zombie? How horrible!" Erec hoped that none of the splashes around him got too close.

"Or you'd become indestructible. Or maybe both." He cackled.

Being indestructible sounded good, but there was no way he'd risk touching this water. The raft was pulling up to the other shore, and soon washed onto land.

"Thanks," Erec said. "When I'm ready to go back across I just call you, then?"

"I'll know when you're here. I'll come to you. As long as you can pay for the trip, you can go back to the other side."

"But I already paid you!" Erec fished around in his pockets. They were empty.

"Good day."

"Wait—how much does it cost to cross?"

"A piece of gold."

"But I paid you two before. . . ."

"Your choice."

So, he was supposed to take two coins—one to cross the River Styx and the other to come back again? "I want one of my coins back."

"Good luck finding it."

Erec knew that there was no way he would ever get his other ring coin back again. Now was he stuck for good in the Underworld? A chill went through him as he thought about his fate. But then he tried to forget about it. He was supposed to be doing this, right? Or was he? The Fates wouldn't let him do this if he'd really be stuck forever. He shivered, and tried to focus on his task ahead.

He would do his best to disarm Tarvos. If he accomplished this feat, he would move on to rescuing the souls from the Furies. It seemed overwhelming, but then he would have fixed the worst problems he knew about. He'd be finished. But then he remembered something awful—the contract he had signed giving his dragon eyes to Baskania. He might have to live out the rest of his life blinded. And his visions of doing awful things in the future . . . It was too much to think about. *One thing at a time,* he thought. There was a bull to deal with first.

CHAPTER TWENTY
A Test of Cleverness and Chance

SPARTACUS WAS WAITING when Erec climbed off of the ferry. "It's nice down here, isn't it?"

Around them were endless fields swirling with mists. There was little light on this side of the river, and even after Erec's eyes had adjusted to the dimness, the place still had a foreboding look. Shapes passed through the mist, formless spirits that, unlike Spartacus, had lost their original appearance.

Even though the fields were wide open, it had the feel of a

prison. Erec felt claustrophobic even though he was outdoors, as if something unseen was pressing on him.

"Why are those spirits here?"

"I asked one of them." Spartacus shuddered. "This place is a trap. It's where some of us end up if we spend too long haunting earth as a ghost after we die. I don't know how much time that is, but I don't want to end up one of these guys."

Dark shapes appeared nearby, popping out of crags and around rocks. They came closer to Erec on all fours, steadily, leering grins on their faces.

"What are those things?" Erec asked.

"Night Panthers." The boatman nodded at the beasts. "Inside they're all lizard, but their shape and fur look like jungle cats. Don't let them get too close to ye." He winked at Erec. "They love to eat dragons best of all."

Erec stepped back reflexively. He wondered how the boatman knew that he had some dragon in him. "Let's go," he said to Spartacus. "This place give me the creeps."

"All right. But don't expect the next area down here to be much better."

Spartacus picked him up and they flew through the fog over endless terrain. Erec was glad that Spartacus knew the way—it would have been impossible for him to get around alone here. As they flew, the temperature grew hotter and hotter. Spartacus didn't seem to notice, but Erec was dripping sweat. It reminded him of Aorth—and he wished he was wearing the air-conditioned UnderWear that people used down there.

The waving grasses gave way to sand, and soon they were flying over desert. The sky was a deep blood red, and the sands that he could see through the mists were black. "This is it," Spartacus said in Erec's ear. "The Desert of Eternal Heat."

"I can see why it's called that. This is miserable."

"Is it? Hmm. I can't tell." Spartacus landed on a steaming patch of black sand. "The Suction Pits of Despair are just a few paces that way." He pointed. "I thought we could talk about what we're going to do once we get there."

It was hard for Erec to form words in the extreme heat. "I . . . can't . . ." He had to get into that cave before he could even think straight. The red sky looked oppressive in the boiling heat, and the sulfur smell was even worse.

"Well, hullo there," said a crisp British accent. "I can see that we have some visitors here today." A man stood before them, briskly dusting off his long white lab coat. He tapped a pen against a clipboard in his hand, apparently oblivious to the heat. "Wonderful. Wonderful. Let's see . . . Erec Ulysses Rex and Spartacus Kilroy . . . no middle name, Spartacus?" He looked right at the ghost as if he had no problem seeing him at all.

Spartacus answered, unsure if he would be heard, "Um, no."

"Fantastic. Well, we have it right, then." He tapped the clipboard, pleased. "Let's see. . . . Welcome to the Underworld, herald of the past and birthplace of the future." He spoke fast, as if listing oft-repeated lines. "It is the policy of the Underworld that all visitors must be inspected for communicable illnesses, dreaded diseases, poxes, curses, and hexes. Underworld citizens retain rights that will supersede your own when you are traveling here, and you must be advised that an inability to return does not constitute citizenship. Please heed the advisory that the earth elements here can change without warning, and also that their impact on humans is unpredictable. You may come away a somewhat different person if, and I say *if*, you return home again. And finally, it is agreed by the powers that be that each visitor be given a test of both cleverness and chance, and if they fail then they should never have come here, their visit will be void ipso facto, and all rights to return home shall be relinquished." He smiled pleasantly. "Are we all clear?"

THE SECRET OF ASHONA

Clear was the last thing that Erec was. It was hard to even focus on this man's words in this sweltering heat. He just shook his head, no.

"Wonderful. Well, as long as we're all straight, it's time to administer your tests. Right?"

"What tests are you talking about?" Spartacus asked.

"The cleverness and chance tests. Your quid pro quo for getting out of here, you see. Which of you would like to take the tests? I assume it will be Erec, as Spartacus will be able to leave at will, but you will not."

Erec was about to fade, so he raised a hand. If he didn't do the test now, there would be no hope at all for him.

"Excellent. Erec, I'll first administer your cleverness test. Right. Now, let me ask you a simple question, and you answer to the best of your ability. If you needed to get your scepter back, and your life depended on it, what would you need to do in order to obtain it?"

It took a moment for Erec to absorb the question in the blistering heat. How would he call his scepter back to him? He knew the answer—he had programmed it so that both he and somebody else had to say that he was ready to use it again. But his senses were still together enough to know not to answer and give away his secret. . . .

"Wonderful! You are correct. Thank you for sharing that information with me. Now, are you ready for the test of chance?"

"But I didn't say anything. . . ."

"A technicality. I don't require the spoken word to hear you loud and clear. Those details will be critical if, and I say *if*, you end up becoming a permanent resident here."

So, this man could read minds, then? Erec worried why he wanted to know about the scepter—and what he would do about it. *A permanent resident? That better not happen. . . .*

The man produced a small table with a tap from his cane. On it were six glasses of water. Erec's thirst overwhelmed him, and he wanted to gulp down each of them.

The man waved his hand over the table. "There are five rivers in the underworld, and two pools. Of course, one river and pool are connected, so that makes six waters that contribute to our spectacular landscape."

Erec thought the landscape was less than spectacular, but he kept his mouth shut.

The man continued. "In these cups, we have water from each of these rivers or pools. You may choose only one to drink, and whatever befalls you from that drink will be your fortune. Here are the waters of . . ." He pointed to one glass at a time. "Acheron, Cocytus, Plegethon, Lethe, Styx, and Mnemosyne. Which would you choose to drink?"

Erec was so thirsty that he wanted to drink all of them at once. But he hadn't lost his mind. It was obvious that some of those liquids would do horrible things to him. For instance, there was no way that he would drink the water from the River Styx, that was for sure. But the other ones were a mystery to him. Would some of them actually be good for him? How would he know?

Maybe Spartacus could help. Erec couldn't ask him out loud . . . but Spartacus could read his mind. Maybe Spartacus could read this man's mind as well and let Erec know which water to drink! He concentrated. *Spartacus, could you read his mind and tell me what to do?*

Spartacus looked at him and shrugged, shaking his head.

"Oh, and absolutely no cheating," the man said. "Of course a simple ghost can in no way read the mind of a Shadow Demon."

A Shadow Demon! Of course. One of the books in the library mentioned that Shadow Demons were like police down here, and something about "If you want to leave the Underworld you'd better follow their directions wisely."

The Shadow Demon yawned. "Police. What a petty comparison. Now, pick a water, let's go, make it snappy. We don't have all day, now, do we?"

"Do I get any clues?"

"Now, now, Erec. If you had clues, it would not be a game of chance, now, would it?"

There had to be a way that he could get out of this. Maybe the Shadow Demon was lying to him, and he didn't really need to do this to leave the Underworld again. . . .

"Quite sorry, chap. If it were only that easy. Rules are rules, you see, and it's like this—you drink or you stay here forever. And I really don't think you want that, now, do you?"

In his haze, Erec remembered something about Shadow Demons. He was human now, not safely a ghost—and it would devour him if he didn't walk right through it. Even if the thing turned into a hideous creature, he would not be afraid. All he had to do was gather his courage. . . .

The Shadow Demon yawned again as Erec walked through him. "Was that fun, now? I hope you enjoyed that little effort on your part. Yes, you have made it so that I can't eat you. But guess what? I wasn't going to eat you. So you've really changed nothing at all. Now, if you'd please pick a glass of water we can get on with things. It's becoming a bit of a long day."

Erec sent a thought to Spartacus: *Maybe we should go into the Suction Pits of Despair and find Tarvos. We'll see what happens if we ignore this guy.*

The man sounded annoyed. "Now, listen here. I've spent quite a bit of time helping you both through this difficult period of change that you're going through. There are rules to be followed, though, and I don't advise that you take matters into your own hands. It's like this. You pick and drink now, or I go, and you never get out of here. I'll do whatever you like, but this is your final chance." He crossed his arms expectantly.

"Okay, let me think." Erec pointed to the water from the River Styx. "I'm not drinking that one."

"All right, then." The Shadow Demon tossed the glass over his shoulder, and the water melted into the sand with a hissing noise.

"What would that have done to me?"

"Styx is hate. We'll leave it at that. Your choice, now?"

The water looked the same in each cup. Randomly he pointed to one, but then had a horrible feeling that he should not drink it. "Not that one either."

The Shadow Demon threw the cup into the sand. "That was Acheron. Sorrow. Next?"

"Hate and sorrow . . . are there any good ones in there?"

"It's all in your perspective." He waved over the four remaining cups.

Erec thought about using the Awen of Knowledge—one of the small balls that hung from the Twrch Trwyth on his neck. It would give him the answers to everything he needed to know. He knew that he needed to save it for something incredibly important, but wasn't getting out of the Underworld alive the most important thing?

"Wrong again." The Shadow Demon shook his head. "If you use the Awen of Knowledge, you'll learn that it's too late for you, and that you are doomed to stay here in the Underworld forever— because using it will take the chance away from our game of chance. It is a sure way to lose."

Erec pointed to one of the cups. At first he thought that he was drawn to it, but then he immediately felt fear. "No, I'm not drinking that one either."

"Shame." The Shadow Demon tossed it on the sand. "Mnemosyne. Memory. It would give you clarity."

Erec felt at a loss. He should have gone with his initial impression. None of the other cups seemed right. Disappointed, he said, "Okay. I'll take that one."

The Shadow Demon handed him a cup, smiling. He tossed

THE SECRET OF ASHONA

another cup into the sand. "Cocytus. Lamentation. You would not have liked that one." And then the final one. "Plegethon. Fire. Painful, but it would have added to your dragon powers."

Erec stared at the glass in his hand. "What is this one?"

"It's from the River Lethe. I hope you enjoy it. Don't forget, you need to drink a whole mouthful if you want it to count." The Shadow Demon vanished, leaving Erec with the cup.

Something was wrong. Erec knew that the liquid would be bad for him to drink. Maybe it had been the smile on the Shadow Demon's face. Maybe it was his own intuition. "Should I do this?" he asked Spartacus.

"I don't know. I hate the idea of you drinking that. But that book said the Shadow Demons in charge here get to decide who stays permanently." He shook his head. "I wish I could drink it for you."

"It sounds bad either way. If I don't drink it I'm stuck here. And if I drink it something bad happens to me . . . and I'm stuck here." There had to be a way out of this. Could he escape on a technicality?

Then he thought of one thing that might work. . . . He set the drink on the ground and acted fast before the Shadow Demon could respond, if he was still around.

Nee-way. He imagined being a spider again, hoping that he could control what happened to him.

It worked. The world around him stretched and grew, and the cup became huge in size. Erec landed on one of its corners, grasping on with his many legs. He had to be careful not to fall inside—drenching himself in the water might be fatal. But if he could take a mouthful when he was spider-sized, then that should count. That tiny sip might not affect him once he was human-sized again. Anyway, it was worth a try.

Keep an eye on me, Spartacus, he thought. *Don't let me fall into this stuff.*

He had to lower himself . . . and without a moment's thought he began to spin a web. It was so natural that he didn't even have to think about it. It was a short web, and just the way to move downward, like climbing a step. To be extra safe, he reinforced the strands twice, and wound some of his feet in knots of it before he lowered himself. It amazed him how similar the stuff looked to the Substance.

The water looked darker than it should, but at least it had no smell. Erec got as close as he could, but then he hesitated. Was he making the right decision? What would this do to him?

Then again, there was really no choice. He lowered his face to touch the liquid from the River Lethe, and filled his mouth. Before swallowing, he raised himself to the top of the cup, balanced on the rim near his web. Terrified of what would happen, he made the decision and swallowed. . . .

It was very hot when he awoke. How long had he been asleep? The sky was red. Interesting. Skies are red. He was sitting on a white thing, but didn't know what it was. He also wasn't sure what the liquid was inside of it, but something told him that liquid might be cooling on a hot day like this. Should he jump into it, then? That would make him feel better.

"No!" a voice shouted. "Don't go in there!"

Who was making that noise? Erec eyed the water again. Time for a dip . . .

But before he made it into the liquid, a giant hand scooped him away. "Erec! What are you thinking?"

Erec? he thought. *Who is Erec?*

"Oh, no!" the voice said. "This stuff made you forget everything? You don't even know who you are now?"

That thought had not even occurred to him—who he was. Who was he? He looked himself over. Eight thick, jointed, hairy legs, and a nice round, solid body . . . He was a spider, obviously. It was nice that the voice had pointed that out. He must have forgotten.

But it was very hot here, and he wanted to go for a swim. *Nice to meet you,* he thought. *Whoever you are.*

"Wait a minute!" The voice sounded excited. "Say, 'Nee-way.' Try saying it—or thinking it. It might help you."

It seemed that the voice was talking to him. Strange that thinking something might help him. But he did need help—he sure was hot. *Nee-way.*

Things around him changed fast, shrinking. The liquid got much smaller, and the man who had been speaking became closer to his size. And he looked familiar too. . . .

"Spartacus!" Erec threw his arms around the ghost hard enough to pass right through him. He could feel Spartacus hugging him back. It was a relief having his memory back. Thank goodness that tiny spider sip wasn't affecting him now. "That was strong stuff. I hope I don't forget everything each time I become a spider again."

"I doubt that—it's probably lost in your system by now."

"I hope so." He wiped the sweat pouring off his face. "Let's get out of here. You said the Suction Pits of Despair are that way?"

Spartacus nodded, relieved. He looked into the waters of Lethe left in the cup. "I'm keeping the rest. It might come in handy." Spartacus gestured toward the Suction Pits. "You first."

Hot sand bubbled around Erec's feet. He remembered that the Suction Pits were quicksand, and now he worried that he might melt from heat when the sand covered him completely. It burned his skin as he sank into it, then began to pull him faster as he plunged downward. Right before his face was sucked under, he took a deep breath of the hot, humid air.

He was boiling and suffocated, sand pressing in on all sides. He was still moving, but had slowed now. Where was the bottom of this thing? If only he would plunge through and pop out into Tarvos's cave . . . but instead he seemed stuck. The Suction Pits of Despair was the right name for this place, he thought.

It was too hard to hold his breath any longer, so slowly, with terror, he let it out into the sand. Maybe if he sucked in slowly he could get air again . . . but sand flew into his mouth and nose. He started to choke.

Something tightened around his ankles and yanked him downward. It hurt as hot sand shoved against his body, digging into him. But soon he fell through a hole into the cavern.

Instead of dropping to the floor, he was set down lightly by Spartacus. "Some entrance," Spartacus said. "If you didn't have a ghost with you, you'd never have made it through."

"Thanks." Erec collapsed on the floor, taking deep breaths and spitting out sand. "That was awful. At least it's cool in here."

They waited for Erec to catch his breath and calm down. He recognized this place from the last times he had been here. It was definitely Tarvos's cave.

Someone was talking around the other side of the corridor. Tarvos was probably about to change someone into a Golem. He walked closer, quietly, Spartacus drifting beside him.

Tarvos growled. "Well, I don't like it. I don't need a babysitter, especially some human kid. If the Shadow Prince doesn't trust me, then he should find someone else to work for him."

A familiar voice, with a mild New York accent, spoke fast. "It's not like that, with the Shadow Prince. I've known him for hundreds of years, and I trust him completely. But he wouldn't be doing his job if he didn't look over our shoulders. He's just watching out for us, that's all."

Who was that? Erec wondered. He sounded so familiar. . . .

"I don't *need* watching out for. I'm Tarvos!"

"And we all understand that. But this boy, Ward Gamin, has been specially chosen to spend some time here with you. Now that you've amassed your magnificent Golem armies, the Shadow Prince wants to make sure that they aren't misdirected . . . especially since you have the Master Shem now at your disposal."

Ward Gamin was there? Erec had just seen him at the Diamond Minds of Argos. It seemed the Shadow Prince liked to put him in dangerous places.

Tarvos grunted. "If you leave him here, I just might turn *him* into a Golem."

"I'll have to ask you not to do that. Please understand that we're just trying to make things work out smoothly. We're planning our attack now on Otherness, and before you know it, you and your Golem hordes can get out there and go nuts. It's just a little bit of time that we'll have to wait, so things can fall into place."

"How long?"

"A week from now, tops. With the help of our own armies, you and your Golems can wipe out Otherness in two weeks. Then, with the captives we get in Otherness—the ones willing to join us—we'll turn next to Upper Earth. The plan there is easy. One country at a time. The Shadow Prince has it all under control. He owns the airlines, boat and train companies, and he can shut down transportation in minutes. Then he can stop communication, because he has control of the telecom, cable, and Internet companies. Last week he purchased all of the Internet search engine companies in Upper Earth, so at the flip of a switch, the Internet will be almost unusable.

"And then . . . freedom for you, my friend. Baskania was thinking about giving you Australia—it's a huge continent on Upper Earth where you can be ruler over all who live there. There are bulls there too—and you can bring as many Minotaurs as you want from Otherness. Really nice place."

Erec peeked around the corner, curious who had been talking. He glimpsed Ward Gamin in his oversized jacket. Next to him was someone in red ermine and a crown. . . . It was King Pluto, his uncle who had unfortunately been swayed by Baskania. Erec drew back behind the cave wall before he was seen.

Ward sounded timid. "Your Majesty? Didn't the Shadow Prince

want me to search for Queen Hesti? I mean, I don't mind staying here, but I was supposed to do that—"

"No worries. Hesti had a kind of thing for dragons, and we thought that she might be hiding in their caves in Otherness somewhere. We were thinking of sending you to look. But there's no rush—if you ... I mean, when you finish this job you'll go there next. It is important that we find Hesti. I'm sure you know why."

Erec's fists clenched. Queen Hesti was his mother—and she had been missing ever since his triplet siblings disappeared. So Baskania was looking for her, too?

A memory came back to him—one that had been lost for a long time until he got his memory chip back from Connor.

Erec and Elizabeth sat on their mother's lap. She bounced them up and down on her knees and sang a silly song about dragons. Then she became serious. "I want you both to remember that dragons are beautiful, wonderful creatures. There are a lot of people who are afraid of them, and who would be happy to slay them from fear or greed—because dragons' lairs are full of riches. But the best thing that a dragon can give you is its friendship. Someday, I will take you to meet some dragons, and you will see for yourselves how noble they are."

"Daddy said he helped one of the dragons once. He saved its life," Erec said.

Queen Hesti gave them a hug. "That's true, Erec. When you are grown-up kings and queens someday you will protect the dragons, won't you?"

"Yes, I will!" Elizabeth hugged her mother.

"Me too," Erec said. "Maybe I'll get to be a dragon someday!"

Erec smiled. His mother must have had no idea at the time that he actually would become part dragon! He wondered for a moment about why it was important for Baskania to find his mother ... and then another of his memories was jogged.

THE SECRET OF ASHONA

Erec was lying in bed in the nursery, his brother and sister in their beds nearby. Queen Hesti sat on a tall velvet chair overlooking all of them. Her hair was a mess of red curls today—Erec liked it this way, even though it looked different every day. But her soft green-gray eyes and high cheekbones stayed the same. She was beautiful, tall, and regal, and it seemed to Erec that she could do absolutely anything.

"Someday you three will be the next rulers of our kingdoms," she said. "And I will have an important part in that. You can't become kings and queens unless I am there to pass on the crowns to you. Daddy once had that power, but he gave it to me for safekeeping. So now I have a big job to do one day."

"Why did Daddy give you the power?" Edward asked. "Why can't I have it?"

Queen Hesti laughed. "Maybe someday you all will, when your children are old enough to rule. But our good friend, the Hermit, said I should be the one to be in charge of it. Just in case something happened to Daddy, he said."

"What does the power make you do?" Erec asked.

She smiled. "It passes the leadership from father to son, uncle to son, and aunt to daughter. We could have made it work in lots of ways, but I decided that I'd pass it along to you by my kiss."

Elizabeth laughed. "Mommy has magic kisses!"

Soon all of them were laughing and singing silly songs about magic kisses. Erec remembered thinking that when Mommy put them to bed, they always got to stay up extra late and have fun.

The memory hurt. Erec felt pangs of loneliness, missing his mother and siblings. But he also wondered about what he remembered. His mother was the one that would pass the crown from his father to him—and also to his siblings? Did Baskania know that too? Erec would have to find her, for sure, by the time he finished his quests.

In the meantime, he had a bull to conquer.

CHAPTER TWENTY-ONE

A Drink in the Desert

SILENCE FILLED THE CAVE. Erec peeked again to make sure King Pluto had left. Ward Gamin stood pressed against the wall, terrified, while Tarvos scratched the dirt floor with a sharp hoof.

"Hmmm." Tarvos's deep voice echoed through the cavern. "I could turn you into a Golem—it would be a shame to waste you. But I'd rather just fry you on the spot." He snorted. "Show the Shadow Prince I don't need to be watched by one of his lackeys."

"I'm sorry—really." Ward sounded desperate. "I'll just stand here quietly and mind my own business. I won't get in your way. . . ."

Tarvos snorted. "You're already in my way."

Laughter echoed from the walls of the cave. Erec was sure it was from the cranes that stood on Tarvos's back.

"'Ear that?" one said. "He thinks Tarvos will let 'im live. In't that amusing?"

Erec couldn't let Ward get destroyed right in front of him. He'd already saved him once at the Diamond Minds pits, and it looked like he would have to again. Without wasting another moment, he ran around the corner and into the cave. Everyone stopped and stared at him.

It took Tarvos a moment, but then his eyes hardened in recognition. "Erec Rex? You ran in here to save this boy—I can see it in your thoughts. It's too late for him. I'll spare your life one more time, though, since you helped me so much. But you better leave and not come back."

Tarvos could read his mind—luckily he had been thinking about Ward, but he knew he had better act quick before the bull caught on to his plan. Instantly, he sprang into the air and landed on Tarvos's shoulder, grabbing one of his horns.

"Whoa, Nelly!" Spartacus jumped onto Tarvos's other shoulder with a grin. "You don't waste any time, kid."

"What?" The bull waved a hoof up near his head. "What are you doing?" He pointed a hoof at Erec. . . .

Erec was overcome with dizziness. He collapsed and sank over Tarvos's neck in a swoon. A ray of red light shot from Tarvos's hoof over his head. What was happening? It felt like Erec's eyes were spinning in his head. Had Tarvos done something to him . . . ?

Erec blinked, and everything was green. Big ropes of Substance hung around the room. Erec's dragon eyes were out. So it wasn't Tarvos, then. Erec was having a cloudy thought. He waited to hear what it commanded him to do.

"What's going on?" Tarvos roared, enraged and confused. "I can't read your mind anymore."

Erec flopped on the bull's shoulder with relief, his strength returning. Tarvos couldn't read his mind now—was that because he was part dragon from his cloudy thought? Tarvos swatted at him, and he jumped to the bull's other shoulder. The three cranes looked him up and down. He had to work quickly.

"How did you do that? Is your head a complete blank?"

Erec started to grab the bull's horn, then stopped. If Tarvos couldn't read his thoughts, maybe he could take advantage of that and slow down. "Sorry you can't read my mind anymore. Something got messed up when my old memory was put in."

"But I was just reading it a minute ago." The bull growled. "You were wanting to save Ward. Then boom! Your thoughts disappeared."

"Yeah. Like I said, it's all messed up." He tried to think how to calm the bull down.

"You 'ear that, Mage?" one of the cranes said. "He got his ol' memory bags back again. Me wonders who had 'em. Did some sprite stole 'em or somepin?"

Tarvos frowned. "Well, boy? Answer the question. Had a sprite stolen your memory?"

Erec laughed, relieved that he had the gift of time. He wasn't getting any commands from his cloudy thought—maybe it was just here to protect him in this way. "No sprite, just some kid named Connor Flannigan."

The bird preened. "Wha'dya do then, hit 'im over the head and pound it back out again? I'm sure it's no' easy to get memory out of someone, issit?"

"Not at all." Erec grinned. "Luckily the Memory Mogul did all the work for me." Talking about his memory distracted Tarvos, so Erec slid down his shoulder, closer to his horn. But then he saw a look of interest in Ward Gamin's eyes. . . .

Ugh! He felt like kicking himself. Why had he mentioned his

old memory in front of Ward? He hoped Ward would keep his mouth shut about it.

"I came back to help you, Tarvos." Erec hung his feet in front of the bull's massive shoulder and leaned closer to his head. "I'm sitting up here to whisper and keep things private. You know."

"Help me? You already got me the Master Shem—what else could you do? I'll just finish off this pathetic human. No *boy* is in charge of Tarvos!"

"I wouldn't do that yet," Erec said. "That's what I came here to tell you." Ward searched Erec with his eyes, practically begging him for help. Erec gave him a smile and a wink. "You're going to want to keep this kid alive, especially after you find out what's going on."

There was a low rumble coming from Tarvos that Erec assumed was curiosity. Even the cranes kept quiet, listening.

"Baskania is trying to trick you. You can't trust him. You see . . . this kid isn't really here to watch you. He doesn't know it," Erec added, as Tarvos could read Ward's mind. "But he is in trouble. Baskania wants him to die. But the three Fates really like this boy a lot. They said that whoever kills Ward, here, will be cursed forever. So Baskania hoped that you would do it. That way *you* would be the one cursed by the Fates."

Tarvos shifted uncomfortably. "The Fates? Is that true? That Baskania will pay for this. How dare he risk my life?"

A crane said. "Are 'umans startin' to tell the truth all of a sudden? Why believe 'im?"

"Erec Rex is different," Tarvos said. "He said he'd bring me the Master Shem, and he did. He said he would get his soul back, and he did. Plus, I'm no fool. Even though the Shadow Prince puts a shield up, I can still tell some of what he's thinking. And it's all about himself."

Erec put a hand gently on Tarvos's horn. It would be easier to trick Tarvos rather than fight him.

"You're exactly right. Ward over there has a time bomb inside of him, so you better get him out of here soon. Baskania wanted to make sure that you got the blame for killing him, even if you didn't do it. Ward will blow up down here and the Fates will blame you. Listen to his chest and you can hear it." Erec winked at Spartacus, and thought, *Use those rocks to make a ticking noise.*

Tarvos frowned and scooped up the stupefied Ward. Spartacus grabbed two pebbles, then zoomed to the bull's ear. Erec could see Ward's shirt moving as a steady click came from that spot.

"Hmm." The bull set Ward down. "I did hear something. A time bomb? Would it be a magical one, then? Could it hurt my cranes?" The cranes squawked and flapped, flustered.

"Yes. So be very careful. And there is something even worse. Remember the Master Shem that I gave you? There was a problem with it."

"A problem? What is it?"

"Have you tried using it yet?"

"Just once. I made all the Golems raise their hands, then sit. It worked like a charm."

Erec shook his head and whistled a low note. "You got lucky. Baskania took it before I gave it to you. He set it with a timer. After you use it for ten minutes, one of your cranes will die. In another ten minutes the next will be killed . . . and then the next. And after that— you. I felt bad leaving it here with you. I'm the one who brought it, it was only right to give you fair warning."

Tarvos frowned, anger steeling his face. "You've come back to make it up to me."

"I have. That Master Shem is already controlling you, too. Which horn do you keep it in?"

Tarvos pointed to his left.

"Do you want me to show you something? Look what Baskania is going to do to you. He's programmed you so that with one word your horns will unscrew themselves. I'll show you—the Master

334

Shem will come to me all on its own." He winked at Spartacus. "Baskania won't need you at all anymore. You've spent all of this time building a massive Golem army. He's going to let the Master Shem destroy you and your cranes, then steal it right back from you." Erec pointed at Ward. "Plus, you'll take the fall from the Fates for killing this boy."

Tarvos was growling. "When I get out of here I'll find the Shadow Prince and tear him limb from limb, before I use the Master Shem even once!"

It was hard for Erec to suppress the smile on his face. Baskania would be in for a nasty surprise. But he couldn't leave Tarvos with the Master Shem and the Golem army.

"I'll show you how easily Baskania can take your Master Shem, and then I'll give it right back to you. Watch this." Erec moved away from his horns and snapped his fingers. *Unscrew them, Spartacus!* he thought.

Spartacus hovered over the bull's head and started to twist both at the same time.

"What?" Tarvos batted his hooves in the air, passing right through the ghost. "How is that happening?"

The tough skin over Tarvos's horns was no problem for Spartacus's strength. In a moment both were off, one in each of his hands. The ghost grabbed Erec under his arm and sailed into the air.

"Aargh!" Tarvos screamed, enraged. His mouth was trying to form words, unsuccessfully, as he had lost his ability to speak. He lunged at Erec, swiping with an iron-hard hoof.

Spartacus jerked Erec out of the way and around the corner as the bull charged after them. Panicked, Erec grabbed Spartacus, but his grasp flew through the ghost. As they flew, he stuck his fingers in one of the horns and, with relief, felt the Master Shem.

Cranes attacked from all angles, pecking and clawing. They pulled at his clothing, holding him back while Spartacus tried to fly him away. Erec covered his face, batting them away as he could, when Tarvos dove at him, slashing with teeth and hooves. Spartacus yanked hard just in time.

Save Ward.

Erec had forgotten he was having a cloudy thought until he heard the command. He tried to tell Spartacus, but two cranes pulled him back again. Before he could break away, Tarvos butted his hornless head into his side. Erec flew into the wall, and slid to the cave floor.

"Are you okay?" Spartacus picked him up.

Erec nodded. "Get Ward."

Tarvos snarled and dove again, but Spartacus was faster. He grabbed Ward by the arm. In a series of twists and turns, the ghost maneuvered both boys around the cranes and bull until they were out of the cave.

Sand burned and scraped against Erec and Ward as Spartacus yanked them through the quicksand. Going back up suffocated Erec more than going down had. Sand shot into his nose and mouth as he tried to suck in air. Choking, he pulled his hands toward his face, but there was no way to move them there. He kept his fingers locked over the horns, to keep their contents inside. Everything hurt. . . .

Finally, Spartacus dropped them onto the boiling ground of the Suction Pits of Despair. Erec collapsed, heat baking through his skin even worse than before. Ward was lying on his back next to him. Spartacus waited for them to stop gasping and coughing, and then held a glass of water out to Ward. "Thirsty?"

Erec blinked a few times, absorbing the situation. There was nothing else to drink in sight. Ward would gulp it all down, and Erec would be left dying of thirst. "What about me?"

Spartacus raised a finger to his lips. "Ward can't hear me, silly. He thinks a glass of water is floating here on its own. Tell him you

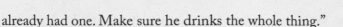

already had one. Make sure he drinks the whole thing."

"What? Spartacus—I'm thirsty too."

Ward stopped spitting sand and turned to look at Erec. "Who are you talking to?"

"Nobody. Just myself."

"Whatever." Ward immediately focused on the glass of water. "Whoa." He reached for it.

"Save some for me," Erec said, afraid it would be gone in a second.

Spartacus sounded annoyed. "Erec, that's not regular water. It's the glass you sipped from when you were a spider. You know, from the River Lethe. It will wipe Ward's memory clean, just like a newborn baby."

"Unh—" Erec reached for the glass, now thinking about knocking it out of Ward's hand to protect him—even though the water looked amazing. Ward must have thought Erec was trying to take it from him, so he brought it straight to his lips and took a big sip.

Spartacus pushed Erec away. "Let him drink it all. He heard everything you said in there, remember? All about how you got your old memory back from Connor Flannigan. And he saw you take the Master Shem and both of Tarvos's horns, too. In the other horn you have all of Tarvos's magical powers. Don't you think Baskania would want to know all of that?"

Erec was glad that Spartacus could read his mind. *Why couldn't you just have told me what Ward was thinking? Maybe he wasn't going to spill the beans to Baskania. I mean, we saved his life. You'd think he would have kept a secret for me.*

"Who knows. I couldn't have followed him around forever to make sure he didn't say anything. Now we're safe."

Ward had obviously forgotten to share the water with Erec, not that Erec wanted it. "I want some more. Where is more water?"

Erec looked Ward over carefully, wondering if the drink had taken effect yet. At least it wouldn't harm him. In fact, since Baskania was putting Ward in so many dangerous situations, maybe forgetting everything would help him. Ward wouldn't even know to go back to Baskania again. Erec could find him a safe home somewhere. . . .

Ward dropped the empty glass in the sand and looked at Erec with wonder. "Who are you? Where are we?" Then he scanned his environment. "It's so hot here."

"It's okay. My name is Erec, and we're in a big desert in the Underworld. It's time to go home now, okay?"

"Good. I'm hot." Ward frowned. "Where is my home? I can't remember where I live."

"You live in Alypium. Don't worry, I'll find it for you."

"All right." Ward looked contented. "Let's go now. I don't like this place."

Spartacus picked the boys up and flew over the desert until the landscape changed to dark marshes and mists. It wasn't until they reached the River Styx that Erec remembered the problem about the gold coin. If only he had kept one when he crossed the first time, he would have no problem getting back again.

"Do you have any gold coins on you?" he asked Ward.

Ward fished in his pockets. "I don't have anything."

Spartacus set them on the shore. Gray spirits drifted through the white mists, and the smell of sulfur filled the dark air. "I don't know what to do. There is no way I can get either of you back through that atmosphere. It must have been designed to keep people from crossing by themselves."

In the distance, a figure approached from across the water. As it grew closer, Erec could see that it was the boatman who had taken him across before. Maybe he would know what to do—although he had been far from helpful the first time.

The raft of bound-together logs washed ashore. Fingers that looked like little white worms wiggled around the edges, making Erec shudder. The boatman's worn canvas hood was pulled over his head. Bits of skull and cheekbone showed though his sloughing skin and grizzled black beard. "Welcome to the Underworld," he said again, drawing out his vowels and sounding just as loony.

"Thanks." Erec nodded, trying not to stare at his protruding hollow eyes. "We need to get back across. . . ."

"I need payment to take ye." The boatman pounded his stick onto the beach.

"A gold coin?" Erec asked.

"Yup." He giggled. "Or ye'll be stuck here forever, mate. Is that wha's going to happen?"

Erec tried not to get angry. "Is there anything else I can pay you with?"

The boatman scratched his chin, thinking. "I suppose I could take this boy's spirit." He motioned at Ward. "Ye can leave 'im with me as payment."

Ward pointed to himself, questioning. "Me?"

The boatman nodded. "Deal?"

"No deal!" Erec was disgusted. "We both need to cross. Is there anything else you'll accept?"

"Nope. Just a gold coin." The boatman grinned.

Spartacus stuck his hands into the boatman's pockets, searching for coins, but all he pulled out were worms and dirt. The boatman giggled.

Erec sighed. "Can you tell us where we can find a gold coin in the Underworld? Because we have to get home."

"There is a place. . . ." The boatman looked into the distance. "Not a very nice place, but a place, nonetheless."

"Yes? Where is it?"

"There is a Carnival of Darkness up in the Dunes of Distress. Ye might be able to win yerself a coin there, if yer lucky."

The Dunes of Distress. Not exactly the name of a dream vacation spot. But Erec had to play the odds in the Carnival of Darkness if he wanted to see his home again.

CHAPTER TWENTY-TWO
The Carnival of Darkness

EREC WAS AGAIN THANKFUL that he was traveling with a spirit who was able to find his way practically anywhere. He was carried with ease by Spartacus, along with Ward, over hills that looked like slimy oil slicks, then above a flat terrain with the appearance of gelatinous globs of goo.

"I hope we don't have to land in that stuff," Erec said.

Before long, they flew over dunes of black sand. Unlike the desert they had just been in, it was freezing cold. Spartacus set them

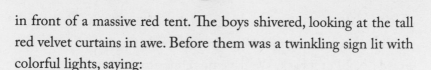

in front of a massive red tent. The boys shivered, looking at the tall red velvet curtains in awe. Before them was a twinkling sign lit with colorful lights, saying:

WELCOME ONE AND ALL TO THE CARNIVAL OF DARKNESS. STEP RIGHT IN AND TRY YOUR LUCK!

"Try your luck at what?" Erec said.

A skeletally thin man with a pencil mustache and long pointed beard stepped around the curtain. He wore a black stovepipe hat that was over a foot tall, with a red ribbon tied around its base.

"Why, try your luck at luck, my friend. Are you here to play? Because we have some glorious prizes in store for you!" He ushered them into the tent.

It was warm inside, and good smells filled the air. The room was dark, as its name suggested, but of all of the places in the Underworld, this seemed the best by far. Popcorn stands mingled with fried dough booths, and carnival games were everywhere. A huge, brightly lit Ferris wheel spun at one end of the tent, and a carousel with cheerful music echoed from its center. People were laughing and talking. . . . Erec realized that this was the first time he had actually seen people in the Underworld. Maybe this was where they all hung out. He didn't blame them.

"Wow." Ward looked around slowly. "This is nice. Is this my home?"

"I don't think we should stay long," Spartacus said. "Something is fishy about this place."

Erec didn't have that feeling at all. In fact, he was hungry. "Let's get a snack first. I haven't eaten in forever!"

He walked up to a brightly colored booth with racks of pizza under warming lights. It smelled heavenly. "How much for a piece?" Erec realized that he had no money at all.

"One gold coin." A bald man working behind the counter smiled. "Would you like a piece?"

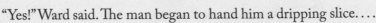

"Yes!" Ward said. The man began to hand him a dripping slice. . . .

But Erec realized that it might be a trick. He shouted over the crowd, "No! Put it back. We have no money to pay you."

"You could owe me." The man winked. "It's no problem."

"Okay." Ward put his hand out.

"No." Erec pulled Ward's arm away before the pizza touched it. "We can't." He dragged Ward from the booth, against his protests. If they were lucky enough to earn a gold coin, the last thing he needed was for this man to take it away because they owed him for pizza.

"Good thinking," Spartacus said. "Let's see if we can earn some change."

People walked by, eating snow cones and slurping sodas. They seemed to be having a great time. But when Erec took a closer look at them, he jumped with fear. Their eyes burned glowing red, like fiery coals, and their teeth were sharp and pointed. It was obvious that they were not human at all. . . .

Spartacus noticed them as he heard Erec's thoughts. "They are undead. Living, but without souls or spirits. Kind of like zombies, but these seem more controlled, like something is animating them. I can tell you there is only one thing that all of them are thinking, though, now that I'm paying attention to it."

"What's that?" Erec wasn't sure that he wanted to hear it.

"You don't want to know," Spartacus agreed. "Should I tell you anyway?"

Erec nodded.

"They are hungry. And they all hope that you mess up so they can feast on both of you."

Chills went through Erec. This place no longer looked carefree and fun. He inched closer to Spartacus as they walked, trying not to look at the burning eyes of the ravenous undead around them.

Ward seemed not to notice, however. He focused on the food

THE SECRET OF ASHONA

that was everywhere. "I want that." He pointed to the cotton candy. "And that." He motioned at the huge salted soft pretzels hanging from a string nearby.

Erec took him by the shoulders. "Promise me something, Ward. This is very important to remember. You can't eat anything here, okay? I'll get you whatever you want when we get home again. But right now, don't touch the food."

Ward shrugged. "All right." Erec decided that he had better keep a good eye on him, anyway.

The huge tent made the carnival look even darker than it was outside. Tiny lights twinkled at the roof, giving the appearance of stars. It would have been beautiful if it weren't for the horrifying people inside. They walked by the Ferris wheel which was spinning extra fast, its riders screaming.

Something yanked Erec around the middle. He shot backward, stumbling, from the pulling around his waist, arms reaching toward Spartacus. "Help!"

A man with a tall stovepipe hat, like the one who let them into the tent, removed his large curved cane handle from around Erec's midsection and winked. At least his eyes weren't bright red, Erec thought. But he was terrifying nonetheless—probably just because he seemed so happy here. The man gestured to the Ferris wheel. "Step right up, boy. Are you game to try something new? How about a fantabulous ride on our Wheel of Fortune? Nothing like it anywhere else, I assure you."

For the first time, Erec noticed two huge black arrows, one long and one shorter, built into the side of the Ferris wheel. They both were hinged at the center and spun at the same time the wheel did, but the small one went in the opposite direction of the large one. It gave the appearance of a crazy clock with its hour and minute hands whirling the wrong ways.

As the ride slowed, the arrows did as well. Soon they all stopped. Lights turned on, blinking along the edges of the long arrow. It pointed at one of the cars with passengers in it that had been whizzing around a moment ago, and that car lit up as well. The two people—a man and a woman, if you could call them that—inside of the car looked excited, and began jumping up and down, rocking the small car precipitously.

The smaller arrow had stopped as well, and now it was pointing to some words printed along the side of the ride. A stream of red lights turned on along the smaller arrow, and then the words lit up as well.

BURN.

Erec was fascinated. There had to be some meaning to this, he was sure. The people in the small car looked excited. Would they get something as a prize?

But, instead of a prize, streams of flame shot out of the seats that the figures sat in. Erec could see them well—they were not high up—and they were soon engulfed in fire. There was a smell of burning flesh. Amazingly, the two people in the basket continued to cheer and dance around, although Erec wondered if they were actually struggling to escape.

All of the glowing-eyed undead figures in the other basket cars watched them with interest. Soon the flames petered out, and the two riders were nothing but charred skeletons with glowing red orbs in their eye sockets. It became clear that they were still alive—or at least not dead. The skeletons stood in their seats, cheering, arms above their heads.

It occurred to Erec that they should be afraid of falling out of the ride from their antics. At the same time he realized that falling couldn't possibly hurt someone who happily lives through being burned alive. It was such a horrific spectacle that Erec was stunned.

He could not remove his eyes from the victims—or winners.

He wondered what other fates lay in store for the riders. There were eight segments on the side of the wheel for the short arrow to point to. They read:

BURN.

SHRED.

ACID.

GOLD COIN.

LIFE IMPRISONMENT.

CHEW.

CHOP.

GOLD COIN.

Gold coins? If this was how he was supposed to risk earning one, then he wanted none of it.

Spartacus looked equally horrified. "Chew? I can only imagine what that means, with these starving undead all over the place."

Erec shuddered.

The man with the tall hat patted him on the shoulder, making him jump. "Ready to take a chance at the wheel? We have wonderful prizes, as you can see. Maybe you'll even win a gold coin! Think of all that you could do with a gold coin." He smiled leeringly, and Erec could see that his teeth were just as sharp and pointed as the undead, even though his eyes were not glowing red. Erec backed away.

Spartacus said, "He's no better than the rest of them. He just has coverings over his eyes."

The thought made Erec shake with fear. One of those . . . things had spoken to him? He had to get away fast. . . . But, then again, where else was there to go? Would he have to spend the rest of his life in the miserable Underworld because he was too afraid to try to earn a gold coin here? Or would he end up dead, burnt to a crisp? There was no good answer.

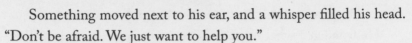

Something moved next to his ear, and a whisper filled his head. "Don't be afraid. We just want to help you."

Erec jumped. It was the man with the tall hat. How had he gotten so close without Erec noticing?

Ward seemed not to mind the man at all. "Do you have some food I can eat?" he asked.

"No," Erec whispered harshly, pulling Ward away.

But the man followed them, offers of French fry baskets and plump donuts in his hands. "Please, help yourself. Just one gold coin apiece."

Ward began to reach, and Erec snatched his hands away. Even though the food looked and smelled far better than normal, it terrified Erec. "Come on. Let's see what else is here."

Booths with carnival games lined the sides of the tent, and the undead flocked to them, spinning wheels and tossing hoops over bottles. Rows of Kewpie dolls hung from strings along the tops of the booths, as well as odd things such as eyeballs and ears, floating in jars of liquid. A winner of a ball toss pointed at the jar of eyes, and the booth worker tossed one straight into his mouth. The thing made a hideous squishing sound as the man crunched into it, almost causing Erec to throw up.

Another hatted man waved them toward a smaller tent. "Come inside, and see the one and only Freak Show of the Bizarre. Be dazzled by our snake woman, her body is made entirely out of snakes. Watch her eat the mouse man alive! Only one gold coin, and you will be treated to delights seen nowhere else in the world. . . ."

A carnival barker seemed to be shouting just to them. "Step right this way. Age-guessing here. Let me try and guess your age correctly, and if I fail you win a gold coin. Right this way." He wore the same tall stovepipe hat that the others did, and had a long, thin face.

Did everyone know exactly why Erec was here? It seemed like

they all taunted him with exactly what he needed—a gold coin to get back across the River Styx and home again. Maybe this was where everyone was sent who couldn't pay the toll. Why else would someone come to this awful place?

At least the age-guessing stand didn't seem to have as dire consequences as the Wheel of Fortune Ferris wheel. He walked slowly to the barker and eyed the empty stand covered with red velvet in front of him. Before stepping on it, he asked, "How does this work?"

"Such a cautious child." The barker chuckled. "It's a simple game. I guess your age, and you win . . . or not. That's all."

"And if you guess my age wrong I get a gold coin?"

"Exactly."

Erec had his doubts. If the man was able to tell what he wanted, he probably could guess his age without a problem. "And if you get my age right?"

"Oh, you know, just quid pro quo. I get the return of the favor. That type of thing."

"What favor? What happens?"

The man cleared his throat. "We get to keep you, that's all. You become one of us. Nothing to worry about at all, my boy. You win either way." His thin lips curled into a smile, showing his long, sharp teeth.

Erec stepped back. "One of you? No thanks." He grabbed Ward's arm and walked away, Spartacus at his side. "I bet there is no way here to really win a gold coin. What are we going to do?" If only he hadn't wasted both coins the first time across the river. He felt like an idiot.

"I don't see any way out of this," Spartacus said. "I can't get you and Ward across the River Styx. And there is no other way back home again without a coin." He scanned the booths. "A lot of these signs offer gold coins to winners, but losing would be horrible. Look at that." Spartacus pointed to a sign at an apple-bobbing booth listing body parts that would be given up for failed attempts: LIVER, KIDNEYS, PANCREAS, SPLEEN, HEART, BRAIN.

"That's awful." Erec pulled Ward away. "These things are just waiting to devour us."

Ward looked around innocently, like a child. "Can we play some games?" Erec saw a tray of food coming closer to Ward's dangling hand. He whisked Ward away from the dangerous temptation.

"No. These games are bad."

"What about that one?" Ward pointed to a small stand where a short, dark-haired woman stood, her hair in a ponytail. One of her eye coverings had slipped, revealing glowing red around its edge.

At first it looked like she was running a ring toss, but when Erec got closer he saw that instead of throwing rings, the players had to fling long bones into the eye sockets of three rows of skulls that were nailed onto a board in order to win.

"I can help you," Spartacus said. "You throw and I'll make sure it goes the right way."

That sounded like a good idea. Erec read the sign.

BONE TOSS

TOSS THREE BONES INTO THE EYEHOLES AND WIN A GOLD COIN!

TOSS TWO BONES INTO THE EYEHOLES AND LOSE A GOLD COIN.

TOSS ONE BONE INTO THE EYEHOLES AND LOSE YOUR LIFE.

TOSS NO BONES INTO THE EYEHOLES AND BECOME A PERMANENT RESIDENT!

Even with Spartacus helping him, Erec was terrified of losing. Becoming a permanent resident likely meant being gobbled up by these zombie creatures and becoming one of them forever. But there was no other choice he could see.

He walked up to the creature in the booth. "I'll give it a try."

She smiled, baring rows of sharp teeth, and handed Erec three smooth white bones. They were each about the size of one of his arm bones, he thought. Were they originally from people who came here and had turned into zombies?

The undead woman gestured toward the skulls, and stepped back, a look of contentment on her face. All of a sudden, everything around them had stopped. People who had been walking and talking, others who were playing games at booths—all paused and turned to stare at Erec.

He nodded, trying to keep an eye on Ward at the same time. Even if this game was not rigged, it would have been impossible to win. The bones would have to be thrown at exactly the right angle to make it into the eye sockets, and even then they would bounce out when they hit a piece of bone that split the eye socket in two.

But Erec had help, so he crossed his fingers and picked up one of the bones. He lifted it overhead, and aimed, and then threw. . . .

As the long bone left Erec's fingers, he could feel it swerve in the wrong direction. One miss would lower him one gold coin—a loss he could not afford, as they were nearly impossible to get. More misses would be a disaster.

Spartacus, with ghostly-quick reflexes, grabbed the bone as it sailed by. He yanked it in the air as it flew—but it wasn't easy for him. He managed to tug hard, wedging the bone deep into the eye socket of one of the skulls. A rickety sign behind the woman in the booth lit up with one blinking red light bulb showing one successful hit.

"Phew." He wiped his brow. "That thing was programmed to miss by a long shot."

Eyebrows went up all over the carnival. More undead gathered with interest. Some licked their lips with long, pointed tongues. Erec was sure they thought he was bound to lose and become their dinner.

He rubbed his hands together, and picked up another long bone.

"Let's do this." He raised it behind his head and threw it, worried less about precision this time.

Spartacus grabbed it and plowed the thing through the air. It was even harder now to steer, but he pulled while propelling it forward and managed to thrust it into another eye socket. With a buzz, the second blinking red light flashed on in the sign.

Nobody cheered. Instead, the crowd pressed in, silent and drooling. Ward watched with quiet interest.

"Here goes nothing." Erec picked up the third bone. This time it yanked unexpectedly from his hand, and soared out of the booth. Spartacus almost lost it, and had to make it curve through the air toward its target. He groaned from the effort, and Erec worried he might not make it. But, just as it neared the edge of the table, Spartacus gave a final yank and jammed it into one of the skulls' eyeholes.

The third light blinked on the sign. A strange noise filled the air, and it took a moment before Erec recognized it as a mass, communal growl. The creatures around them were not happy, as they might be losing a meal.

Erec wondered if they were going to accuse him of cheating. It seemed obvious from its curved path that the bone had not flown from a simple toss. But then again, they were cheating even more, pulling it in the wrong direction. Playing by the rules had nothing to do with the game here.

But he had won. He put out his hand, about to ask for the gold coin—

"Look at that. It changed." Spartacus pointed to the sign.

BONE TOSS

TOSS FOUR BONES INTO THE EYEHOLES AND WIN A GOLD COIN!

TOSS THREE BONES INTO THE EYEHOLES: LOSE YOUR LIFE AND BECOME A PERMANENT RESIDENT.

TOSS TWO BONES INTO THE EYEHOLES: LOSE YOUR LIFE AND BECOME A PERMANENT RESIDENT.

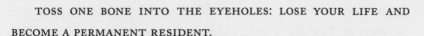

TOSS ONE BONE INTO THE EYEHOLES: LOSE YOUR LIFE AND BECOME A PERMANENT RESIDENT.

TOSS NO BONES INTO THE EYEHOLES: LOSE YOUR LIFE AND BECOME A PERMANENT RESIDENT!

A man in a tall stovepipe hat held another bone out to Erec.

"I won," Erec protested. "Where's my gold coin?"

The man pointed to the sign. "See? It says that you have to throw four in to win."

"But the sign changed! What if it changes again?"

The man smiled craftily and set a gold coin on the counter of the booth. "There it is, boy. All yours if you can make this last throw. Go on, take the bone."

Erec eyed the coin, and then the sign again. With Spartacus helping again, maybe he'd finally get what he needed. He wrapped his fingers around the bone, but as soon as he touched it, it yanked backward.

Spartacus was in front of him, in the wrong direction to catch the thing. Erec, terrified of losing and being devoured, gripped hard, and held on tight. There was no way that he could throw it. The bone catapulted him backward, and he sailed over the crowd, holding on to it like a hang glider.

Red eyes followed him as he flew in the opposite direction of his target. It would be impossible for Spartacus to steer him now that he was this far away and moving so fast. It was hard enough before when they were much closer. He should never have tried this. Now it was too late.

Something sailed by him, even faster than he was going. It was Spartacus, and he was holding something. . . . The spirit soared in front of Erec, and in mid-air held the thing in front of the bone.

It was a skull. Spartacus jammed it hard onto the bone in Erec's hand.

At that instant, a moment before they would have smashed

against the wall of the tent, the skull with the bone in it dropped to the ground. Erec fell with it. Hordes of red-eyed creatures crowded in, looming over him, teeth bared.

"Time to go!" Spartacus called. He pulled Erec by the hand up and over the crowd.

"But we need the coin!"

"I got it!" Spartacus had Ward wrapped in his other arm. "Let's get out of here!"

The angry fiends let out a mass shriek of despair and rose off the ground in flight after him. In unison, they dove at him and Ward, grabbing and biting. It felt like a pack of hawks attacking from all sides.

"I don't like this," Ward murmured. "Ow . . . I'm bleeding."

Erec didn't like it either. He began to feel faint, and worried that he was going to pass out. Was he being eaten already? There were nips on his legs. . . .

But then a familiar voice entered his head, and it was one that he was never happier to hear.

Rise and spin.

It was not what Erec expected to hear from a cloudy thought. But he would not have questioned it even if he could resist its command. He broke away from Spartacus with new ease, his dragon power making him bigger and stronger. Wings sprouted from his back and he flew upward, then spun. . . .

Grab the Substance. Hold it tight and spin faster. Make a Substance Web.

Erec did as he was told. When he had been a spirit, he had been able to hold on to the Substance with every bit of his being, and tie all of it together into a tight web. But even as a human, Erec found that he could grip some of it. Not with his hands, or every bit of him as he had before. It was more with his mind, his concentration.

Was this what Baskania was like with the Substance? Able to move it at will? As Erec pulled, yanking and twisting it into knots, he could feel its resistance.

Speak to it.

Of course. That made complete sense. He was making the Substance do something against its will. The least he could do, as he had done before, was to ask its permission.

Substance, he thought, *I need your help. I have to spin you into a web so that I can get out of here alive. I think it's the only way Ward and I will make it back. I'm sorry that I have to do this.*

It was as if the Substance heard him and agreed, for in a moment it was helping him. If before he had been able to pull and twist it into tangles, now it was grasping him and forming itself into a full web. With his dragon eyes out, Erec could see the thick ropes of it knit together, surrounding the zombielike creatures in the tent.

The only problem was that the creatures did not seem held back by the Substance Web at all. They had been batted away by Erec's tough, scaled arms and legs as he spun, but otherwise they flew freely. Erec could not see Spartacus or Ward, and called out for them. . . .

Spartacus shouted back, "We're okay. It's not easy, but I'm keeping Ward away from these guys so far. Where did you go?"

Erec flew toward the voice.

Dive and spin.

He did as commanded, whirling and throwing off attackers in mid-air. They were all teeth and glowing eyes, the rest of them became a blur. . . .

Spartacus was in front of him now, holding Ward in his arms like a rag doll. He was full of cuts and gashes, but he was breathing. The moment that Spartacus and Erec saw each other, they soared together toward the door of the tent.

Once they reached the opening, the Substance Web took effect. It contracted, pulling back. The bodies of the creatures were not held by it, in fact many still ran or flew after Erec and Ward. But, with his dragon eyes, Erec could see that the lights in the insides of the creatures were whisked right out of them. The red in their eyes disappeared as the living parts of their beings were yanked away from their bodies.

Some of the figures dropped, some ran on, confused, until they hit a wall. Others fell upon one another, attacking.

Spartacus glanced back at them, mystified, then he smiled. "I never would have thought of a Substance Web. Good idea."

"I was just following directions. Hopefully now we can get out of here!"

CHAPTER TWENTY-THREE

One Gold Coin

IT WASN'T LONG before the three were back at the shores of the River Styx. Erec was relieved. Finally he would get out of here! This place was horrid. He still had the Master Shem and Tarvos's power source in their horns in his pockets, and he was finally starting to feel victorious.

The boatman approached, a dark figure on the waters. When the raft slid ashore, he winked at Erec from under his frayed canvas hood. "Welcome to the Underworld."

Couldn't the crazy loon find a better thing to say? They had already been here awhile. The guy needed to develop a vocabulary, Erec thought.

"We need a ride across the river," Erec said. "We have a gold coin now."

The boatman nodded. Erec stepped aboard the raft. Spartacus lifted the still drooping Ward on board and set him in the one chair strapped onto the wooden logs. Erec sat at the base of the chair. He would have to be careful not to let the waters that lapped onto the raft get on him.

But the boatman held a hand up in the air. "Only one may ride."

Erec's eyes met Spartacus's. What was he hearing? This could not be happening. The boatman had made it sound like they needed only one coin to get back. There was no way they would ever escape if they needed another one.

"No, really. It's okay. I don't need a chair. We only have one gold coin, so we'll just share the ride."

The boatman did not move. Erec thought, in fact, he looked gleeful under his thick, scruffy beard. "Only one may ride."

"Well, what should we do, then?" Erec began to feel angry. "I overpaid you once. We went out and got a third coin, just to pay you again. There is no way that we can get another one. Can't you give us a break?"

The boatman didn't answer, just stood still. It was obvious that nothing was going to make him move with two people on his boat.

Spartacus grabbed the boatman's stick and gave it a push into the mud. Erec filled with excitement, thinking they were finally saved ... but no matter what the ghost tried, the raft would not budge. What were they supposed to do? Leave Ward here, clueless and unaware, to wander in the Underworld until he died of thirst, or something worse? Maybe they could just leave him here a short while, then come back with more coins—enough to safely get both of them out.

"That sounds good," Spartacus said. "But look." He pointed,

and in the distance three shadowy night panthers approached, fangs bared. "I could stay with Ward to protect him, but if you go, there is no way you'll ever find your way back alone."

"So what do we do?" Erec was pacing now, keeping an eye on the night panthers. "Maybe leave me here with them and you can take Ward back. At least I might turn into a dragon and defend myself."

The idea of being left alone in the Underworld sounded awful. But it seemed like the only possibility.

"Bad idea." Spartacus shook his head. "You're not invincible. And who knows how long it will take us to get back, or if something will happen to us? What if I'm called by Baskania and have to serve in his army? I won't be able to resist that—you remember that pill? You'd be stuck here forever."

Erec shuddered. He knew Spartacus was right. It seemed hopeless. He climbed off of the raft and left Ward alone there, but Spartacus did not drop the coin into the mouth of the waiting corpse on the boat.

What if . . . ? A thought occurred to Erec. If he morphed into a spider, maybe the boatman would not notice he was onboard. He caught Spartacus's eye and held a finger up to get his attention. He pictured himself as a spider, and then he thought the word.

Nee-way.

The world around Erec grew upward at incredible speed, as he shrank to miniscule size. There were his eight jointed, armored legs, as he remembered them. In a moment he remembered how to use them, and started the long crawl toward the raft. Now that he was small, it would take forever for him to get there.

But Spartacus was watching. He picked Erec up and set him on Ward's shoe. The boatman did not seem to notice.

"Okay, then?" Spartacus said. "Can I pay you now?"

The boatman nodded. Erec was glad that the boatman was able to hear Spartacus. Maybe it was because he was the gatekeeper of the

Underworld—he had to sense everything there. Spartacus dropped a coin into the open mouth of a shaggy male corpse on the raft. It smiled and slid into the dark waters.

But the boatman did not move.

"Go on, then." Spartacus gestured out toward the water. "Take him across."

"Only one person."

Erec's heart sank. Even though he was this tiny, the boatman still would not bring him across with Ward? At least Spartacus had made it over the river as a spirit. . . .

And then another thought occurred to him.

Nee-way.

Erec imagined himself as a soul. In a moment, he felt himself evaporate.

He had forgotten how lonely it felt to be a soul, alone and apart from its spirit and body. It was a horrible feeling. But if Spartacus was able to cross the river as a spirit, Erec might be able to cross as a soul. Either by himself, or together with Spartacus.

The urge to join him was overwhelming. Erec flew straight into Spartacus's empty soul. It was hard to communicate—he could not speak at all—but Spartacus knew that he was there. In seconds they were passing through the compressed atmosphere above the river, breaking up into little particles, yet crossing all together. Underneath them, the boatman pushed Ward across the water.

On the other side, Erec and Spartacus waited for Ward to arrive. Erec waited a while to become human again, hoping he was helping Spartacus feel more normal again. Then he stepped outside of Spartacus and thought, *Nee-way.*

Human again, he pulled Ward off of the raft. They were all safe now, and on their way home.

❄ ❄ ❄

Erec felt in his pockets for the two bull horns. He was glad they—and his clothing—survived the trip. Apparently, inanimate objects passed through that tight atmosphere much more easily than living things. The Master Shem was still resting inside of one horn—Erec would always recognize it. The tiny scroll was made of ancient-looking parchment, and it was the size of one of his fingers. So small, but so powerful.

In the other horn was a small, soft ball. It was warm and a little mushy. Erec was careful not to accidentally poke a finger through it. When he looked carefully, it moved just a little bit, looking alive, like a little brain. This was Tarvos's power source, given to him by the sorcerer ages ago. Without it, he was just an extra-large bull.

Spartacus dropped Ward off at his old ranch, to be watched by Erec's old friends, Kyron and Artie, who were living there. Then he flew with Erec to Rosco's apartment. Rosco was pacing, his face pulled tight, fists stuffed into his pockets. When he saw Erec, he looked stunned for a moment. Then he pulled him into the kitchen and spoke quietly. "Do you know how worried I've been?"

"I'm sorry." Erec felt awful. "I know. I just didn't want to risk your life." He grabbed a glass of water and sat down.

"I got all the way to the cave that led to the Underworld. But I couldn't find my way through. It was pitch black, and my MagicLight wouldn't even work in there. I was so scared you might need me that I tried to find my way by feel, and then I fell down a huge pit. If I couldn't fly, I'd still be there." He put his hand on his stomach. "I had to give up. But I felt like I was abandoning you. And I have to say, I'm really angry. You could have been killed!"

"Rosco, that's awful. I'm glad you're okay. But I'm fine. If you came with me, we would never have gotten out. . . ."

Rosco collapsed into a chair, and put a hand up. "Hey, it's over. I'm going to try to put this out of my head now. Never again, okay?" He covered his eyes with his hand.

Erec did not answer, not able to promise that he would take Rosco everywhere. In fact, there was no way that Rosco would be able to go see the Furies, which was what he had to do next.

Rosco peeked between his fingers. "So . . . what happened?"

"I got both of Tarvos's horns! Also the Master Shem, and Tarvos's power source." As he said it, Erec began to gleam. He had done it! It had been so hard getting home again, and so exhausting, that he had not really enjoyed his victory.

Rosco's eyes widened. "You are kidding. . . . Are you serious? You actually disarmed Tarvos the Great? What are you, some kind of superhero?"

"Nope. Just lucky. Spartacus did most of the work." Erec told Rosco about making Ward drink the water from the River Lethe. "So he's kind of like a newborn now. He's at Spartacus's ranch. I guess we'll leave him there for now. He'll be okay."

Rosco frowned. "I don't know. But something bothers me about this—"

Before he could finish his sentence, Rosco took a deep breath and howled, chin up to the ceiling. It was so loud that Erec had to step back.

"We have to go." Rosco stood. "The Shadow Prince wants me to bring you to him right away. Let's take the Port-O-Door."

Erec was glad that Baskania had not tried making Erec come by commanding him personally. Hopefully he had given that up. Even though the pill that put Erec under Baskania's control didn't fully work, it was not pleasant to resist.

Rosco led Erec to the Port-O-Door, and Spartacus followed. They walked out into the Inner Sanctum of the Green House in Alypium. Passing a series of rooms, they came to a large office filled with hundreds of candles, Baskania at his huge carved wood desk. King Pluto stood at his side, and President Washington Inkle trembled in fear next to them.

Rosco bowed low, and then rose stiffly. "Master."

Erec could not read Baskania's face any more than Baskania could read his mind. The two stared at each other for a few minutes, wondering. Had King Pluto seen Erec in Tarvos's cave? Erec thought he had been so careful. He had waited until Pluto was gone before he had spoken to the bull. The only person who had seen him was Ward. . . .

Baskania rose, a huge smile on his face. "Erec! I am delighted to see you again. I have become more and more impressed with your talents. Look at you—a trip to the Underworld and you've arrived back with no problems at all."

Erec froze inside, but he tried not to show it. How did Baskania know? Rosco may have been uneasy, but he looked completely calm. Spartacus, on the other hand, paced back and forth across the room. Erec wished he would stop. Even though nobody else could see him, it was making Erec nervous.

Baskania strode forward and patted Erec on the head. "It's so nice that you are alive and in one piece again. You have proven useful to me constantly, helping me with one thing after the next. What a good boy you are."

The Shadow Prince's words worried Erec, but Erec had no idea what he was getting at. He stayed quiet and waited.

Baskania began to count things off with his fingers. "First, you gave me the scepter. Granted it's gone again, but soon you will return it to me safely. Next, you offered me both of your dragon eyes. A nice touch—and thank you. I do look forward to using them. Then you offered yourself as a blind follower. But when I made you my servant, and allowed you to keep your sight, what did I get?" He paused dramatically. "Loyalty? Servitude?"

Erec could feel his heart pounding. He had no idea what Baskania knew, other than that he had been in the Underworld, but it didn't sound good.

"Oh, no. Erec Rex, you've offered me something far better than that!" He laughed, and snapped his fingers. Connor Flannigan appeared, bound in black rope from shoulder to toe. "You gave me your old memory. The one that you were missing."

Erec's stomach dropped to his feet. How did that happen? Erec had the memory back himself—Connor didn't own it anymore.

Connor looked stunned, eyes darting around the room in fear. "I gave my memory back to the Memory Mogul," he said. "It's too late. I don't have it anymore."

"Oh, but you do." Baskania gloated. "One never really gets rid of a memory, true?"

That left Erec thinking. What was Baskania talking about? He was sure Connor had given back his memory, just like Erec had removed the memory that used to give him nightmares once.

And then Baskania said something that made Erec's breath stop. "But the most exciting thing that you have given me so far is Bethany Cleary's younger brother. You know, the one who will be able to teach me the secret of the Final Magic. You, Erec Rex, have put him right into my hands." He tilted his head back and cackled with glee.

Erec could not believe his ears. This was a sick joke. Was Baskania making it up to upset him? Was this his way of confusing Erec, so that he could learn something from him? He looked around for Bethany's brother. Was he here somewhere?

Baskania chortled. "Are you trying to see if I'm hiding the boy here now? Not yet. But I have all that I need now to find him." He patted Connor's white hair.

Everybody in the room was trying to absorb what Baskania was saying, but it seemed like only he knew. He paced the room, wringing his hands, a big smile on his face. At one point, he walked straight through Spartacus, who was also pacing. That made Erec nearly jump out of his skin, but Baskania did not notice the ghost at all.

Finally he stopped in front of Erec. "I'm sure that you want to know more, and it will be my great pleasure to tell you. First, as you suspect, I know everything that happened in the cave with Tarvos, after Pluto left. Which means that I know that on top of all of the other amazing gifts that you have given to me, you also have a Master Shem, and Tarvos's magical power source for me as well." He held out a hand. "Thank you for those, my boy, and for everything else."

Erec froze, unsure what to do. He had no doubt that if he resisted, Baskania would overpower him and take both of them easily. But, then again, he couldn't give Baskania the key to the Golem army! He was planning to lay siege to Otherness and Upper Earth. There had to be a way to stop this.

Spartacus had an idea. "What if you start to give those things to him, and I'll grab them and fly out the window. I'll hide them somewhere."

That sounded like a great plan—and the only way to solve all of the problems at once. Relieved, Erec fished in his pockets and pulled the Master Shem from one of the horns. He held it out toward Baskania in his open palm.

Spartacus swept down and scooped it up. To the rest of the room it must have looked like the object came to life on its own, flying suddenly toward the window. . . .

And then it stopped, mid-flight. After hanging in the air for a second, the Master Shem was whisked out of Spartacus's hands and straight into Baskania's.

It took a moment for Spartacus to notice what had happened. He tried again to take it from the Shadow Prince, but this time only got it an inch away before it returned again.

"Very good, Erec." Baskania nodded. "I remain more and more impressed with your mind, if not your magical skills. But don't worry, your abilities will improve with time and my teaching, even though they will never match mine." He examined the object that he held intensely. "You were right to get this, Erec. This will be much better held by me directly, not by that stupid beast. I shall keep it with my other treasures." He stuffed the item into his pocket.

If Baskania knew exactly what had happened in the Underworld, then he knew that Erec did not take the Master Shem just to give it to him. What kind of game was he playing here?

Baskania dusted his hands together. "As I was saying, I was privy to the happenings inside of Tarvos's cave. And I am completely impressed, my boy. You went there on your own to obtain all that vast power. And you succeeded! I watched you use magic in that cave that I did not know you possessed." He pursed his lips in thought. "You didn't tell me, your master, that you were going to steal those things. In fact, you could well have ruined my plans for your own gain.

"But then there was more! I learned that you had been to the Memory Mogul, and found your old, lost memory again. How clever of you. And how handy for me. But what I truly admire is the way that you operated on your own. No regard for me." Baskania pointed to himself. "Only for what was good for you."

Regardless of the fact that Baskania sounded pleased, Erec was sure that he must be infuriated. He had caught Erec red-handed try-ing to ruin his plans. How could he be happy about that?

Baskania sat on the edge of his desk with a sigh. "It has been so long since I have found a follower with true bravery and spunk." He gestured to Rosco. "My advisor here had that at some point, for sure, which is why I've ended up respecting and trusting him so."

Rosco returned a smile to the Shadow Prince.

"But you are something else altogether. You do not cower before me. You are not afraid to further yourself at my expense. No worries—" Baskania held a hand up. "I am not at risk of you actually ruining any plan of mine. I am more than capable of keeping you under check.

In fact, this has been a delight." He bounced the Master Shem in his palm.

Erec was amazed. It seemed that Baskania was serious—he was happy that Erec had broken into Tarvos's cave and stolen the Master Shem. He truly was that impressed by it. . . .

Baskania looked at Erec with respect. "And see what you've given me. I now am holding the Master Shem, which gives me personal command over the massive army of Golems that Tarvos created. And I'll be able to do wonders with his power source. And you—I now have someone to actually teach. No offense, Rosco—you still are close to my heart. But what spunk!"

Erec, oddly, was feeling slightly proud of himself. It wasn't often that people patted him on the back for anything he had done. And it was true—he had been pretty brave. Erec was doing it to help others, though—Baskania was wrong about him just wanting power. But it felt nice to get complimented for once. Usually people just complained when he messed up. . . .

"Like I said, so many gifts at once. The scepter, your dragon eyes, Tarvos's magic, and now your old memory." He smiled. "Which gives me Bethany's brother. Perfect!"

CHAPTER TWENTY-FOUR

Reliving Old Times

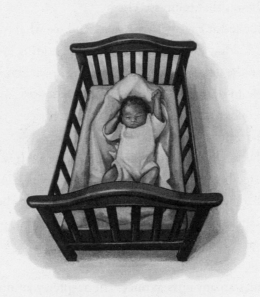

EREC CLOSED HIS EYES, completely losing what Baskania was saying—even though his words made Erec boil. Erec had given Bethany's brother to Baskania? It was bad enough that he had handed him his dragon eyes, the Master Shem, and everything else.

He took a deep breath, trying to calm down. At least Baskania wasn't blowing him into pieces. He had to ask questions. How would Baskania know what happened in that cave? The only other person there was Ward, and Spartacus made sure that he forgot

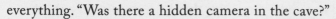

everything. "Was there a hidden camera in the cave?"

Baskania laughed so hard that he bent over. "You could say that."

And then it all made sense to Erec. He had completely forgotten. Ward! Ward Gamin had given Baskania one of his eyes, so the Shadow Prince was able to see through his other eye at any time. In fact, that was the whole reason that Ward was left there—to keep watch on Tarvos for him. Maybe there was even an alert for Baskania, somehow, to look through Ward's eye when he sensed that something was going on. That must have been it.

Spartacus figured it out at the same time. He stomped around the room shouting names at Baskania. He was so loud to Erec that he was terrified that everyone else would hear, even though they showed no signs of it.

It was bad enough that Erec had lost the Master Shem to Baskania. But there was more that he needed to know. "If you heard that Connor had my old memory, and I got it back from the Memory Mogul . . . then why is he here?"

Baskania patted Erec on the shoulder. "Because I like you, Erec. I really do. I never thought that I would say those words. But you have become a sheer pleasure now that I have gotten to know you. It helps that you finally came to your senses—even if it took a little help from the Furies—and decided to become my pupil. But that is not answering your question, now, is it?

"Yes, I learned that you found your old memory, and that Connor Flannigan here was its holder. He used it for years, had it removed, and now you have it. So, if I did not care for you so much, I would simply use your brain to explore your missing memory and find out what I need to know. But rather than strap you down and take days, or longer, fishing things out of your mind—" He gestured to Connor. "I'll simply do it to him. He has all of the same memories inside of him still."

Connor let out a gasp of protest.

Erec did not understand. Not that he wanted to have his brain probed through, but . . . "I thought once a memory was taken out, it was gone. I had a memory taken by the Nightmare King and now it doesn't bother me anymore."

Baskania tilted his head. "What was the memory? Can you tell me?"

The memory was nothing really important, nothing Baskania didn't already know. "It was just someone else's memory of a bad childhood that I was given once. But yeah, I could tell you about it in detail . . . if you want to hear it."

Erec realized that he was talking to Baskania like he might a friend. It even felt a bit like Baskania was on his side, which he knew was completely wrong. This man was his worst enemy. He had tried to kill Erec many times in the past. But now that Erec knew him better, he didn't seem quite so bad. It was almost confusing.

"It doesn't matter what the memory was," Baskania said. "What is important is that you could still repeat it all now. You still *remember* it. It's a funny thing about memories. If your original memory was removed, it's gone. That's that. But if you get someone else's memory, you think about it on your own, it becomes your memory as well as theirs. So when the other person's memory is removed, your own memories of that memory stay . . . if that makes sense."

It made perfect sense. Connor's memory was removed, but he had lived with it every day for so many years that it was part of his own memory as well. He could repeat every bit of it. "I still don't understand. Why do you want my old memory?"

Baskania winked at him. "Dear boy. I admit, I already know most of what happened in your early days. Either I had tabs on it, or I orchestrated it. But there is one thing—or one person—who has evaded me. The prophecy said that the secret of the Final Magic is hidden in the mind of the smallest child of the greatest seer of

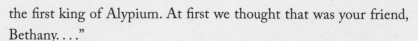

the first king of Alypium. At first we thought that was your friend, Bethany. . . ."

Anger filled Erec as he remembered the torture that Bethany had been put through by this man. He felt like a traitor for even speaking to him. But then again, he was ordered by the Fates to serve Baskania. It was all so strange, he did not know what to think. He tried to focus on what Baskania was saying, not how it made him feel. "So, you wanted my old memory because of the prophecy?"

"Exactly!" Baskania shouted. "Now that we know that Bethany had a younger brother, all I have to do is look in your old memory from that time and I'll be able to find out all about him."

It was true. "I knew Bethany when I was young—she lived in the castle. So maybe I knew her younger brother. . . ."

"And now I will know as well. Thank you, yet again, Erec."

Erec's heart sank. He had made one awful mistake after the next. He wanted to kick himself for being such an idiot.

Unless . . . could there be a way for him to head things off before Baskania found Bethany's brother? It would take Baskania at least a few days to sort through Connor's memory—it had taken weeks to pore through all of Bethany's when she was captive. Maybe Erec could figure it out first. He would find Bethany's brother and save him.

He could not wait to get out of here, go home and sift through his old memories. But he had to keep up a good front with Baskania. "I'm glad it all worked out. And I'm sorry that I did those things without asking you."

"Don't be sorry. I would have said no, of course. And then where would we be?" Baskania ruffled Erec's hair. "Forget sorry, boy. And forget asking. If you have to ask, you're no better than the rest of them." He gestured to President Inkle, who shuddered.

Erec resisted feeling good. Why was it that Baskania sounded so much nicer now—more human? "Let me know what you find out, then, okay?"

Baskania made a motion as if he was tipping a hat to Erec. "Of course. And thank you again for the many gifts today." He nodded curtly at Rosco, who walked over to Erec.

"Time to go, kid." Rosco kept up a tough front, but Erec could see that he was flustered. Rosco ushered him back through the Port-O-Door and into his apartment. "We need to talk."

Spartacus appeared, and he was irate. "How could we have forgotten that Baskania was looking right through Ward Gamin's eye? I can't believe he knew everything! I tried so hard to pull the Master Shem out of his hands. But he was much stronger than those zombie things in the Underworld were. I can't believe the power he has . . . more than a spirit even!"

Rosco, who hadn't heard a word of what Spartacus said, looked angry. "You are so lucky. Do you realize how that could have gone? I was sure you would be dead, imprisoned, blinded, had the life sucked out of you . . . but not complimented! If people disobey him he doesn't take it lightly. The Shadow Prince really likes you. I don't get it."

"Thanks, Rosco. I'm that unlikable?"

"You know what I mean." Rosco sank onto his couch, stunned. "All I can say is he's rarely like that. It's true you've given him everything he's ever wanted, and all at once, too. That's enough to soften anyone up." He shrugged.

"And all of those things are going to cause a lot of damage, hurt a lot of people." Erec's shoulders drooped.

"I know. If it makes any sense, the Shadow Prince sees what he's doing as the greater good. He doesn't value individual human lives. Instead he thinks the pursuit of knowledge is bettering the world."

"The pursuit of knowledge? How about his crazy need for power?"

"You're right. He has that, too. But he doesn't see it that way. The Shadow Prince is a student of time and magic, and he's dedicated his life to reading and learning everything there is to know." Rosco sighed. "He disregards people, and does horrible things. Even he knows that power is his main goal, I think now. But I bet he doesn't admit it to himself."

Erec felt like he was about to cry. "I've messed up again and again. I need to make things right, and I don't even know how. Before I do anything else, I need to remember who Bethany's brother is before Baskania finds out."

Rosco nodded. "That's a great idea. Then we can try to save him before it's too late."

"Wish me luck."

Erec lay down in a quiet bedroom. *Bethany's brother.* He wondered what Bethany was like as a little kid. Last year in New York they had thought they were meeting for the first time. Both of their early memories had been taken away.

But now his was back. He was excited to remember Bethany when she was little. Had they been friends? What if they had hated each other? Erec hoped that he didn't remember anything awful that would make him like her less, like if she had punched him in the nose every time she had seen him, and stolen his favorite toys. He couldn't imagine, though, that anything she did then would affect him now.

But what if thinking of her as a very old childhood friend changed the way that he felt about her now? He really liked what they had—it was like friendship but more than that too. Like having a girlfriend, in a way, but not so serious and corny. Would she seem more like a sister after this?

Erec pushed all of those thoughts out of his head, and instead focused on his old memories that were new to him again. He didn't

know if it would be hard to remember the right thing, but he thought back to a day when they were little, living in the Castle Alypium. *Ruth Cleary, Bethany, Pi . . .*

"Bethy! Bethy! Bethy!" Erec's sister, Elizabeth, rolled around the nursery floor in delight. Her favorite friend was coming to play in the nursery today—one that they didn't see all the time.

Erec wasn't so excited. "Not her *again." All that girl ever wanted to do was play pretend magic games with Princess Pretty Pony. She never wanted to try Zoom Zoom Undie-Ball with Erec and Prince Muck-Muck. Stupid girls. Some of them could be really fun, but not this one.*

Bethany skipped into the nursery with her mother. She sang, "I'm going to be a mommy. I'm going to be a mommy."

Her mother, Ruth, patted her on the head. "That's right, dear. We only have to wait five more months and you'll be a big sister."

Bethany plopped on the floor with Elizabeth and picked up some crayons. "No, I'll be a mommy. Princess Pretty Pony will be our sister."

That memory was too early. But how strange remembering Bethany as a little girl! She had been so cute, with dark curls waving all around her face. Erec laughed, relieved that it had not changed his feelings about the current Bethany one bit. He tried to think about a later time, after her mother had the baby. Sifting through his thoughts, it seemed that that was toward the end of his new memory—not long before it had been removed.

One stray image hit him—

Someone brought Bethany to play in the nursery, but it was not her mother. In fact, she had been taken here a lot of days in a row, it seemed. And she wasn't happy about it.

Whoever was dragging her here—was it a maid?—had to pull her by the arm into the room and slam the door shut. "Listen to me, you . . . you little girl. This is no way to act. I am in charge of you today and you get to come play here with your friends. Now be a big girl and act nice. Okay?"

Bethany stuck her tongue out at the maid. "I hate you! I don't want to play here. I want to play with Mommy!" She stamped her foot.

The maid was having none of it. "Mommy is tired now, because of the new baby. She was up all night again. Now she needs her sleep today, so you are going to stay here."

"I want my Mommy!" Even though she wasn't his best friend, Erec felt bad for her. Every day she had come in here crying.

The maid left, and Bethany broke down bawling, just like she had the other mornings. "I hate having a baby! I hate the baby! He's stupid. All he does is cry and sleep, and he takes Mommy away all the time."

Erec was glad that he didn't have a baby. He wanted to help Bethany. "Let's throw the baby away! I hate babies too." He never knew before that he hated them, but looking at Bethany he certainly did now.

A smile lit on her face. "Yeah! I know where he sleeps! And I know how to get back home all by myself."

"Can Clio do it with us?" Erec glanced at today's nursemaid, one of his favorites. She was helping his sister pick up her crayons.

"No! Grown-ups don't let us touch the baby. They just make us go to our rooms and be nice to the baby. We have to throw him away all by ourselves."

Erec started running in big circles around the room, excited. He stepped on his sister's crayons by accident as he darted by. Some of them broke, and others sprayed across the floor. She began to cry, but Erec only noticed that for a moment. He was going on an adventure!

Bethany caught up to him, running too. "Let's go!"

He stopped and bragged, "I snuck out before." Clio had told him all about it, but he didn't remember. She said that once Erec had left again and again from the nursery. She said it was a bad thing, but it sounded exciting. *And now he was going to do it again with a friend! He put a finger over his chubby little lips. "Shh."*

They tiptoed to the door. Erec turned the knob, just like he saw big people do. When it opened, the two ran out. After they were safely down the hallway they jumped up and down, screeching. Bethany darted into another hallway, and Erec tumbled after her, laughing and kicking the walls. "This is fun!"

"Whee!" Bethany trotted ahead of him, a big grin on her face. "We're going home!"

Erec looked around at the unfamiliar rooms they passed by. "Home?"

"This way!" Bethany jumped as she ran, pointing. "I saw how to go."

After a few minutes, Erec was tired and he stopped. Bethany looked like she was going to go on without him, but then she turned and walked back to his side. "Is you hurt?"

"No. I'm tired. I want Clio."

Bethany took his hand. "Get Clio later. We're throwing out my baby. Remember?"

She was so nice that Erec forgot about Clio. "Okay." He smiled.

They walked hand-in-hand—or actually Bethany pulled Erec's hand—until she found the door to her family's apartment in the castle. She opened the door and pulled Erec up a flight of stairs and down a hall. "Shhh! Don't wake up Mommy!"

Erec figured that they would grab the offending baby, wherever it was, throw it into a garbage can, and then everyone would be happy. Then someone nice would walk him home. And give him a snack.

But it wasn't so easy. First of all, the baby was in a kind of tall cage. Bars were all around its bed, and they reached so high that Erec could not even touch the baby, let alone pick it up. And then second of all . . .

"What are you two doing in here?" A woman in a maid's uniform whisked Erec high into the air. He and Bethany each dangled from one of her arms, far from the bad baby.

THE SECRET OF ASHONA

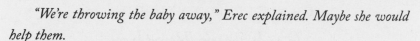

"We're throwing the baby away," Erec explained. Maybe she would help them.

"What?" The woman shook them in the air. "Now, you two rascals shouldn't sneak around like this." She lowered her eyebrows at Bethany. "I'm sure your mother won't be happy." Then she glared at Erec. "And as for you, they're going to have to step up security in that nursery again. Now I've seen it with my own eyes. You are truly a sneaky little one, you are."

Bethany glared at the woman. "Put me down! I want my mommy!"

"Not this time. I believe you were both to be watched in the castle nursery, and that is where you are going. Now, say you're sorry to your little brother, first, okay? I don't want to hear any more of this 'throwing away the baby' nonsense."

She held both children over the crib to apologize to the baby, who had no idea that anything had been said, and couldn't have understood a word of what was happening.

Erec looked down at the infant. "What's he called?"

The maid smiled fondly at the infant. "We call him Tre, after his daddy."

The baby didn't look so mean. Maybe he shouldn't be thrown away. There was just a bit of curly fuzz on his head, and he actually was kind of cute. Bethany must have been wrong. In fact, the baby looked a little like Bethany's big brother, Pi. Erec loved to play with Pi. He showed him how to throw basketballs and played running games with him. . . .

Erec's eyes popped open in shock. Bethany's little brother did look a little like her older brother, Pi. He looked like Bethany . . . and someone else, too. Everything clicked inside his mind. Why hadn't he thought of this before? It was all so clear now. He had to fix things right away before Baskania found out what he already knew, and to save Bethany's brother from a terrible fate.

CHAPTER TWENTY-FIVE
Bethany's Brother

ROSCO STEPPED BACK when he saw the look on Erec's face. "What happened to you?"

"I know where to find Bethany's brother. We need to protect him. Let's go straight to Ashona so I can talk to Bethany first. She needs to know this. Then we all can help hide him."

"I'll go with you. We should hurry—who knows how long it will take the Shadow Prince to figure it out too." He opened the Port-O-Door, and Erec followed him inside. "Take this Port-O-Door back separately from me if you need to. I have other ways I can get around."

In another minute they had checked in at the desk and were walking through the big doors into the beautiful Castle Ashona. Erec led Rosco, with Spartacus following, to the suite where his family was staying.

June was surprised to see them when they opened the door. She rushed over and threw her arms around Erec. "How are you? I've been so worried. . . ."

He hugged her back. "I got my old memory back, from the Memory Mogul."

She pulled away and looked hard at his face. "You remember everything now?"

"Mostly. I mean, if I give it time, then it all comes back."

She hugged him again, and ruffled his hair. "That's a lot to take in, I guess."

"Luckily it's not all pouring into my head at once. It comes in spurts. But there is one thing I found out—who Bethany's brother is." He threw her a meaningful glance, and she started to stammer. But Erec held a finger up. "I have to tell her."

June shook her head. "That's not a good idea. He's safe now. Let it be."

"Well, he won't be safe for long. Baskania has the same memory that I do, and it's just a matter of time before he comes and gets him on his own. We need to hide him. But Bethany has to know what's going on."

June looked stunned. She took a breath and nodded. "She's in the library. It's down the hall and to the right—"

"It's okay. I know where it is, Mom."

"Come back when you're done and we'll all figure out what to do. I'll talk to King Piter."

Rosco let Erec go into the library alone to talk to Bethany. She was the only one there, so she was easy to spot. "Hey, Bethany!"

She took one look at Erec and came running. She started to throw her arms around him, but then stopped short. "You're not a ghost again, are you?"

"Nah." He grinned. "Go ahead."

She gave him a hug, and then pulled him into a chair next to her. "So, you were with Baskania? How did it go? Oh, I'm *so* glad that's done now. We can celebrate! I want to hear every detail." She stopped and looked into his eyes. "I was so mad at you for leaving. And I was scared every day that I'd never see you again." She took a breath, thinking about it. "I thought that when I finally saw you, I wouldn't even speak to you. But now that you're here, it's all evaporated. I'm just so glad that you're back." She hugged him again, and then looked into his eyes. "What's wrong?"

"I'm so sorry, Bethany. I didn't mean for you to go through all of that. It hasn't been fun for me, either." He wanted to tell her about the Underworld and his meetings with Baskania, but that could wait. There was something else that could not.

She put a hand on his cheek. "What's wrong?"

Erec choked up for a minute, and then he cleared his throat. "I found your little brother."

Her eyes flew wide open. "My *brother*? Where is he?" She grabbed Erec's shoulders and jumped up. "I have a brother! I can't wait to meet him!"

He bit his lip. "You already have." Erec could feel his eyes well up with tears.

Bethany looked concerned. She held Erec's hands and sat down next to him again. "I have? Where is he? What's his name?"

It was hard to get the word out of his mouth. Erec tried to speak, but he had to shut his mouth again. Then he managed to say it. "Trevor."

They sat for a moment in stunned silence. Bethany's gaze drifted into the distance in disbelief. But then they snapped back into focus. "You mean his name is Trevor? Trevor what?"

"Trevor, my brother."

She shook her head. "No. That's not possible." But then she glazed over again. "Is it?"

Erec nodded. "I got my old memory back. Remember Connor, that crazy kid in the contests in Alypium who was always saying that he was really Erec Rex? He had my early memories."

She thought hard for a minute, then drew in a breath in shock. "You are *kidding*!" She clapped her hands together. "I always thought that he was insane for saying that. That explains a lot."

"We talked him into giving my memory back to the Memory Mogul, and I have it now." He smiled for a moment in victory, but his smile faded fast. He wanted to wait a minute before he told her the bad news. It wasn't fair to give her a brother, and then take him away one minute later. If only it were different.

"So . . . you got your old memories back, and you remembered that Trevor was my brother?"

He laughed. "Yeah. I never thought about how we used to know each other when we were little. But it makes sense. We both lived in the Castle Alypium, and our parents worked together."

"Wow." Bethany's cheeks turned pink. "Did we like each other then? It's weird to even think about that."

"I'd say we did. You were more friends with my sister. You know, Princess Pretty Pony." He laughed.

Bethany frowned. "Do you think you could remember the names of your missing triplet brother and sister?"

"I did! They were Elizabeth and Edward."

"All *E*'s. Like your father, Pluto, and Posey are all *P*'s."

"I guess so." Erec felt like he was putting off the inevitable, but he couldn't tell her about the danger yet.

"So, Trevor is my baby brother," she said in wonderment.

Erec laughed again. "You didn't like him so much back then. You know, the jealous sib thing. You and I were planning a big mission to go throw the baby in the trash can."

Bethany clapped a hand over her mouth. "Are you kidding? I can't believe that we were fellow adventurers even back then." She giggled. "I'm glad we didn't hate each other."

Erec looked down. "I just hope that you don't hate me now."

"Why?" Bethany pulled a knee up to her chest and wrapped her arms around it, shivering. "What is it?"

He shrugged. "It's not good." Erec pinched his lips together tight, not wanting to let the words out. He wished that he hadn't even brought it up—although that was the reason that he was here. Bethany had been so upset for so long, because of him. Now he was going to ruin her first few decent moments.

"Is something wrong with Trevor?" She began looking around as if wondering where he was. "Does he know yet?"

"I wanted to tell you first. You're going to have to hide him. And not tell me where he is. I had to let you know as soon as I found out, but Baskania isn't through with me yet. I have to go back there. And . . . he has my memory too."

"You mean . . . he knows about Trevor?"

"He will soon. He took the same memory from Connor, and he's looking through it to try to find out who your brother is. They have whole teams of people there working on it. You have to hide Trevor before Baskania finds him. And it could be soon."

"Why can't you help me? I trust you."

"I don't trust me." Erec closed his eyes.

"I don't understand."

"There was something that I saw when I looked into my future before. I was working for Baskania . . . and I handed Trevor over to him. I didn't even know then that he was your lost little brother. It was bad enough that I was giving my *own* brother to him. Now it's even worse. Trevor is the kid he needs for all of his awful plans."

Bethany slumped into her chair, eyes wide with shock. Then she looked at Erec sharply. "Why would you even believe you'd give Trevor to that monster? I know you, and that is the last thing you would do. Either the vision was wrong, or you're going to get possessed. Maybe we should hide you, too."

"I wish that would work. But I have to go rescue those souls still. I'm going to learn a spell to stop time, and then I'm going back to Alsatia. . . ."

Bethany stared at him a moment, then shook her head, uncomprehending. "I don't even know what you are doing anymore. It's like you're living a whole new life. . . . Okay. I'll go find Trevor and hide him. If you think it's safer I won't tell you where he is. I just can't believe he's my brother. . . ." She paused. "You know what? He does look like Pi, now that I think about it, with his red hair."

"I thought so too. And he was named after your dad."

"Tre?" She looked sad. "I wish I could remember my dad."

"Maybe someday we'll find your old memories too. But having them is almost worse. I miss everyone now that I never even knew about before."

Bethany looked upset. "So, you're leaving again, then? And I guess I can't come with you?"

"I'm really sorry, Bethany. If there was any way it could be different, I would love for you to come. But the only way you can even get to Alsatia is by dropping onto a huge spike and dying. . . ."

"You're going to *die* again! Erec—you can't do that! You've gotten really lucky twice now, but I just know that if it happens again it will be forever. Last time—"

"There's another way. I can get in to Alsatia without dying. It's the same way that I got out of the Underworld—by turning into a soul."

"You went to the Underworld? And you can turn into a soul? Is this some new magic you learned? I don't know anything going on with you anymore."

She was getting more upset, and Erec could understand why. He decided to fill her in on everything, starting with his first meeting with Baskania.

At the end her mouth was hanging open. "You poor thing! You need a break. And you need help! I wish I could go back with you to Baskania, and then to Alsatia."

"Knowing that you are safe here helps me the most."

She thought a moment. "Not that I'm trying to talk you out of this . . . but I actually feel bad for the three Furies. I mean, it's horrible that they have all of those innocent souls as prisoners. But sending the Furies back to Tartarus . . . I mean, they're going to be miserable there for eternity. Plus they've really been helping you—and they aren't waging war on the Fates and destroying humans now."

"You're completely right. I've been trying not to think about that, because I feel so bad for those trapped souls. I was in there with them and I can tell you the pain they are in. But the Furies *have* been great to me. I'm a total traitor sneaking in there and sending them back to Tartarus. They'll be suffering there forever."

"Yeah, and you know what would happen if they escaped again? They would kill all of humanity in revenge. I don't think they'd like humans so much anymore."

"You know, I wasn't thinking about that. But there's something worse. Once Baskania finds out that they're in Tartarus again, he'll be thrilled. He'll gather up three thousand people right away and retry his plan to free the Furies—for a price."

"It would put us all right back where we started again—about to die because the Furies will be set loose by Baskania. They would be released soon to serve him and destroy the world."

They both sat in silence, absorbing this. Erec had no idea what he should do now. His whole plan seemed ridiculous. As much as he could not stand seeing three thousand souls suffering forever, what could he really do about it? Maybe they were fated to be there forever, sacrificing themselves in agony for the sake of the rest of the world.

"I'm really glad I talked to you," Erec said. "I would have made a horrible mistake if I sent the Furies back to Tartarus. By the time I realized that, it would have been too late." He smiled. "Good thing you're so smart."

She winked back. "You're not too bad yourself. We're just better as a team."

"I guess I shouldn't go back there, then. The only thing I don't understand . . ."

"What is it?"

"My quest is still not done—the segment on my Amulet of Virtues isn't lit up. I know that's what I'm supposed to do. And why would the Fates have talked about me freeing those souls? They're the ones who first said something about me sending the Furies back to Tartarus. If I wasn't supposed to do it, then they would have said that. It just doesn't make sense."

"When do those Fates ever make sense?" Bethany laughed.

Erec did not say anything, but he didn't agree. They might not make sense at first, but before long they always were right. At least Trevor would be okay. Erec was so relieved that he had figured out who Bethany's brother was before Baskania did. Now he would be safe. "I have an idea. The last time I looked into the future, I saw myself giving Trevor to Baskania. I'll try it again, and this time I'll see what will happen to Trevor when you hide him and don't tell me where he is. I want to make sure he'll be safe that way, so we're not taking any chances."

"Great idea. I still think there is no way that you would ever really give your own brother—or mine—to Baskania though."

Erec, on the other hand, had no doubts that his visions of the future were correct every single time. But things should be different now. He asked himself, *Show me what will happen if Bethany and my family hide Trevor somewhere safe, and they don't tell me where he is. Show me Trevor's future then.*

Erec closed his eyes and imagined himself entering the dark room inside of his mind. It had been a while since he had been here, and he had almost forgotten how nice it was . . . how calm. It felt great to relax after worrying so much for so long. He didn't want to leave this place, but at the same time he could not wait to see what the future showed him. He hoped he would see Trevor safe and sound, far away from the Shadow Prince.

So he entered the smaller room inside of the one that he was in. It was even darker, more peaceful. There was the box that contained all of his knowledge sitting on a table. He allowed himself to rest a hand on it and feel the warmth, excitement, and wonder that it contained. Once again, it gave him the feeling that everything would work out just fine. He hoped this time that the feeling would last after seeing Trevor's fate. Erec pulled the soft cord that hung between the two windows and pulled the shades open to watch.

Trevor was alive—he was breathing, at least. But he was strapped down to a table, metal cones inserted into his head. His eyes were closed, and it was hard to tell if he was unconscious or just resting. But there was a look of agony on his face.

Baskania stood over Trevor's body cackling with glee. "I have done it! I have found the answer that I have waited for my entire life!

The Final Magic." He rubbed his hands together. "If I had only known all along how simple it was. It took a child, a very wise child, to be able to see the connections that I was missing all along.

"A toast!" He lifted a glass of purple liquid that looked to Erec like dragon blood. "A toast to my great future! And to the memories of Erec Rex—may he rest in peace. Thank you, Erec, for giving me such wonderful gifts when you were alive."

Trevor began to stir. He opened his eyes, but when he saw Baskania, tears formed, and he shut them again tight.

"He wakes." Baskania rubbed his hands together. "What a great opportunity to try out my new powers." He reached in a pocket and withdrew a long silver knife, and in a second he slit Trevor's throat. "Right through both carotids and jugulars." He wiggled the knife a little more. "That should do the most damage."

Trevor's eyes flashed open in horror as blood spurted out. He was unable to speak, and in a moment he drooped and then lay on the table, dead.

"Now, let's see if this works." Baskania waved his hands in the air over Trevor's body, and closed his eyes, murmuring.

Trevor's body jerked, and then he opened his eyes. He was alive again, blood spurting more out of his neck now that his heart was beating. In a moment his eyes closed again, and he died.

"It worked! Starting life on my own. What a prize! I'm glad that we found you, Trevor. It was so easy, too." Baskania *stared greedily at him as if he was about to devour him. "And once again . . ."*

He waved his hands over Trevor's body, eyes closed, and Trevor awoke from the dead again, with a start. This time as soon as the blood began to spurt from his neck, Trevor faded away and died.

Baskania laughed wildly. "Look at that! Bringing life to the dead! I can animate anything now!"

He waved his hands over Trevor again, awakening him only to die another instant death. It was obvious that Baskania had cut Trevor's throat so he would die immediately, making his spell easier to test. He had no intention of saving Trevor at all.

Finally, Baskania dusted his hands together and left Trevor dead on the blood-soaked table.

Erec yanked the shades shut and stepped out of the rooms fast. He could not believe what he had seen. This was the worst situation of all. Trevor dead . . . Erec dead . . . and Baskania with the greatest power in the world. This could not happen.

"You can't hide Trevor from Baskania. It won't work." Erec was panting, but could not tell Bethany the horrible details. "Baskania will find him, and everything will go wrong."

"What else can we do, then? If I *don't* hide Trevor then Baskania will get him too, right?"

Erec had not thought about that. What other options were there, aside from Bethany hiding her brother, or not hiding him at all? If Erec hid him, he would likely turn him over to Baskania before long—like he had seen in his other vision.

But then something occurred to him. What had happened to Trevor in his original vision? Erec had given him to Baskania, saying that he was worthless. And then in another later vision, Erec had proposed killing Trevor by throwing him into a trash compactor. Although that was horrible too, it at least was better than this. Baskania had not seemed to get the information from Trevor that he needed.

It was confusing, and Erec wanted to make sure he thought it out correctly. Baskania would find Trevor on his own, or Erec would bring Trevor there himself. Those were the only choices. The outcome seemed better for Trevor—and everybody—if Erec was the one to do it. At least he wasn't lying dead in a pool of blood in that vision.

How was he supposed to tell Bethany that, though? And why would it even make a difference how Baskania found Trevor?

Bethany's face was pale. "You're supposed to bring him to Baskania yourself, aren't you?"

"How did you know?"

"Look at your face. I don't have to be a math genius to realize there are only three options here. And two of them—me hiding Trevor, or not hiding him—lead to the same thing."

Erec nodded. "I just wish that I knew how to make this work out the best. If I turn Trevor in myself, Baskania doesn't seem able to find the information he needs."

"Could it be a time thing?" Bethany asked. "Maybe if you turn Trevor in, Baskania doesn't keep him as long."

Erec's visions flooded his mind. "I don't think that's it. It could be other things. If you hide Trevor, then I'll die too. I stay alive the other way."

Bethany gasped. "Why didn't you tell me that before? That settles everything. You have to take him there. If only we can figure out a way to keep him safe . . . somehow . . ."

A voice in Erec's ear made him jump. "I have a way."

Spartacus! Erec had not seen him in the room until now. "Have you been here this whole time?"

Bethany looked at him in surprise. "Me? Of course I have—what are you talking about?"

But Spartacus shook his head. "Nope. I had a little errand to run. All the way back to the Underworld. I hope you appreciate it."

"What? Why would you go back there again?" The idea made Erec cringe.

"Who are you talking to?" Bethany shivered. "You're acting weird."

"I'm sorry. Spartacus is here."

Bethany's eyes flew open wide. "The ghost?" She wrapped her arms around herself. "Where is he?"

Erec did not know what it was that made ghosts so much scarier to people when they were invisible. "He's right next to me . . . and he might have an idea."

"Might?" Spartacus plunked a glass of water in front of Erec.

"Thanks." Erec wondered how the ghost knew that his throat was dry . . . but then again Spartacus could read his mind. He picked up the glass to take a drink—

"No!" Spartacus shouted. He ripped the cup from Erec's hand before he took a sip.

Bethany watched in wonder as the glass appeared and jerked itself back to the table. "What's going on?"

As if she could hear his answer, Spartacus said, "I'll tell you what's going on. I went all the way back to the Underworld and brought back water from the River Lethe. Took a lot of planning, too—I'll tell you that."

"How did you . . . ?"

"I had to bring two gold coins so the boatman would transport the cup across the river and back again. Be glad you didn't have to see the River Lethe. You wouldn't have been able to drink this stuff if you had."

"So, what are we going to do with it?"

THE SECRET OF ASHONA

Spartacus waited a moment for Erec to put things together. "Trevor . . . ?"

A thought settled into Erec's mind. "Oh! What a great idea!"

"What is going on?" Bethany was starting to look annoyed.

"This might be the answer." Erec pointed to the cup. "Spartacus got it from the River Lethe in the Underworld. When you drink it you forget everything you ever knew."

"Isn't that what Ward drank?"

"Yeah. I had a sip too, when I was a spider. But if Trevor drinks it now . . ."

Bethany's face lit up. "He wouldn't know anything anymore. He might be useless to Baskania, then!"

"Exactly. Great thinking, Spartacus! This has to be the answer. It fits right in with me calling Trevor useless in my vision when I'm giving him to Baskania."

"Thanks, Spartacus!" Bethany blew kisses to where he stood.

"Aw, shucks," the spirit said. "Tell her it's no problem."

"Let's go find him!" Bethany ran out of the library, Erec and Spartacus following behind.

Rosco was waiting outside the door. He joined them as they walked down the hallway. "Did she take it okay? Any ideas where we're going to hide her brother?"

"I'm going to turn him over to Baskania."

Rosco gave Erec a sideways glance. "Real funny. What are we going to do with him? And where is he?"

"Bethany's brother is Trevor."

Rosco's eyebrows jumped to the top of his forehead. "Trevor? As in . . . your brother Trevor Rex?"

"Yeah. But he was originally Trevor Cleary."

"No way . . ."

"I looked into the future. Trevor and I both die if I don't bring him to Baskania myself. But we're going to give Trevor the same stuff to drink that Ward had, so he won't be any help to Baskania. I think this is the only way."

Rosco thought that over awhile. "It will look really good for you if you hand Trevor to the Shadow Prince. I'd play it up, and get all the credit you can. That will only help you later."

Bethany found Trevor in the open aquarium where he liked to spend time. It was attached to the wing where they stayed, and had both closed containers of different types of fish, and open ones leading straight into the ocean. There was enough food in the boxes that plenty of ocean fish swam in and out. One whole wall of the room was glass, and its view of the ocean floor was magnificent.

Trevor stood before the glass wall, counting softly to himself.

Bethany ran up behind him and threw her arms around him, making Trevor jump. "It's so good to see you!"

Trevor's face turned red, and he stumbled, pushing away from her. "Um . . . yeah." He looked around the room as if trying to think of something to say, but could not.

Trevor had always had a hard time communicating, but he had a lot going on under the surface. Now it was all starting to make sense. Trevor *was* special, but Erec never realized until now just how special he was. He was probably a math genius like Bethany and Pi. Maybe even smarter than they were, since he was the only one able to help Baskania figure out the Final Magic. Erec knew that Trevor liked patterns and codes, and that he thought he could predict things. But he was so quiet, never sharing his predictions with anyone, that it had seemed more like pretend than anything else.

Right now he didn't look so bright at all, stammering and pink. He was more than a little confused about the sudden attention. Everybody was staring at him.

Bethany put a hand on his shoulder. "Do you remember hearing about how I had a little brother? And how I was looking all over for him, but I didn't know who he was?"

Trevor nodded silently.

"You're him."

He stood looking at her, as if she had announced that it was dinnertime, or what the weather would be that day. Erec wondered if what she had said had sunk in at all. But then Trevor slowly nodded.

Bethany threw her arms around him again, and this time Trevor let her stay that way for a while. "I'm so happy I found you," she said.

"Me too."

"What were you looking at in there?" Bethany left an arm around him as they turned to look through the glass.

Trevor pointed. "Those fish. The white ones."

"They're pretty. Do you like the way they look?"

"I like their patterns. I think they're talking to each other that way."

Bethany gazed at the fish a while, thinking about what he said. "I wish I could see it, Trev. But I bet they are. Someday will you teach me about the patterns?"

Trevor nodded.

Erec came up to him, holding the cup of water from the River Lethe. He felt horrible about letting Trevor drink it. All of his memories would be gone forever now. It seemed so unfair—but then again, all of this was unfair. And Trevor forgetting everything was better than Trevor dying in a pool of blood.

He wanted to give them another minute together before destroying everything, so he stood waiting. Nothing was said between Bethany and Trevor, but it was still meaningful somehow, just for the two of them standing there together, knowing.

Erec told him what he was going to do, because it just seemed right. "Things are going to be a little messy for a while, okay, Trevor?"

His stomach clenched. How would he ever be able to do this to his brother? But then again, how could he not? "Baskania knows you are Bethany's brother—or he will soon. I have to give you this drink so you forget everything that you ever knew. It's the only way to make it so you won't be able to help Baskania. And it might protect you from him too. I'm the one who's going to bring you to him. I want you to know that now, or I wouldn't feel right doing it to you later. But when I looked into the future, it was worse if I didn't do it this way."

"It's okay." Trevor smiled bravely. "I know you would only protect me."

That didn't help. Erec's hand holding the cup began to shake, slopping some of the water over the sides. How in the world was he supposed to lead his brother into the worst place in the world and hand him to someone who wanted to kill him? For a moment he thought he just wouldn't do it . . . until he remembered the alternate visions of the future.

Tears formed in Erec's eyes. Trevor put an arm around his brother. "Don't feel bad, Erec. You're doing the right thing." He patted Erec's shoulder. "I may forget who you are, but when everything is done again, can you tell me all your stories? I want to remember to love you."

"I will." Erec gave Trevor a hug, and then handed him the water. "Sorry about this, kid."

Trevor held the glass for a moment. "Am I going to live?"

Erec paused, thinking. "If I have anything to do with it."

"Okay, then." Trevor held up the glass and finished every last drop.

CHAPTER TWENTY-SIX
A Terrible Gift

EREC THOUGHT ABOUT how to tell Baskania about Trevor. He was nervous. Rosco was right—if he was going to make this work, he had to be careful, and try to make himself look as good to Baskania as possible.

They waited outside the large carved oak doors to the Inner Sanctum of the Green House, until a blind servant opened the door. "He is ready for you now."

Erec and Rosco walked inside. Baskania looked up expectantly, five eyes across his forehead.

Rosco grinned. "You're gonna love this boy even more today than yesterday. He just doesn't stop. As much as he used to be a thorn in our sides, now he's making up for every minute. . . ."

Baskania perked up. "Yes? What is it, Erec? Are you ready to go see the Furies and get my scepter back?"

"Soon," Erec said. "But I thought you'd like something else I found for you in the meantime."

"Something more? You're right, Rosco. This is interesting. What else?"

"Bethany Cleary's brother."

Baskania's hands flattened on his desk, trembling. "You found him?"

"I searched through my new memory and I'm sure that I know who he is."

"Wonderful! I can't believe our luck with you lately! Where is the boy—do you know his name?"

"I know his name, where he is . . . and everything about him. And I'm happy to bring him here to you—unless you want to send your own people to do it. I thought it might be easier if I got him, so you could avoid King Piter and Queen Posey trying to fight you off."

"King Piter and Queen Posey . . . so the boy is in Ashona, then? Do the king and queen know he's there? Do they know who he is?"

"They all know. It's Trevor Rex. I guess he used to be Trevor Cleary."

Baskania's mouth dropped open a little, and all of his eyes focused on Erec sharply. Erec was sure that Baskania was trying to read his mind. He couldn't blame him—Erec was handing over his own brother and his girlfriend's brother. It was probably more than the Shadow Prince could believe. But Erec had to make it all seem real.

"You mean your adopted brother, Trevor?" Baskania looked like he was about to drool from anticipation.

"That's the one." Erec laughed. "I can't believe I'm actually telling this to you. I guess I really am on your side now."

Baskania crossed his arms and leaned back in an almost fatherly manner. "That, Erec, is a great thing for both of us. We will help each other from now on. You and I will be like one together." A slick smile spread across his face. "I think you are right. You should bring Trevor here yourself. We'll keep it all quieter that way. I'll send a few guards to wait outside of the Castle Ashona for you." He held up a hand. "Not that I believe you're going to try anything funny, like hiding him."

"Why would I do that? If you want to send someone else, that's fine with me. Maybe Rosco could do it."

"No, not Rosco. I want *you* to bring him here. I think it would be a nice touch, actually."

Erec felt like throwing up. Baskania wanted them to be "like one," but was also ready to slaughter his baby brother—and Bethany's. But he managed a smile and a nod. "When would you like me to go?"

"No time like the present." He thought a moment. "But I'd like to show you something first. Come with me." He held a hand up when Rosco started to follow. "Just Erec."

Baskania led him down a short hallway to a door with no knob. He waved a hand in front of it and it opened with a groan. Then he waved Erec inside.

"This is where I keep some of my favorite treasures." He looked around with appreciation. "Some of the finest items through the centuries are in this room." He picked up a small silver tube resting on a shelf and looked at it fondly. "Take this little thing, for instance. It looks innocent enough, no? But would you believe it was the first method I ever used for inserting eyes into myself?"

Erec tried not to cringe as he thought about it.

"Maybe someday you, too, can have more eyes of your own. I

would say you would be perfect for that kind of responsibility, being in charge of groups of people. I won't want to do this forever, you know."

Was he talking about passing the evil-villain torch down to Erec now? Erec remained stock still and nodded.

"I was thinking . . . you have done wonders for me lately. In so many ways, as well. And going to Ashona to collect Trevor, well . . ." He looked around the room. "I'd like to give you something as a token. Maybe this." He set the silver tube down. "Or anything that you like, with a few exceptions, of course. Here is a love magnet. The most powerful one on the planet." He picked it up. "I have no need for it. You may find it fun."

"What's this?" Erec saw a small plastic flower that sat on a shelf.

"Nothing much. It's an eternal water source—really only a token, because there's not much use for it." He tapped the center of the flower's face and water sprayed into Erec's face until he tapped it again.

Erec laughed and wiped his face off. "That could be fun too."

"Here's a good one." Baskania pointed to a portrait on the wall. "This painting absorbs your aging process. Just reset it to your face, and all the years of your life will show up on the portrait's face, leaving you eternally young. Nice, if you care about shallow things like that."

That did not appeal to Erec at all. But something else caught his eye. For some reason he was drawn to it, even from across the room. Nothing about it seemed special—it looked like a kind of steel mousetrap. "What is this?" He pointed at it, afraid to touch.

"Ah, that is another good one. It's a projectile magic launcher. It will send a spell anywhere—any kind of magic at all. I was planning to use it to destroy Tartarus when the Furies were there, after they agreed to my terms. It was easier to let them escape that way then by collecting all of those people for their souls."

"Why didn't you use it then?"

THE SECRET OF ASHONA

"I didn't have a magic source strong enough to blast through their cave, even with its help. In the past I've had tokens and totems that would have done the trick. But they're hard to come upon, and I didn't have any at the time. You can imagine, it would take something quite powerful to help the Furies out of their prison."

Erec considered it a moment. "I'd like this, please. If that's okay."

Baskania picked it up, and put his hand on Erec's head. "Take it. I doubt I'll need it again, and if I do, I know where to find you. You might enjoy sending spells to places in Upper Earth from your home here in Alypium."

Erec pocketed the contraption and thanked Baskania. As they walked back, he slid his hand in to touch it again. It felt right, somehow, as if he was meant to have it.

When they returned to Baskania's office, he pressed a red button on his desk. A general popped into the room within a minute.

"Sir?" He stood at attention.

"Have two guards take Erec and Rosco here to the Castle Ashona. Erec will go in alone and come back out with a boy—Trevor Rex, or actually Trevor Cleary. Bring them back to me straightaway."

"Yes, sir." The general clicked his heels together and disappeared. Moments later, two guards led Erec and Rosco to the largest Port-O-Door that Erec had ever seen. It was one of a giant line of immense Port-O-Doors that filled a gigantic wall of the Green House. What was Baskania planning to send through these doors? Entire armies?

Moments later, they stood in the entryway that led into the Castle Ashona. Erec walked through the desk area and slowly made his way to the suite where his family was staying.

He thought for a moment about telling June what he was about to do. How in the world could he, though? She would never let him take Trevor there, even if Erec told her about his visions. June had her own ideas, and didn't put enough stock in Erec's visions to do something that sounded that ridiculous. Erec wondered if she had even noticed that Trevor had forgotten everything he ever knew. He was so quiet he probably seemed like his normal self, especially if Bethany was helping him figure out his way around.

It took a while to find Bethany and Trevor. Finally someone pointed Erec to the wat-air beach attached to the side of the immense entry room. Erec watched quietly while they talked, looking at the fish flying through the strangely blue air and flickering back and forth through the wall that separated the room from the ocean. A starfish crept slowly up to Trevor's shoe and put a tiny foot on him. Trevor smiled and picked the thing up, turning it over. Bethany pointed, teaching him something, Erec was sure.

Soon he could not stand waiting any longer. Watching them was too painful. "Hey, guys!" He gave Bethany a sad smile.

"Hi Erec. Hey, Trevor—do you remember Erec?"

Trevor shook his head.

"He's your brother!"

"My brother?" Trevor looked interested. "And you're my sister. So you're her brother too?"

Erec laughed. "No, Trev. You're Bethany's real brother. You and I are adopted brothers. June adopted both of us a long time ago."

"But Erec still loves you just as much as I do," Bethany said.

Why did she have to go and say that? Erec could feel tears forming in his eyes again. This was already going to be the hardest thing he ever did. If anything happened to Trevor because of him, if he ended up losing his brother, he would never forgive himself.

Erec pulled Bethany aside to talk to her in private, out of Trevor's earshot. "What are you going to tell June?"

"I guess I'll just tell her the truth." Bethany shrugged. "It will be too late for her to do anything about it."

"She'll kill you."

"It won't be as bad as what you two will be going through. I've been spending some great time with Trevor. He forgot all of his old ideas about patterns, but I can tell they'll come back. I mean, he notices things that I never would. I bet in a few years he'll be right back where he was before."

Erec really hoped so. "I got something from Baskania that might help with the Furies." He touched his pocket. "I have the feeling it's what I needed to find there. It doesn't look like much, but it can send magic from distances. I'm getting an idea about how I could use it to solve the problem of the Furies and the captured souls, but I'm not sure yet."

"I'm crossing my fingers for you." Then she whispered, "What about Trevor? Is there some way we can break him out after Baskania gets him?"

"I've been thinking about that, too. Try not to worry. Right now it's important that I keep Baskania happy and off of my back. I don't want him watching me too closely. Things might work out okay . . . but it's going to take a lot of luck."

"Are you going to tell him that Trevor forgot everything?"

"No. He'll figure it out soon enough . . . or think that something has always been wrong with him."

She nodded. "If you know too much about it, Baskania might think that you did it."

Erec felt bad enough as it was, without thinking about what he really had done to his brother. But for now he had to keep playing the game and hope it all came out for the best. He patted the contraption in his pocket that would send magic all the way to Tartarus. Then he walked back to Trevor. "C'mon, kid. We gotta go somewhere awful. A man, Baskania, is going to look through your mind and see what you know. And I'm going to try and help you, okay?"

Trevor nodded. "Okay." He took Erec's hand.

When Erec arrived with the guards and Rosco back at the Green House, he tried to put his game face on. He could not risk looking suspicious by caring too much about his brother. Knowing how hard it would be to do, Erec ruffled Trevor's hair. He didn't want to say too much—Baskania would see anything Erec said now as he looked through Trevor's memory. But he did risk a quick "I love you, kid. I always will."

Then he whipped his hand from Trevor's grasp and grabbed him by the wrist. "Let's get this over with, you stupid kid." He yanked his brother hard, making him trip as they walked through the luxuriously decorated Green House.

Trevor looked up at Erec with big brown eyes, confused. "Why are you doing this? Let me go."

Erec gripped Trevor's wrist harder. "That's enough from you. Come with me." His mouth winced into a fake smile. "I would never do anything to hurt you. Remember that."

Trevor shook from head to toe as Erec dragged him down the hallway. He knocked on the tall wooden doors of the Inner Sanctum. When they swung open, he shoved Trevor inside and walked in behind him.

"Look what I have for you." Erec grinned at Baskania.

"Wonderful!" Baskania beamed. "What a treat."

"Enjoy him." Erec dusted his hands off with a grin. "Thanks again for letting me serve you. It's my pleasure."

Baskania laughed with glee. A silver cage fell out of the air and over Trevor. Trevor put his little hands on the bars and gazed through at Erec with sad eyes. Erec felt a twinge of grief, but he pushed it aside. He had done what he needed, and that was all that mattered.

"How about a dragon?" Erec suggested. "I know one that I can deliver here. I thought that would be a nice next gift for you."

Baskania strode over and patted Erec's head with his hand. "Boy, you have turned out to be a pleasure for me. I'm so glad that we've gotten to know each other better and moved past that bad time we used to have."

Erec was pleased. Baskania was happy now, and that's what was important. Things just might turn out all right after all—if he played his cards right.

Rosco was not pleased when they were back at his apartment. "I don't like this, Erec. Not one bit."

"I don't either—believe me. It's not like I wanted to hand my brother over to him. But what else could I do? Trevor would die if I didn't. And Baskania trusts me now. I've seen that Trevor won't die right away, and maybe we could save him for good." But the minute he said that, Erec felt sick. What was Trevor doing right now? He shuddered, not really wanting to know. But he would do whatever it took to get him out.

A thought slid into his mind like an icy snake, making him shudder. What about his vision of the future where he told Baskania to throw Trevor into a trash compactor? Why would he do that? He couldn't . . . he wouldn't . . . unless he could think of a way to turn that into something that might help Trevor. . . .

But, then again, didn't that mean Trevor would be okay until Erec returned to talk about the trash compactor? At least he was somewhat safe.

"That's not what I'm talking about." Rosco ruffled his own hair with his hands, upset. "It's terrible about Trevor, but I get it that there's no choice. I've been thinking of ways to protect him there. But there's something else, Erec. I'm starting to worry about *you*. I'm not liking what I've been seeing one bit."

"What are you talking about? Me going to release the souls?

Because I've had some other thoughts about that—"

"No. Not the souls—although that's also driving me crazy. I don't like what's happening between you and the Shadow Prince."

Spartacus, who had been hanging out silently, jumped up and pointed at Erec. "Aha! I'm glad Rosco said it, because that's been bothering me, too."

"Huh?"

Rosco said, "Listen, I know what it's like to be a kid, and finally have someone pay attention to you. Look up to you, even. Baskania knows how to get followers—real followers who will do anything for him. And he doesn't do it by being a jerk to them. Baskania . . . if it makes sense for someone so crazy, evil, and selfish . . . well, he actually cares about people who are close to him, higher-ups who serve him. He cares about you—I can see it. And that's dangerous. When someone that powerful heaps on the praise and starts giving you gifts, it's hard not to like them back."

"Are you saying that I'm becoming friends with the Shadow Prince?"

Spartacus clapped his hands together. "See! You would never have called him the Shadow Prince before. Only Baskania!" He looked at Rosco for confirmation, and then got frustrated that he couldn't be heard. He pointed at Rosco. "Tell him I said that! Tell him, Erec! I want to know what Rosco thinks about that."

Erec ignored Spartacus. "Listen, I'm not going to be friends with . . . Baskania. You do realize I hate his guts, right?"

"I don't know," Rosco said. "I saw the way you were talking with him. You were losing your resolve, I think. That's how it starts. I lived through it, remember?"

Spartacus picked Erec up and held him onto the ceiling, to the surprise of Rosco. *"Tell him what I said!"*

"Okay! Just put me down, then . . . Rosco, Spartacus wants to

THE SECRET OF ASHONA

point out that I never used to call Baskania the Shadow Prince before now. Are you happy?"

"Yes." Spartacus put Erec on the couch.

"He has a good point."

"See!" Spartacus looked delighted.

"I'm just telling you, from the outside you started looking a little starstruck, a little appreciative. That's how it began with me. It was all great at first. Who would start a friendship with someone like that if it wasn't great? He was supportive, noticed my abilities, and let me know it. He gave me things—he can be really generous. But, before long I found myself doing things back for him. And even though they made sense in a twisted way, some of them were truly awful. He trusted me and relied on me. And in turn I committed murders, hurt people, stole things. Acted in ways I never thought I could do. And I became the Rosco Kroc you know—the one who Oscar went back in time to get rid of and do everyone a favor."

"The Rosco Kroc I know is a great person. It doesn't matter what you did in the past for that guy. I know he can con people. You were a kid, and all alone back then too. There was nobody else that you trusted. It's not like you went out on your own and did all of those things. Someone who you believed in was telling you to do them. But you're my friend again now. The past is the past."

"I don't know that I can ever make up for what I've done. But I'll try."

Erec held a hand up. "I'm not getting sucked in by him, don't worry. Even when he starts to make sense, I think of what he's done to Bethany, what he could do to Trevor . . . and I'll never get those images out of my head."

"Good."

"I just wish I knew what to do about the Furies. Talking to Bethany, I realized that freeing all the souls would be a huge problem.

If the Furies go back to Tartarus, Baskania would give them more souls again, like last time. He'd retry his plan to let them out if they serve him. The Furies would be released and would wipe humans off the face of the planet, like they were planning to the first time—and I'd be the reason they hate humans. We'd all die, basically."

"You're right."

Spartacus dropped the spell book on Erec's lap. "Guess it's over, then. You went to all that trouble to get Tarvos's horns. Do you still want to learn the time-stopping spell now?"

Erec could hear the tension in the ghost's voice. It wasn't until now that he thought about how all of this affected Spartacus. He had given up his own soul to let Erec have his back. He deserved to have his soul returned—just like all of the other specters that had lost theirs. He never complained about it, never talked about how bad it felt being soulless—but Erec knew what it had been like.

In fact, Spartacus wouldn't be around much longer. The only reason he was here was to help Erec free the souls. Soon he would go to the Furies and see if they would destroy him, or ask Aoquesth to do it. He had made that clear.

"Spartacus—I'm sorry I haven't talked to *you* about this. You're the first person that I should have discussed it with. This was our plan together, from the beginning. . . ."

"Hey, don't worry about it, kid. I hadn't thought about all of that stuff either, but it's true. Of course Baskania would just release the Furies again, and they'd be all ready to go back to their old plan of killing everyone on the planet. Not a great option."

"But I'm not giving up on those souls yet either."

"Are you crazy?" Spartacus shot him an incredulous look. "I've given up. See? All done. Finished. Next problem."

"There has to be a way. I've gotten something from Baskania that might help us."

"You mean that mousetrap thing? I was there when he handed it to you. But even he said that he didn't have anything powerful enough to destroy Tartarus with."

"I have something that might work." Erec pulled the little pink brain out of his pocket.

"What's that?" Rosco asked.

But Spartacus's eyes widened. "You still have Tarvos's power source? I thought that you gave it to Baskania."

"He took the Master Shem, and he asked for this, but then he got sidetracked with Connor and my old memories, and he never actually took it from me." Erec explained to Rosco, "This was the thing that gave Tarvos the ability to collect all the soulless people in the world and turn them into Golems."

"Wow." They all stared at the little pink thing for a while, wondering if it had enough power to do the trick.

"I don't even know how to use it."

Rosco picked it up and looked it over. "Well, it's a power source. Usually that just means it increases your current load of power. So if you're holding it in your hand, and you try to do magic, it will be amplified."

"So, if I wanted to blast a hole in Tartarus, the prison of the three Furies, then . . ."

"What?" Rosco looked at Erec sideways. "Isn't that a little much? I mean, even Baskania couldn't do that with his abilities alone. He needed to find a super-powerful magic item to use."

"But this is super-powerful. Maybe it will be enough." Then Erec had a better idea. "If it amplifies people's powers, then why don't you use it instead of me? You can do a lot more than I can."

Rosco looked at the pink thing skeptically. "It would have to multiply what I could do by thousands in order for that to work."

"Well, just think of all that Tarvos could do from this alone. He wasn't even magical without it. This let him speak, point a finger at you and kill you if he wanted . . ."

Rosco studied the brainlike thing for a while. "I guess that would be amplification by thousands of times." He smiled. "I guess it couldn't hurt to try. But as far as who has more magical ability—I know far more magic than you do, maybe more than you ever will. Who knows, though, which of us has more inner strength? There is no way to test that, because I've just had far more experience."

"You use the thing. We can't be that far off from each other, anyway. Both of us can do things that most people can't, like finger magic."

"I'm happy to give it a try. Let's see that power source."

Erec handed it to Rosco, who gingerly held the small pink brain. He lifted his finger and flicked it toward the wall.

A fifteen-foot fireball shot out of his finger. Everything was fire and heat all around them. Crashes and explosions filled the air, and smoke blinded them all. All around, they were engulfed by flames.

Rosco said a few words with both of his hands out, waving in front of him. In a moment, the fire was gone. Along with it, most of his apartment building had been eaten away. The couch that they were sitting on was charred, and the floor under it was black, but the side of the floor near the far wall was gone. All of the walls on that side of the apartment were missing now, and Erec looked straight out into the air, as if they were sitting on a perch in the sky.

CHAPTER TWENTY-SEVEN

Amplified Magic

ROSCO LOOKED AROUND him in shock. "I can't believe it. I just tried to send a little test flame out toward the wall. A little test flame!" He took a deep breath and looked around. "I'm going to try to fix this myself, but it might take time."

Spartacus was gone, but he returned a moment later and shook Erec's shoulder. "Tell Rosco everyone is okay. He's worried sick about it. Not a lot of people were in the building, and only one person was stuck. She was under collapsed floorboards that fell from above her, but I got her out okay. Other people are upset, but nobody is hurt."

"Spartacus just saved one person, and he said everyone else here is okay."

"Thank him for me. Thanks, Spartacus."

The spirit bowed. "All in a day's work."

With renewed vigor, Rosco waved his hands around and began to reconstruct things as they were. Spartacus helped, and even Erec tried to pitch in with the little magic he could do.

"Why don't you try using the mousetrap thing to fix this place? I mean, it also amplifies what you can do. . . ."

Rosco's face lit up. "Great idea! It would take forever to get this place back to what it was this way. Let's see how this thing works." He pulled the lever back and held it up, concentrating. Then, he let go. . . .

All around them, boards started flying. Wood morphed so that the black charred bits dissolved and the old paint sprung back on again. Erec sat in wonderment as the floor underneath him reconstructed itself, and walls put themselves together again.

Rosco looked just as stunned. "I barely did anything."

"Is this like the scepter?" Erec picked up the mousetrap device. "Do you feel rushes of power from using it?"

"Not at all. It does everything by itself, without me. I just gave it a tiny push."

In a moment, Rosco's apartment looked just as it always had. He tapped the mousetrap. "This thing is far more powerful than I imagined. Just think what you could do with something like this."

"Yeah—like crack open Tartarus."

"I don't know about that, though. Yeah, everything was amplified like crazy. But Tartarus . . . that's put together to keep the three Furies captive. Can you imagine how strong that place has to be?"

"That's why we have this." Erec held up the little brain thing.

"Imagine using these two things combined. This makes you thousands of times more powerful by itself. Then when you use the mousetrap, the whole thing will get amplified like crazy, and we can send that massive lump of destruction all the way to Tartarus. Think about it."

Rosco was thinking about it. But then Spartacus had an idea. "What if I did it?"

That was something new. Spartacus, as a spirit, had far more power than any human, Baskania aside.

"Let's see what you can do with this." Erec handed the mouse-trap machine to Spartacus.

Rosco saw it floating in the air in front of him. "Spartacus is going to try using it? As a spirit? Wow. *That's* going to be something to see. Tell him that he'd better be careful. I barely sent a tiny flame out and the whole building went up in blazes—and he's going to have far more power in him than either of us would."

"Tell Rosco that I can hear him—he can talk to me directly. It makes me feel like I'm not in the room when he does that." Spartacus was eyeing the brainlike pink thing. "I should try using them both together. You know, just to see what I can do."

"Be really careful. If Rosco used Tarvos's magic source when he sent a flame out, and he also used the mousetrap thing, it would have burned the whole city down."

"Oh, no." Rosco shook his head. "Tell Spartacus not to use both of them. Even without his spirit powers it would be far too much."

Spartacus raised his arms over Rosco's head like claws and gritted his teeth. "He's doing it again. Just like I'm not here." Before Erec knew it, Spartacus had Tarvos's power source in one hand, and Baskania's gift in the other. "Just one drop of rain. That's all I'm going to make. And I'm going to send it all the way over the ocean out there, miles from the edge of Alypium. One drop."

Erec followed behind him and looked out the window. "How are

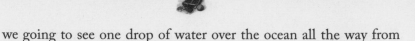

we going to see one drop of water over the ocean all the way from here?"

Rosco followed Erec. But before he reached the window, water surrounded them everywhere. Currents above and below him whipped Erec around. Pieces of the apartment complex swept by, along with furniture and rugs. In moments, the walls washed away, and some of the water drained out onto the street. But not fully, because the floods outside were already so high that there was nowhere for the water to run.

Erec was outside now—he was pretty sure—but still part of the same giant flood. There were moments where his head surfaced enough to catch breaths, but luckily he had Instagills so it wasn't an issue. He was more worried about crashing into the other things whipping around in the water. It filled the streets and the entire city of Alypium as far as he could see.

Spartacus had obviously missed his mark completely, causing the magic to work in Rosco's apartment instead of over the ocean. He wondered if people had been hurt or had died from this disaster, and where Rosco was.

Then, in a flash, all the water vanished. Everything was bone dry. Erec was sitting on a patch of grass by a sidewalk, broken trees around him on the ground. A woman was coughing and gasping nearby—but at least she was alive. Buildings were collapsed, pieces of furniture strewn around.

Soon, Spartacus was at his side. "Did you *see* that? There was a *solid water wall* over the entire ocean! For a minute I thought the sea rose up and overflowed into the sky, but then I realized it was the other way around. Water filled the whole atmosphere!"

"Yeah? Well, what about what happened right here in Alypium? Like in Rosco's apartment?"

"This was *nothing*. You should have seen what it was like out there where I sent the spell."

Erec looked around, amazed. "Is everyone okay?"

"I flew around like crazy and rescued a few people who were in trouble. There were some problems. . . ." He looked guilty. "But I took care of most of it. Luckily nobody died—but a few people were close, though."

"You probably should use that thing to put the city back together again, like Rosco did."

Spartacus eyed the mousetrap suspiciously. "This is strong enough to let me do anything. . . . But rebuild a whole city?" He shrugged. "I'll try." He concentrated, holding the brain in one hand. Then he pulled the lever on the mousetrap back and let it snap down again. In a minute, building materials and furnishings flew all around them, restoring themselves into order. The ghost blinked, a shocked look on his face. "I barely even gave it an effort. . . . Look at this thing work!"

In minutes, the city looked as if nothing had ever happened to it. Spartacus grabbed Erec by the arms and took a leap—in seconds they were back at Rosco's place.

Rosco was sitting on his couch, stunned. "Just one drop of water, huh?"

Erec nodded. "I can't believe it either. If anything is going to destroy Tartarus, Spartacus could if he uses both of those things together."

"With these two things a *mouse* could destroy Tartarus." Spartacus laughed. "If I put all of my effort into it, that cave will crumble. It's going to be simple."

Erec gave Rosco a grin. "Spartacus thinks that crumbling Tartarus will be easy!"

"It won't be that easy," Rosco said. "Tell him that the Furies' cave is strong enough that even they can't blast it open. It's magically reinforced. He'll have to use every ounce of his strength, even *with* the mousetrap thing and Tarvos's power source, to have a chance."

Spartacus pointed at Rosco. "He's doing it again. Talking like I'm not even in the room." In a second, Rosco's chair was whipped out from under him, sending him falling to the floor.

Rosco got up, stunned. "That made him upset? He has to know the facts. If Spartacus is not willing to try his hardest with this, let me do it instead."

"I'll do it right. Don't worry." Spartacus took the magical objects to the window and sat on the ledge. "I also have a much better sense where to aim this thing than Rosco would. Tartarus is *that* way from here." He pointed out and down into the dirt. "I can tell its exact location. And if this mousetrap sends magic distances, right where you want it to go, I won't just aim it that way. That would destroy everything in its path, and also not leave as much oomph when it gets to the right spot. I'm going to throw it there with this thing—I can tell how to make it work. . . ."

Spartacus played with the contraption for a minute and then held a hand up. "Tell Rosco to keep his mouth shut for a minute, so he doesn't distract me."

Erec held a finger to his lips, and Spartacus stretched the metal bar back like a bow and arrow. Erec had no idea it would even do that. Spartacus frowned intently, squeezing Tarvos's magic source in the fist that held the metal. His whole face squeezed in concentration, and he released the bar. Noise resounded from it, sounding like a jet engine passing through the room.

"Done!" Spartacus said, cheerily. "I sent the whole massive blast to just the right spot. I gave it more power than a thousand humans could, all put together. There is no way that Tartarus is still standing." He handed the items back to Erec, satisfied.

"Did he think it worked?" Rosco watched Erec put the things back in his pockets.

"He's sure it did." Erec felt relieved. Now he could free the souls and not worry about imprisoning the Furies again. If they got sent to Tartarus, then they would just fly right back out again. Everyone would be happy.

"Ready to go to Alsatia?" Spartacus tapped his toe on the floor.

"Now?" Erec thought a moment. He had everything he needed. "I can't just leave Trevor with Baskania though."

"I've checked on him. He's hooked up to . . . well, let's just say he's okay. They ghostproofed him, I'll tell you that, or he wouldn't still be there. Baskania's taking no chances."

"If something happens to me in Alsatia, I won't be able to save Trevor."

"I'll figure something out just as well as you could," Rosco said. "He's my number one priority. We have to give the Shadow Prince a little time to realize that Trevor knows nothing. As soon as he does, he'll become less interested in the boy. That will be the time to get him out of there. Soon, I'm sure . . . But I'm still not happy with the idea of you risking angering the Furies."

Erec could not help feeling excited, though. The time was right, and things had actually come together. He could do what he had been driven to do since he got his own soul back—free the other souls. And once he rescued Trevor—there had to be a way—then he could finally go home. He would be done.

He looked at his Amulet of Virtues. The seventh segment had not lit up yet—but he was sure that it would after he did this.

"One last thing you need." Spartacus waved the spell book in front of him. "Learn that time-stopping spell."

Erec grabbed the book. He wouldn't get far freeing the souls if he didn't know this one—it was a big part of his plan.

Time—Stopping Spell

Not for the fainthearted, once mastered, this spell can be used for many purposes—the best of which is to have fun! How many times have you wanted to see what was written on the teacher's answer key during a test . . . or your quarterly review that is hidden facedown on your boss's desk during a meeting? With this time—stopping spell and a snap of your fingers, you can stroll over and take a peek at your leisure, and nobody will be the wiser. Bullied at school? Not for long, with this spell in your repertoire. As soon as someone starts to pick on you they will find themselves in front of the room with their pants down, or with a pie in their face.

Some may use this spell to gain wealth the easy way. It can make the life of a criminal one of ease and comfort. Others may choose to do good and help others with their new powers. The choice is yours. This spell will magnify your influence on your world.

There is a paradox to beware of, however! Be careful when you perform this little gem. If someone else in your universe performs this spell at the exact same time as you, time will stop for both of you. This will keep time stopped permanently, as nobody will be able to start it back up again. In this situation, it will be up to the Fates to fix things . . . if they desire to give humanity another shot after flubbing up completely. The best prevention for this is to not overuse the spell.

THE SECRET OF ASHONA

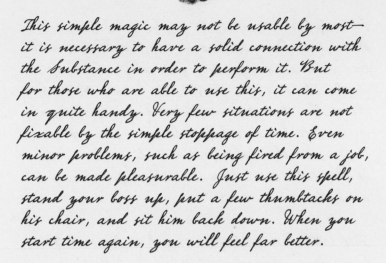

This simple magic may not be usable by most—it is necessary to have a solid connection with the Substance in order to perform it. But for those who are able to use this, it can come in quite handy. Very few situations are not fixable by the simple stoppage of time. Even minor problems, such as being fired from a job, can be made pleasurable. Just use this spell, stand your boss up, put a few thumbtacks on his chair, and sit him back down. When you start time again, you will feel far better.

Warning: Long-term stoppage of time is not recommended. If the user dies before starting time back up again, humanity will be on permanent hold.

Rosco tapped the words at the bottom of the page:

Warning: The Fates, as well as certain other supernatural creatures, are not susceptible to the stoppage of time, and will continue on with you during that fragment.

"This means the Furies, I'm sure. I don't know what your plan is, but if you're going to stop time so you can get away with something in front of the Furies, it's not going to work."

Erec thought about that for a moment. "That's not it, exactly. We should be okay. I'm stopping time to trick the door of a storage facility—it's alive and knows what's going on." Erec looked at the details of the spell.

In order for the spell to work, you must obtain a talisman of a living foe. Very small foes such as mosquitoes generally will not work. The stronger the foe, the easier to work the spell. The talisman must be grasped firmly in the left hand, while holding a pair of sharp scissors in the right. After reading the words of the spell, the talisman and scissors may be discarded.

This incantation does not need to be committed to memory. However, it is advised that you read and understand this page in its entirety. The spell may be said up to an hour in advance of time stoppage and may be performed silently. After it is recited, simply snap your fingers when you are ready for time to come to a halt for those around you. If you touch somebody while you snap, then they also will be immune to the time stoppage while everybody else appears frozen around you. Snap again when you are finished and time will immediately start back up—to the joy or dismay of those around you.

TIGGLEDY PIGGLEDY HIGGLEDY POE
I TOOKUND DE TALISMAN OFFEND A FOE
MIRANDA, MIRACTRA, MINSTANSILO BLAST
EUSTANCHIA MIRANCHIA TIME BALLIDO CAST

At the bottom of the page were a number of provisions, including:

If you are not adept at snapping your fingers, think twice before using this spell. Time may be stuck permanently if you cannot adequately snap to end it.

Erec snapped his fingers a few times for practice, and had no problem at all. The spell was very different sounding from the other one he used. It almost sounded like a strange version of a nursery rhyme. "I guess I'll try it out now and make sure I can do it."

"I keep scissors with me in case I need to stop time." Rosco handed them to Erec. "They're pretty sharp, so you won't have any problems."

Erec held one of Tarvos's horns in his left hand and the scissors in his right. He read the spell out of the book—the last line was a little hard to pronounce, but he thought he had it right. Then he put the scissors and horn down.

"I'm all loaded up and ready to go. I'd better see if this works." Erec snapped his fingers.

Everything froze. The look on Rosco's face was comical, as if he was about to say something, or blow a kiss. Even Spartacus was paralyzed, floating in the air.

What should he do? It seemed a shame to stop time and not change anything at all. He strolled around a bit, looking in drawers, but then he felt nosy. So instead he went in the kitchen, took sliced turkey out of the refrigerator, and made three sandwiches. He brought them back into the living room, sat down, and took a few bites before snapping his fingers.

Rosco said, "I guess you should try here, but be careful."

"I already did it." Erec grinned.

Rosco looked at the sandwich in front of him in amazement. "You did, didn't you? That was quick—I mean, how much time did you spend? You had to make the sandwiches. . . ."

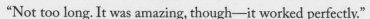

"Not too long. It was amazing, though—it worked perfectly."

"Thanks for the food," Spartacus said, laughing. "I'm not sure just what I'm supposed to do with it."

"Oops, sorry. I forgot about the ghost thing. I'll eat it for you." Erec gulped down the extra sandwich, and copied the words of the time-stopping spell onto a scrap of paper. "I think it's time for me and Spartacus to go see the Furies."

Saying the words made his stomach tighten. What would happen if he never came back? Everything was ready, but he was still afraid. Instead of thinking about what could go wrong, he tried to look ahead to being home with his family again.

Rosco finally seemed to understand that he could not go to Alsatia with Erec and Spartacus, unless he wanted to die on Mercy's Spike. As soon as Erec said he was ready, Spartacus put the scissors and horn into Erec's pockets and zoomed them straight to Pinefort Jungle.

Erec stood on the ledge and looked down at the giant spike. The sharp rock needle pointed up at him ominously, and it terrified him. As a spirit it had been interesting impaling himself and waiting to see what would happen. There had been nothing to lose—nothing that could hurt him. But now that he was alive, it was another story.

His plan seemed solid, but there was some risk. He was going to morph into a soul so he would be safe. But once he body-planted himself on the deathly rock below him, if he somehow morphed back along the way, he'd be a goner. He would have to be really careful to stay a soul, and not say or think *Nee-way*. How long would he be able to remain in the form of a soul?

But it was a risk he would have to take. Spartacus had given his own soul up for him, and hadn't complained about it once. All of those other spirits and souls were suffering too, and Erec had promised that he would put an end to it.

"I guess I should say the time-stopping spell now," Erec said. "Then I'll just have to snap my fingers to start and stop it when we're there."

Erec took the scissors out of his pocket and held one of Tarvos's horns in his other hand. He fished out the spell and read it out loud. *"Tiggledy Piggledy Higgledy Poe, I tookund de talisman offend a Foe, Miranda, miractra, minstansilo blast, Eustanchia miranchia time ballido cast."* He put the scissors and the horn away. "Hope that worked."

"We'll see." Spartacus looked down at the spike, knowing that Erec was afraid of it. "You go first," he said gently. "That way I'll be here to help you."

Erec nodded. "What about this thing?" He held up the Calamitizer weapon that he had carried since he was in the Hinternom, training for Baskania's army. "Do you think it will come with me? You never know if we might use it. But we'll definitely need that." He pointed to the Rapid Transitator—Spartacus's weapon that he kept slung over his shoulder. "You were able to bring that with you before."

Spartacus nodded. "Everything I had came right with me. I'll take your Calamitizer, just in case."

Erec handed it to Spartacus, then looked down at the looming spike of rock. It was time to try morphing into a soul. He closed his eyes and ran the word through his mind. *Nee-way.*

Everything around him shot high into the air, growing a mile a minute. He was tiny again, and he lost sight of the spike. There were his massive armored legs again, all around him. . . .

He was a spider again? This was not a time for mistakes. He had to get this right, and hope that there were no problems, because then it would be over for him forever. . . .

Think about becoming a soul. *Nee-way.*

Erec grew again, but with a funny feeling, like something huge was missing from him. He was wobbly and floating, as if he were perched on a tiny branch that could break any minute and send him plummeting. He was vulnerable, unprotected.

"Let me help you." Spartacus guided him down to the spike and pushed him all the way down to the middle. Soon he followed after Erec.

Everything began to spin. The last time he had experienced this, as a spirit, it had not bothered him at all. But as a soul it was making him sick. He was dizzy and confused, and it seemed like it never was going to stop. Soon he could feel himself fly off of the spike and into the air, floating fast, and very far away. . . .

Alsatia looked completely different to Erec as a soul. Before it had seemed beautiful, like a vision from the deepest recesses of his imagination. Now, all around was nothing but barren rock. Deep crevices wound through it like cracks on the top of a tray of brownies. Maybe those were the spaces between the treetops that he had stepped over when he saw this place as the roof of a rainforest.

Erec could sense immediately that there were no other lone souls here. This was a place for spirits whose souls were contained safely within them. Spartacus probably felt at odds here too, as a soulless spirit.

Well, hopefully that would not last for long. There were three thousand suffering captives here, and by the end of the day they should all be free. That was, unless Erec and Spartacus failed.

They had thought it through so well, though, and even practiced. The souls—poor things—were already bound together in a Substance Web from their last visit here. They would simply go into the storage facility, which they had already been given permission to enter by the Furies, and then Erec would stop time with his spell. Spartacus would use his Rapid Transitator to take the clump of souls and transport them within a fraction of a second as far away as he could. Then they would flee before starting time again, before the storage facility door was aware to even alert the Furies.

Hopefully, the three Furies would get sucked straight to Tartarus as soon as the souls were free. They wouldn't be able to chase Erec and the freed souls. But instead of being imprisoned, they would see that their jail had been busted open. They would be free, and then they would have no reason to be angry.

Erec had thought about going straight to the Furies and asking them to release the souls themselves. But they would likely say no. Even if Tartarus could no longer contain them, they might feel that they owned the souls and want to keep them to be safe. If they knew Erec wanted to rescue the souls, he would be denied access and it would never work.

But Erec could not go straight to the storage facility without the Furies knowing that he was there. So he had come up with a reason for their visit.

"This way," Spartacus said. "The Furies are past the rabbit burrow, in that huge hillside over there. This way—let's go around the fox dens and those hedgehogs playing over there."

Erec decided not to tell Spartacus what the place they were in really looked like. *Let him have his illusions.* It must have been nicer than what Erec was seeing. They went over two hills of dark rock and entered a split crevice in the side of a stone cliff.

Spartacus jumped over boulders and stepped around gaping cracks with ease, commenting now and then about the snake nests and frolicking bunnies. Erec wondered if Spartacus actually believed that snakes and baby bunnies were living together in peace.

The three Furies were living in a cave that looked exactly like the one they had been locked into in Tartarus . . . except here the roof had been blown wide open. Erec remembered from before that they kept flying in and out of the place, and now he understood why.

He figured it must feel great to have their freedom now. He supposed all of those eons locked away there made them want a place just like it . . . except wide open.

This time, the Furies looked exactly how Erec remembered them from the first time they met. Even though they were not gorgeous princesses, or immense birds, they were even more impressive in their true forms. They were huge, mostly due to their gigantic faces. Batlike wings flapped behind them, extending from the backs of their heads. Under the wings were small feather-covered, human-shaped bodies that seemed too tiny to support their heads. Long, radiant curls swirled in the air behind them, flowing from their heads, limbs, backs, and wings. It was as if the hair had a life of its own—Alecto's red, Tisiphone's black, and Megaera's white.

But most impressive was their eyes, which pierced through Erec like knives. The energy that radiated from the superhuman creatures was breathtaking. It was as if they were far too immense to fit into their own bodies and were about to burst into supernovas right in front of him. When Erec had first met them, they were putting out so much anger that their feelings alone had almost flattened him. But now a calmness spread through the room. Was that from his influence, or was it Alsatia itself that was making them feel so much better?

Erec reached instinctively for his Amulet of Virtues and the Twrch Trwyth that hung from chains around his neck. He was glad that even as a soul they had accompanied him here. He had to remember to keep his mind clear. Luckily, Alsatia made it harder for the Furies to read his mind, but they might if he raised their suspicions in any way.

It all seemed good, but if Erec had known what would happen next, he might have turned right around and gone back home again.

CHAPTER TWENTY-EIGHT
A Hard Choice

CLEAR YOUR MIND. *CLEAR YOUR MIND.* Erec wanted to do all that he could to make sure that the Furies did not read his thoughts.

"Erec Rex and Spartacus Kilroy. Well, what a nice surprise. The only human we will waste our time with. And his friend." Alecto seemed far calmer than Erec remembered her.

"Look at that," Megaera said with a laugh. "First he comes here as a spirit without a soul. After we send him back to life, he now returns as a soul without a spirit."

"What brings you two here?" Tisiphone asked.

Erec was ready with his answer. "I'm really sorry to bother you, but I have a favor to ask. You three have been wonderful to me. You gave me my life back, and I am so thankful for that. But there is one more thing I would really love. Baskania made me sign a contract that would let him take my dragon eyes away from me whenever he wants them. Could you make that contract not work anymore?"

He waited expectantly. It had seemed to Spartacus and him that this was the perfect excuse for their visit. Plus, Erec would be glad to keep his dragon eyes.

"There is a problem with that, you know," Tisiphone said. Her voice echoed through the cave. "You signed a blood oath. We can break it, of course, but it is the same issue as the pills that you asked us to remove from you before—the ones that let Baskania control you. He will be aware the moment those bonds are broken. It may be a problem, or it may not. But he will know that you have severed those connections with him."

"I don't mind. I just want to keep my dragon eyes safe." Erec had another idea. "And since you're doing that, maybe you could remove that pill from both of us too. Baskania will know already something is up." He tried to keep his mind blank beyond this thought. If this made enough sense, the Furies would probably not bother reading in further.

"If that's what you want." Alecto smiled. It was amazing, Erec thought, seeing her happy in this form. The Furies really had changed. "It is done."

"Done?" Erec looked down at himself. Was it possible, so quickly?

"Very possible," Tisiphone said. "The contract with Baskania is no longer valid. And the pills are now gone forever."

Erec gulped. She had read his mind so easily. But they were only his surface thoughts. He had to keep the deeper ones hidden. . . .

Megaera laughed. "Baskania knows already that something is up. But it's funny—he's all excited. Seems like he thinks that you are here to get your scepter from us and give it to him?"

They all started laughing.

"Like you would do that," Alecto said. "You're not crazy."

"Baskania thinks you are his protégé," Tisiphone said. "He knows that we have helped you get out of your deal with him. But instead of being angry, he is thinking you are smart and crafty like he is. That man really likes you, Erec."

Erec tried to keep his mind a blank, but it was hard. What a crazy situation this was! His worst enemy was considering him a best friend, or a son. And Erec was the crafty one. . . .

"You are the crafty one," Tisiphone laughed.

They were reading his mind so easily now. He had to keep it clear. But it was hard to make conversation with an empty head. "You are reading Baskania's mind from here?" It wasn't what he would have chosen to say—to call attention to their mind-reading abilities when he was trying to hide something—but he was not letting himself think freely.

"Of course," Megaera said. "Anytime we think of someone, we know what is going on in their head. Unless they are here in Alsatia. Then their thoughts are hidden, unless we make an effort."

Erec suddenly worried that the Furies might have thought of *him* before he was here, but he pushed that thought out of his head as well. It seemed best to change the subject before they demonstrated their mind-reading skills on him or Spartacus. "Thank you so much for letting me keep my eyes . . . and giving Spartacus and me our freedom! I'm glad you seem to be happy here. Do you think you're going to stay in Alsatia, then?"

"We've just been speaking about that," Alecto said. "When we first arrived, right after you freed us with your own personal sacrifice, we still had some anger and jealousy. But the peace you showed us with your Awen of Harmony let us get past all of that. We realized the only way to have the kind of life we want is to forgive, and to think about the future instead of the past.

"We came to Alsatia to have privacy from our sisters, the Fates. They were aware of that—it was no secret. We needed time to clear our heads and decide what to do. This is also thanks to you. We would not have even given ourselves this gift of time had it not been for your influence. It has been difficult, though, to decide how to handle our long imprisonment from the Fates. It is a hard thing to forgive."

"But we have a goal now, you know?" Megaera chirped. "To feel good again, like you showed us with your Awen charm."

Erec was amazed that, as a single human being, he could have had influence over these great creatures. And he also felt like a heel doing something they would not like behind their backs. But at least it would not end up hurting them in the long run.

"There is one other thing," Erec threw in. "When we are here, is it okay for us to visit the souls again in your storage facility? Spartacus is missing his." This was where keeping a blank mind was the most important—Erec hoped Spartacus was able to do it as well.

Tisiphone frowned. "Seeing your soul will just make things harder, Spartacus, when you leave again."

"I don't think so." Spartacus shook his head with a smile. "I'm happy to just visit it for a little while. I really want to see it, you know."

Tisiphone would have none of it. "No. That is not a good reason to be with your soul again. It would not end well for you."

She sounded final. This was not what they had expected, and unfortunately they had not thought of a back-up plan. Erec had to get back into that storage facility again. . . . "I thought that Spartacus could have his soul back again for a while. I'm going to make a trade with him, and I'll stay in there until he's had some time with his own soul again."

Spartacus turned to him sharply, surprised. This was not part of the plan.

"That is very kind of you," Alecto said. "But you are a giving person." She smiled. "I will allow you to both do this one time only. It is not good to become dependent on having your soul back. But for Erec—go ahead, spend as much time as you like. And whenever your friend Spartacus wants to come back for you, we will welcome him."

They thanked the Furies and went down what had previously looked like stairs—and now looked to Erec like a jagged slope in the cave rock—to the storage facility. Spartacus remembered the way, even though this place now looked like a forest glen to him. Soon they were at the bottom in a craterlike cavern. A round trapdoor sat in the center, sparkling and glittery. This was the only thing that looked the same as it had before—and it was completely out of place in the stone. Erec knocked, and the door swung open.

First Spartacus, then Erec descended into the darkness of the storage facility. The door swung shut behind them, leaving them in complete blackness. The souls inside were still bound together in a tight Substance Web. Most of them were crying, scared. It had been bad enough being locked up here, away from their spirits. But now they were held tight, with no space to move. Erec could see how badly frightened they were.

Never was he more glad that he had come back to free them. These beings did not deserve an eternity of suffering. As a fellow soul, he felt for them even more than before.

And they looked different to him too. Last time they were like sticky, goopy globs that fastened themselves onto him, like leeches. But now they glowed in all the colors of the rainbow, astoundingly beautiful. He wondered if he looked that way to them.

"Are you ready?" Spartacus winked. One of his hands was on the door, ready to knock.

"No!" Erec rushed to his side. "Wait a minute. There is something we need to talk about. You were going to go to the Furies or Aoquesth after this, so they would destroy you. So you wouldn't be in service to Baskania forever. But now the pill is gone—"

Spartacus nodded. "I know. Thanks, Erec. You saved me from that. Now if I get my soul back, I'm free. I hope it's easy to find after we release them, but I'll keep looking."

"What are you going to do then?"

Spartacus smiled. "I guess what I was meant to do from the beginning. Go wherever I'm supposed to go. Spirit and soul together."

Erec felt a huge weight lift. Spartacus would be saved. "Thanks for everything. I couldn't have done any of this without you."

"My pleasure, kid. I'd give you a hug, it's just that . . . you know."

Erec laughed. As Spartacus was a spirit without a soul, and Erec was a soul without a spirit, a hug wouldn't be the best idea. "I'm going to miss you, Spartacus."

"Miss you too, kid." He ruffled Erec's hair—or the gummy part of the top of his head where hair once had been.

"All right. Let's do this."

Spartacus knocked on the door and waited for it to swing open.

Erec looked at his fingers, and wondered for the first time if they would even snap, now that he was a bodiless soul. There was only one way to find out. He grabbed Spartacus by the wrist so that he would not be affected if time stopped. Then Erec pressed his thumb and middle finger together and snapped. . . .

The squirming, crying souls froze. The room was silent.

Moving fast, Spartacus pointed his Rapid Transitator to the mass of souls and pulled the trigger. He then aimed outside of the door and shot again, aiming at the far wall and concentrating. Then he pulled the trigger again. In a flash, all of the souls disappeared from the dark room. The door of the storage facility did not slam shut or react at all, so time must have stopped for it as well. When Erec turned to look, the souls were in the cave now, outside of the storage facility, still motionless. It had worked! Erec could not believe it.

Spartacus took off his jacket, and underneath were rows of rocket-propelled grenades strapped to each arm. A grin lit up his face as he spread them like wings. "Stand back, kid. Here goes nothing." In a moment, streams of grenades flew through the air and blew chunks out of the side of the cave. "Woo-hoo!" He grinned, bounding forward to the gap. He took aim once more at the group of souls and then fired, shooting another time far away through the hole in the cavern.

The souls were gone. Spartacus bolted through the cracks in the cave after them. The Substance Web still bound them together, but Spartacus could release them by cutting the web with a silver knife. That way they wouldn't drift too far apart before Spartacus found his own soul.

Loud, agonized howls filled the cave. It was happening. Erec snapped his fingers to restart time. It obviously had not paused for the Furies, whose wails were shaking the cavern. Rocks broke from the walls and cracked on the floor around him.

He had to get out, fast. Erec sped toward the hole that Spartacus blasted through the wall, sharp rock scraping against his fingertips. He was almost there . . . so close . . .

But it was taking too long. Something was sucking him in the wrong direction. He flew backward up the cut slope of the cave and straight to the large open rocky platform where the three Furies stood.

Cracks shot up the stone columns and through the remaining

walls. Boulders tumbled to the ground, barely missing Erec as they rolled by, crashing into hundreds of pieces.

One moment later, the bundle of terrified, writhing souls was before them as well.

Erec closed his eyes in disgrace. He had made a complete mess of things, and had solved nothing at all.

At least Tartarus was busted open.

The Furies screeched in despair, their voices ear-shattering. Alecto's long red hair stood behind her like flames. Erec took one glance at her face and had to look away. The anger seething from her was too much to take.

She screamed, shrilly, in the voice from when they first met. "You deceived us! We trusted you, a mere stupid human, because you showed us something good. I didn't even bother reading your mind when you came here. But you tricked us. You stole our souls and condemned us to a life of torture!"

"Wait!" Erec pleaded. "You have the souls back . . . and I fixed Tartarus so you can get out any time you want. . . ."

A powerful wind blew through the cave, sweeping Erec off of his feet. The Furies' hair stood straight on end, pulled by the wind, and rocks flew up into the air currents. Someone grabbed Erec around the middle—was it Tisiphone? Her hand had grown, and the Furies were huge now compared to before.

All three Furies were yanked into the air, Erec in Tisiphone's grasp. They tumbled and sailed into a bright light . . . and then darkness.

The squeezing fingers released Erec, and he tumbled onto the hard stone floor of another cave. This one looked familiar. . . .

It was Tartarus. The first place that he had ever seen the Furies. The place where he had given his life for them. And here it was.

Intact.

Not even a tiny hole had broken through the prison here. There was not one pebble on the ground. All of the might that Spartacus mustered, all of it magnified by thousands, had not made even a single crack in Tartarus.

The Furies gazed around them in despair, howling with rage and sadness. The souls struggled against their web, confused and miserable.

And Erec had done all of this. He had taken these immensely powerful, supernatural creatures from their home, where they were learning to get along with the world, and put them into a place of eternal misery and captivity. Even the souls were no better off. . . .

"You are right," Megaera snarled. "This *is* all your fault."

On top of it, as they were no longer in Alsatia. The Furies would read his every thought with no effort. There was nothing he could do now. He sank to the floor in shock.

But one thing did not make sense. If all of the souls were here, why were they still captives in Tartarus, then?

"Because," Tisiphone snarled. "They're *not* all here. Your friend, Spartacus," she spit the name out, "managed to get his own soul out, as well as one other, before we took this group back. If it didn't happen so fast, I would have figured it out and caught them, too."

Spartacus got his soul back? That was one thing for Erec to feel great about. He deserved it.

But if he only hadn't, then the Furies would still be free. And Erec would still be free. And the Furies would not hate humanity again and want to kill everyone. And the world would not be in danger when Baskania decided to release the Furies in trade for them serving him. It would take only a few more souls and the Furies would be out again.

What would they do to Erec, in the meantime? Wipe him off the face of the planet? No . . . he was a soul now. They would use him with the other souls for their escape from this place. Maybe if Baskania gave them an extra they would destroy him. If not, he could look forward to an eternity as a hostage in a dark room, missing the rest of himself.

"You are correct, Erec," Alecto said. "You have made a lot of big mistakes."

Erec was surprised that her voice sounded calm. He looked up at the Furies in wonder.

They were no longer screaming. In fact, they almost looked peaceful. Their bodies were smaller, their bat-wings calmly flicking behind them.

This was as much of a shock as the fact that Tartarus was still in one piece.

Alecto spoke. "People aren't perfect. Even we are not perfect, so how could we expect it from you? The only thing I want from you is goodness, and that you still have. You have caused us problems, Erec. Bigger problems than you know. I, for one, will not accept any favors from Baskania. He would demand we promise him something in return, and we do not go back on promises. So, even though we are only one soul short of escape, we are likely going to remain here for eternity, unless a stray soul happens to wander by."

Erec's heart sank. There went his last chance to ever see the light of day again. But, then again, this was excellent news. The Furies were not going to help Baskania. Erec waited, still trying to gauge how angry they were.

"You were a stupid boy." Tisiphone shook her giant head. "But we were stupid as well."

"Now, now, Tisi," Megaera said. "Don't be so hard on us. Or him. He's just a boy."

Erec felt even worse. He had put them in a horrible situation . . . and the Furies were being so *nice* about it. Erec deserved to be demolished after this disaster he caused.

"Listen to him," Megaera said. "He thought it would be different. He actually thought this place would be blown open so we wouldn't be trapped."

They all began to laugh, which really shocked Erec. For a moment, they almost sounded like their sisters, the three Fates.

Tisiphone giggled. "As if some human spell could break though bonds that *we* couldn't escape from."

When she said that, Erec realized how stupid he had been. What was he thinking?

"The kid wasn't against us," Alecto said.

"Not much good that does us," Tisiphone commented.

Erec had the unnerving feeling that he was eavesdropping on a private conversation, but there was nowhere he could go. This was the way it would be forever—Erec listening in on the Furies' conversations until they finally happened on another soul for their release. He thought about trying to morph himself back, but he realized that wouldn't really change anything.

No, he would never be free. He would remain a prisoner of theirs for eternity, keeping them from returning back to Tartarus the next time.

Erec thought of the last time he had been in this cave. At least he had done the right thing then. By just using the correct Awen on his Twrch Trwyth chain he had been able to show them what peace and harmony were like. The Twrch Trwyth was powerful enough to even help the Furies. . . .

And it was still hanging around his neck! What Awen balls were left there? Erec tried to remember. He felt for the boar-shaped glass vial and the three crystal balls that were remaining on it: the Awen of Knowledge, Beauty, and Creation.

Maybe one would work now in some way? The Awen of Knowledge would let Erec know exactly what he should do right now. And it also would tell the Furies what they needed to know. It might be the perfect thing. . . .

"Are you insulting us?" Tisiphone asked him.

"Huh?" Erec was confused.

"You think that we don't know what to do? That your Awen of Knowledge is something that will tell us something that we haven't thought of already?"

Erec realized it sounded ridiculous. "Sorry."

"Our heads are not clouded by anger now, so we can think clearly. We are able to look at all sides of this—which is why we are not going to leave here as soon as we could. Because we don't want to owe Baskania. Your Awen of Knowledge would add nothing for us, or for you. You have nothing else to do."

It would be a long eternity of the Furies reading his every thought and putting them all down. Why would Erec try to change things if they already knew it was impossible? He tried to imagine settling in here, floating in the air forever, lonely without his spirit. Right now it wasn't so bad, but given time he would soon be grieving his lost parts. The other souls here were miserable. Which reminded him—

"Could you please take the Substance Net off of the souls? They're feeling worse all bound up."

Alecto nodded. "He is right. There is no need for these poor beings to suffer even more." She paused. "It's funny, when we were collecting souls the last time we were here, I don't remember noticing they were upset."

Megaera nodded. "How could we? We were much too upset ourselves to see it."

There was silence for a moment. Then the Substance Web was broken. The souls drifted apart with relief. Now the colors inside each one shimmered even more. They were truly beautiful.

The Furies were watching them too. "I'm not sure it's right," Tisiphone said.

"I know." Alecto's curls waved around her face with a life of their own. "They will be sad forever with us."

Erec wondered what they were considering. Surely the Furies would not volunteer to stay in this prison forever just to free this group of souls. Would they?

"You know," Tisiphone said. "We never finished that discussion from the other day."

Megaera nodded.

Alecto said, "I wonder if we ever would have. It wasn't bad there, in Alsatia. We might have gone on forever that way."

Megaera looked wistful. "Now we may have to go on forever this way."

Hearing that made Erec feel worse. He had ruined everything.

"I suppose it doesn't matter now." Alecto had a strange look on her face. "But for completeness, I want to decide what to do. No more putting it off, sisters. It's time to make a choice."

Megaera yawned. "Already? It seems so early for all of that."

But Tisiphone agreed. "We should have done it right away when we got to Alsatia. We had freedom there, and privacy."

"But what good was the freedom?" Alecto said. "What did we do with it? What were we going to do?"

Tisiphone nodded. "Exactly."

Erec wished that he understood. It was like the Furies were having a conversation that made sense to everyone except for him.

Alecto sighed. "Must you think so loud, Erec Rex? We are talking about what our plans will be once we are free again. *If* we are ever free again."

"Do you mean when you get the extra soul and you can leave here?"

"*If* we leave here. Now that we're all calm—again thanks to your first visit—we feel that there would need to be a good reason for us to leave. Otherwise it would not be worth causing these souls to suffer forever. Looking at them with fresh eyes, I feel rather bad for them."

Erec could not believe his ears. They were valuing the lives of the souls more than their own?

"Not more than our own," Tisiphone explained. "But valuing them nonetheless. What were we doing with our freedom, anyway? Not much more than we are doing here. Yes, it's a bit claustrophobic." She looked around. "But at the same time, it's home."

"It would be nice to fly in and out, though," Megaera said.

"It would," Alecto agreed. "But at the price of these beings?" She gestured to the souls.

"Is that what you are trying to decide, then?" Erec was trying to fit the pieces of their conversation together.

"No," Tisiphone smiled. "That is something that we all agree on. We will only keep the souls and try to leave if there is a good reason. There is something else, though, that we have put off discussing. It is important, even if we stay here forever. It's . . . our plan."

"Your plan for what?" Erec was confused.

"What to do when we get out," Alecto said. "*If* we get out."

Erec had no idea what they were talking about. "Didn't you say that you weren't doing much when you were free in Alsatia?"

"We hadn't decided yet," Megaera said.

It seemed that the conversation was going in circles. Doing what? Planning what?

Tisiphone looked at Erec sternly. "It has to do with our sisters. The Fates. We had not yet decided if we should forgive them."

"I still think that there is no rush," Megaera said.

"But there is a rush," Alecto disagreed. "It is not as easy living here as it was in Alsatia. Now that we are here, it won't feel right to be in limbo like we've been. Our minds won't be right until we answer this question. And our minds are all we have here. I'm tired of waiting. The choice is simple—do we take revenge against the Fates for imprisoning us? In this case we will keep the souls until we find one more, let our anger build, then fight until victory is ours. Or should we forgive our sisters and move on with life? Then we will set these poor souls free and resign ourselves to an eternity in Tartarus."

It seemed a terrible choice either way. Who would commit themselves to an eternal life sentence in jail? But then again, the other option of fighting the Fates sounded just as awful. Violence, death . . . but what was worse, that or eternal captivity?

Alecto laughed. "Erec here has a keen grasp of our situation. But there is one thing you are missing, Erec."

"What's that?"

"Happiness. You showed that to us, remember? It may have been brief, but you gave us a taste of the way things should be when you used the Awen of Harmony in this very cave. You may not realize it, but that little glimpse of contentment changed everything for me— for us. It has become our goal now. Why choose strife and anger if it will only take us further from our purpose? Happiness can be attained anywhere, not just in a place of beauty or freedom."

"And unhappiness can be attained anywhere too," Megaera added. "We had unhappiness when we were free, long before the Fates locked us here."

"What would you do, Erec?" Alecto asked.

Erec could not believe his ears. The three Furies—these intensely powerful creatures—were asking his opinion? He thought hard for a minute. What would he do? He knew how bad it felt to be wronged, and how hard that was to let go. Also he could not begin to imagine signing up to be locked away forever. But he kept coming back to one thing. "It's terrible to think about. I would hate being in your shoes, and I'm sure I wouldn't handle it as well as you. But I wouldn't have a choice. I would be stuck here, miserable, forever. There's no way I could choose freedom at the expense of three thousand others, so I would free the souls. And I wouldn't even want to hurt sisters that

I was so angry at. I'd forgive them, or just avoid them, maybe. But that's just me."

The Furies looked at each other silently. Finally, Alecto said, "I think Erec spoke for all of us."

One of Megaera's eyebrows shot up. "Wouldn't it be odd, and funny, if the Fates locked us here for that reason—so that we would eventually figure this out?"

"That sounds like them, you know," Alecto said.

Tisiphone giggled. "You know, this decision has made me feel better already, like I'm a million years younger."

Suddenly, the three started laughing. Their glee was so contagious that Erec and many of the other souls floating around the room found themselves chuckling along.

Their laughter grew and grew until the entire cave began to shake. The Furies were growing, enlarging in size until they took up most of the cave.

"So, we've decided then, sisters?" Alecto asked.

The other two nodded.

"It's a deal, then. Erec, thank you for everything. We are letting you go, along with the rest of the souls here. We Furies have learned our lesson—and from a little boy, no less."

A ray of sunlight fell on Erec. It looked like a spotlight, as if Erec had just taken center stage and was about to burst into song. But there was no stage . . . so where was the light coming from?

They all looked up. A large crack was forming in the ceiling of Tartarus. It grew larger until chunks of rock began to clatter all around them. The sun shone heavily all around them now, causing the Furies to sparkle with radiance.

Nobody spoke, but all eyes were glued to the roof of the cave. It was as though they were witnessing a miracle. Tartarus was breaking open. And none of them had done a thing to make it happen. Erec had just talked to the Furies, giving his opinion. They had just agreed with him and made a decision. . . .

So, that was it, then? Their decision had broken Tartarus open?

The three Furies gazed at one another in wonderment. The Fates were letting them go. Erec wondered if this place was programmed to cave in once the Furies decided to live in peace. Or maybe the Fates were listening as they spoke, and chose to give the Furies their freedom. Erec had no idea, but he was sure they had a hand in what was going on.

Chunks of rock dropped in larger pieces, shattering as they fell and filling in the cave with boulders and soot. The souls were taking last looks at the Furies before darting through the opening in search of their long-lost spirits. Erec hoped they all found them. Watching them leave, he felt a hot burst of longing for his own spirit and body. He thought the word *Nee-way* and tried to morph back, but nothing happened.

Maybe he had to return through Mercy's Spike in Alsatia before he could return to his normal form. But instead of going now, he remained with the Furies a little longer. Even though the roof of their former prison was completely open now, they still stayed as if glued to the spot.

Alecto looked up at the blue sky overhead. "We have it all now, sisters. Freedom *and* happiness. And that is thanks to the Fates, and to Erec Rex. We would never have seen what we needed to if it wasn't for you. And we would never have listened to you if our sisters had not locked us away for a while."

Tisiphone's mouth was open in awe. "This is the greatest gift of all."

Megaera just laughed, and her laughter caught on with her sisters and then Erec, until all of them were lost in a sea of merriment. If Erec had his human body he would have been gasping, his sides hurting from laughing so hard.

When they finally calmed down, Alecto said, "Erec, thank you again. You have freed the souls here, and you have freed us forever. You will always be special to us."

"Look, he is missing his body and spirit," Tisiphone said.

"I'll take care of that. It's my pleasure," Alecto said.

In a blink, Erec was whole again—body, spirit, and soul. It felt so good. He had almost forgotten what it was like to be covered by a solid frame, not drifting, missing his other parts. The only problem was that since he was no longer a floating soul, the big chunks of rock rolling down the cave walls and smashing around him were now dangerous and scary.

"We'll get you out of here," Tisiphone said. "You might not be seeing us again. But we'll always remember you, Erec. Wish us good-bye, and then I think it's time for you to have a rest with your family."

Before Erec could say good-bye, the cave was gone in a blink. He was in a room inside . . . somewhere. It was deathly quiet compared to the loud avalanche he had just been in. Things around him seemed soft and comfortable. The bed he was on was covered with pillows. But even though he was safe, Erec felt empty.

The Furies were much larger than life. They were so awe-inspiring that he had been a tiny, meaningless grain of sand in their presence. They were so terrifying that nothing else should ever intimidate him again. They were so brilliant that they made humans look like ants, trailing after one another in mindless streams. Yet, at the same time, they were flawed, which made Erec realize that even the best that the world has to offer is still not perfect.

He would miss them.

CHAPTER TWENTY-NINE
The Other Scepter

BETHANY WAS IN THE LIBRARY bent over a stack of books. Erec watched her for a moment before he realized that she wasn't reading at all. Tears fell from her cheeks onto the open pages, and her shoulders shook.

He rushed over to comfort her, careful not to make her jump in surprise. "Bethany? Are you okay?"

She sniffed, then threw her arms around him. "Erec! You're back!" She hugged him a minute before asking, "How's Trevor?"

Erec's heart sank. He had felt so good, so relieved about the souls and getting his own body back in one piece. He had thought that he would be stuck in Tartarus forever, and never see his family again. But thinking about poor Trevor brought all the sadness back. It was time to get him away from Baskania.

"I haven't seen him. I was just locked away in Tartarus with the Furies." He told Bethany everything that had happened.

She gazed at him in awe. "I can't believe they got out of there. So everything worked out, then."

Erec nodded, still dumbfounded at the turn of events. "Yeah. It all worked out just right."

"Look!" Bethany picked up his Amulet of Virtues and showed it to him. "Your seventh segment is lit up!"

And it was. The seventh pie slice on his gold disc glowed a bright, sparkly gold, with a small black symbol printed on it. Erec closed his eyes and made his dragon eyes come forward. When he opened them, the room was green and he could see thick tangles of the Substance hanging in the air. He was now able to read what the symbol said.

"Bravery."

He laughed right away, then thought about that for a while, letting his regular eyes slip back into place. Had he been particularly brave? He guessed that he had—going to his death like the Fates had told him to do. He had not put his own safety first when he tried to save the captive souls. He was terrified the whole time, but he just didn't let it stop him.

He smiled a minute, thinking that maybe he did deserve to be called brave.

But then he remembered about Trevor and his smile went away. It was time to save him.

"What did you see in the future about Trevor?" Bethany asked. "He was still alive when you went back, right?"

"He was, but he wasn't looking good. For some reason I was still Baskania's friend in that vision. I was giving him the scepter, which is hard to believe. But, you know what was weird? I told him that I had gotten it back from the Furies for him. That doesn't even make sense. The Furies never had the scepter to begin with. It was just something I made up so he would leave me alone for a while."

Bethany frowned in thought. "So, in your vision you were telling Baskania a lie. Maybe you weren't under his spell, then. I wonder if it was some sort of plan."

"Why would I give Baskania the scepter as part of a plan?"

"Maybe so you could get back in there? You want him on your side to help get Trevor out."

That actually made a lot of sense. Baskania was fully aware that Erec had removed the influence of the pill from himself and from Spartacus, and also that Erec broke his blood oath that let Baskania take his dragon eyes from him. Baskania might also know that the Furies had gone back to Tartarus and had been freed forever—Erec wasn't sure about that. And he was expecting to get that scepter back from Erec now.

If Erec sauntered in and tried to kidnap Trevor from the Inner Sanctum it might not go well. But if he came with the scepter as a gift . . .

"But that would be crazy," Erec said. "Yeah, I'd get Trevor out of there. I saw in the vision that Baskania will get totally absorbed with the scepter. I could probably do anything then. But how can I give it to him? I just can't—"

"I know!" Bethany bounced up and down in her chair, excited. "We could use the fake scepter! Then it won't matter if he keeps it."

"That sounds great—but he would realize that it was a phony right away. And we'd never get out of there, then."

"I could program it to work for him." Her eyes sparkled. It made

Erec happy to see her feeling better, even though he was skeptical. "It can't be as powerful as the real scepter, but it does work. Remember how Cutie Pie filled that whole room with sardines? I mean, if it does things for him, then he won't get suspicious right away. Maybe that will be enough. You could even make a trade for Trevor that way."

Erec thought about making a trade. That might work, but it would blow his cover as Baskania's protégé. If Baskania considered Erec a friend he could get away with more. . . .

Was that possible, though? Baskania had forgiven him for stealing the Master Shem—in fact, it seemed he liked Erec even better after that. He was proud that Erec was crafty and wily like he was. And he wasn't afraid that Erec would really get away with anything if he was watching over him.

That was it. He would go back to Baskania with the peace offering of a scepter—only it would be the fake scepter. When he was there, he would plan an escape for Trevor. Maybe Baskania would think that Trevor had been killed, but really Erec could secrete him away. . . .

"The trash compactor!"

"What?" Bethany looked completely confused.

"I need to figure out a way to make Baskania think that I'm getting rid of Trevor for good, when I'm really sneaking him out of there. In my vision I gave Baskania the scepter—and it worked for him—and then got Trevor into some kind of trash compactor. That would be perfect. I could sneak him out in that thing."

"It doesn't sound safe at all. What if it gets turned on and smashes him?"

"I know. But it has to look like we're really doing away with him for good."

Erec wished that Spartacus was still around to help him. It was so much easier to do things with a silent, powerful, invisible friend. He would always miss him.

"And what makes you think that I'd leave you high and dry?"

Erec almost fainted when he heard Spartacus's voice. "Is that really you?" He looked around, and there stood Spartacus right behind him. He jumped up and threw his arms around his friend, forgetting that they would sail right through him.

Bethany watched Erec clap his arms together with a big grin on his face, and looked at him like he was crazy. "What are you doing?"

"Spartacus is back!"

"I never left. Thanks to you I have my soul again. I can't believe how amazing it feels to be in one piece. And I don't have to be Baskania's servant anymore, since that pill is gone. I'm free, the way I'm supposed to be. I couldn't be better."

"Did you hear what happened with the Furies?"

"I did—as soon as you disappeared I tracked you to Tartarus. I was waiting outside, trying to figure out how I could possibly rescue you. But there was no way I could get in without the Furies taking my soul and escaping, so I just waited and listened."

"Why didn't you go on to . . . wherever you're supposed to go?"

"That's the funny thing about being a ghost. When there is something left unresolved, you have the choice to stay around for a while and help settle it. So, that's what I'm doing."

"You're staying on earth to help me?"

"Of course. You helped me, didn't you?"

"Wow. Thanks." Erec was at a loss for words.

Bethany chimed in. "Spartacus is going to help rescue Trevor? Thank you, Spartacus!" She hugged the air near where Erec tried to hug Spartacus. Erec laughed when he saw that she was hugging the space next to the ghost, one of her arms passing through his midsection.

"Wait a minute." Erec had a sobering thought. "Baskania is going to want my eyes again when I'm there. He knows that his contract with me for the eyes is void, so there is no way that he'll let me out of there with them again."

"Could you just sneak out fast with Trevor after he has the scepter?" Bethany asked.

"I don't think so. This whole thing is a game, and the minute he suspects that I'm faking, then it's up." Erec's heart sank. He remembered that in his vision of the future everything had gone black. He was going to have to trade his eyes for his brother. It was as simple as that.

But really, that was no choice. He would just learn to live with it. "Spartacus? Could you make sure that there is a trash compactor in Baskania's Inner Sanctum? I saw it when I looked into the future, so there should be one there."

"Yup. If not, then I'll put one in. And I'll scan the place to see where we can sneak Trevor out."

"Thanks."

Spartacus disappeared.

Bethany was all smiles. "I thought I'd never see either of you again. Now everything seems like it will be perfect."

Erec wasn't so sure that it would turn out perfect at all. In fact, there was a good chance he would never see Bethany again—even if he did make it back home.

Bethany pulled the fake scepter out of her closet. Erec was surprised she had brought it with her.

"I never leave magical objects behind, even silly things like this. But I did take Cutie Pie's hair out of its base, so it won't work for her anymore. She was getting fat from the sardines, and she completely stunk up the apartment."

"How does it work again?"

"The Druids said that all I have to do is put a few hairs in here and then it will work only for that person. . . ." She froze, staring at the thing. "Wait a minute. How are we going to get Baskania's hairs?" Her smile disappeared.

Erec thought about it. "Maybe Spartacus could yank some before he comes back? Or find Baskania's hairbrush somewhere?"

It seemed hard to imagine that Baskania ever brushed his hair or did anything that mundane. He probably fixed it magically with a permanent spell. What if his hairs were inaccessible?"

But Bethany was happy again. "Great thinking, Erec! All we need is to put it in—"

"Wait! I have a much better idea!" Erec had used scepters enough to realize that there were ways of getting around problems like this. "We'll use one of your hairs. *You* command the scepter, and tell it that it should do what Baskania orders it to do. That way you can tell it to only work for him for a short time. Maybe twenty minutes—long enough for us to get out of there safely. And then you can tell the scepter to fly away from him and come right back here to us."

"That's a great idea! Then he won't be able to keep it. Who knows if he'll be able to get much magic out of the thing, but I'd rather not leave it with him too long just in case."

Another idea perked Erec up. "I'm going to give Baskania my dragon eyes. I have to—it's the only way that I can convince him to trust me. If I don't, he'll just take them anyway. Let's program the scepter to get my eyes back when it leaves Baskania, and put them back into me."

Bethany looked dubious. "You would trust this joke scepter with something as important as your eyes?"

"I don't have a choice. We have to give it a try."

Bethany stared at him. "You're really serious, aren't you? I can't imagine giving up my vision."

A look passed between the two of them, and Bethany nodded solemnly. She plucked two hairs from her head and slid them into the small slot at the base of the scepter. Erec marveled at how much it resembled his own. But when he put out a finger to touch it, he felt nothing at all, instead of the massive drawing power that the other held over him.

"That should do it," Bethany looked it over. "Let's see. I guess I just tell it what to do?"

"Try it."

"Okay. Scepter, Erec is going to bring you to Baskania. When Baskania takes you, then you are to do whatever he commands you to, just like you are his scepter. But in twenty minutes, you need to come straight back here to me. Okay? And also, if Baskania takes Erec's eyes when he's there, you need to take his eyes back from Baskania twenty minutes later and put them right back in Erec—and make sure that they work for him again too. Then you can go back to not doing anything again, and just stay in my closet. And make my hairs disappear from you then, so nobody can make you do anything until we plan it next."

All of a sudden, Bethany's eyes bugged out. Her hands spasmed on the scepter as if she was being electrocuted, and her hair blew around her head like the Furies'.

Erec didn't know what to do. Was the thing backfiring or blowing a circuit? He tried to yank it from her hands, but her grip on it was far too strong. It didn't even look like she noticed he was trying. Finally, her face relaxed, and in a burst of energy Erec ripped the scepter from her grip.

Bethany spun around and glared at him with a look of pure hate. It made him jump—he had never seen her like that before. But then she calmed down and looked embarrassed. "I'm sorry. I don't know what came over me. Why were you trying to take my scepter away?"

"I wasn't. But it looked like it was hurting you, so I thought I better get it out of your hands."

"It didn't hurt. I could feel the magic working, though. It kind of felt . . . good."

"I know all about that." He laughed. "Just don't do it again. Even if this is just a fake one, it still might be addicting."

She smiled. "I know that it worked, though. It kind of told me that. So I think we'll be okay."

Spartacus appeared, looking somber. "You're coming in the nick of time, kid. Are you ready to leave now?"

"Yes. What's happening there?"

"I'll tell you the reason that there is a trash compactor in the Inner Sanctum. It wasn't your idea to throw Trevor into it, it was Baskania's. He's got him there now, and he's making his last threats to see if Trevor will help him. Baskania knows that Trevor's mind is messed up. He's already searched through all of his memory—what little new memory there is after all the old stuff was gone—and he can't find anything. He's suspicious, too, that you were the one that did something to Trevor. Luckily Trevor had no memory of what happened—he can barely keep yesterday's events in his head, the water of Lethe was so strong. So the Shadow Prince can't be sure."

"I'm going to really have to play it up to get him back on my side."

"Offer him the world. When he sees you have the scepter, he's bound to forgive and forget."

"What else can I offer him besides my eyes and the scepter?" Then Erec thought about the Amulet of Virtues and the Twrch Trwyth hanging around his neck. He wouldn't give those away, and it was too late to ask the scepter to bring them back later. He would offer Baskania something else to throw him off track and make him forget about the things hanging on Erec's neck.

Spartacus answered his thoughts. "Why don't you leave the Amulet of Virtues and the Twrch Trwyth here?"

"I can't take them off. The Amulet protects me. And they are supposed to stay on me, always."

"Good luck, then. Are you ready?"

"Yes. Bethany, thanks for programming this thing." He picked up the scepter. It was strange holding one that looked so much like his but did nothing for him. "We have to hurry."

"Good luck." Bethany looked like she was thinking.

"She wants to come, but she knows it's not safe." Spartacus said.

Erec felt guilty, as he was eavesdropping on her private thoughts. "It's okay, Bethany. I'll have Trevor back really soon." He thought about how little time they had spent together this last horrible month. "I promise I'll take you somewhere, just the two of us, after all of this is over. We could use a little adventure of our own."

She grinned. "Thanks, Erec. I'm just going to keep thinking everything will be okay, and maybe I'll make it through being alone, waiting here again."

Erec smiled at her as Spartacus grabbed his shoulders and sailed with him to the Port-O-Door in the Castle Ashona.

A blind follower opened the heavy oak doors to the Inner Sanctum. When Erec told him who he was, and that he would like to speak to the Shadow Prince, the poor man had gasped in shock. He stumbled back in his heavy, hooded robe, then turned and plodded to his master. Moments later, he returned and swung the doors open wide. "Please come in. The Shadow Prince will see you now."

Erec strolled into the room. Hundreds of candles reflected sparkling light over the ornate gold chandeliers and furniture. The sole eye on Baskania's forehead today swept its gaze over Erec, stopping at the gold scepter in his hands.

Erec could feel the tension in the room. Trevor looked up at him with hope. Next to him was a trash compactor, a huge guard standing next to it.

Baskania tilted his head. "Well, look who has come back to visit." Erec could tell that Baskania was trying to read his mind, unsuccessfully.

Erec had to play this perfectly. He cracked a grin. "I wasn't going to stay away for too long. Just learning from the best, that's all."

Baskania cocked an eyebrow, listening. It seemed that he was not going to make a sudden move for the scepter, probably because he thought that Erec could use it against him.

"I brought you a few gifts." Erec wagged the scepter in the air. "Peace offerings. And also an apology. I did a few things I shouldn't have when I was with the Furies. Like take away our contract where you would get my eyes. It was too hard to resist. I was there, and I could do it, so I did." He tried to sound cocky. "But, like I said, I came back. There's too much for me to learn here. You've been really good to me. And when I was reborn from the Furies, I saw a whole different side to you." He shrugged. "So maybe I shouldn't have done that with our contract, but I'm going to make it all up to you now."

Baskania's eyes widened with delight, gazing at the scepter. "What do you have for me?"

Erec looked at the scepter and tapped on it. But then he glanced back at Baskania. "For one, I have some news for you. King Piter and Queen Posey are in Ashona now. Two royals and another scepter there. Just thought you'd like that information."

Erec knew full well that that was no news to Baskania. But it seemed best to start slowly. He pretended to notice Trevor for the first time. "Did you get what you needed out of him?"

"No." Baskania's voice soured. "He was useless. Someone erased his mind."

"I know who it was, I'm sure." Erec crossed his arms, confident. "King Piter said some kind of spell when I was taking Trevor out of Ashona. I didn't know what he was doing, but that must have been it."

A look of realization crossed Baskania's face. "So you didn't . . ."

"Me? I'm just trying to help you." He laughed. "And occasionally myself."

Baskania beamed. "Well . . . what a good boy you are. I'm glad to see you are still using your head."

Trevor was crouching, arms around his knees, and shaking head to toe. Erec laughed cruelly, and gave him a kick. "Worthless piece of garbage."

Trevor stared at him with big eyes, in disbelief. Tears rolled down his cheeks.

"Look at that. He's useless." Erec smirked, then kicked Trevor into a large box that was on its side on the floor. He looked up at Baskania and laughed. "Let's throw him in that trash compactor to be crushed. Trash is all he is, anyway."

"That's fine." Baskania looked at Erec greedily. "Now, let's see what else you have for me today."

"This." Erec held the scepter out to him. "It's yours again. I got it from the Furies for you. This time nobody will take it away. Why don't you take my dragon eyes first, so you don't forget? Once you are using the scepter, you'll be thinking of other things."

"Good thinking, boy." Baskania's whisper was tight with greed. "Here we go."

The room went black. Erec felt the scepter lift out of his grip.

"*This is it!*" Baskania's voice echoed. "Oh, it's so good to have you back in my hands again. I've missed you, lovely. Let's see what we can make you do now!"

Erec could feel the electricity spark in the room and screams echoed from outside. What was Baskania doing with the scepter?

He could not even imagine. But it was definitely working for him. Bethany had been able to program it right. Now hopefully it would go back to Bethany again soon. Erec just had fifteen minutes to get Trevor out of there.

He felt a hand on his arm. "Spartacus?" he whispered.

"It's me," Spartacus said. "I entered one of the guards and made him pick up Trevor and drop him into the trash compactor. It was perfect—the guard thought that Baskania was making him do it, and Baskania's completely distracted now. I'm going to pop back into the same guard and make him wheel Trevor out of here in that thing. I'll get you in a minute."

Erec nodded. He could hear Baskania murmuring to the scepter. ". . . and then you will finish my plans to let me conquer the world. You will bring me the rest of the . . . Ashona . . ." Erec wished he could catch everything, but it would probably be too horrifying, anyway.

Someone grabbed Erec's arm with a heavy hand, and Spartacus whispered, "It's me . . . in the guard. Let's go before Baskania finishes with that thing."

In the hallway outside, Spartacus stepped out of the guard, who sounded surprised. "What do I do? I can't tell if the Shadow Prince wants me to cart this kid to the trash."

Erec couldn't see, but he knew the guard was talking to him. He said, "I'm supposed to do it. That's why you grabbed me and brought me out here. Get it? Now go back inside."

"Yeah. I guess." The guard sounded nervous. Erec could hear him stumble back into the Inner Sanctum. Baskania was still talking to the scepter when the guard opened the door.

"Let's get out of here!" Spartacus had Erec and Trevor out a window before Erec could even answer. He flew them to a Port-O-Door that he had left in a tree in the woods of Alypium. It was nauseating being carried through the air blind—Erec could not wait to get his eyes back again. Spartacus pressed the buttons to go to the Castle Ashona. Thankfully he was not trying to drag Erec and Trevor there through the ocean water.

When the inner door of the Port-O-Door opened, Spartacus walked through it easily. But when Erec tried to pass, he was stopped by what felt like a glass wall. Trevor must have hit it too, because he made a noise and sounded like he was rubbing his face.

"Come on, you guys." Spartacus looked back at them impatiently. Finally, he took Erec and Trevor by the hands and pulled them, making them slam hard into whatever the thing was.

"Ow!" Trevor rubbed his face. "What pulled me into that invisible wall?"

"What's going on?" Spartacus squinted until he saw what it was. "Is this stopping you guys? It looks like glass or thick plastic. Sorry. I didn't notice it here before."

"That's okay." Erec wished that he could see what the thing looked like. Then he remembered the little he had heard Baskania talking to the scepter while he was in the room. "I think Baskania did something to Ashona—he said something, but I couldn't make out the details."

A look of realization crossed Spartacus's face. "You're probably right. I wonder what he's up to, closing this place off."

"We aren't going to be able to get in there now." Erec began to worry about Bethany and his family. How would he see them again? How would they know that Trevor was okay?

"I'll tell them," Spartacus said.

"But they can't hear or see you."

"I'll get a piece of paper and write on it. Bethany knows what's going on. I'll fill her in on what happened, and tell her Trevor is okay."

"Good." Erec waited until Spartacus returned.

"She's really happy," the ghost said. "She thanked me and said to thank you. The girl can't wait to see you again, kid. She really misses you."

"I miss her, too."

"Yeah, I know. I told her that."

"Thanks."

All of a sudden, Erec could see again. His eyes were back. "Look!" He pointed to his face.

"The scepter worked, then." Spartacus grinned. "I guess it's back with Bethany now."

"What are we going to do?" Erec put a hand on Trevor's head. Trevor looked up at him with frightened eyes, and he gave his brother a hug. "It's okay, Trev. All that bad stuff is done. I'm here now, and I'm not going to let anything happen to you. And I'm sorry about how I acted in that place—I had to fake being mean."

Erec had not even had time to feel relieved until this moment. All of a sudden, reality came rushing to him—he had saved Trevor! Everything would be okay now. The Furies were free, the souls were free, Trevor was free. Erec had even finished his seventh quest—bravery. Even if he could not see Bethany and his family immediately, things were all good, and everyone was safe.

He wondered how long it would be before he could see his family. Why was this barrier around Ashona anyway? In a flash of fear, he wondered what Baskania had done with the scepter. Did he do this because Erec had pointed out that King Piter and Queen Posey were staying here? Baskania already knew that, though. Maybe he was holding them hostage for Queen Posey's scepter. . . .

"I guess we should go to Rosco's place," Erec said. "We can wait with Trevor there until Ashona opens up."

Spartacus nodded and took them back through the Port-O-Door

into Alypium. Moments later, Erec and Trevor were sailing through the air toward Rosco's apartment.

"He's in there," Spartacus said. "And I get the sense he's not happy. I can't read his mind clearly from here."

Spartacus was right. Rosco was pacing the floors when they arrived. He looked up at Erec with relief. "Thank goodness you're here—and you're okay. I've been worried sick."

"About me?"

"Yes . . . and more than that too. Baskania is attacking Otherness now, and he's going after Upper Earth next. He showed us his plans in a meeting—he's starting with Europe, then moving down into Africa, and then North and South America. The guy's got it planned down to how each town and each city will fall, and the timing of his Golem army crushing everything. He owns all the bridges. And all the transportation—the trains, airlines, buses. He's bought them all. Plus, he has half the police around the world on his payroll. And with Eye of the World taking over the United Nations, its army overriding the rest of the nations' militaries, nobody can even put up a fight. He's obsessed about these details for decades, and the guy isn't one to forget a detail."

Erec absorbed this in shock. Just when he thought everything was okay, Baskania was waging war? Or was it even war if nobody could fight back? It was more like Baskania smashing a bug with his thumb—and Erec's world was the bug.

"Did you say Golem? Baskania is going to use Tarvos's Golem soldiers to destroy the world?"

Rosco nodded. "After the scepter you gave him disappeared—and your dragon eyes—he wanted to strike immediately. He was angrier than I've ever seen him."

Erec went from feeling victorious to wallowing in guilt. He was the one who made Baskania angry enough to attack. He handed the Master Shem to Baskania to command the Golems.

"What can I do?"

Rosco looked at him strangely. "Do? You really think that you alone, a single kid, could do something about a large-scale attack on the world? We're talking millions of people involved here, most on Baskania's payroll in one way or another. Armies, businesses, 'peace' forces. One person couldn't change anything."

"I don't know about that," Spartacus said. "You've changed a lot already."

Erec knew that was true. But what would he do? The first thing that occurred to him was to consult the three Fates. They would know exactly how Erec could help.

"Exactly," Spartacus said.

Rosco buried his head in his hands. "Part of Otherness is already gone. The only group that held out in that area is the dragons. They're going after the clowns next."

"The clowns? Danny and Sammy—I mean Derby and Shalimar?"

"Yeah. It makes me sick too."

"We can't let that happen. I'm going to talk to the Fates now. Would you watch Trevor for me while I'm gone?"

Rosco clicked on his television, and Trevor was drawn straight to it. "Wow. This is cool. I'll learn all kinds of things." He plopped on the couch in front of it. "I'm hungry."

Rosco laughed and went into the kitchen. "Coming right up!" He winked at Erec. "Sure, I'll keep an eye on him. Go talk to the Fates if you want. It can't hurt. Let me know what they say."

"Thanks."

Before Erec could say good-bye to Trevor he was flying through the air again. Spartacus was not high on patience, he thought.

"Hey, you wouldn't be either if you were hanging out on earth for one reason alone. Let's get to the bottom of this and fix it. Not to rush you or anything."

"Of course not." Erec laughed. "It's okay. I remember what it's like to be a ghost. And there's nothing I'd rather do now. Baskania is about to attack Danny and Sammy with the clowns, so we have to hurry."

They landed in front of the mountainside in Delphi, Greece. The Oracle, the stone well that allowed him to speak to the three Fates, was just up a winding path by the edge of a bubbling brook. It wasn't until he was gazing into the deep dark waters of the stone well that he remembered what he had to do. It was time to use his dragon eyes again to see another vision of the future. Erec was thankful again that Baskania had not taken his eyes.

He pictured himself going into the small dark room in his mind. What would he see this time? With all of the mess with the Furies he had forgotten the other terrible images he had seen before in his future. Would he still do those horrible things? Maybe now things were different—that was all that he could hope.

The room was relaxing, though, and he soon forgot all about everything that bothered him. When he felt ready, he opened the door to the smaller room inside of the first one, and went in. There was the box that held all of his knowledge. There were the windows. All he had to do was pull the cord and open the shades. What was his mind going to show him this time?

Erec was charging forward on the fastest horse that he had ever heard of. His view on all sides was a blur from the speed, but that didn't matter. All that he focused on was in front of him. The Flame—the powerful, huge lance—was poised in his grip, ready to spear his target. Nothing would stop him now. He couldn't even slow down if he tried.

Faster now, and faster. His aim was true and steady, and he was almost there. In seconds, the image of what he was going to destroy was right in front of him. The tip of his lance zoomed inexorably toward . . . Bethany. . . .

Erec yanked the cord to pull the shades down. *What?* This could not be happening—now or in the future. He would never, ever hurt Bethany. The whole thing did not make sense. She was his best friend, and even more than that. What in the world would be happening in the future that would make him do terrible things to people and hurt the one he cared about most?

No. For the first time since he had seen visions of his future, Erec refused to believe this one. It simply would not happen. He stepped out of the dark rooms, opened his eyes, and looked down into the well water.

"Fates?" he called. "Can you hear me? I need to talk to you."

There was a chorus of squealing, and shouts of "Erec!" "He's back!" "Our hero!"

It was great to hear the Fates happy again. The last time he had come here they were acting like they had had enough of him.

"Thank you, Erec!" a voice said. "You, like, saved our sisters! That is so totally rad. Alecto, Tisiphone, and Megaera are sooo happy now. And they're not prisoners of themselves anymore."

He grinned. At least that was one thing he had accomplished. "I'm glad it worked out."

"And now you want us to, like, tell you what to do about the Golem army," another voice said.

There were titters in the background, and someone said, "As if that was his only problem."

Erec's ears perked up. He had more problems than that? Would they never end?

"If you want things to work out right, then you need a little dip in the toilet water," one of the Fates giggled.

It took Erec a second to realize she was referring to Al's Well.

"Like, duh!" said another. "Draw a quest and work with fate, not against it. It's, like, your only hope."

"So, if I do my next quest I'll be able to stop Baskania from conquering Otherness and Upper Earth?"

"Yeah, like, maybe you can stop that and also something even worse for you. But only if you don't totally mess things up. If you, like, follow your *brain* and your *heart*, then just maybe you can win."

Follow my brain and my heart, he thought. Well, that's all he could do. "Can you help me get to Al's Well again, through the waterways?

There was more giggling. "Um, like, ya, I guess. I mean, we always like to help our hero."

Erec hesitated a moment before jumping into the well water. He had to pick his eighth quest now? Was it going to lead him on a wild goose chase like some of his other quests had? What if it was dangerous, or made him die again?

He pushed his fears aside and looked at the water. Whatever it was, he would have to deal with it. Not only was Baskania about to destroy Otherness and the whole human world, but something *worse* was going to happen? And he could stop whatever it was if he did things right. There was no question he had to do what the quest told him to do.

As he jumped into the water of the well, a thought popped into his head. What if the "worse" thing had to do with some of his visions of the future? What if it was him turning evil and doing horrible things? Maybe he could stop that, too, and things would work out okay after all.

CHAPTER THIRTY

The Choice to Become Evil

*Ride the mythic horse of
the elements to victory*

T HE WATER AROUND EREC quickly changed from the
burning hot/freezing cold liquid of the well to normal water. He whizzed through waterways, around
turns, and down suction drops until things started to
look familiar. Before he knew it, he was again under
Al's Well, looking up through the white porcelain commode . . . and
directly into Al's face, which broke out into a big grin.

"Well, lookie here! It's Erec Rex again. Great ta see ya, kid. I
heard you pulled off a doozy with that last quest of yours. Pretty
brave, I'd say."

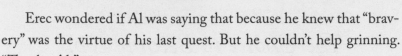

Erec wondered if Al was saying that because he knew that "bravery" was the virtue of his last quest. But he couldn't help grinning. "Thanks, Al."

"You know, the Fates recommend that ya sign Janus's paper before you get the quest." He shrugged apologetically.

"I think it's more than a recommendation. Seems to be the only way it works," Erec said. "It's no problem. I'll be right back."

Erec dove into the large pipe that ran under the Labor Society building. He knew exactly which way to go now. Minutes later, he swam under the row of toilets, and was looking through the sink grate into Janus's room.

Unlike last time, there was no music or noise. In fact, dead silence filled the room. Where were the people who attended Janus's neverending party in Erec's honor? Did they not like him anymore? He wondered what happened.

"Janus?" he called through the sink grate. "Are you there?"

There was a sharp sniff, but no answer.

"Janus?" Erec would not be able to break through the wall where the sink was, so he hoped that Janus would hear him.

A shuffling noise started, and then grew closer. In a moment, Janus peered down at Erec's eye, which was pressed up against the base of the sink.

Janus jumped in shock, and then turned a pale greenish color. "Who is that?"

"It's me. Erec."

"That's impossible." Janus spoke sharply. "Erec Rex is dead."

Erec poked his hand through the hole and wiggled his fingers. "I'm not dead. Look at me—I'm fine."

"That's not what I heard." Janus looked skeptical. "I have it from several good sources that you . . . I mean, that Erec Rex has passed on." A sob broke loose from his chest, and he held a hand over his mouth until he quieted down. "My purpose in life is over, unless Erec's siblings surface and take on the quests. But it is a sad time indeed, when such a noble and courageous future king is no longer with us."

"I'm back, Janus. I'm here. And I'm ready to do my next quest."

"Stop making fun of an old man. Now go and leave me alone!" Janus turned and walked away, leaving Erec's line of sight.

"Come back! It is me. I can prove it. I was brought back to life. Just give me the pad and I'll show you."

There seemed to be hesitation on the other end. There were pacing noises and a few murmurs and grunts from Janus. Finally he came back into sight with the paper pad. "I suppose it won't hurt to let you try. You do sound oddly like Erec. But if this is a joke, I'm turning you in!"

Erec took the pen and reached through the opened sink hole, then signed the paper pad. Immediately his name cut deep into the paper, cracking it open. Light shone through the breaks and into the room.

"Oh!" Janus stared again at Erec's eye through the hole. "You're alive! *You're alive!* I'll have to let everybody know. The party can start again!"

"Great." Erec loved the idea of people that were all on his side. So word had gotten around that he was dead? Well, maybe those people would be happy now. "Thanks, Janus. I'll see you later!"

Swimming away, Erec hoped that he would actually *not* see Janus later. He wished that this was the last time that he would ever have to draw a quest. As far as he was concerned, once the damage that he had started was cleaned up, and he had done what he could to save Upper Earth from the Golem army, then he would relax forever with his family and Bethany, and leave any new messes to someone else.

When he got back to Al's Well, the water was freezing and

burning again, although not quite painful. Al looked down with interest as Erec waved his hand through the liquid around him. Soon, something warm touched his fingers, and he grabbed it. It was the quest paper.

For a minute he hesitated, and then he read its words.

Ride the mythic horse of the elements to victory.

Erec read the quest again, surprised. It said nothing about him dying, or doing something awful or dangerous. In fact, the very words of the quest suggested that he would succeed—ride the horse to victory. From his recent experiences, he would not have been surprised if the quest had said something awful like, "Ride the mythic horse of the elements to a sure death," or "to mass destruction," or even "to the disappointment of everyone you know." This sounded wonderful! All he had to do was find this mythic horse—which, the name suggested, might not be so easy—and then he would be victorious.

Al looked at the quest paper with approval. "Not bad, kid. Sounds like fun, even. Good luck with dat thing."

"Do you know anything about the mythic horse of the elements?"

"Nah. Never heard of it."

Erec pocketed the quest and thanked him. He dove back into the water, the Instagills in his wrists opening so that he had no problem breathing. He wondered if Ashona was opened up again, because what he really wanted to do now was to talk to Bethany about this new quest. Maybe she could help him figure out who the mythic horse of the elements was. He wondered again why Baskania had sealed Ashona off . . . and then he had an idea. Once he had been able to go in and out of Ashona through the very waterways he was swimming in now. If only he could figure out a way to get back there again . . .

"What you need is someone with a spirit's sense of direction."

Erec's head swiveled toward the sound. Spartacus floated next to him with ease.

"You didn't think you could lose me that easily, did you? I was waiting up there with Al for a while, until I realized you weren't about to come out. So, you want to go to Ashona through the waterways? Follow me."

Instead of merely swimming in front of Erec, Spartacus grabbed hold of his hand and yanked him forward until they were traveling at rocket speed. They passed up turns and tunnels so quickly it was hard to see what they were going by.

In a moment, they stopped before an immense round opening. It was about twenty-five feet across, and at the top a sign glittered, ASHONA.

"You found it!" Erec was surprised, given how fast they had gone.

Spartacus pursed his lips with a trace of humor. "You doubted me?" He sighed with frustration. "Come on, then." He swam through the opening into a huge tunnel.

A smile lit on Erec's face. He had found another way to get back to Bethany and his family! He dove forward, but in a moment his head hit something that felt like glass. "What's this?" He ran his hand over it. It was hard to see underwater, but after looking a while he could detect a faint ripple where the barrier was. He swam in all directions, trying to go around it, but the entrance to Ashona was completely blocked.

"What are you doing?" Spartacus asked, but then he answered his own question by reading Erec's mind. "Not again. So it's closed this way too?"

Erec was disappointed. "I just want to talk to Bethany and my family. I'm tired of doing everything alone."

"Alone?" Spartacus huffed. "What am I? Meatloaf?"

"I'm sorry." Erec tried to refocus. "Do you have any idea what the mythical horse of the elements is?"

"No. If I did I would have told you already. But I can help you try to figure it out."

"I guess we can go back to Rosco's apartment." There was no way that he would spend time at his father's house in Alypium now. Baskania would no doubt have people looking for him there.

Spartacus nodded. In moments, Erec was speeding through the tunnels again, then flew out into the warm air of Alypium. Soaking wet, he soon was freezing as he sailed through the air with Spartacus into Rosco's place.

There, Trevor was watching television and taking Rosco's house apart. Piles of food were scattered around the house. But Rosco was nowhere in sight.

"Hmm." Spartacus glanced around. "I'll see what he's up to. Be right back."

"Hey, Trevor." Erec helped himself to an open bag of potato chips. "How's it going?"

"Great! I'm learning all about these things." He held up a handful of silverware. "I figured out what these are for." He demonstrated how to use a knife like a seesaw on top of another knife. Then he laid a fork over top and pushed down on the knife, catapulting the fork off of the table. "Isn't this a great thing to have around? Another thing that it does is this. . . ." He scooped up a bunch of spoons and let them fall to the ground. "What you do is guess how they're going to fall. They make shapes on the floor. If you do it enough, you can start to know what will happen the next time."

Erec laughed. But before he could respond, Spartacus sprang through the wall. "We have to get out, fast." He grabbed Erec and Trevor, and jumped with them out the open window.

Trevor's eyes were wide but unquestioning as he flew through the sky with the ghost. It seemed that wiping out everything he knew made him less prone to surprise.

"What's going on?" Erec asked. "Is Rosco okay?"

Spartacus nodded. "He's fine. But Baskania is on the warpath in

Otherness now, and in a complete rage about you. He's sending people to search through Rosco's things in case Rosco was hiding something— like you. Baskania doesn't know what to make of things. You were so convincing when you were there, but now his scepter is gone, as well as your eyes—and Trevor, who is still alive, despite what you said about killing him. So Baskania doesn't believe you anymore, of course." They flew for a while, then Spartacus asked, "Where should we go?"

Erec had no idea. Who else might be able to help him figure out what to do? He thought about his old friend, Jack Hare . . . but he lived in Aorth.

"That's not a problem." Spartacus winked. "I'll even get you there with a Port-O-Door, so you don't have to go through miles of dirt and rock."

"Gee, thanks." In a moment, Spartacus pulled Erec and Trevor into the Port-O-Door in King Piter's house, shutting the door behind them. He pushed a few buttons on the map, bringing Americorth North up before them. His fingers moved so quickly on the map, Erec could not follow them. Then the door opened into the searing heat of Aorth.

Erec began to protest—they had no air-conditioned UnderWear to keep them cool. But his words were lost in the searing heat. Spartacus didn't notice at first, then he frowned and flew faster. But the wind in that blistering temperature did not cool Erec down. It was like being blasted with oven air.

Spartacus dropped them in front of a doorway, then flew straight through the door. One moment later, he opened it from the inside. Dizzy, Erec and Trevor fell into the blast of air-conditioning without even considering how it was rude to enter without knocking. Spartacus slammed the door shut, and Erec and Trevor collapsed on the carpeting.

"Erec? Is that you?" There were footsteps and voices.

Erec cracked his eyes open, too parched to speak. His old friend, Jack, looked down, confused. "Hey, Erec! Trevor! What's going on? Why aren't you wearing UnderWear? Are you two crazy?" He waited a moment, but since Erec was still speechless, he said, "That's cool you came to visit. I've been thinking about you—was just going to write you a letter. Sorry I'm not that good at writing. But I hope you were having a good summer break."

Erec nodded. "Um . . . yeah." His voice croaked. "Do you have some water?"

"Yeah—sorry!" Jack rushed away and back with tall glasses of ice water for Erec and Trevor. His parents and sister said hello and brought out chocolate chip cookies.

Finally Erec was able to retell to Jack's family everything that had happened. After he finished, they sat in stunned silence. Then Jack's father roared, "I knew it! I knew the Stain triplets weren't meant to be kings. The craziness Damon's caused here in Aorth is unbearable. We have to bow any time we see someone in the government. And we're whipped like slaves in the street if one of them wants us to do something. It's insane. We're planning to move to Upper Earth just to get away from this mess—if we can get our papers." He rubbed his forehead. "Now you're saying that Baskania is going to mow through Upper Earth and Otherness?" He stared up at the ceiling. "I hope that horse thing can help fix all of this. I just wish that there was something I could do."

Erec had an idea. "Do you have e-mail or the MagicNet here?"

"Sure—we have both." Jack's mother looked pale. "Do you need to use them?"

"Can I use your e-mail to talk to my family?"

"Of course." She led Erec down the hall, and everyone followed.

Erec had never used e-mail here himself. "How do I get my family in Ashona on the screen?"

A skinny, dark-toned arm reached around his and tapped a few keys on the keyboard. "Maybe you could get your family on the screen in Ashona. Or the screen on your family in Ashona. Or Ashona on your family on a screen."

Erec spun around to see the Hermit giggling. He wore a massive plastic flower on the top of his head like a hat—the pink petals drooping down over his face and head, and the long stem sticking straight up from the top. Other than that, there was very little covering him, except for a hot pink bathing suit. Regardless of how he looked, Erec was thrilled to see him.

"Hermit! I need to talk to my father, and Bethany. Hey—do you know where I could find the mythic horse of the elements?"

"If it's mythic, then how do you know it exists?"

The Hermit posed the question so simply that for a moment Erec worried that there was no such horse. But then he realized that the Fates would not have sent him out to do the impossible. "It has to exist. What is it, though?"

"The question of the century." The Hermit faked a serious pose, stroking his chin. Then he threw his arms out and laughed. "Oh, well. Guess that's for you to find out, and then for you to find out."

Typical Hermit answer, Erec thought. It made no sense at all. But at least he had connected their screen to a young woman with short red hair in the Castle Ashona. "Can I help you?" She looked brightly from Erec to the Hermit.

"I need to talk to my father. King Piter. Can you put him on?"

"So you're ... Erec Rex?" She peered into the screen. "Okay. Hold a moment."

The screen went blank for a few minutes, and then the king's face flashed in front of him.

"Erec! Are you okay?" Piter clasped a hand over his chest. "Bethany told us what you were doing. I was so worried."

"I'm fine. And the Furies are fine now. How is everything there?"

The king's brow wrinkled with worry. "Not good, I'm afraid. Someone sealed off Ashona, and I think I know who it is. Baskania is the only person evil and powerful enough to do this. He must have found out how he can control Posey's scepter from far away. That is the only thing we can think of—she still can't use it at all. This is going to be a problem if we can't figure out a way to stop it.

"The Secret of Ashona might keep us safe, if Posey can figure out a way to communicate with it. She used to talk to it with her scepter. Swimming down to it in person is too dangerous. The Secret will devour anyone who approaches it, except its ruler. That used to be Queen Posey, while her scepter was working for her. But that's probably not the case anymore. So, we're in a fix here. We're trying to keep it quiet so there isn't mass panic.

"Nothing can go in or out at all. We're going to run out of supplies soon. We can't even fish for food from the ocean. And our oxygen supply . . . well, it's not going to last forever. I can feel the air getting thinner. We're okay for now—don't worry. Posey and I are thinking of ways out of this."

Erec could not believe his ears. His family was trapped undersea with their food and oxygen running out? "I'm sure Baskania put that seal around Ashona with the fake scepter that I gave him. I had no idea it would cause this much of a problem. I'm so sorry. I'll try to help figure out a way out of this." It occurred to him that this must be what the Fates were talking about when they said there was a worse problem than Otherness and Upper Earth being attacked.

The king was quiet for a moment. "Don't come here. There is absolutely nothing that you can do. Posey is the only one who has a chance to fix this, I'm afraid." He sighed. "Even if you were king and used your scepter, it wouldn't work. Are you sure you're okay?"

"I'm fine, Dad. But there might be something I could do. I drew my next quest. The Fates told me it would fix everything. Even the 'worse problem'—which has to be Ashona sealing up." He held back from going into detail about the battle Baskania was planning. If his father knew that Erec was going to fight against Baskania's military, he might blow a fuse. "I need to find the mythical horse of the elements. Do you have any idea what that is?"

The king frowned in thought. "I'm not sure. Mythical horse of the elements? The only horse I can think of is not really a myth—it's very real. But you couldn't ride it, anyway."

"Why not?"

"It's called the Dragon Horse of Fire. She's a beautiful dragon horse mare in Diomedes's stable. The mare used to be quite a legend. People called her mythical, I remember that. She's the only horse I've heard of that comes close to what you're looking for."

"Great! The Dragon Horse of Fire. I guess fire could be called an element—that has to be right! Where is Diomedes's stable?"

"Forget it, Erec. You can't ride her."

"What are you talking about? I have to."

"No." The king shook his head. "You wouldn't survive the ride. And don't get any ideas—the mare wouldn't even let you try. She'll only take on riders that are evil."

"Evil? I'll pretend I'm evil—I did that with Baskania. Or I'll think bad thoughts before I ride her."

"That won't work. She's smarter than that. You'd have to do something evil. And recently, too. That is the only way. But don't even think about it. She's unrideable."

"I don't understand. Why is she like that?"

"They say she was once a regular dragon horse. You've seen them—they're brilliant and beautiful. But her evil master kept giving her more and more powers, making her do terrible things to people. Eventually, the horse killed him and became her own master.

By then, she felt more powerful than any human. She would ride for nobody. She was her own horse.

"She kept on collecting human powers, and the more she could do, the smarter she got. She became a mind reader, among other things. But in order to stay free and keep people at bay, she enchanted herself. If anyone rides her, their life and magical ability get sucked straight into hers. Nobody could survive the trip.

"At least, to the mare's credit, she won't ride just anyone to death. She only lets evil people try, I guess it's her way of doing a favor to the world."

Erec was stunned. He got off of the computer, asking the king to let Bethany know what was going on. "What am I going to do?" he asked the Hermit.

The Hermit pondered this. "Stand there and act confused? Pick your belly button, maybe?"

That was no help. Erec looked at his choices. He could give up on his quest, and let Baskania take over the world, or he could ... try to become evil. But even then, would he survive the ride? It sounded so strange, not like something he should try.

Then again, it was his quest. If riding that horse fixed things ... Erec still didn't understand how stopping the Golem army could save his family trapped in Ashona, but he knew the Fates had a funny way of working. Erec just hoped it would do the trick.

How would he become evil? It sounded so crazy. What was he supposed to do—go around hurting people so he could do his quest? That's when it came back to him—all his visions of being a horrible person, and the awful things that he did. Was that why he stole candy from kids and robbed a family? But when it came to charging at Bethany with a lance—no amount of evil would make him do that. Ever. He had to make sure that he kept control over himself.

"I can help, you know," Spartacus said. "If you have to do evil things, nobody said that I couldn't go around after you fixing them again."

That sounded like the best idea Erec had heard. "You mean, if I take things from people, scare them, and ruin their stuff, then you'll make it all better again?"

"Why not? Let's try it. First we should take a look at that Fire Horse. What do you say?"

That sounded wonderful. Everyone was looking at Erec like he was crazy for talking to the air, except for the Hermit who seemed perfectly fine with it. "Sorry, guys. I have to go. Would it be okay if you watched Trevor here for a while?"

Jack's family was happy to keep Trevor. Erec found himself whisked back into the baking heat before Jack's father could push an UnderWear suit into his hands. Before he had time to complain, though, Erec was inside of the Port-O-Door, which opened again into King Piter's house.

Erec fell into the cool air, breathing deeply. He had not been outside long enough to fry, but even that quick blast of intense heat was hard to handle.

Spartacus asked, "So, are you ready to become evil?"

It sounded like a ridiculous question. "Not really." He laughed. "Where is that Dragon Horse of Fire? Do you know where Diomedes's stable is?"

"It's on the outskirts of Alypium, not far from here. Want to try your first shot at being a villain there?"

Erec sighed. "I guess it's as good a place as any. Let's see that horse first, and figure out what we need to do."

CHAPTER THIRTY-ONE

The Dragon Horse of Fire

I T WAS AN EASY RIDE to the stable under Spartacus's arm. When Spartacus set him down, Erec stepped back in wonder. Before them was the largest and most beautiful horse that he had ever seen. Black, like the dragon horses that had belonged to the Stain boys, her eyes glowed a flaming red, and fire occasionally streamed from her nostrils. But this horse was three times the size of the others, and her face looked more intelligent. Her tail swished fast and hard, sounding like a whip cracking through the air.

Erec stayed far away. He had a feeling the mare would incinerate

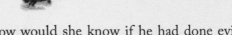

him if he got too close. How would she know if he had done evil things, anyway?

But Erec could hear her thoughts in his head as loud as words. *You want to ride me, fool? Go away before you hurt yourself.*

"Won't you let me try it, just once?"

Of course not. Leave now if you want to live.

Erec could feel himself lose it. This horse could let him try to ride now, but she had to stick to her dumb rules. So he'd have to go do evil things instead for no reason. He was beyond frustrated. "I have to stop Baskania from taking over Otherness and Upper Earth! The three Fates sent me here—I'm supposed to ride you!"

There was a pause. *I see you are telling the truth. But I'm not sure that the Fates have really chosen me. The mythical horse of elements? That might be someone else.*

Erec calmed down. At least she sounded reasonable. "I don't know. My quests never tell me exactly what to do. The Fates don't make things too easy for me. But you're the only horse anyone could think of."

You're supposed to ride me into battle? She paused. *But Baskania is planning to do that. He knows the only way. Beyond that, I pick and choose who I let on my back. But I despise Baskania and I would not stand by and watch Otherness get destroyed. I would much rather that you rode me.*

"So you will let me try, then?" he was excited. "Even if I'm not evil?"

It's not possible. I only let evil humans ride because it kills them. Any who fancy themselves rotten enough to hop on me die right away.

"But I'm supposed to be able to do this. I have dragon eyes and some dragon blood, so that might let me survive."

I doubt it, but climb on and see.

Erec wondered how to get on the tall horse. But before he had time to worry, Spartacus was setting him on its back.

In seconds, Erec felt drained. He slumped over its neck, and everything went black.

Before long he opened his eyes, and was lying on the grass. "What happened?"

Your ghost friend lifted you off of me—just as I was trying to shake you to the ground to save you. You will never be able to ride me. Not even a foot. It is a shame—there used to be a way.

"What was it?"

A stream of fire blasted from the horse's nostrils. *There was a gem in my stable that would let me carry a human if I wished. It was a special stone, huge, sparkling, and beautiful—like a blue diamond. It's called Levrium. But Baskania took it. When he uses the Levrium he will ride me and I will have to obey. He is planning to use me soon to lead the battle into Lerna.*

"Lerna?" Erec sat up. "That's where my friend Tina lives! Do you think I can get the Levrium stone back?"

That would be wonderful. A man near here is hiding my Levrium stone for Baskania. This man has hurt a lot of people. He is the one who told Baskania about me, and offered my services. I'm sure he's getting a fat reward. But I don't know where he keeps the stone.

"What's his name?"

Kev Hunter. He lives in one of the larger houses in the town nearby.

"No problem," Spartacus said. "I'll just get the stone for you. Stay here, Erec."

The horse seemed to have no problem hearing Spartacus. "You can't do that, unless you're the one to ride me. The stone will work for the person who steals it back only, now that it's been taken from me. Erec must get it himself."

Erec nodded. "I'll find Kev Hunter, then. Spartacus, you can show me where he is." The man's name was familiar. "Is he related to Ajax Hunter, Baskania's servant?"

THE SECRET OF ASHONA

They are brothers, but not on good terms. Kev wants to take his brother's place. He struck a deal with Baskania to brainwash the kids in town to give him their eyes—which would leave them to be his blind servants. Baskania gave him a mind-control formula and made it into candy. Soon the kids in town will be turning in their parents if they don't follow Baskania's orders, and stealing money for Baskania's cause.

"I heard Baskania talk about that! He was going to make people into his slaves with it. This Kev Hunter is sick to go along with it. I have to find him. And I'll take that candy away when I get the Levrium stone." Erec stormed away with Spartacus close behind. He was so close now to finishing this quest. There was no way that he was going to let Kev Hunter ruin it.

And then he remembered one of the visions that he had been having . . . taking lollipops away from kids. That's what it was about, wasn't it? What a relief. At least he wasn't so bad after all.

"Would you like to lead the way, or should I let you know where you're going?" Spartacus asked, following Erec.

Erec could not help but laugh, even though he was upset. "I have no clue. Go ahead."

The outskirts were dingy. Some of the shacks were propped with broken rakes and bent ladders. They passed a park full of children playing, their mothers looking on with smiles and chatting with friends. Erec walked closer, missing being younger and carefree, when he saw a few kids gathering around a dark-haired, slightly balding man in a yellow shirt. He was waving some kids over toward the bushes, and handing out lollipops. . . .

It all seemed to happen so fast. Kids were showing their candy to the other children and soon most of them were grasping small handfuls.

It was happening—and it was disgusting. How could this guy try to turn happy little kids into robots? In a moment the man was gone,

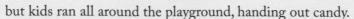

but kids ran all around the playground, handing out candy.

Anger seared through Erec, making him shake. "Give that to me!" He dove at the kids with a snarl. A low growl escaped from his throat as he grabbed candy from their hands. People stared at him with wide eyes, as if he were a maniac. But there was no time to stop—so many kids, so much candy. And he had to take it all!

Mothers darted toward their children, trying to save them. But Erec could run faster than they could. One of the toddlers was surprisingly strong, and Erec struggled a while before yanking the sweets out of his hand. His mother looked equally confused and terrified. Right behind her was a kid about to put an opened lollipop right into her mouth. Not when Erec was there—he'd get it first! Shoving the mother out of his way, he snatched the sucker out of the little girl's fist, leaving her crying and rubbing her hand.

A few kids got knocked into one another as lollipops in their hands sailed into the air—Erec grabbing each one. Some kids still sat on the swings. They looked small and defenseless—taking their candy would be easy. He scooped the lollipops straight from their little fists.

One of the mothers stepped forward, outraged. "What's wrong with you? These are little kids. . . ." She tried to grab his arm, but he shoved her back. There was still a lollipop he had missed, and she wasn't going to get in the way. "Ow! Somebody call the police. This guy's crazy! Let's get out of here, Dougie."

The last kid was older, and he struggled with Erec before letting go of his lollipop. Erec hadn't meant to trip him, but the kid ended up on his face, his cheek cut and bleeding.

That wasn't important. Erec had all the candy now, so he patted his pockets and turned away. He had won—he had taken every child's candy in the whole park. But it wasn't enough. Now he had to steal something else. . . .

Nothing was going to stop him on this mission. He followed Spartacus's gliding strides, frustration growing with each step. It was bad enough that Baskania was causing so many problems—why did people like this Kev have to make it worse?

Spartacus stopped suddenly.

Erec said through his teeth, "Which house is it?"

"That one." Spartacus pointed at a white-painted brick house on a hill, looming over the others. It figures, Erec thought, that Kev Hunter would have the only big house on the outskirts of Alypium.

"Let's go." Erec started walking toward the house, but Spartacus didn't move.

"It's not in there."

"How do you know that?"

"I can read minds, remember? This was an easy one, even from this far away. Kev Hunter is in there, gloating about handing all the candy out. He'll be testing his control over the kids later today." Spartacus laughed. "Looks like he'll be disappointed. I hope they scratch the project and send it back to the drawing board. But he's also thought about the Levrium stone. He's excited that Baskania will use it and he'll get the credit. He hid the thing well. Typical, it's making someone else miserable now. Guy hijacked a poor family that lives out in the woods, and set a bunch of Squirler Trees all around them, so they can't get out and nobody can get in. Kev told them to keep the Levrium stone with their most valued possessions, and protect it with their life if they ever wanted to see the outside of their house again. Unbelievable."

"What are Squirler Trees?"

"They're like massive Venus flytraps—except they'll eat any living thing, no matter how big. And they give off an aura that makes you angry just being close to them. They say that if the trees don't snap you up themselves, you could die of rage just being nearby.

I guess your brain hemorrhages or something. Their branches are strong and they bend like snakes to grab animals or people. Then they roll you up and squeeze, sucking the life out of you. Generally something you'd want to avoid."

He headed into the woods, and Erec followed, ducking under vines and stepping over rocks. "I'm going to take you as far as you can go before you get to the Squirler Trees. But be careful if you find yourself getting angry."

After a short hike, Spartacus stopped. "Stay here. I'm going to see this family for myself." He bounded away, leaving Erec in the woods. He was right—Erec began to feel uncomfortable and grumpy just standing there. It came on fast and hard. Soon, anger didn't even describe how awful he felt. It helped that Spartacus had warned him, but his mind kept thinking of other people to blame, especially Kev Hunter.

Spartacus reappeared, looking even more somber. "The family is terrified. Kev threatened them with death if they speak to anyone. They won't open the door for you, I'll tell you that. You're going to have to break in. And they hid the Levrium stone with their jewelry." He thought a moment. "I wish I could just get it for you, but at least I'll keep an eye on things." He thought another moment. "You'll need something to help you. Let me see what I can find." Moments later, he returned with an ax. "This will have to do. You can use it against the Squirler branches and also to break into the house."

"Break in?" Erec had a sense of déjà vu, sure he had seen the ax before.

"It's your only choice."

Erec sizzled with annoyance. Why did this have to be such a pain? He tried to remind himself that the reason he felt this way was from the Squirler Trees, but it didn't matter. He wasn't even under their canopy and he was miserable. Would it get worse when he was

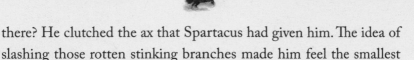

there? He clutched the ax that Spartacus had given him. The idea of slashing those rotten stinking branches made him feel the smallest bit better. He couldn't wait to chop and destroy them. . . .

"This ax will mess up those Squirler Trees?"

"If you swing hard and fast enough when you run. Don't worry—I'll keep you from getting caught if you mess up. I'd take you over the trees, but that would be worse. They surround and cover the house, and then you'd have to go through too many branches at once. This way you just have to avoid the ones that come down to the ground."

"I'm ready." Erec looked at the dirt path ahead. The trees that lined it were still, limbs reaching to the sky. It was hard to imagine them attacking him. But when he stepped forward, he noticed a branch slowly dip in his direction. He aimed with his ax and chopped the end off just as it reached him. Fury raced through his mind, making him feel crazy. It was hard to remember what he was here for—he just wanted to take the ax and chop every tree in the forest to the ground.

"Hurry up!" Spartacus pushed Erec's back. "If you wait here they'll all attack at once."

Tree limbs began reaching toward him, and he slashed them hard, chopping their ends off as he went. It was difficult to focus through his wrath. He kept forgetting why he was there and diving at the branches—even ones behind him. It wasn't hard to defend himself, maybe because he was enjoying the fight. Branches fell to the ground all around him.

"Go!" Spartacus yelled. "You're almost there!"

Erec ran fast, holding on to the ax and swinging it wildly. He was sweaty and out of breath. Anger and hate surged through him. Before long he came to a small house made of logs. He knew that he had to break into it. Erec raised the ax above his head and brought it down onto the door, splitting the wood. He yanked it out, then did it again. Pieces clattered to the ground as he kept chopping.

In a rage, he reached inside and unlocked the knob, then flung the door open with a growl. Before him, a family trembled. The mother held a young child tight, his arms wrapped around her neck. An older girl clung to her knee, crying.

The father stepped in front of them, arms out in a gesture of protection, but his hands shook badly. "Leave us alone. You can take anything you want from here. I don't care what happens to me, but stay away from my family."

"Jewels. Necklaces. Watches." Erec squinted around the room. "Where do you keep them?"

The man stuttered, upset. "D-don't take any of those. Please. Anything in the whole house is yours—but don't steal our jewels."

Erec swung the ax back over his shoulder, aiming at the man's neck.

"Sorry!" The man stepped back in shock. "I'm sorry. Go ahead. They're upstairs in my wife's dresser. But we don't have much. T-take what you want."

Erec shoved past them and went upstairs. He rooted through drawers, dumping out piles of clothing and old notebooks. There was no stone in any dresser drawers—the man had obviously hoped he wouldn't find the Levrium stone. Erec yanked everything off of shelves and out of closets, until he spotted some rows of boxes under folded scarves. Paydirt. He tore the lids off, revealing a few thin gold chains, chipped fake pearl earrings, and a plastic-looking brooch. He tossed these to the floor in haste. Underneath was a large box, and in it a brown paper bag. Pulse quickening, he pulled out a glittering gemstone as big as his fist that shone in hundreds of shades of blue— from the brightest hue of the sky to the darkest shade of midnight.

This had to be it. He pocketed the huge gem, and scrambled down the stairs. His anger had faded now that he had been in the house for a while, and he felt awful about how he had treated this family. This was the vision he had seen when he had looked into his future with his dragon eyes—and it had been correct. He had been horrible, but at the same time he got the Levrium stone back.

This should have made Erec feel better, but instead things seemed worse. For, if all of his visions of the future were coming true, what about the one where he was riding toward Bethany about to stab her with a huge lance? She had no way to protect herself from him, when he came at her that fast—she wouldn't have even been able to run away.

He tried to shake the image from his mind. The family was still huddled together, terrified, in the front room of the house. It wasn't going to help much, but Erec figured that he better make amends for being so violent and destructive before. He dropped the ax at his feet and said, "Look, I'm really sorry—"

In an instant, the father made a lunge for the ax. He held it over his head, aimed right at Erec. "What did you take?"

In shock, Erec cowered under the sharp blade. But then a second later, the ax yanked backward and the father flew toward the wall behind him—with the help of Spartacus.

"Get out of here now!" Spartacus yelled. "These people will do anything to get that stone back. I'll hold them for you."

Erec bolted from the house and through the trees, dashing between reaching branches. This time he had no ax to swing, so he sometimes had to dart backward and around to avoid being grabbed. The faster he ran, though, the more infuriated he became at his entire situation. Where was Spartacus, anyway? This was ridiculous, having to go through this all by himself. . . .

Something yanked his waist, and then Erec flew into the air. A tree limb wrapped itself tight around his middle as he floated up. He seethed in anger. How could this happen now? It was pathetic.

But instead of curling into the top branches, Erec shot forward in the air. The branch held him like a stiff python, but it was taking him straight forward and out of the grove. That didn't make sense. Erec looked behind and saw Spartacus holding the other end of the tree limb. He had broken it off and was flying Erec to safety. Other branches reached toward them, but the ghost was able to expertly weave in and out until they reached safety.

The branch around Erec squeezed him tighter, seemingly unaware that it was no longer attached to anything. It was hard to breathe. The thing dug into his waist, and it hurt. Finally, Spartacus severed its coils, and the branch fell away.

Before he could tell Spartacus off for taking so long, still angry from the influence of the Squirler Trees, Erec found himself hurtling through the air back to the Dragon Horse of Fire.

"I got that poor family out of there—sorry it took me a while. There is no time to waste. I've been focusing on the minds of everyone, and I'm getting better at reading thoughts from far away. Baskania just came to collect the Levrium stone from Kev Hunter and the family—we got it just in the nick of time! He knows it's gone, and he wasted no time, shot himself straight back into battle. He's approaching Lerna now, and it will fall fast if we don't hurry."

"Lerna! I hope Tina is okay!" Erec gripped the Levrium stone tightly. The time and distance away from the Squirler Trees let him feel more rational. He had to get on that horse fast and do whatever he could. Moments later, Erec and Spartacus were at the stable in front of the immense dragon horse with flaming red eyes.

I see you found the stone. Thank you for returning it, Erec.

He nodded. "Will you take me to Lerna so we can stop Baskania? My quest was to ride you to victory. I have no idea what to do, but I guess we'll see when we get there."

Put the stone in my saddle pocket and climb on.

THE SECRET OF ASHONA

Erec dropped the huge sparkling blue stone into a small pocket in the horse's saddle. It would have been nearly impossible to mount the mare if Spartacus did not lift him. But this time, Erec did not feel drained. In fact, he felt great.

Before saying another word, the mare reared back, pedaling her hooves toward the sun. Erec almost flew off, but managed to grab the horn of her saddle. Then she raced forward like lightning. Erec wove first one hand and then the other through her mane, clinging on for dear life. He pressed flat against her back, eyes squinting against the wind. The countryside became a blur as they shot past.

The horse's strong muscles rippled beneath Erec as they rode. Her black coat shimmered in the wind. The green and brown blur below them became a rippling blue for a while—Erec realized that they must be charging over a lake. This horse could ride on water? Then again, the thing was so strong, it probably could do anything.

The landscape around them blurred more as the mare cantered faster. A giggle in Erec's ear made his skin jump. He cocked his head to the side . . . but maybe it had just been the wind. He wanted to look over his shoulder, but all he could do was hold on. Something squeezed itself into his hand, still tightly gripping the horse's mane. He was stunned to see it was the ax he had left in the house on the outskirts of Alypium. Another hand gripped it too—and Erec followed its arm with his eyes until he saw Spartacus Kilroy, floating alongside of the galloping mare.

Spartacus was on his side in the air, a hand propped under his chin. He was letting himself be carried by the horse, tugged by his hand on the ax.

Erec tried to understand why Spartacus had given him the ax, but it was too hard to talk into the wind.

Spartacus heard his thoughts. "Sorry, it was the first weapon I could find. I'm still carrying the Calamitizer and Rapid Transitator too, in case we need help."

Erec nodded, trying to grip the ax and the horse hair at the same time. Soon it was easier as the animal slowed to a trot. They were in the wilderness of Otherness now—Erec saw a dragon soar overhead. As they sauntered through a clearing, a sound from the distance echoed like thunder—only it kept growing louder. Soon, it burst through the woods in a flurry of hoofbeats and crashing feet.

Before Erec's eyes was the largest army he could ever imagine. Rows of soldiers on horseback broke through first, followed by hordes of giant sand creatures with blocklike features: the Golems. Through the middle of the Golems and flanking them on the sides were foot soldiers, more on horses, and sad-looking Cyclopes who looked unsure why they were there. Machinelike creatures on wheels, cannons jutting from their faces, followed behind, and scattered through the army troops.

At the end of the cavalcade marched rows upon rows of Spirit Warriors, with a few specters thrown into the mix. Spartacus gripped his shoulder, and Erec knew they were sharing the same thought: This is where they both would have been if not for the help of the three Furies. At least, no matter what else happened, he had done right for them.

Leading the army was a face that Erec could never forget. Eyes blazing in all directions, Thanatos Baskania headed the cavalcade with glee. Waving something above his head, a wild grin on his face, he galloped on a huge black steed with blazing red eyes.

Baskania's horse looked just like Erec's, only much smaller. Erec now realized why the Fates told him that he had to ride the Dragon Horse of Fire into battle. He was now a match for Baskania.

At the same time, Erec realized what Baskania was holding in the air—it had to be the Master Shem. He was commanding the

Golem army, and was about to use them for more destruction when they reached Lerna.

Erec fixated on Baskania's hand. There lay the key to saving Otherness and Upper Earth. There was the way to keep Danny and Sammy safe, as well as the rest of the clowns—and Tina and her family in Lerna too. The rest of the army was powerful too, but the Golems were unbeatable destructors that could not be injured. And maybe, somehow, stopping this would save his family from dying in Ashona.

He had to get that Master Shem back. Everything in his life centered around this one small object in the hand of his worst foe. There was nothing that could stop him from fighting for it. Every person he cared about in the world would be affected by this, and they were all counting on him.

Erec eyed the ax in his hand, hoping that it would be enough to do the job against his enemy.

"Don't forget," a voice said in his ear. "I have some things up my sleeve too."

Erec remembered that Spartacus had the Calamitizer and the Rapid Transitator. "Maybe you could use that thing to take the Master Shem now?"

Spartacus aimed the Rapid Transitator at Baskania and squeezed its trigger, then pointed in the opposite direction and shot at a tree. Erec watched in wonder, waiting to see the Master Shem transport itself to the tree.

It did not. The thing tugged sideways in the air, but Baskania easily resisted Spartacus's weapon. Baskania, however, swung around to look straight at Erec. Horror and rage swept over his face.

"Um, I guess that wasn't the best idea," Erec said. "I can't give him time to think. Let's go."

With a mere nudge, the mare under him charged straight at

Baskania. The world around them disappeared into a blur. The sudden jolt made Erec lose his grip on the ax—but he wasn't sure what he would have done with it anyway. Chop Baskania's hand off? Instead he rushed ahead, focused on the Master Shem.

Spartacus's voice in his ear seemed amazingly clear and calm in the midst of the rushing wind and intense speed. "Well, the Rapid Transitator didn't do the trick. Want to try the Calamitizer, then?"

There was a click, and the giant mare slowed to a stop. It took a minute for Erec to orient himself to his surroundings because everything looked so strange—almost upside down. Golems toppled overhead through the air. Horses spun backward on their sides. The sky was full of kicking soldiers, crashing into one another on their way back to the hard earth. Trees bowed as if they were made of rubber.

Erec's mare was amazingly able to resist the forces around her. And he was surprised that Baskania and his horse also stood still on the ground about fifty feet away, gazing at the spectacle. It was as if the two of them were the only fixed points around which everything else revolved.

"Go, girl! Let's get that thing." Erec nudged his horse again, and she took off. Baskania looked at Erec and his horse, and seemed to think that it wasn't worth the risk to fight him. He darted the other way, into the middle of his army. Soldiers were dusting themselves off and mounting their horses again. Golems untangled themselves from piles on the ground and stood up to march. But now they no longer headed toward Lerna. Instead, all of the Golems turned toward Erec, marching inexorably toward him as their target.

There was no time left. It was attack or be mauled by Golems. Erec's horse jumped over smaller ones in her way, diving expertly between Golems. Erec slid as far forward onto her neck as he could without falling, grasping her mane for dear life. He reached an arm out and focused on Baskania's hand. *Charge!*

In a flash, Erec and his mare were beside Baskania. He reached for the Master Shem, and with amazing precision, his horse put him in just the right spot. He clenched the magical item with all of his might, and then his horse raced forward.

But even though Erec gripped the Master Shem so hard that his hand almost ripped off, it did not come with him. Baskania still held the thing, glaring at Erec. He pointed, and smoking black daggers shot through the air toward Erec's chest. The mare expertly dodged them, then turned again to face their enemy. Baskania sent more smoking daggers toward Erec, then darted to the far side of the Golem army. More sand creatures were reaching Erec now. They completely blocked him from Baskania, and Erec wasn't sure how long he and his horse could hold out against them.

How was he supposed to do this? Baskania obviously used some sort of spell to keep the Master Shem stuck to his hand. Erec needed more help. He looked up at the sky, then he remembered . . . Aoquesth. His spirit dragon friend had said Erec could call him anytime. . . .

He closed his eyes and said, "Aoquesth," and in moments the dragon ghost zoomed down from the clouds. With his shining dark purple-red scales and black spines he looked just as he had in life. He smiled. "Glad to help, old friend." Even with patches over both of his eyes, the dragon spirit could see just as all ghosts could. Aoquesth blew a burst of fire over the Golems that were closing in, setting a few of them to flame.

Erec grinned. "Thanks. We need to get the Master Shem. It's attached to Baskania's hand."

"There's only one way to do it," Aoquesth said. "Dive for it again. Your horse is smart enough to get you in just the right spot. As soon as you grab hold, stop time. I'll be touching you, so I won't be affected."

"I'll keep a hand on you too," Spartacus said.

Erec grabbed one of Tarvos's horns in his left hand and found the scissors to put in his right. He fished out the spell he had jotted down, and read it out loud. "*Tiggledy Piggledy Higgledy Poe, I tookund de talisman offend a Foe, Miranda, miractra, minstansilo blast, Eustanchia miranchia time ballido cast.*' Okay, ready."

The mare raced toward Baskania so fast Erec could barely hold on. Her speed gave them extra force to shove between Golems and soldiers. She found Baskania, and Erec spotted the Master Shem still waving in his hand, commanding Golems. His horse expertly maneuvered to the right spot, and even as Baskania's horse moved away, she kept right alongside. Erec reached closer to the Shem . . . closing around it . . . then grasped it in a death grip.

It was hard to let go of the mare's mane without falling so he could use his left hand. He squeezed tight with his knees and snapped. . . .

All movement around Erec and his horse stopped. His mare ground her hooves into the ground, muscles flaring, so she could come to a full stop and hold still. It was nightmarish, Baskania stock still at his side, his eyes boring into Erec's like frozen beacons of hate.

"Good job, Erec. Now, don't move." Aoquesth's claw reached toward them. In a second there was a slice and the sound of a tear and popping as the claw cut through bone. . . . "Now run!"

Erec had the Master Shem in his hand. His horse charged, and only after Erec was safely away did he snap his fingers again. In a last glimpse, Erec saw Baskania's face change from forceful arrogance to shock and horror. But Erec and his horse were one, and they did not stop galloping until the sounds of the Golem army were far behind them. When they finally slowed down, Erec looked at what he held.

Attached to the Master Shem was Baskania's hand.

He shuddered and screeched all at once, dropping the thing to the ground. But then Spartacus grabbed it and stuck it back into

Erec's hand. "Use it, quick! Turn the Golems against Baskania, and against one another, so he doesn't follow us out here and get it back!"

Erec nodded, and addressed the Master Shem, hoping it would work. "Do it! Golems, attack Baskania. And destroy one another completely! Now!"

Spartacus flew away, then returned with a smile. "Done! Baskania buzzed off, and the sand things are shredding each other up. There will be no more Golem army to worry about!"

Erec dropped the Master Shem—with Baskania's hand on it—into the dirt, and asked his horse to crush it. Baskania would never forgive him for this! Gone were the days of pretending he was a friend. Erec was sure the Shadow Prince would create a new hand for himself, but he'd never get the Master Shem again.

As the realization of what happened sank in, he felt like cheering. Everyone was safe now! Could this have helped Ashona, too, like the Fates said it would? His family might have died in there. He had to go back right away and make sure things were all right.

"Right on it, boss." Spartacus grinned. "I was thinking the same thing. We'll check and see that everyone is safe. But according to the Fates it should be, so who am I to question?"

Erec wished he shared Spartacus's confidence.

CHAPTER THIRTY-TWO

The Secret of Ashona

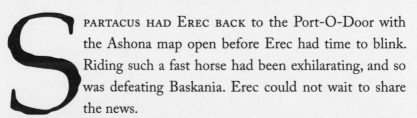

SPARTACUS HAD EREC BACK to the Port-O-Door with
the Ashona map open before Erec had time to blink.
Riding such a fast horse had been exhilarating, and so
was defeating Baskania. Erec could not wait to share
the news.

The ghost swung the inner door open into Ashona, but he hit
something and bounced back into the vestibule. A strange look
crossed his face. "I don't understand." He reached to touch something in the air, pushing his fingers in and out of the doorway.

"What's going on?" Erec stretched his fingers out to feel. Just like last time, an invisible wall stood between them and Ashona. "This is still here? I don't get it."

Spartacus sighed. "I'm afraid it's much worse. Before, I had no problem crossing through the barrier—just like I can pass through anything. But this is different. This"—he tapped the obstruction—"is compressed more than any earthly material. I might be able to squeeze through, but it would take a long time. I have to push hard against the fabric of this thing." Demonstrating, he shoved his finger forward. It moved just a speck.

A chill ran through Erec. "Why do you think it's like this now?"

"I don't know, but the barrier is growing stronger."

This was the last thing that Erec wanted to hear. "I don't understand. That last quest was supposed to have solved all of our problems." He lifted the Amulet of Virtues off his chest, expecting the eighth segment to be lit up. It was not. Erec stood a moment, staring at the thing.

"I don't know." Spartacus frowned. "I thought you were done too."

"I need to talk to my dad and find out what's going on in there."

Spartacus nodded. In a moment, the outer door of the Port-O-Door flung open and Erec was flying in the air in Spartacus's arms. They arrived at Rosco's apartment before Erec had time to wonder where to go.

Rosco was not in, but Spartacus let them inside. Erec found his MagicNet e-mail. After pressing a few buttons, a young man's face appeared on the screen, sweat beading on his brow. "Can I help you today?"

"I need to talk to my father in Ashona—King Piter."

"Oh!" The man looked excited. "Wow. Okay, then. Here you go."

In a moment, several faces flashed onto the screen in a sequence, looking Erec over, then transferring to someone else. Finally a gray-haired woman appeared. "You're Erec?" She looked skeptical.

"Yes. Can I speak to my father, please?"

For a moment it looked like the answer would be "no," but then she said, "Hold."

King Piter's face popped on the screen. His face was beet red and he was panting, sweat streaming down his brow. "Erec—are you okay?"

"I'm fine. I finished the quest . . . I mean, I thought I did. But you were supposed to be safe when I was done. We couldn't get into Ashona again. You're still trapped?"

The king took a moment to catch his breath. "Still." He nodded. "Worse now. The air is almost used up. Most of us are sleeping so we don't need as much oxygen. But it's hard to sleep now that it's so hot and uncomfortable. The pressure is horrible—almost worse than the lack of air."

Erec was horrified. "What pressure?"

The king wiped his forehead. "Ashona is alive, Erec, and it's malfunctioning. It's keeping everything inside itself closed off. The seal is getting tighter, and it's starting to pulse and crush us. Like a headache coming from outside of your body. Maybe we're feeling its heartbeats. Whatever it is, it's getting bad.

"Ashona has served Posey since she created it with her scepter five hundred years ago. It's a wonderful place. Because it's alive, it protects us from the sea and gives us everything we need without our asking. But Posey's power over her scepter is gone, and now she can't communicate with the Secret of Ashona at all. She is going to go to it directly and speak to it—even though that will probably end her life. The Secret of Ashona will devour anyone who comes too close, except the one who controls it. That used to be Queen Posey, but now . . . well, I think we know who has command of her scepter."

Baskania, of course. But how could he have done such strong

magic with the fake scepter? "Is there another way to talk to the Secret of Ashona that is safer?"

The king shook his head. "Not from in here. When Posey reaches it, deep down in the workings of the base of Ashona, it will put her right inside the thing's mouth. She wouldn't even do that safely if her scepter was working. If she was able to go outside she would talk to it from underneath Ashona. But even that would be dangerous without her scepter. So we've spent most of our time trying to make her scepter work again, using spells. . . ." He sighed. "We're really in a fix."

Before the thought was fully formulated in his head, Spartacus was already saying, "No way. Let me do it."

Erec hesitated, then grinned. "That's a great idea! I was going to try to talk to the Secret of Ashona from below, but that's even better. You don't have to risk being killed."

With a nod, the ghost disappeared.

"We'll take care of it, Dad." Before King Piter started to protest, Erec clicked the MagicNet off. It was not up for argument. Erec and Spartacus would do what they had to.

But Spartacus soon returned. "I went underneath the city and found it—the Secret of Ashona is hard to miss when you're down there. It's an amazing creature . . . or whatever you'd call it. But it could not hear me or see me at all. Completely frustrating. I tried to ask it what was going on . . . even went inside of it, but it couldn't detect me."

"What should I do?"

A familiar voice issued from over Erec's shoulder. "Pick your nose? Pick your brain? Pick your battles?"

Erec spun around to see the Hermit standing calmly, wearing nothing but an enormous fig leaf over his lower parts and his winged shoes. He posed like a Greek statue, balancing an apple on one hand in the air.

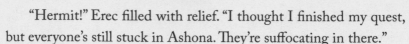

"Hermit!" Erec filled with relief. "I thought I finished my quest, but everyone's still stuck in Ashona. They're suffocating in there."

"Oh, no. Mustn't have that." The Hermit's eyes twinkled with merriment as if he was talking about a kid eating too much candy, and not everyone who Erec loved dying.

"How can we help them?"

"We? So it's we, now that you want something done, is it?" He giggled.

Erec waited, hoping for usable advice.

The Hermit took a bite of the apple with a loud crunch and scratched his chin. "If you have heart, go to the heart of the problem. If you have a brain, though, think first, or you will find yourself all stomach." He hooted with laughter, then finished his apple, tossing the core into Erec's hands.

Erec threw a glance at Spartacus, but when he looked back the Hermit was gone. "How does he do that?"

Spartacus shrugged. "I can't even scoot that fast. What do you think he was saying?"

"Who knows? I should go to the Secret of Ashona myself. I'll have to try to find out what's going on since Posey can't do it from inside. I guess that's what the Hermit means—if I have heart, I'll go to the heart of the problem."

"And if you have a brain, you have to be careful . . . or you'll end up in its stomach, I guess."

"I'm not sure how to be careful with that thing. I guess I just won't get too close to it."

"How will you breathe under there? It's in the middle of the ocean."

Erec flashed his Instagills. "Easy."

"Oh, yeah, that's right. Well, no time like the present, right?"

Erec nodded—and they were off.

Erec had to shout at Spartacus in his thoughts until the ghost noticed that he was trying to communicate with him. They were whizzing through the ocean so fast that it hurt Erec's skin, and he had to tell Spartacus to slow down. Reluctantly, Spartacus changed his pace. Now Erec could see the sea life they were passing. Octopuses and schools of fish grazed against him as he sailed through the water. It was interesting enough to distract him from where he was headed. The bubble city of Ashona was within view, and Spartacus was taking him down along its side, then underneath it.

Erec hoped this wasn't a stupid thing to do. If Queen Posey was not able to speak to the Secret of Ashona without being eaten alive, then why would Erec even attempt it? Maybe he would do everyone a lot more good if he stayed on the outside and found Baskania, made him reverse his command about Ashona. Not that he had any chance of doing that.

But the Hermit made it sound like he should do this . . . at least if he did it right, whatever that meant. He hoped he was interpreting the Hermit correctly—he never really knew what that guy meant.

From the outside, the set of connecting bubbles that was Ashona looked smoky-colored, and pulsating—completely different from the way it previously appeared. Before he was close enough to put a hand on its shell, Spartacus yanked him downward. The city went much deeper than Erec expected.

Spartacus pulled him under a long, flat wall of cobbled metal. Erec reached a finger up to touch it. It was pulsing out as if it were about to burst. The tension inside it must have been enormous to make it buckle out like that. He cringed, thinking of Bethany in there, sweltering, with no oxygen. How much longer would everyone last?

A long way under Ashona, Erec saw swirling, rushing bubbles

circling in the water ahead of them. Even through the water, he could hear a rushing sound, like a whirlpool. Spartacus pulled him closer until he began to resist. *I think this is a safe distance,* he thought.

Spartacus stopped. "You can't even see her from here."

Her?

"Yeah. The Secret of Ashona. It's a woman."

I don't know how close I can go without getting swallowed.

"Well, you can try talking to her from here."

Erec was able to speak underwater, thanks to his Instagills. But in addressing the Secret of Ashona, he wasn't quite sure how to start. "Can you hear me?"

There was no response.

"I think you're going to have to get a little closer, bud." Spartacus pulled him farther.

Erec yanked back, and then tried again to speak to the Secret—and heard no answer.

Like a game of tug-of-war, Spartacus kept pulling one way and Erec kept yanking back. As they inched closer to the swirling torrent ahead, Erec thought about the Hermit's warning. Was there another way he was supposed to prepare for this? He wished he knew.

The Secret of Ashona was approaching fast. Erec was much closer than he wanted to be. At the same time, it was still not responding when he spoke to it. Steadily, he approached, until finally he could see it clearly.

The rushing water of the Secret of Ashona swirled in the shape of waving hair around a woman's face. Inside were clear features. Watery blue eyes fluttered at Erec, and lips smiled. She was beautiful, he thought, straight out of a dream. How could anyone be afraid of her? Calm knowledge and happiness radiated on her face.

Erec asked, eagerly, "Can you tell me what's happening? Everything is sealed in Ashona."

She opened her mouth, and, in a second ... lunged. All he could see were jaws and blackness.

He was devoured.

It was dark in the Secret of Ashona. Erec could still breathe in the water, but he could not see. And there was nothing to hear other than the rushing sound of its whirlpool.

He tried to speak to her from the inside, in his thoughts. *I'm Erec Rex. Queen Posey's nephew. They're having a lot of trouble up there. Queen Posey can't talk to you anymore. Can you tell me how to help them?*

There was no answer.

After a while, Erec could hear Spartacus's voice nearby. "Sorry—it took me forever to get in here. Not easy, this thing. It's almost as tight as the barrier around Ashona. Let's get you to safety."

Erec felt tugging on his arm, and then his legs. But he was not moving.

"Hmm. That's strange." There was a lot more tugging, and then Spartacus seemed to disappear. Quite a while later, Erec heard him again. "I can get out and back in, but it took me a while. I just have to figure out how to get you free."

After a lot more tugging, though, Spartacus gave up.

I'm okay, don't worry, Erec thought.

Neither of them said the obvious—even though Erec could breathe here, he would not last long without food and fresh water. This had been a mistake. It was over for him.

Long after Erec had given up and resigned himself to his loved ones suffering in agony, he heard a voice from above. It sounded familiar. "We need to talk."

For a minute, he thought someone was addressing him. But then the water all around him tinkled into a voice. "You are not my master anymore, Posey."

"I realize that. You need to stop listening to Baskania. You're destroying this place, and hurting everyone inside. We won't be able to live much longer."

There was a pause. "I'm sorry, Posey. I can't help you anymore. In fact, by rights I could digest you right now. But I'll let you go this time, as you were the one who created me. And I have someone else in my stomach now—your nephew, who is delicious."

Queen Posey's voice grew shrill with horror. "My nephew? You've eaten Erec?"

"I am digesting him now. He's quite a tasty morsel."

Erec shuddered. He was going to be digested? He wasn't sure if that was worse than dying of thirst and starvation, but it didn't sound good.

"You must let him go! We need him. He is destined to be the King of Alypium!"

"That is not my concern. I only heed commands of the Queen of Ashona."

There was a pause. "I don't understand. I am the Queen of Ashona. I thought Baskania was giving you orders now."

"Who is Baskania? I know no such person. I am following orders of my new ruler—the one you passed your scepter to by full rights."

"Who is that? Are you talking about 'King' Dollick Stain? Because I can assure you that he is not a true ruler. He could not command my scepter. . . ." She thought a moment. "Or can he now? Is that what this is about? Did that idiot boy make this much of a mess here already?"

"King Dollick Stain? I know of no such person. And he is certainly not my new queen."

Erec was as confused as Posey sounded. New queen? Who could the Secret of Ashona be talking about?

THE SECRET OF ASHONA

Posey spoke slowly. "What new queen are you following?"

"Your successor. The Metamorpher has acted, and passed on your crown."

"The *what?* The Metamorpher is here? Hesti? How could that be?"

Erec immediately recognized his birth mother's name. Hesti was here? In Ashona? For a second he was excited, but then remembered that he was stuck and couldn't find her, and she would die with everyone inside of Ashona. His mother had the power to pass the crown from one generation to the next. But could she do it randomly like that? Why would she? And who was the next queen—did that mean that his lost triplet sibling was here as well? He wanted to find his mother and triplet sister so much he could explode. But he was stuck in the Secret of Ashona permanently.

Posey took a few breaths, trying to calm down. "Thank you for letting me speak to you. But there is a problem you should think about. Your new ruler is in Ashona, it seems. If you continue to follow her command—whatever that is—then you will kill her as well."

The Secret of Ashona was silent for a moment. Then she said, "That is true. It may be a problem. But she has given me no other commands. I have to follow her orders."

"Can I give you one last order?"

"No, Posey. You may not. I am sorry." It sounded like the Secret of Ashona was truly sorry that its new queen would die.

"What was her request for you, exactly?"

"My new queen touched her scepter and commanded to me, 'I want things to stay like this in Ashona forever. I wish nobody would leave, ever, and that absolutely nothing could get in or out.'"

Who would have said that? Erec wondered. It didn't even make sense. The person sounded like she had no idea what she was wishing for. But if she was in control of Posey's scepter, why didn't she fix everything now?

"I have an idea," Posey said. "We both agree that it would be terrible for your new . . . queen to die because of a mistake. There is a way for you to reverse a spell. Why don't we do that?"

"That demands a sacrifice."

"I understand. I will be the sacrifice."

Erec listened with shock. His aunt was volunteering to sacrifice herself to reverse this spell?

"But who would sacrifice you? It would have to be someone from the outside. Nobody except you can live in the water long enough to do it."

"Erec Rex can—if you let him go. He has Instagills."

There was a pause. The two understood completely what was going on, even though Erec had no clue. So, the Secret of Ashona might let him go, but then he would have to sacrifice his own aunt? He could never do that.

The tinkling voice around Erec spoke. "That might be possible. He would have to ride the Horse of the Elements, and use the lance there. This is how this sacrifice will take place. Piercing the shield around Ashona with the lance will break it open. But it will not work unless it goes straight through the heart of a living sacrifice to reverse this spell."

Erec felt lightheaded in the swirling waters. He had to ride the Horse of the Elements? That is exactly what his quest told him to do. So the Dragon Horse of Fire wasn't what he was supposed to ride? But it had worked to stop Baskania. . . .

Was he supposed to do both things, then? He never knew with the Fates. Riding the Horse of the Elements sounded fine, as did spearing the shield with a lance. But stabbing someone with it and killing them—how could he ever do that? Especially his aunt?

"I will be the sacrifice," the queen repeated.

"No. I won't take you," the Secret of Ashona mused. "You are too important to me. It must be someone else. I'll let your nephew go. He will find the Horse of the Elements in a small cave a mile north of the northernmost point of Ashona. Place your sacrifice at the tip of the shield on that side. Erec should ride the horse at top speed, and stab straight through the shield into that person's heart. All will be well then."

There was a noise as the queen disappeared back into the bowels of Ashona. Erec was tossed around, spun in circles, then spit into the calm water at the undersurface of Ashona.

Erec floated a while, wondering which way was due north. Spartacus was nowhere to be seen. Erec hoped he would come back soon. If Erec took too long, the people of Ashona might not survive.

He thought about what he had heard. His mother was inside of Ashona now—and she was called the Metamorpher? And his lost triplet sibling sister—Elizabeth—was there too? He wondered if she still liked the name "Princess Pretty Pony." Why were they here? They were so tantalizingly close. Once Erec broke through the spell holding Ashona captive, he would search for them right away.

But there was another problem. Even if it was not his aunt sacrificing herself, how would he ever be able to stab through the heart of anyone—killing them? It wasn't possible. Then again, if he didn't do it, everyone would die, wouldn't they? That would be much worse.

Except *he* would be the one killing someone. How could he live with that?

But how could he not? His aunt seemed okay with it. It was the only logical thing to do. It made sense. But it would be the hardest thing that he ever did.

Could he close his eyes? Just pretend he was somewhere else? But if he did that, he couldn't aim through the person's heart. . . .

Just then, Erec froze in terror. As if remembering a distant dream, he pictured the vision he had seen of his future. Rushing forward on a horse, with a lance aimed straight at the heart of *Bethany.*

CHAPTER THIRTY-THREE
The Impossible Quest

THERE WAS NO WAY in the world he would let that happen. No way. Bethany would never die at his hands. He just wouldn't do it. Nobody could make him. Erec crossed his arms and let the current carry him away from Ashona. It was over for them—and for him. He didn't care anymore.

There was something on his shoulder—he looked and saw Spartacus's hand. For a while the ghost didn't say anything, but then he gave Erec a sad smile. "You know, she's going to die either way."

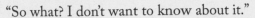

"So what? I don't want to know about it."

"But you do know about it. Pretending it isn't happening doesn't help. Bethany wants to give her life so she can help everyone else. Isn't that a better way for her to die than by suffocation, along with everyone else in Ashona?"

"She wants to be the one to make the sacrifice. That sounds just like her." Erec flushed with anger at the thought. "Selfish," he murmured.

"Selfish! She's giving up her life to save everyone else, and you're calling her selfish?"

"Exactly!" Erec wasn't sure where his anger was coming from, but he was full of it. "She's thinking of everyone except for me! How am I supposed to go on and be happy if she dies here? She should think about *that*!"

Spartacus put his hands on Erec's shoulders and looked him in the eye with sarcasm. "Is this the person talking who gave his own life up to save all of the captive souls—without thinking about how it would affect Bethany? Is this the person who risked going into the underworld without thinking of Bethany? Is this the guy who jumped into the Diamond Mind pit to save five people—"

"All right! All right. You made your point." Erec calmed down, thinking about it. Spartacus was completely right. Erec had done this much more than she had, and it was only with luck that he was still here to talk about it. He had been perfectly fine with himself making that choice—and now he realized it was much harder being the one left behind. No wonder Bethany had been crying when she was in Ashona, not knowing where Erec was or if he was even alive. He felt awful for her. What he had done was wrong. No matter what the risk, he should have let her come and be there for all of it. This was the last time, he decided, if for some reason they both possibly lived through this, that he would ever leave her home to worry.

The only problem was that there was no way they would both live through this. Erec was safe now. And his brother—and Bethany's brother—Trevor was out of danger. But everyone else would be gone. His father, Aunt Posey, Nell, Zoey . . . his heart crumbled when he thought of Zoey in that place with all of the pressure and heat, and no oxygen. Was it too late for her already? How could he be taking his time like this—he had to save her now! And all the innocent people trapped in Ashona.

And his birth mother, Queen Hesti, the Metamorpher.

And his lost triplet sister, Elizabeth.

There was no choice. He would have to do this, for everyone's sake. Even for Bethany's sake. Better she die the way that she chooses than in absolute failure.

This would be the hardest thing he ever did.

Without another word, Spartacus pulled him fast in the right direction. Soon they were at the mouth of a small rock cave. It seemed a horse would not fit inside, but Erec went in to look.

The circular cave was five feet around—with no horse anywhere. But a large, sparkling silver sea horse wagged its curled tail back and forth, darting in different directions around the cave.

The creature cocked its head, looking at Erec out of an eye in the side of its face. Its voice was clear and soft, almost like a whisper. "I know why you're here, little boy. You want to take the spell off of Ashona. You need to use the lance on the floor here."

A thin needle, about one foot long, lay against some rocks. Erec picked it up. It was much smaller than the one in his vision. In fact, it seemed doubtful that it could stab through the shield around Ashona at all. And if it punctured Bethany's heart . . .

Erec cheered up immensely. This little thing wouldn't kill Bethany. If it went into her heart it could hurt her, but there were great doctors in Ashona, like in Alypium. Magical doctors who could fix a small problem like a needle in the heart. There was hope! Everything would be fine. The Secret of Ashona needed a sacrifice, but the sacrifice didn't have to die, did it? Maybe Erec had it wrong. . . .

He grabbed the tiny lance with glee and approached the small sea horse. "Can I ride you, then?"

"Of course." The thing preened its fins with its snout, then breathed what looked like orange liquid onto its back. "Let me finish cleaning up. I want to look nice."

Erec watched it blow orange all over its body. "Is that some kind of paint?"

The Horse of the Elements cocked its head again. "No, little boy. It's fire. I have fire, air, earth, and water inside of me. I will breathe fire at anyone who gets in our way on the ride to Ashona."

Erec almost laughed, thinking about how little a tiny stream of fire would do, especially underwater. But he held back. This animal was saving everyone he knew.

"Go ahead, climb on!" it said.

Erec was as large as the sea horse. He threw a leg over its back and an arm around its neck, the tiny lance in his other fist.

"Okay. Ready, then." The sea horse took off slowly, barely drifting out of the cave. Erec bit his lip to keep from laughing. This was what he had been so worried about? Going at a snail's pace and holding a needle, he wasn't going to hurt a fly. Bethany would be fine. He had never been happier—all was going to be great. Everyone would be freed from Ashona, and he would be able to finally meet his birth mother and triplet sister soon!

The only problem was that they were moving so slow it would take a year to get there. With a mile to go, Erec was impatient. His family was suffering. Someone in Ashona could be dying.

As if on cue, the sea horse sped up a bit, and then a bit more. In fact, Erec was surprised that the thing was able to go so fast, given its size. It didn't seem very strong—Erec's feet hung far below its underside . . . at least they had before. Oddly, the animal seemed to be larger. As they ventured forward it grew even bigger, and moved faster. In fact, it was obvious now—the thing was far bigger than Erec. He could still wrap an arm around its neck, but he had to scoot forward to reach it.

It was getting harder to hold on as the Horse of the Elements sped ahead. The water dragged Erec backward, and he had to angle forward so he did not get tugged off. Holding the lance was harder too. If Erec did not keep it pointed straight, the pressure of the water yanked it to the side. It seemed heavier now, and harder to hold.

Erec looked at the lance with horror. It had grown as well, along with the horse. What had started out a thin, one-foot needle was now a four-foot long, thick blade.

This would not be safe for Bethany at all.

But if Erec had thought he was moving fast before, that was nothing compared to now. The horse kept growing larger and racing quicker until they charged at full speed. Erec could see nothing except bubbles and blur. Water yanked his lance up and down until he wedged its base into the ridges of the horse's neck, keeping it poised straight ahead. It took everything he had to hold the horse and lance at the same time.

They would be there any minute now. Erec's heart thumped. This was exactly like his horrible vision of the future. His lance was now seven feet long, aiming straight at Ashona and Bethany's heart. He thought about stopping time again, but what would that do? As soon as he restarted it, he would either stab through Ashona and Bethany, or not.

How could he do this? But how could he not do it? It was what Bethany wanted. It would save everybody. It would save Zoey. And his mother. And everybody else.

He had to do it.

Ashona rose up fast before him. He could not see where the clear seal around it began, but soon he spotted a lone figure directly in the path of his lance, which was now ten feet long. At first he could only see the dark hair.

But then he could see her. It was Bethany. Ropes held her still, stopping her from changing her mind.

Everything inside of Erec froze. The Horse of the Elements shot forward. Erec gripped hard, poised so he could aim . . .

. . . straight . . .

. . . at . . .

. . . her . . .

. . . heart . . .

NO!

Something broke inside of Erec. Just before the lance stabbed through the barrier around Ashona, and into the heart of his best friend in the whole world, he dove on it. With the weight of his body, he shoved the handle upward, pushing its tip straight down into the water. It plummeted before it even made a nick in the shield.

In the split second that relief flooded through his body, the speeding lance hit rock beneath him. Erec was thrown up through the water, flung from the force of the speed and the weight of the lance. Before the drag from the water slowed him, he was above the edge of the bubble around Ashona.

Getting his bearings again, he swam the rest of the way up to the top. What had he done? There was no way he could kill Bethany . . . so he had basically killed everybody inside, including Bethany. He was an idiot. A failure. Bethany was just as doomed now, and would be miserable in her last moments too.

Was it worth finding the Horse of the Elements below and trying this all over again? He closed his eyes and pictured a repeat

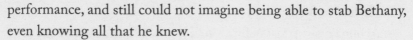

performance, and still could not imagine being able to stab Bethany, even knowing all that he knew.

It was hopeless.

Erec drifted along the upper surface of Ashona, dragging his fingertips along its sealed enclosure. The least he could do was to be there when the whole thing went bad. As soon as he could face her, he would swim to Bethany and wait with her, watching her through the bubble shield even if they could not hear each other.

Erec could see the hallways and passages below him, as well as some open-topped storage rooms. Nobody was in sight. It was so hot and miserable inside they were either sleeping or waiting on lower levels where it might be cooler.

Erec drifted to the pinnacle of the shield. Under him, at the very topmost point, someone was in a room filled with machinery. Out of curiosity, he swam over and looked in. Of all people, there was Nell, his sister, fiddling with gears on a large turbine. She leaned on her walker propped against a wall.

What was she doing? Erec watched until she gave up with the turbine and tried to yank a chain off of its gear teeth.

She was trying to destroy the machinery. It looked impossible, but his brave sister was doing the only thing she could think of to disable the Heart of Ashona. He figured this must be the control room that Ashona needed to function. If Nell dismantled it, the Secret of Ashona would lose its ability to form a force field around the place.

It wasn't a bad idea, but there was no way that it would work. Nell wasn't strong enough to do any damage—Erec doubted anyone could. The only way to help things was for Erec to . . .

He didn't want to think about it. Instead, he distracted himself watching Nell struggle against the machines. She didn't see him, and worked tirelessly in an effort that would amount to nothing.

Erec shoved his hands into his pockets, thinking about the futility of everything.

Something in his pocket scraped against his hand, and he pulled it out. It was that odd mousetrap-shaped device that Baskania had given him. Which made him think of another thing he was carrying— Erec dug deeper and found the little pink brain that had been Tarvos's power source. Just holding it amplified his powers thousands of times, and the mousetrap multiplied it thousands of times more. Erec remembered when Rosco tried to create a drop of water using those two things and had created a solid wall of water that flooded all of Alypium.

For a moment, he held the two objects, wondering if they might be enough for him to break open the seal around Ashona. It couldn't hurt to try. . . .

"You might as well," a voice said in his ear. "But I wouldn't hold my breath. Even when I used them both I didn't make a crack in Tartarus."

Erec was happy to see Spartacus again. It was nice that he could read Erec's mind, so he was spared from repeating the whole painful story. But Spartacus was right. The mousetrap device, even with Tarvos's power source, had not touched Tartarus. Would it work here now? There was nothing else to do but try.

The Amulet of Virtues swung around his neck, its eighth segment still not lit, even though he had ridden the Horse of the Elements. He failed this quest for sure. Then again, was he *really* supposed to kill Bethany? Wouldn't the Fates know that was impossible?

Next to the Amulet, the Twrch Trwyth swung over his chest. Three Awen balls were left on it: the Awen of Beauty, the Awen of Knowledge, and the Awen of Creation. Maybe he should use the Awen of Knowledge so that he would know exactly what to do.

Or maybe—

Erec fingered the Awen of Creation, dumbstruck. There it was, dangling around his neck this whole time. Inside of it was an unmatched power of destruction, and creation as well. It alone might be able to break through anything that existed—even Tartarus itself. But magnified with the powers of the mousetrap device and Tarvos's power source . . .

But why did his quest tell him to ride that sea horse, then, if he wasn't supposed to stab through Ashona? Looking down at the control room underneath him, it sunk in. Maybe he was supposed to do exactly what he did. That would have put him right up here, where he was now, where he had flipped when the lance hit the stone. Maybe this was exactly where he needed to detonate the Awen of Creation—right above the control room.

Spartacus stared at him in amazement. "There is one problem, you know."

"What? This has to work!"

"It might. But unless you can take that thing off of your neck and give it to me, you'll probably blow up in the process."

Erec stared at him, comprehension sinking in. He never had thought of taking the Twrch Trwyth off of his neck ever since he had gotten it. He wasn't supposed to. When he started to lift it off, a terrible feeling came over him. No. He dropped it back onto his chest. It was his to use. Nobody else's.

But then he remembered something else. When he had used the first Awen ball, the Awen of sight, the entire city around him became blinded, obscured by clouds. At the same time, though, he alone was able to see clearly through the mists. Maybe wearing the Twrch Trwyth would protect him from the effects of the explosion.

Then again, the second Awen ball he had used, the Awen of Harmony, gave both him and the Furies complete harmony. It affected him the same as everyone else.

He had no idea what this one would do. All he knew was that he had no other choice.

He looked at Spartacus. "Nell's still down there. Can you get her out of the way? I'm going to try this right here, on top of the control room."

Spartacus nodded. It took forever for him to inch through the tight, thick barrier around Ashona. When he was halfway, he winced. "It's awful in there, even for me. The pressure is horrible. Get ready now—and give me ten seconds after I'm through. That's more than enough time for me to get Nell and everyone in this part of Ashona out of the way. But don't wait any more than that. People won't survive this much longer."

Erec watched Spartacus wedge his way through the force field. Then he gripped Tarvos's power source and pulled back the bar on the mousetrap device. Below him, Spartacus grabbed Nell by the waist and fled from the room—a look of terror filling the poor girl's face.

It was safe now. He had to act fast, but he made himself count to ten. Then Erec twisted the tiny black glass dodecahedron attached to the foot of the boar-shaped Twrch Trwyth vial. Its little stem cracked. A small black trail slithered into the water as he lowered it onto the mousetrap. The Awen ball positioned itself neatly in the crease where the lever was aimed.

Erec pressed Tarvos's power source onto the mousetrap, and hoped for the best. He released the bar. It snapped.

White sparks. Black glitter. Fragments. Pieces of things. Whirling. Banging.

Blackness.

CHAPTER THIRTY-FOUR
Good-bye to a Ghost

G LIMMERS OF LIGHT and dark spun before Erec's eyes. Where was he? The shadows around him were confusing. His brain felt like it had gone through a blender. Was he still spinning through the ocean? Buried under chunks of rock? Were the glimmers little rays of sunlight?

No . . . as Erec's mind cleared, he could tell that the glimmers were light rays through his own opening eyelids. He was in something soft. A bed. White sheets.

Erec moved a finger, and then a hand. Everything was sore, but seemed to be in working order. He was alive—at least he had survived the blast, somehow. But had anyone else?

With trepidation, Erec turned to look around the room. Someone was in a bed nearby, and other people walked around.

"Erec!" Bethany rushed toward him. "You're awake! I was so worried about you. We've all been sitting here waiting with you. You could have died! How in the world were you able to break through the barrier? I thought we'd never make it."

It hurt to speak, but Erec didn't care. "Is everyone okay?"

"Everyone." Bethany wiped Erec's forehead with a cloth. "You've been sweating the whole time you were passed out."

Erec let the relief inside fill him completely. Tears came to his eyes as he thought about what had almost happened. "I couldn't do it, you know. There was no way."

Bethany broke into a sob. She wiped her face a few times. "I wondered about that. I so much wanted to do that . . . you know. To save everyone. Like you do."

"Bethany, don't ever think you have to—"

"I wanted to! But then, at the last minute, I didn't want to. I hoped you would change your mind—I was terrified. It seemed impossible, though. Why would you ever choose to kill everyone there, including me . . . ?"

"It wasn't a choice, like that. There was no choice, really. I just couldn't do it." He was quiet a moment. "But it all worked just right. I guess I had to charge toward you with that lance so I would be shot up to the right spot on top of Ashona to blast through it."

Bethany heaved a sigh of relief. "Thanks, Erec." She lifted the Amulet of Virtues off of his chest. "Another one is lit up."

It was true. An eighth segment was now glowing a brilliant green color. The black symbol inscribed in it was unintelligible, so

Erec shut his eyes and brought his dragon eyes forward to read it.

It said *Instinct*.

"Why instinct?" Erec let his regular eyes out again.

Bethany smiled. "You made the right choice in a split-second decision, didn't you?" She gave him a hug. "Prince Charming saved the day again."

Erec could feel a blush creep over his face. "Who is that?" He pointed to the next bed over, changing the subject.

"It's Nell. We're in the Castle Infirmary in Ashona. A lot of people have been in and out of here in the last few days, treated for heatstroke and injuries. Nell got a little more hurt—I guess she was closer to where the explosion was. But she's going to be fine."

Another voice nearby said, "The people inside were shielded from the blow. The force field absorbed most of the blast." Erec turned to see Spartacus on the other side of the bed. "You looked like you had it pretty bad, though. I thought you'd never survive. The explosion created a massive hole in the ocean floor around Ashona. The old coral reefs are gone, but new ones formed in all kinds of crazy patterns. It looks like a meteor hit there. And I won't talk about the tidal waves crashing into countries around Upper Earth." He shook his head. "It was hard to see clearly, but there was something growing around you during the blast. It was like a green bubble made of leaves . . . I really couldn't tell. I've never seen anything like it."

"What are you staring at?" Bethany asked.

"Spartacus. He's here."

"Oh!" Bethany looked into the air in that direction.

"I've come to say good-bye, you know." Spartacus put a hand on Erec's head. "You'll be okay now, I think."

"I will." Tears came to Erec's eyes again. He was happy for his friend. The ghost was ready to go on to where he was meant to be. But he would miss him, just the same.

"I'll miss you too, kid." Spartacus winked and then he vanished.

"He's gone," Erec said to Bethany. He choked up, unable to speak, as tears streamed down his face.

Bethany held him until he could catch his breath.

"I don't understand!" Erec sat in the throne room with Queen Posey and his father, King Piter. "I want to find my birth mother and my triplet sister. Where are they?"

"I don't know where your birth mother is," Queen Posey explained. "I've had my people search high and low. She was here—the Secret of Ashona told us. But where?—I don't know."

"What about my sister?"

The king and queen exchanged a look. "She's been taken care of," Posey said. "It's nothing you need to worry about."

"Where is she?"

"Safe. We don't want to risk her exposure. We fixed her problems with the scepter. So nobody has to worry anymore. We're all good."

"*I'm* not good! I want to know who she is! We are supposed to be working together, she and I. And whoever my brother is . . . him, too."

King Piter frowned. "There are reasons, Erec. She isn't ready. Just let it go."

Erec could see he was getting nowhere fast—as usual. He shouldn't have expected anything different. But it was hard being this close and not meeting her. Where were they hiding her? If he found her himself, and they could go on adventures together . . .

But the idea exhausted him. An adventure was the last thing that he wanted. In fact, the more he thought about it, the less he even cared who his triplet sister was. What really mattered was that his real family, the ones he knew growing up, and Bethany were safe. Everything was fine, the way it should be. Upper Earth still was in existence, and Otherness, too. Something new was the last thing he needed.

The only thing for now was to relax and do absolutely nothing.

"You ready?" Erec popped his head into the castle library in Ashona. "You don't need to pack books, you know."

Bethany sighed. "You're right. It's just hard to travel without them." She hesitantly lowered an immense subprime geometrical derivatives book to the table. "So, will you tell me now where we're going? Is it somewhere exciting, like the Underworld? Are we going to visit the Furies—or see the Fates in person? I can't wait to have an adventure, after sitting around for so long worrying about you!"

"I'm so sorry about that, Bethany. I'm not going to do that to you anymore. I know how awful it is being unable to help when your best friend is risking their life."

She looked happier than Erec could ever remember. "So, where's it going to be, then? A dragon's lair? Some hidden place in Otherness?"

Erec laughed. "No way. I've had it with risking my life—and yours. I want to go somewhere I've never been. And it wasn't easy getting Mom to agree to this trip either, even though I've been through death and back without her. I don't think I could have talked her into letting me take you to the Underworld just for fun."

Bethany bounced up and down. "Well, where is it, then? Where are we going?"

"Mississippi. And then Alabama. I've never been down south. I've heard it's really pretty there."

"Mississippi? Alabama?" Bethany looked confused. "You're talking about Upper Earth?"

"Yeah. Since it hasn't been destroyed by a Golem army, I figured we might as well enjoy it. It's going to be fall soon, and we're both going to get started with tutors again, I guess. So this is a nice place for us to visit for a few days. You know, we could see the sights, go to the Mississippi Delta . . ."

"And your mom is letting us go alone?"

"Not exactly." He shrugged. "Jam's coming, too. He's bringing the Serving Tray, so we can pig out every day."

"I'm in!" She gave him a kiss on the cheek.

Erec felt himself blush. "I don't even want the crown. Seems like I keep getting pushed in that direction by the Fates—doing one quest after the other. I wish they would just leave me alone. Someday I'll have to find my lost siblings and my birth mother, but I'm through with these quests." He sat in a chair and watched Bethany stuff more books into her bag. "If only we could have a normal life. No more adventure. All I want is to sit around with you and eat doughnuts."

"And brownies."

"And blueberry pie."

"And those really juicy hamburgers that the Serving Tray makes."

"Where is that thing? I'm going to have to find Jam. You're making me hungry."

"Not yet." Bethany put a hand on Erec's shoulder. "There's one thing we have to do first."

And she kissed him on the lips. Erec was shocked, but not too shocked to kiss her back. He could feel the last bits of tension leaving him. All of the worrying about the Furies, about the trapped souls, about Spartacus, about his lost siblings, about Baskania, about the destruction of Upper Earth, about his loved ones dying in Ashona. It was all over now. Finally, he knew, everything was going to be all right.

If you are twelve, you have it:
the Ability to enter people's minds.

It's your choice whether you use it
for good . . . or for evil.

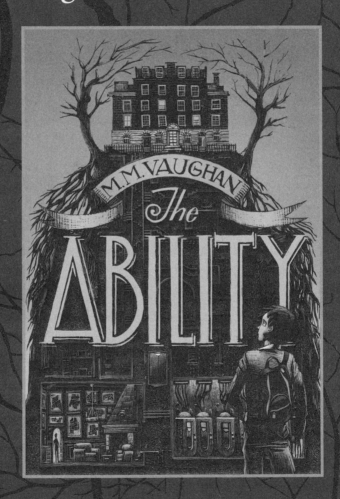